Cassie Hack is the lone survivor of an attack by a slasher called the Lunch Lady...

a slasher who happened to be her mother!

After years of battling slashers and other high strangeness—and paying the price of everything she held dear—

Cassie thought to escape her life of fighting evil.

But the monsters and madmen who threaten the world never rest, and neither can Cassie Hack.

Script by MICHAEL MORECI & STEVE SEELEY

Art by EMILIO LAISO

Colors by K. MICHAEL RUSSELL

Letters by CRANK!

Edits by JAMES LOWDER

Design by SEAN DOVE

Art Direction by STEFANO CASELLI

Series Direction by TIM SEELEY

Cover by STEFANO CASELLI & EMILIO LAISO

HACK SLASH
SON OF SAMHAIN

IMAGE COMICS, INC.

Robert Kirkman - Chief Operating Officer
Erik Larsen - Chief Financial Officer
Todd McFarlane - President
Marc Silvestri - Chief Executive Officer
Jim Valentino - Vice-President

Eric Stephenson - Publisher
Ron Richards - Director of Business Development
Jennifer de Guzman - Director of Trade Book Sales
Kat Salazar - Director of PR & Marketing
Corey Murphy - Director of Retail Sales
Jeremy Sullivan - Director of Digital Sales
Emilio Bautista - Sales Assistant
Branwyn Bigglestone - Senior Accounts Manager
Emily Miller - Accounts Manager
Jessica Ambriz - Administrative Assistant
Tyler Shainline - Events Coordinator

David Brothers - Content Manager
Jonathan Chan - Production Manager
Drew Gill - Art Director
Meredith Wallace - Print Manager
Monica Garcia - Senior Production Artist
Addison Duke - Production Artist
Tricia Ramos - Production Assistant
IMAGECOMICS.COM

HACK/SLASH: SON OF SAMHAIN, VOLUME ONE. January 2015. First Printing. Published by Image Comics, Inc. Office of publication: 2001 Center St. Sixth Floor, Berkeley, CA 94704. Originally published in single magazine form as HACK/SLASH: SON OF SAMHAIN #1-5, by Image Comics. Copyright © 2015 Hack/Slash, Inc. All rights reserved. HACK/SLASH ™ (including all prominent characters featured herein), its logo and all character likenesses are trademarks of Hack/Slash, Inc. unless otherwise noted. All rights Reserved. Image Comics® and its logos are registered trademarks of Image Comics, Inc. No part of this publication may be reproduced or transmitted, in any form or by any means (except for short excerpts for review purposes) without the express written permission of Image Comics, Inc. All names, characters, events and locales in this publication are entirely fictional. Any resemblance to actual persons (living or dead), events or places, without satiric intent, is coincidental. Printed in the USA. For information regarding the CPSIA on this printed material call: 203-595-3636 and provide reference # RICH – 599208. For international rights, contact: foreignlicensing@imagecomics.com. ISBN: 978-1-63215-244-2

D0917226

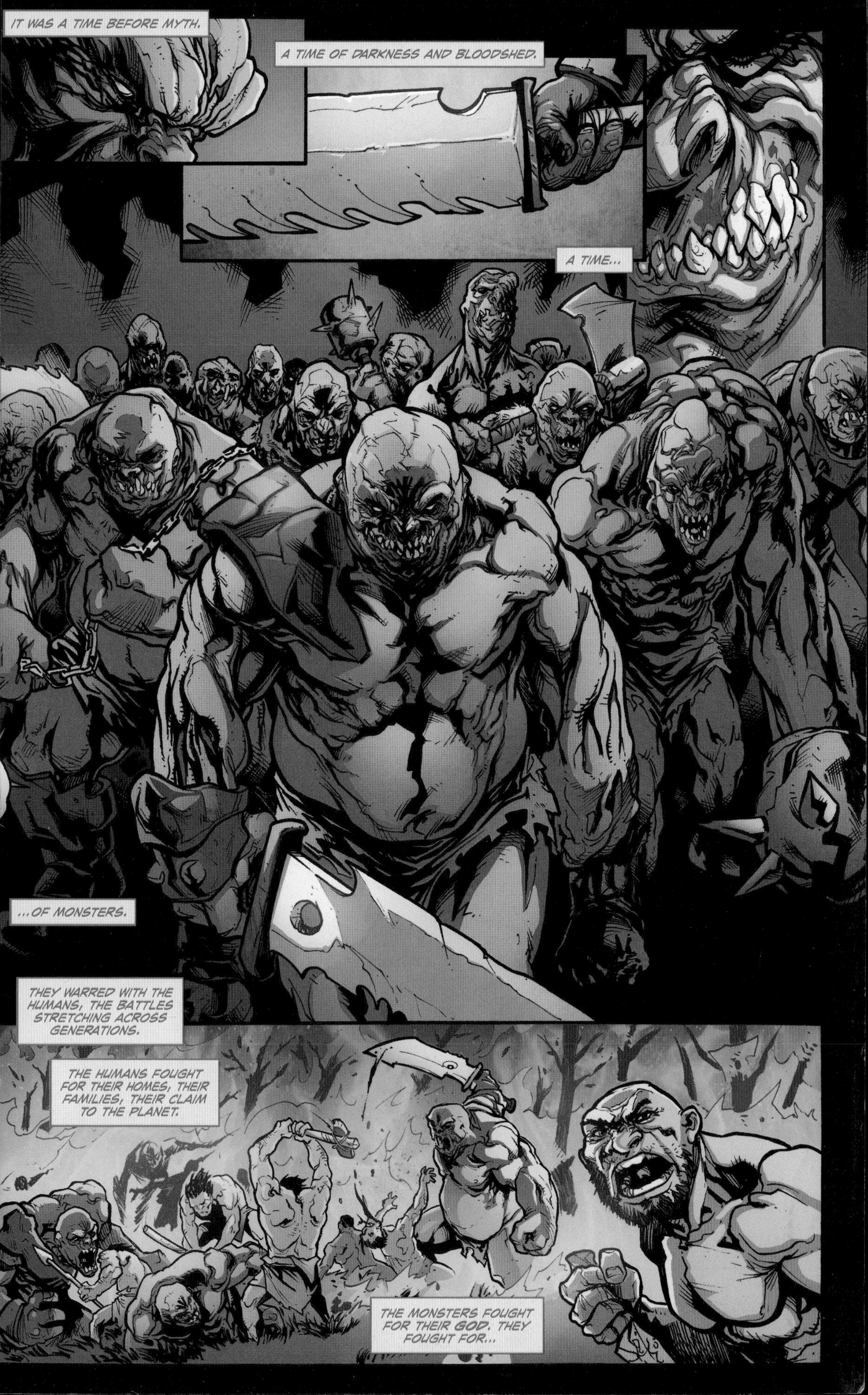
IT WAS A TIME BEFORE MYTH.
A TIME OF DARKNESS AND BLOODSHED.
A TIME...
...OF MONSTERS.
THEY WARRED WITH THE HUMANS, THE BATTLES STRETCHING ACROSS GENERATIONS.
THE HUMANS FOUGHT FOR THEIR HOMES, THEIR FAMILIES, THEIR CLAIM TO THE PLANET.
THE MONSTERS FOUGHT FOR THEIR GOD. THEY FOUGHT FOR...

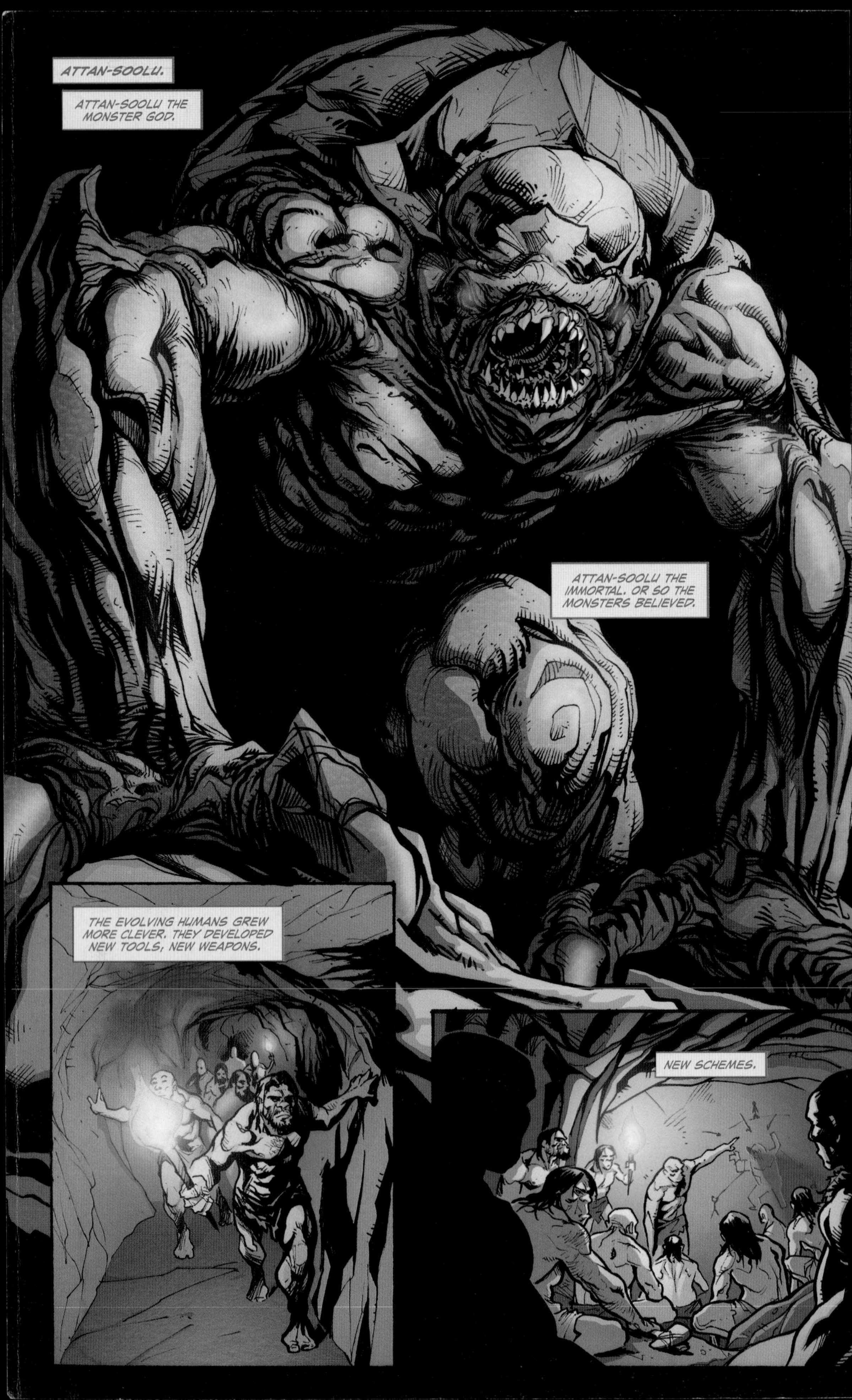
ATTAN-SOOLU.
ATTAN-SOOLU THE MONSTER GOD.
ATTAN-SOOLU THE IMMORTAL. OR SO THE MONSTERS BELIEVED.
THE EVOLVING HUMANS GREW MORE CLEVER. THEY DEVELOPED NEW TOOLS, NEW WEAPONS.
NEW SCHEMES.

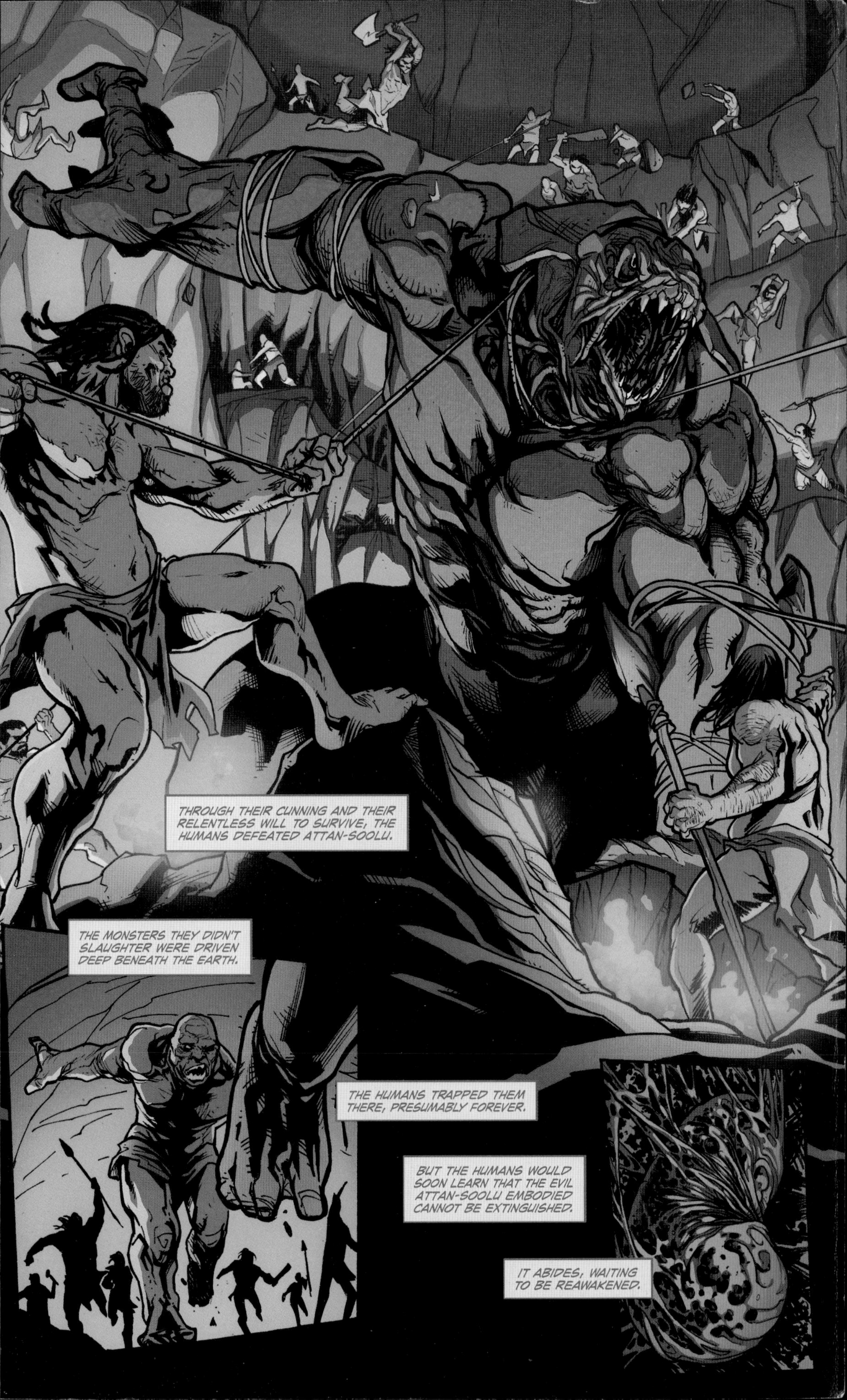
THROUGH THEIR CUNNING AND THEIR RELENTLESS WILL TO SURVIVE, THE HUMANS DEFEATED ATTAN-SOOLU.
THE MONSTERS THEY DIDN'T SLAUGHTER WERE DRIVEN DEEP BENEATH THE EARTH.
THE HUMANS TRAPPED THEM THERE, PRESUMABLY FOREVER.
BUT THE HUMANS WOULD SOON LEARN THAT THE EVIL ATTAN-SOOLU EMBODIED CANNOT BE EXTINGUISHED.
IT ABIDES, WAITING TO BE REAWAKENED.

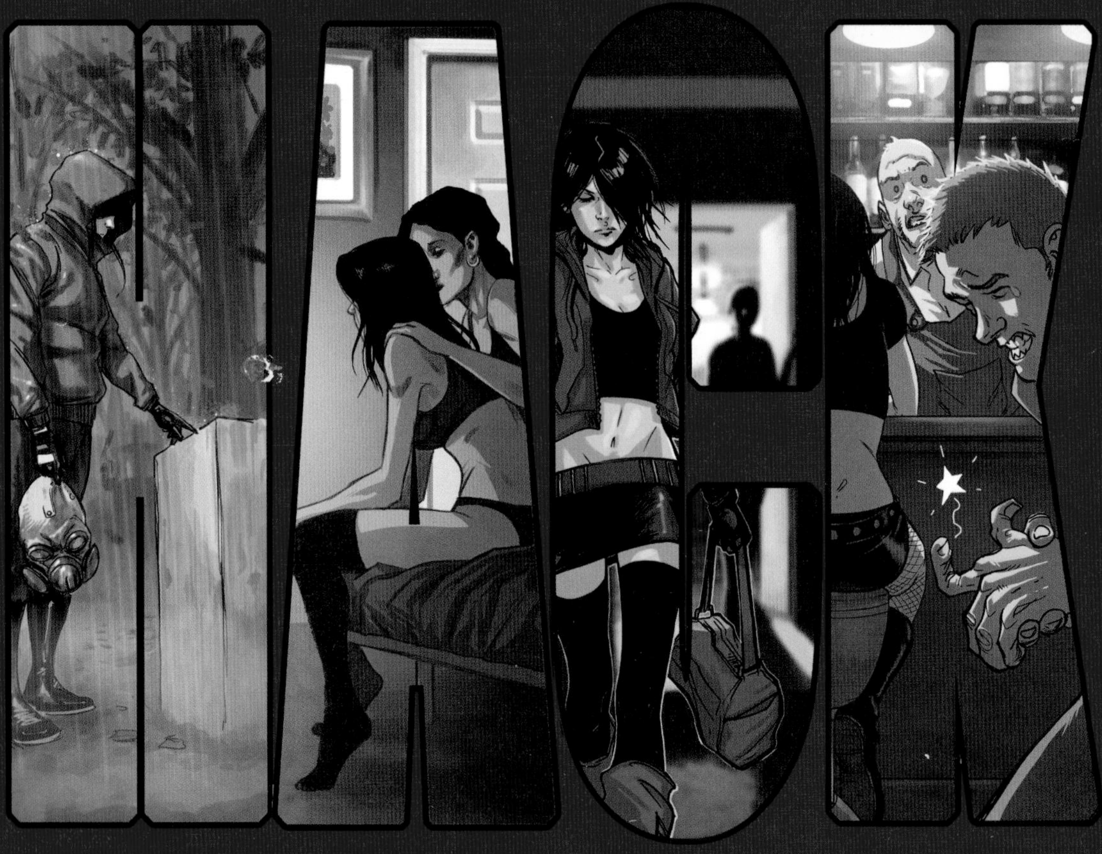
HACK

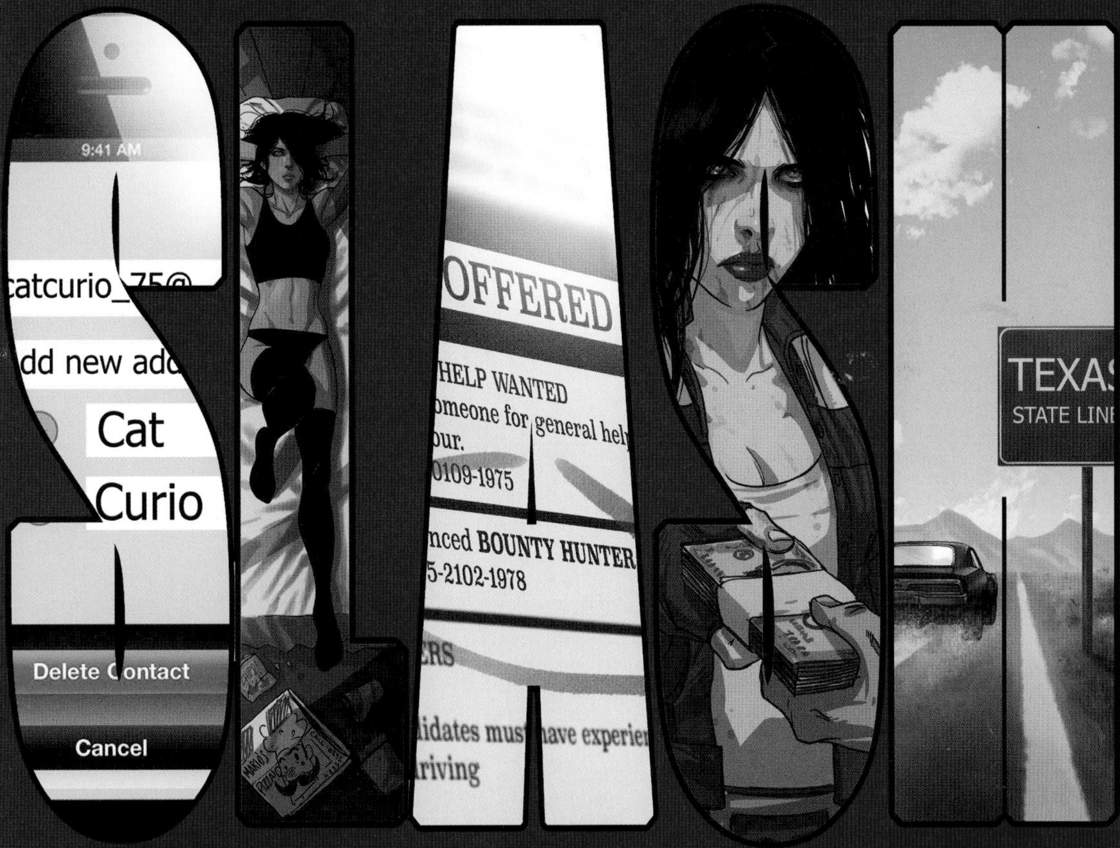

9:41 AM
Cat
Curio
Delete Contact
Cancel
OFFERED
HELP WANTED
BOUNTY HUNTER
TEXAS
STATE LINE

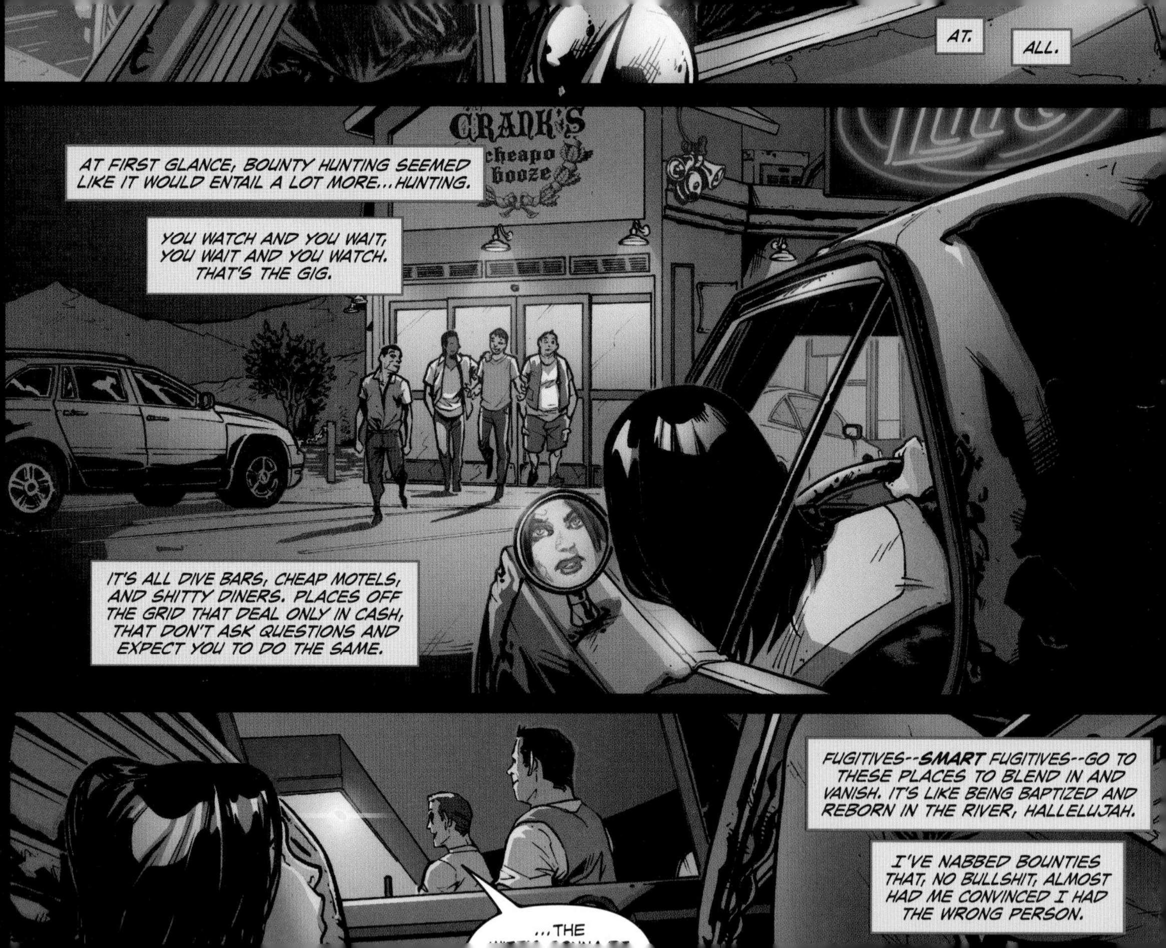
AT.
ALL.
CRANK'S cheapo booze
AT FIRST GLANCE, BOUNTY HUNTING SEEMED LIKE IT WOULD ENTAIL A LOT MORE...HUNTING.
YOU WATCH AND YOU WAIT, YOU WAIT AND YOU WATCH. THAT'S THE GIG.
IT'S ALL DIVE BARS, CHEAP MOTELS, AND SHITTY DINERS. PLACES OFF THE GRID THAT DEAL ONLY IN CASH, THAT DON'T ASK QUESTIONS AND EXPECT YOU TO DO THE SAME.
FUGITIVES--**SMART** FUGITIVES--GO TO THESE PLACES TO BLEND IN AND VANISH. IT'S LIKE BEING BAPTIZED AND REBORN IN THE RIVER, HALLELUJAH.
I'VE NABBED BOUNTIES THAT, NO BULLSHIT, ALMOST HAD ME CONVINCED I HAD THE WRONG PERSON.
...THE

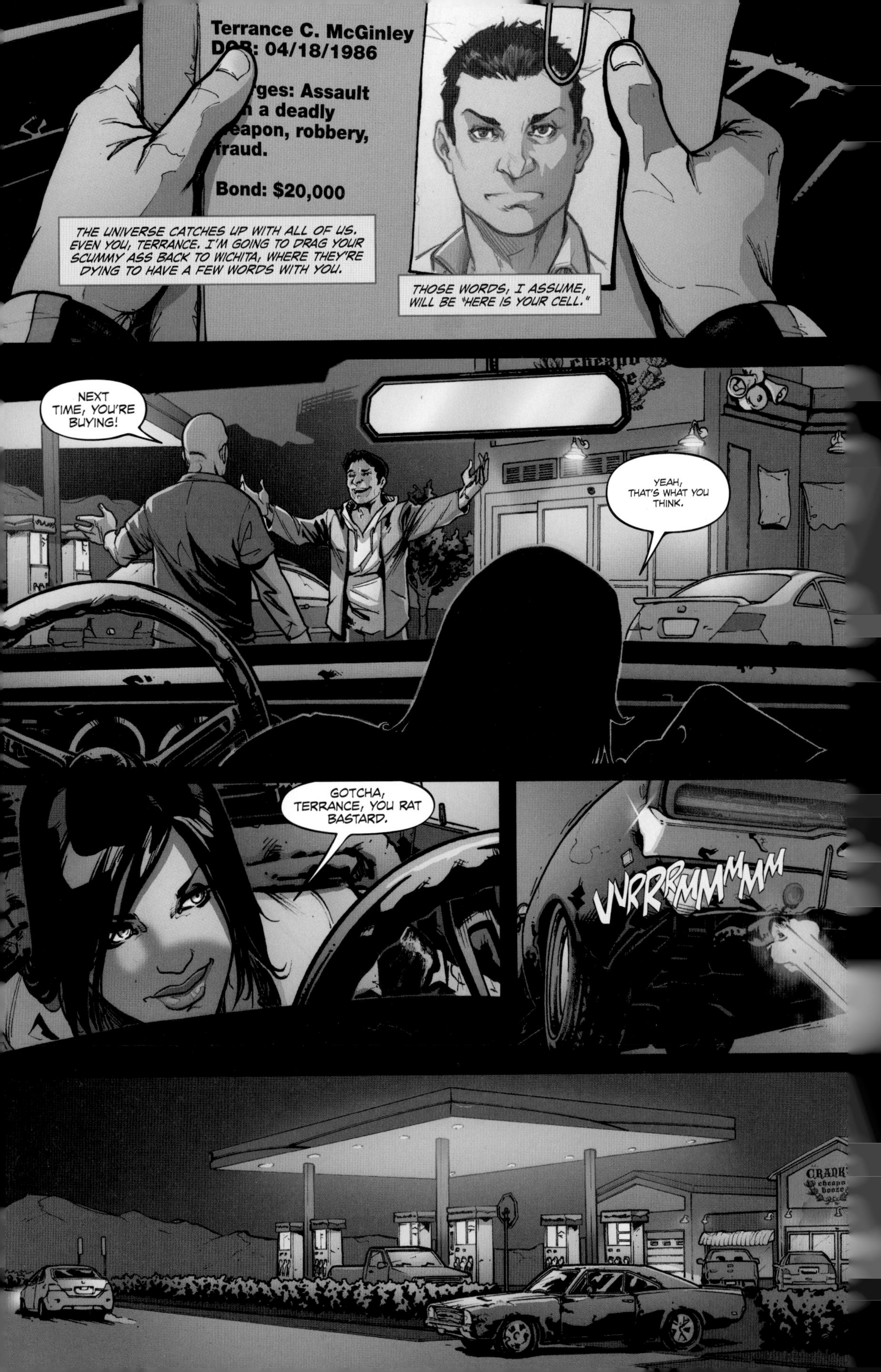
Terrance C. McGinley
DOB: 04/18/1986
rges: Assault
a deadly
eapon, robbery,
fraud.
Bond: $20,000
THE UNIVERSE CATCHES UP WITH ALL OF US. EVEN YOU, TERRANCE. I'M GOING TO DRAG YOUR SCUMMY ASS BACK TO WICHITA, WHERE THEY'RE DYING TO HAVE A FEW WORDS WITH YOU.
THOSE WORDS, I ASSUME, WILL BE "HERE IS YOUR CELL."
NEXT TIME, YOU'RE BUYING!
YEAH, THAT'S WHAT YOU THINK.
GOTCHA, TERRANCE, YOU RAT BASTARD.
VVRRRMMMMMM
CRANK'S
cheapo
booze

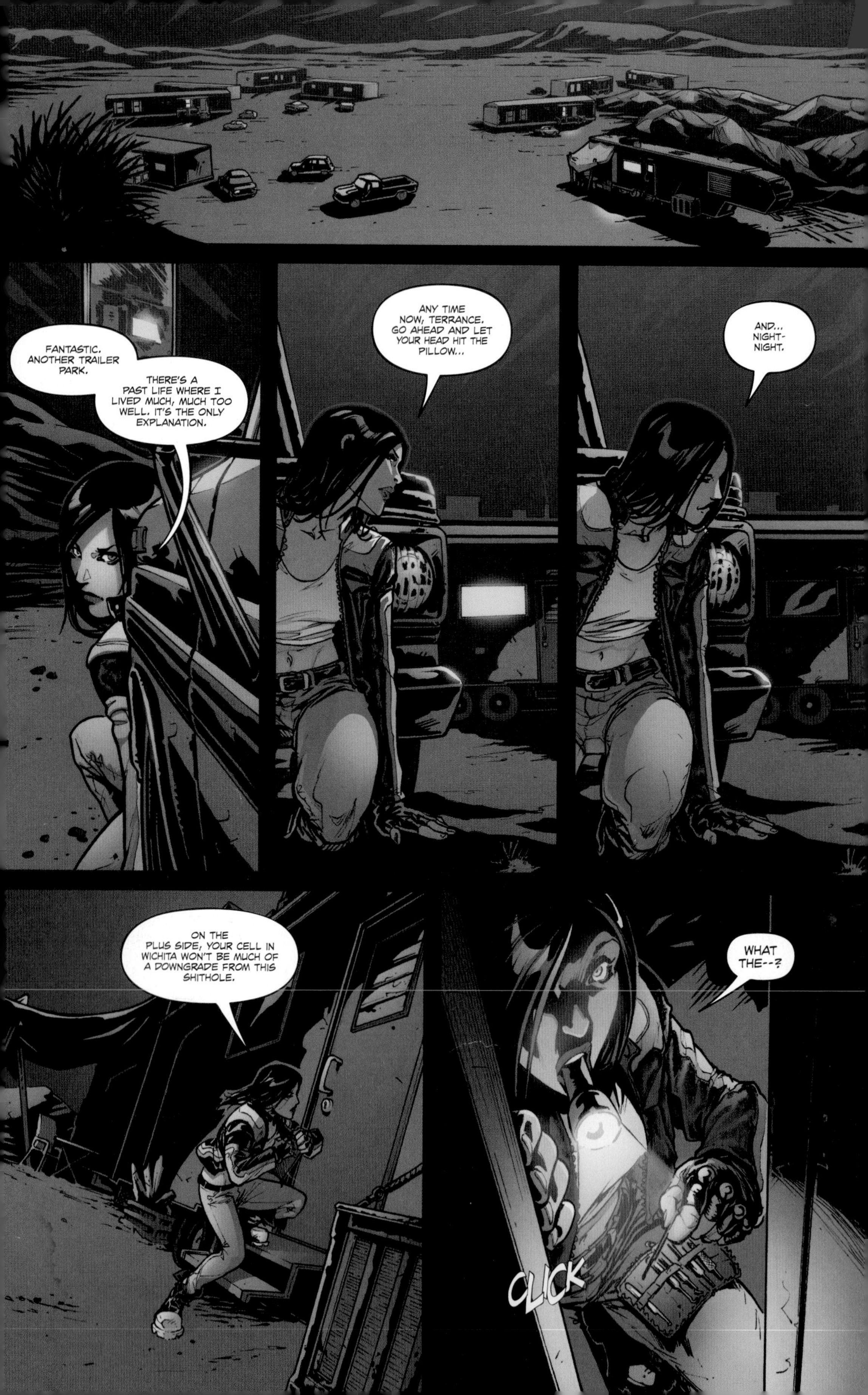
FANTASTIC. ANOTHER TRAILER PARK.
THERE'S A PAST LIFE WHERE I LIVED MUCH, MUCH TOO WELL. IT'S THE ONLY EXPLANATION.
ANY TIME NOW, TERRANCE. GO AHEAD AND LET YOUR HEAD HIT THE PILLOW...
AND... NIGHT-NIGHT.
ON THE PLUS SIDE, YOUR CELL IN WICHITA WON'T BE MUCH OF A DOWNGRADE FROM THIS SHITHOLE.
WHAT THE--?
CLICK

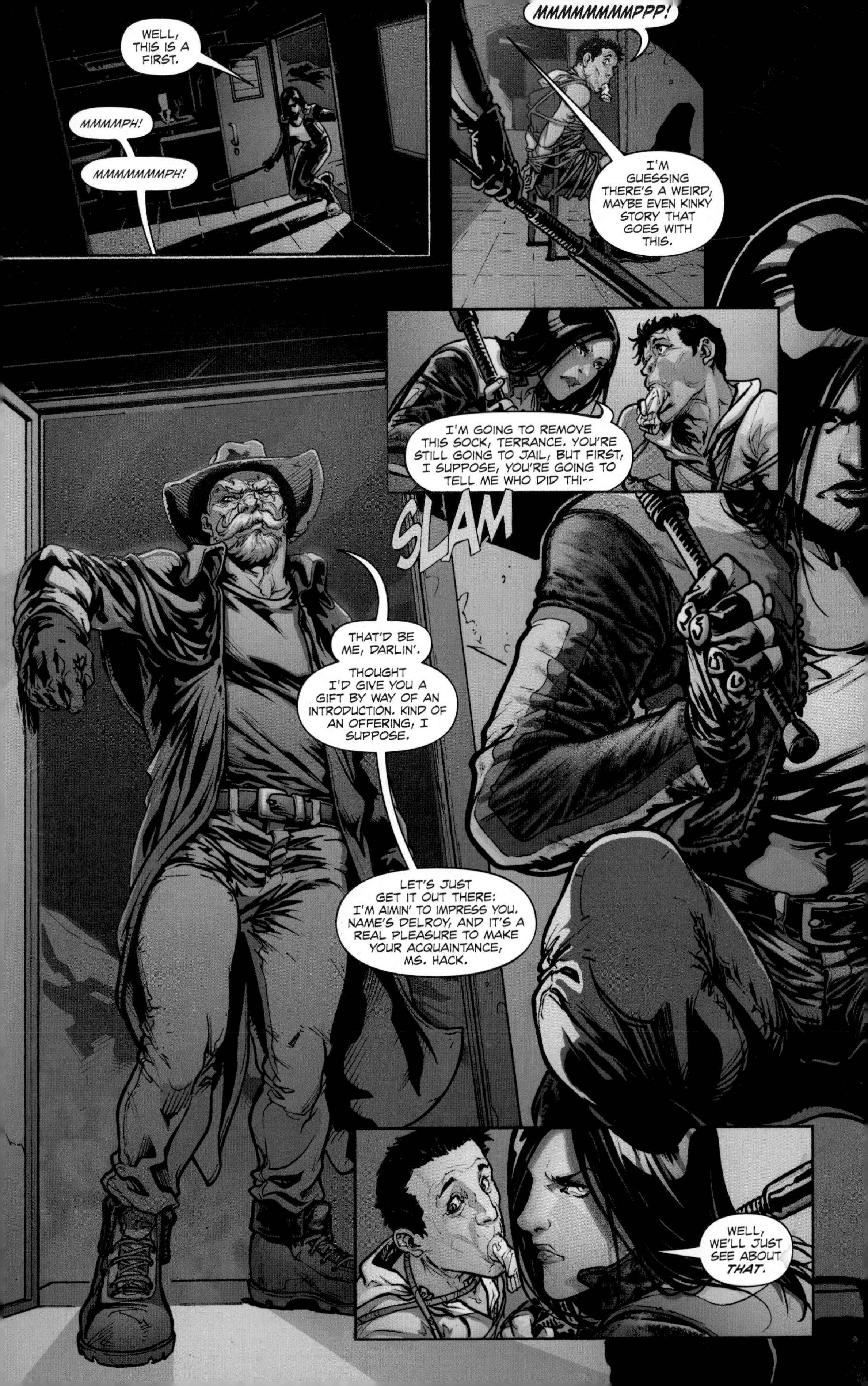
WELL, THIS IS A FIRST.
MMMMPH!
MMMMMMMPH!
MMMMMMMMPPP!
I'M GUESSING THERE'S A WEIRD, MAYBE EVEN KINKY STORY THAT GOES WITH THIS.
I'M GOING TO REMOVE THIS SOCK, TERRANCE. YOU'RE STILL GOING TO JAIL, BUT FIRST, I SUPPOSE, YOU'RE GOING TO TELL ME WHO DID THI--
SLAM
THAT'D BE ME, DARLIN'.
THOUGHT I'D GIVE YOU A GIFT BY WAY OF AN INTRODUCTION. KIND OF AN OFFERING, I SUPPOSE.
LET'S JUST GET IT OUT THERE: I'M AIMIN' TO IMPRESS YOU. NAME'S DELROY, AND IT'S A REAL PLEASURE TO MAKE YOUR ACQUAINTANCE, MS. HACK.
WELL, WE'LL JUST SEE ABOUT *THAT*.

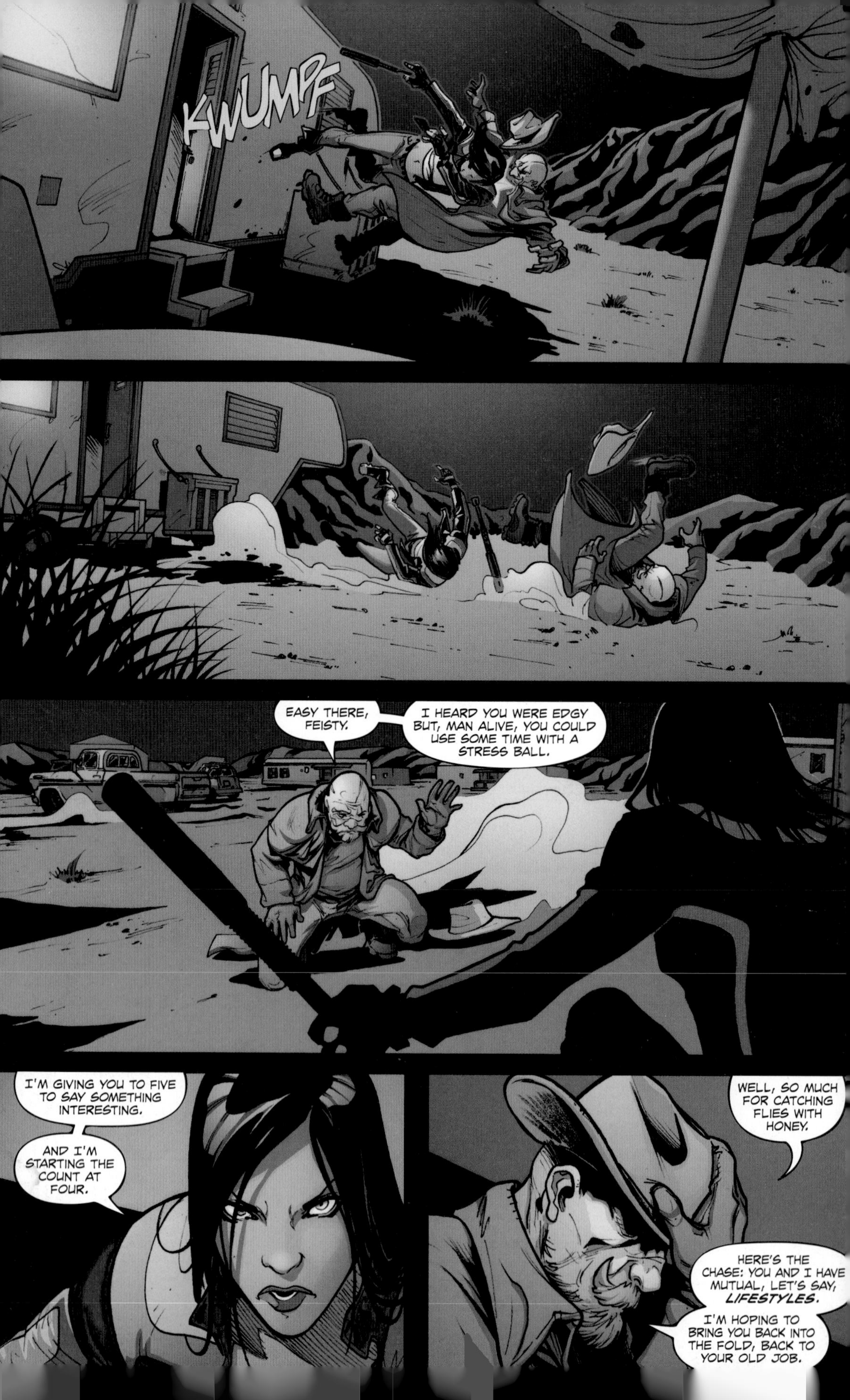
KWUMPF
EASY THERE, FEISTY.
I HEARD YOU WERE EDGY BUT, MAN ALIVE, YOU COULD USE SOME TIME WITH A STRESS BALL.
I'M GIVING YOU TO FIVE TO SAY SOMETHING INTERESTING.
AND I'M STARTING THE COUNT AT FOUR.
WELL, SO MUCH FOR CATCHING FLIES WITH HONEY.
HERE'S THE CHASE: YOU AND I HAVE MUTUAL, LET'S SAY, *LIFESTYLES*.
I'M HOPING TO BRING YOU BACK INTO THE FOLD, BACK TO YOUR OLD JOB.

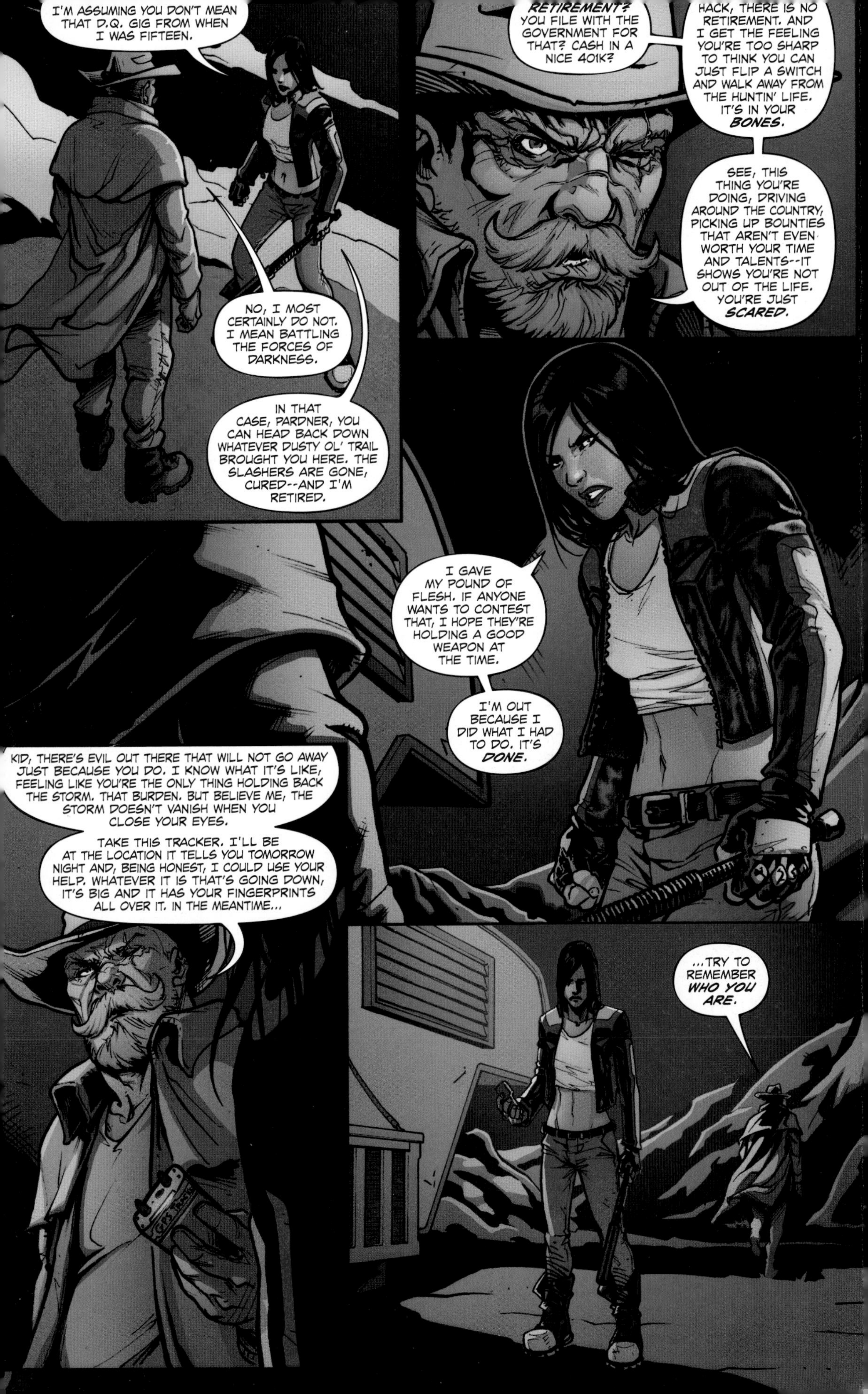

I'M ASSUMING YOU DON'T MEAN THAT D.Q. GIG FROM WHEN I WAS FIFTEEN.
NO, I MOST CERTAINLY DO NOT. I MEAN BATTLING THE FORCES OF DARKNESS.
IN THAT CASE, PARDNER, YOU CAN HEAD BACK DOWN WHATEVER DUSTY OL' TRAIL BROUGHT YOU HERE. THE SLASHERS ARE GONE, CURED--AND I'M RETIRED.
RETIREMENT? YOU FILE WITH THE GOVERNMENT FOR THAT? CASH IN A NICE 401K?
HACK, THERE IS NO RETIREMENT. AND I GET THE FEELING YOU'RE TOO SHARP TO THINK YOU CAN JUST FLIP A SWITCH AND WALK AWAY FROM THE HUNTIN' LIFE. IT'S IN YOUR BONES.
SEE, THIS THING YOU'RE DOING, DRIVING AROUND THE COUNTRY, PICKING UP BOUNTIES THAT AREN'T EVEN WORTH YOUR TIME AND TALENTS--IT SHOWS YOU'RE NOT OUT OF THE LIFE. YOU'RE JUST SCARED.
I GAVE MY POUND OF FLESH. IF ANYONE WANTS TO CONTEST THAT, I HOPE THEY'RE HOLDING A GOOD WEAPON AT THE TIME.
I'M OUT BECAUSE I DID WHAT I HAD TO DO. IT'S DONE.
KID, THERE'S EVIL OUT THERE THAT WILL NOT GO AWAY JUST BECAUSE YOU DO. I KNOW WHAT IT'S LIKE, FEELING LIKE YOU'RE THE ONLY THING HOLDING BACK THE STORM. THAT BURDEN. BUT BELIEVE ME, THE STORM DOESN'T VANISH WHEN YOU CLOSE YOUR EYES.
TAKE THIS TRACKER. I'LL BE AT THE LOCATION IT TELLS YOU TOMORROW NIGHT AND, BEING HONEST, I COULD USE YOUR HELP. WHATEVER IT IS THAT'S GOING DOWN, IT'S BIG AND IT HAS YOUR FINGERPRINTS ALL OVER IT. IN THE MEANTIME...
...TRY TO REMEMBER WHO YOU ARE.

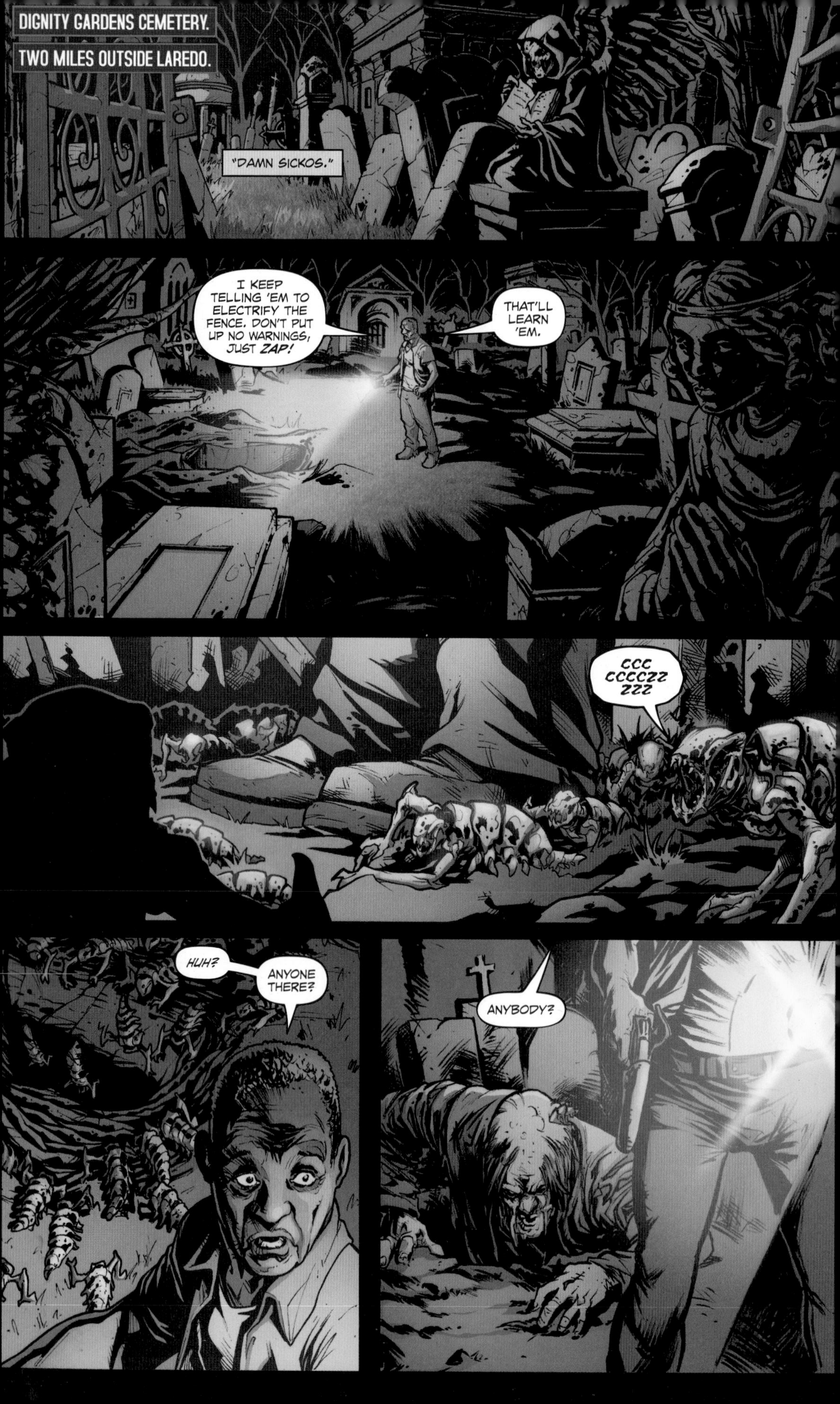
DIGNITY GARDENS CEMETERY.
TWO MILES OUTSIDE LAREDO.
"DAMN SICKOS."
I KEEP TELLING 'EM TO ELECTRIFY THE FENCE. DON'T PUT UP NO WARNINGS, JUST ZAP!
THAT'LL LEARN 'EM.
CCC CCCCZZ ZZZ
HUH?
ANYONE THERE?
ANYBODY?

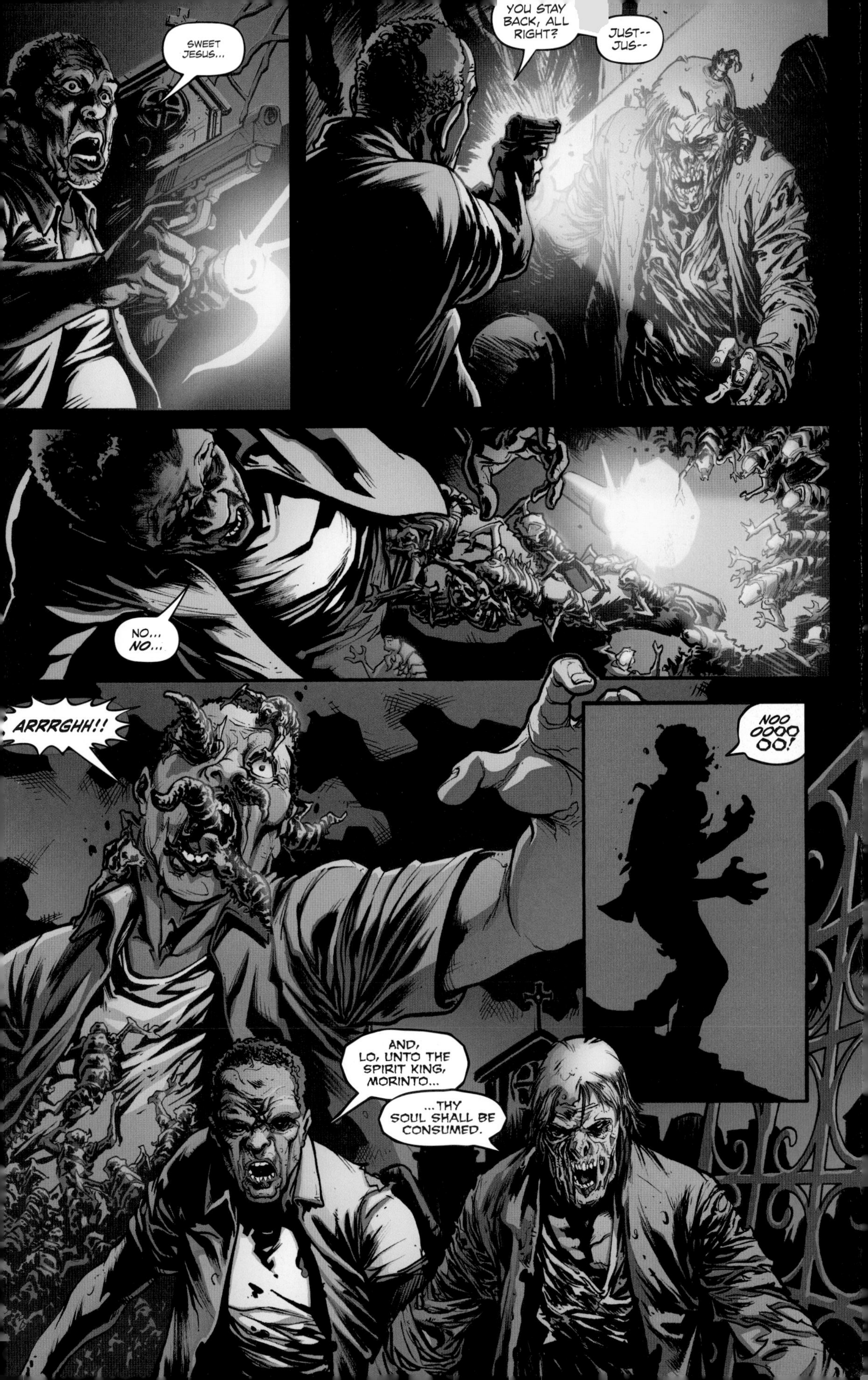
SWEET JESUS...
YOU STAY BACK, ALL RIGHT?
JUST-- JUS--
NO... NO...
ARRRGHH!!
NOOOOOOOO!
AND, LO, UNTO THE SPIRIT KING, MORINTO...
...THY SOUL SHALL BE CONSUMED.

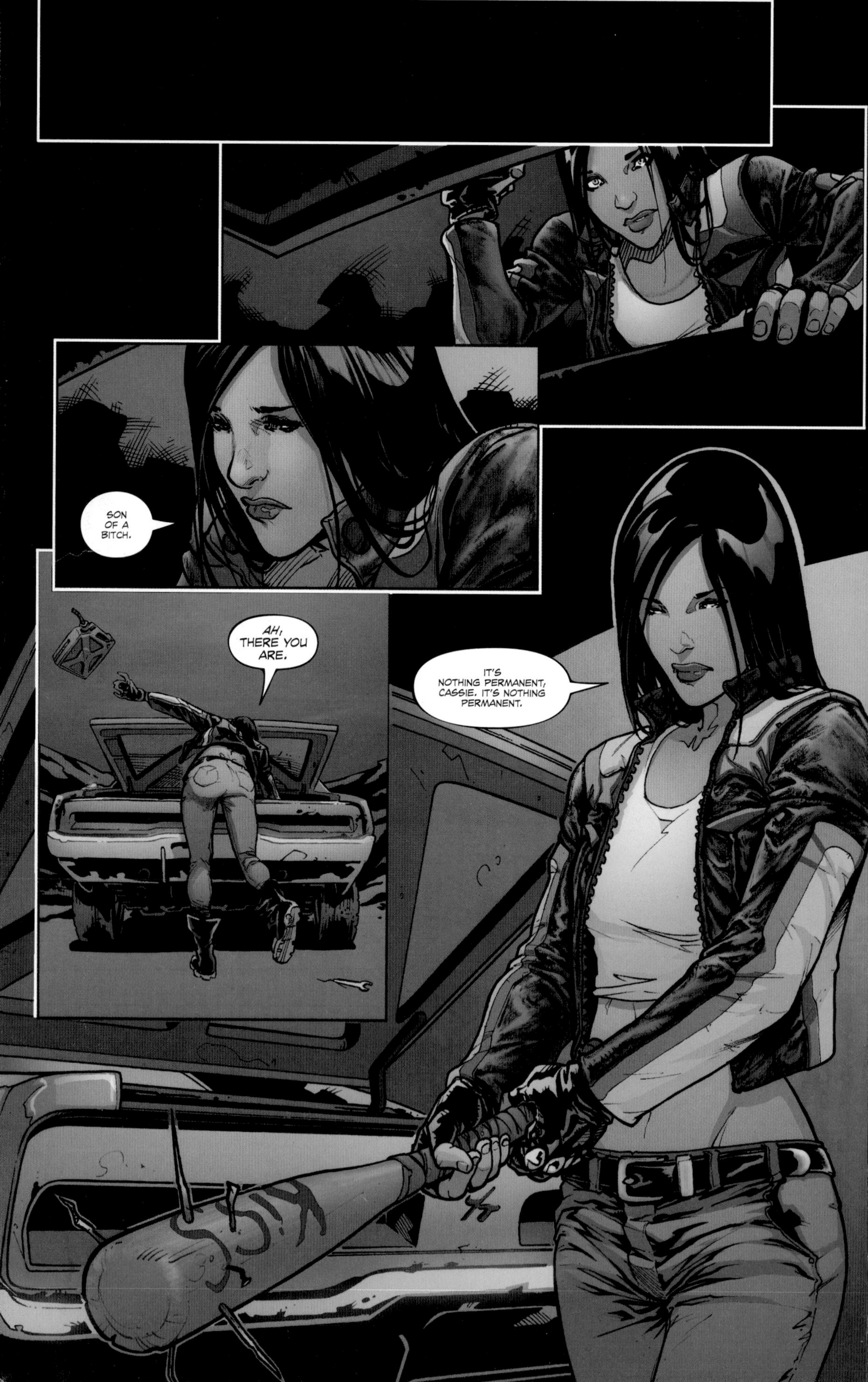
SON OF A BITCH.
AH, THERE YOU ARE.
IT'S NOTHING PERMANENT, CASSIE. IT'S NOTHING PERMANENT.

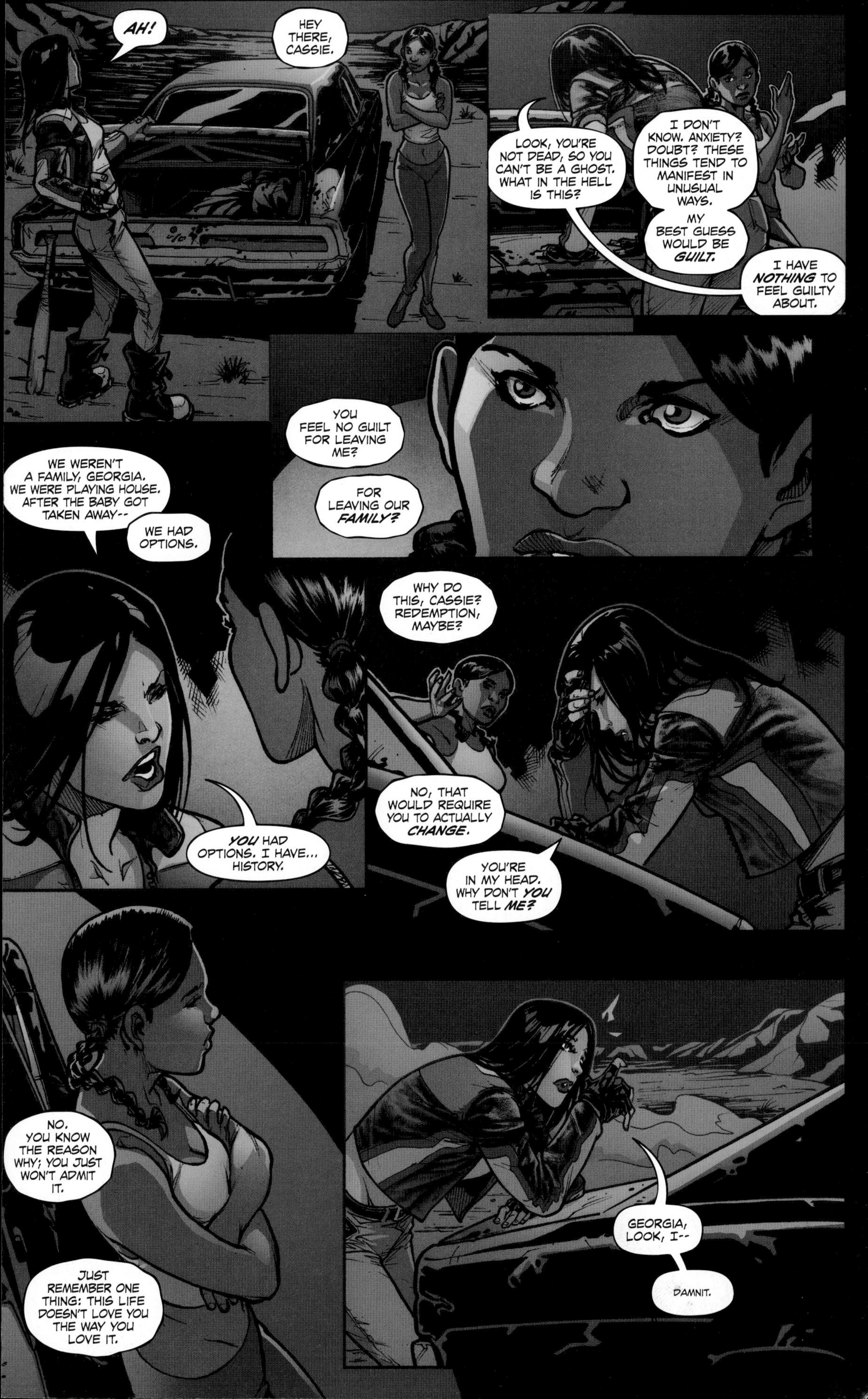
AH!
HEY THERE, CASSIE.
LOOK, YOU'RE NOT DEAD, SO YOU CAN'T BE A GHOST. WHAT IN THE HELL IS THIS?
I DON'T KNOW. ANXIETY? DOUBT? THESE THINGS TEND TO MANIFEST IN UNUSUAL WAYS.
MY BEST GUESS WOULD BE GUILT.
I HAVE NOTHING TO FEEL GUILTY ABOUT.
YOU FEEL NO GUILT FOR LEAVING ME?
FOR LEAVING OUR FAMILY?
WE WEREN'T A FAMILY, GEORGIA. WE WERE PLAYING HOUSE. AFTER THE BABY GOT TAKEN AWAY--
WE HAD OPTIONS.
YOU HAD OPTIONS. I HAVE... HISTORY.
WHY DO THIS, CASSIE? REDEMPTION, MAYBE?
NO, THAT WOULD REQUIRE YOU TO ACTUALLY CHANGE.
YOU'RE IN MY HEAD. WHY DON'T YOU TELL ME?
NO. YOU KNOW THE REASON WHY; YOU JUST WON'T ADMIT IT.
JUST REMEMBER ONE THING: THIS LIFE DOESN'T LOVE YOU THE WAY YOU LOVE IT.
GEORGIA, LOOK, I--
DAMNIT.

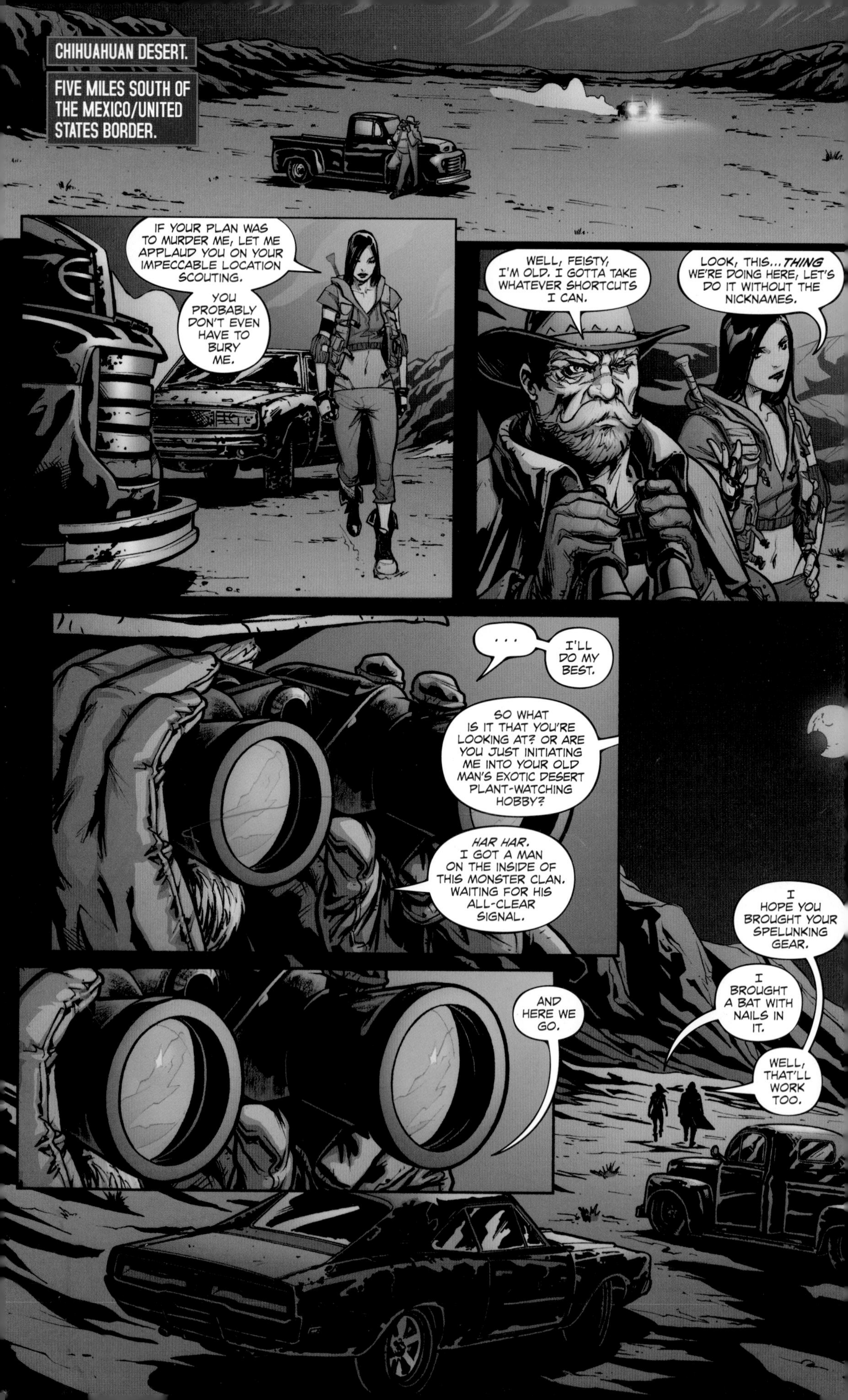
CHIHUAHUAN DESERT.
FIVE MILES SOUTH OF THE MEXICO/UNITED STATES BORDER.
IF YOUR PLAN WAS TO MURDER ME, LET ME APPLAUD YOU ON YOUR IMPECCABLE LOCATION SCOUTING.
YOU PROBABLY DON'T EVEN HAVE TO BURY ME.
WELL, FEISTY, I'M OLD. I GOTTA TAKE WHATEVER SHORTCUTS I CAN.
LOOK, THIS... *THING* WE'RE DOING HERE, LET'S DO IT WITHOUT THE NICKNAMES.
...
I'LL DO MY BEST.
SO WHAT IS IT THAT YOU'RE LOOKING AT? OR ARE YOU JUST INITIATING ME INTO YOUR OLD MAN'S EXOTIC DESERT PLANT-WATCHING HOBBY?
HAR HAR. I GOT A MAN ON THE INSIDE OF THIS MONSTER CLAN. WAITING FOR HIS ALL-CLEAR SIGNAL.
AND HERE WE GO.
I HOPE YOU BROUGHT YOUR SPELUNKING GEAR.
I BROUGHT A BAT WITH NAILS IN IT.
WELL, THAT'LL WORK TOO.

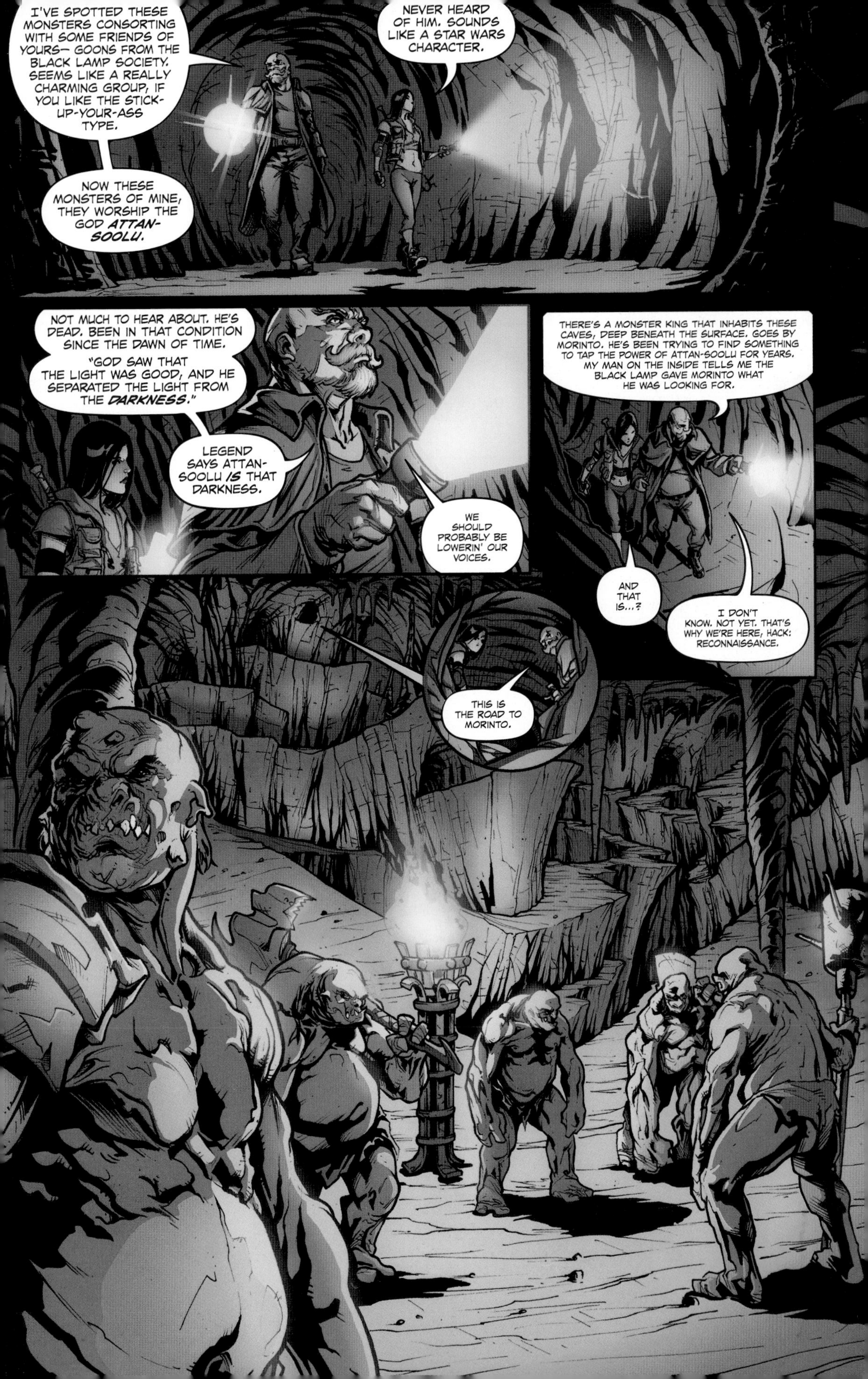

I'VE SPOTTED THESE MONSTERS CONSORTING WITH SOME FRIENDS OF YOURS— GOONS FROM THE BLACK LAMP SOCIETY. SEEMS LIKE A REALLY CHARMING GROUP, IF YOU LIKE THE STICK-UP-YOUR-ASS TYPE.
NOW THESE MONSTERS OF MINE, THEY WORSHIP THE GOD ATTAN-SOOLU.
NEVER HEARD OF HIM. SOUNDS LIKE A STAR WARS CHARACTER.
NOT MUCH TO HEAR ABOUT. HE'S DEAD. BEEN IN THAT CONDITION SINCE THE DAWN OF TIME.
"GOD SAW THAT THE LIGHT WAS GOOD, AND HE SEPARATED THE LIGHT FROM THE DARKNESS."
LEGEND SAYS ATTAN-SOOLU IS THAT DARKNESS.
WE SHOULD PROBABLY BE LOWERIN' OUR VOICES.
THERE'S A MONSTER KING THAT INHABITS THESE CAVES, DEEP BENEATH THE SURFACE. GOES BY MORINTO. HE'S BEEN TRYING TO FIND SOMETHING TO TAP THE POWER OF ATTAN-SOOLU FOR YEARS. MY MAN ON THE INSIDE TELLS ME THE BLACK LAMP GAVE MORINTO WHAT HE WAS LOOKING FOR.
AND THAT IS...?
I DON'T KNOW. NOT YET. THAT'S WHY WE'RE HERE, HACK: RECONNAISSANCE.
THIS IS THE ROAD TO MORINTO.

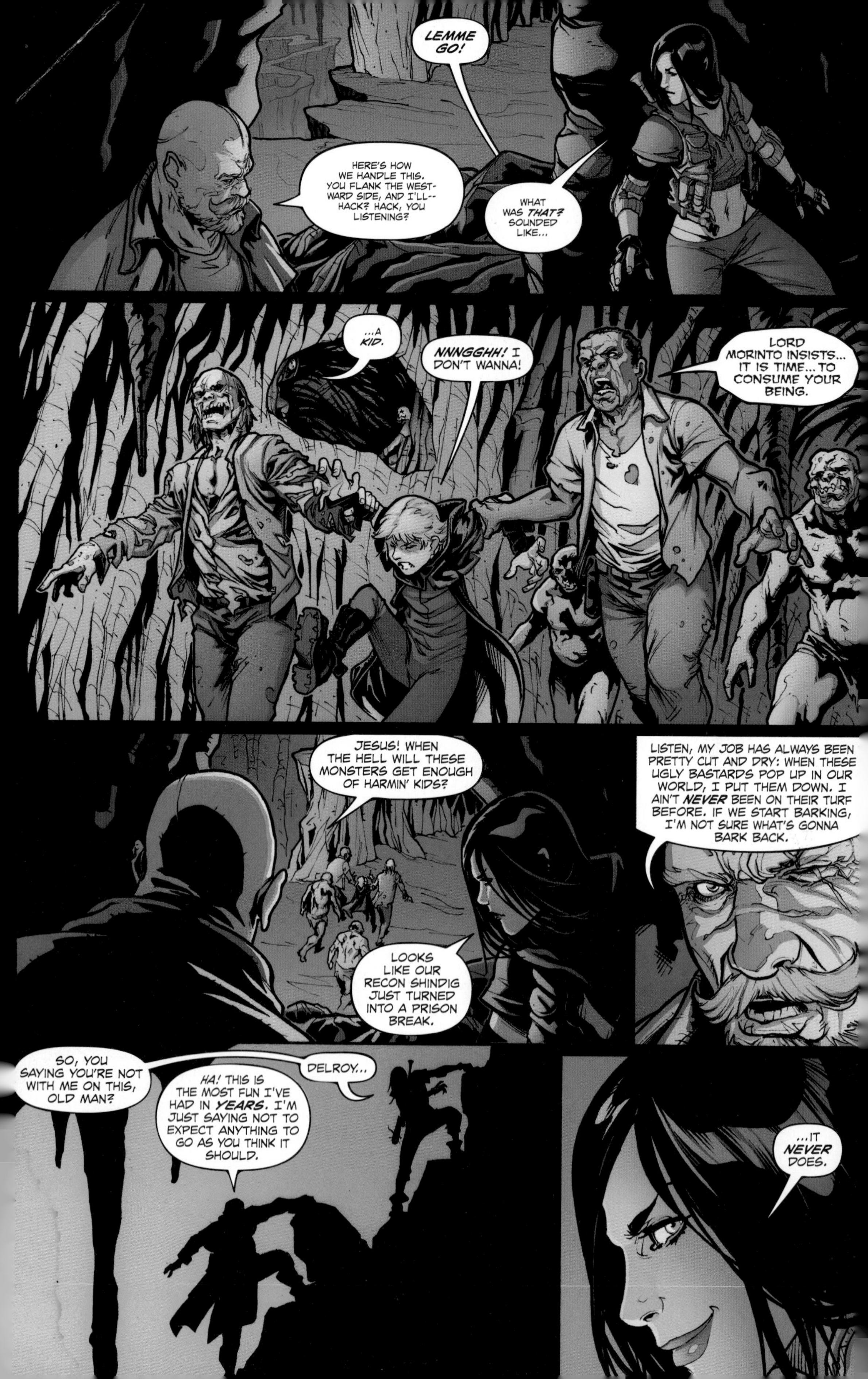
LEMME GO!
HERE'S HOW WE HANDLE THIS. YOU FLANK THE WEST-WARD SIDE, AND I'LL-- HACK? HACK, YOU LISTENING?
WHAT WAS THAT? SOUNDED LIKE...
...A KID.
NNNGGHH! I DON'T WANNA!
LORD MORINTO INSISTS... IT IS TIME... TO CONSUME YOUR BEING.
JESUS! WHEN THE HELL WILL THESE MONSTERS GET ENOUGH OF HARMIN' KIDS?
LOOKS LIKE OUR RECON SHINDIG JUST TURNED INTO A PRISON BREAK.
LISTEN, MY JOB HAS ALWAYS BEEN PRETTY CUT AND DRY: WHEN THESE UGLY BASTARDS POP UP IN OUR WORLD, I PUT THEM DOWN. I AIN'T NEVER BEEN ON THEIR TURF BEFORE. IF WE START BARKING, I'M NOT SURE WHAT'S GONNA BARK BACK.
SO, YOU SAYING YOU'RE NOT WITH ME ON THIS, OLD MAN?
HA! THIS IS THE MOST FUN I'VE HAD IN YEARS. I'M JUST SAYING NOT TO EXPECT ANYTHING TO GO AS YOU THINK IT SHOULD.
DELROY...
...IT NEVER DOES.

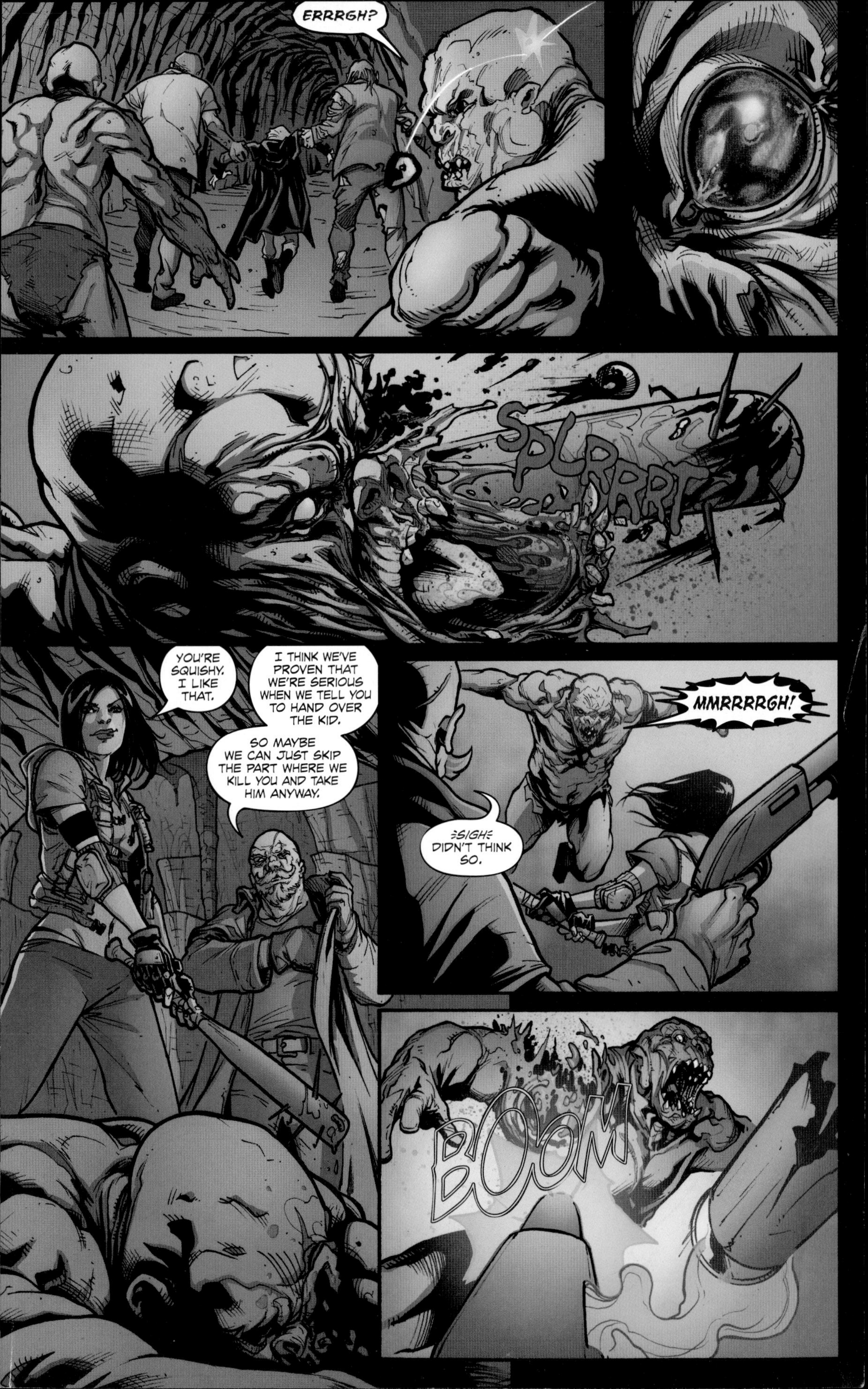
ERRRGH?
SPLRRRT
YOU'RE SQUISHY. I LIKE THAT.
I THINK WE'VE PROVEN THAT WE'RE SERIOUS WHEN WE TELL YOU TO HAND OVER THE KID.
SO MAYBE WE CAN JUST SKIP THE PART WHERE WE KILL YOU AND TAKE HIM ANYWAY.
MMRRRRGH!
SIGH DIDN'T THINK SO.
BOOM

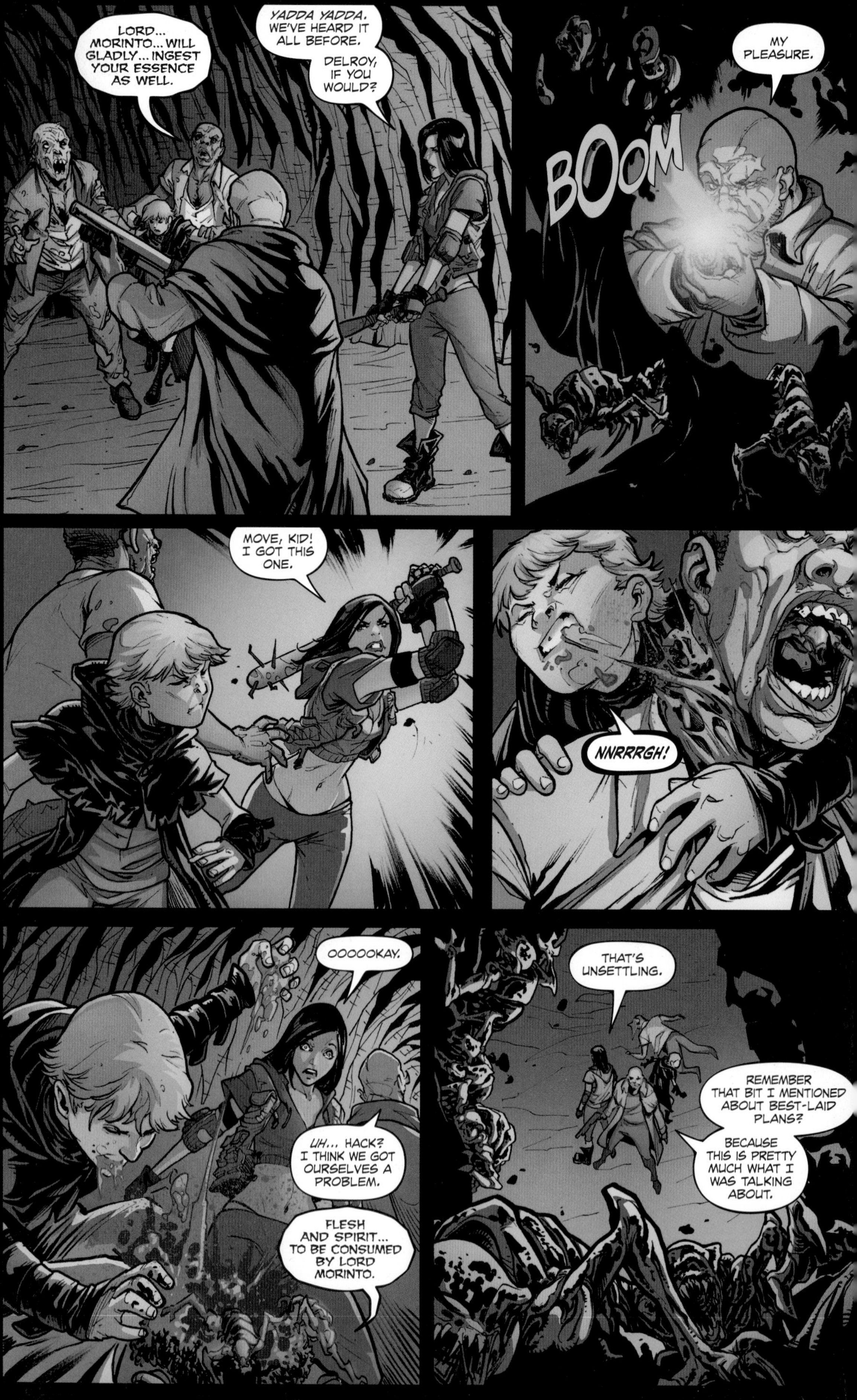
LORD... MORINTO... WILL GLADLY... INGEST YOUR ESSENCE AS WELL.
YADDA YADDA. WE'VE HEARD IT ALL BEFORE.
DELROY, IF YOU WOULD?
MY PLEASURE.
BOOM
MOVE, KID! I GOT THIS ONE.
NNRRRGH!
OOOOOKAY.
UH... HACK? I THINK WE GOT OURSELVES A PROBLEM.
FLESH AND SPIRIT... TO BE CONSUMED BY LORD MORINTO.
THAT'S UNSETTLING.
REMEMBER THAT BIT I MENTIONED ABOUT BEST-LAID PLANS?
BECAUSE THIS IS PRETTY MUCH WHAT I WAS TALKING ABOUT.

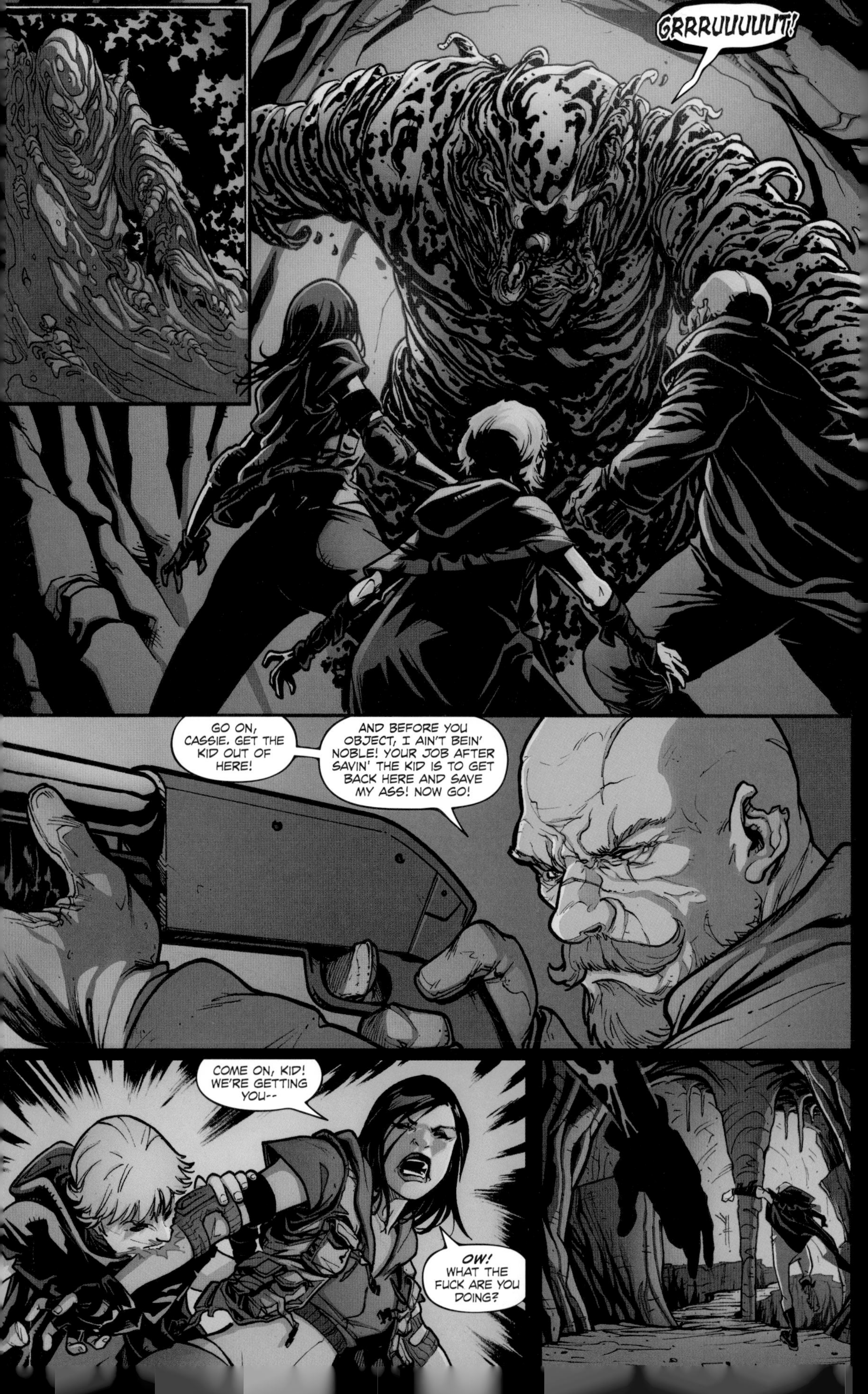
GRRRUUUUUT!
GO ON, CASSIE. GET THE KID OUT OF HERE!
AND BEFORE YOU OBJECT, I AIN'T BEIN' NOBLE! YOUR JOB AFTER SAVIN' THE KID IS TO GET BACK HERE AND SAVE MY ASS! NOW GO!
COME ON, KID! WE'RE GETTING YOU--
OW! WHAT THE FUCK ARE YOU DOING?

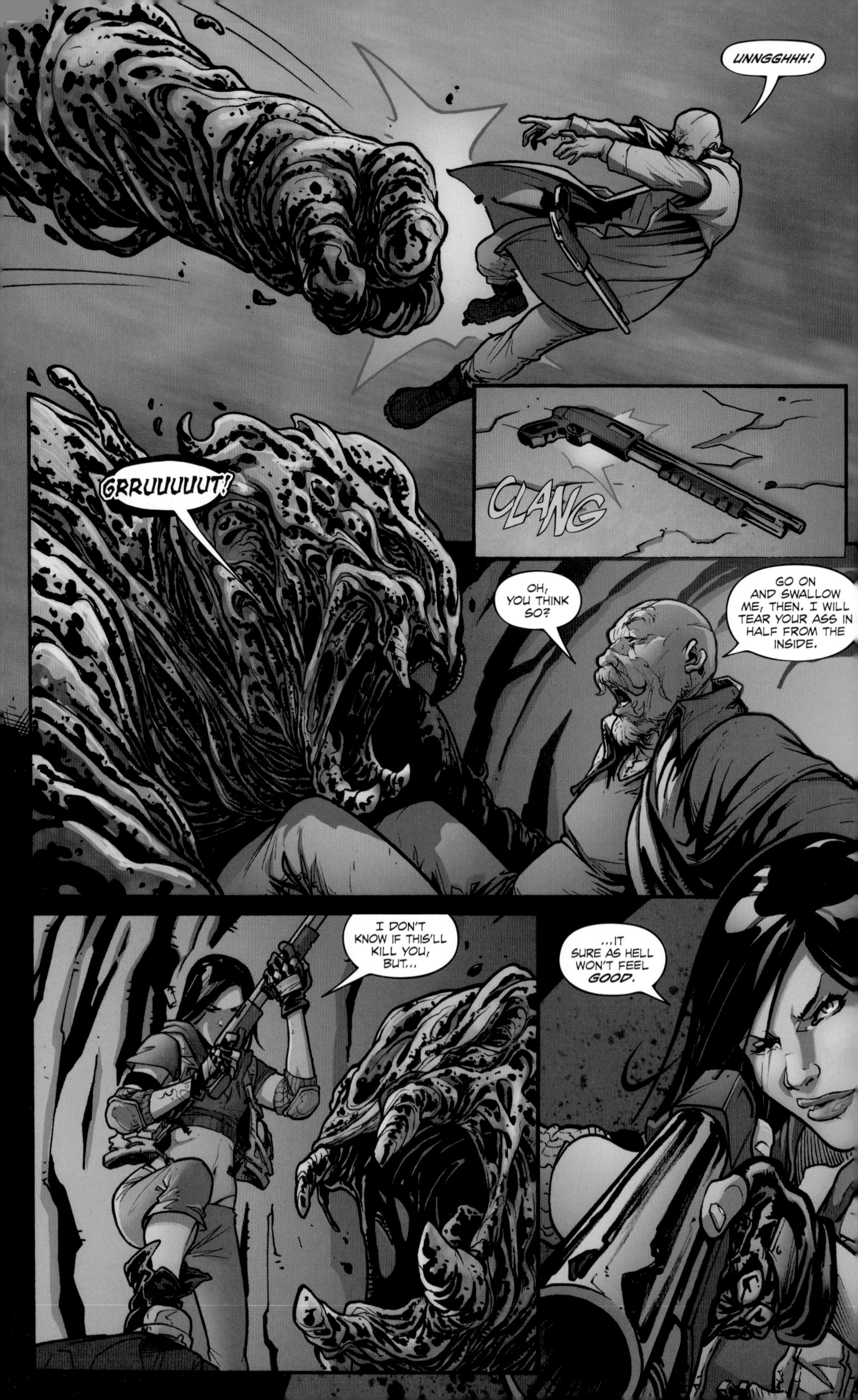
UNNGGHHH!
CLANG
GRRUUUUUT!
OH, YOU THINK SO?
GO ON AND SWALLOW ME, THEN. I WILL TEAR YOUR ASS IN HALF FROM THE INSIDE.
I DON'T KNOW IF THIS'LL KILL YOU, BUT...
...IT SURE AS HELL WON'T FEEL GOOD.

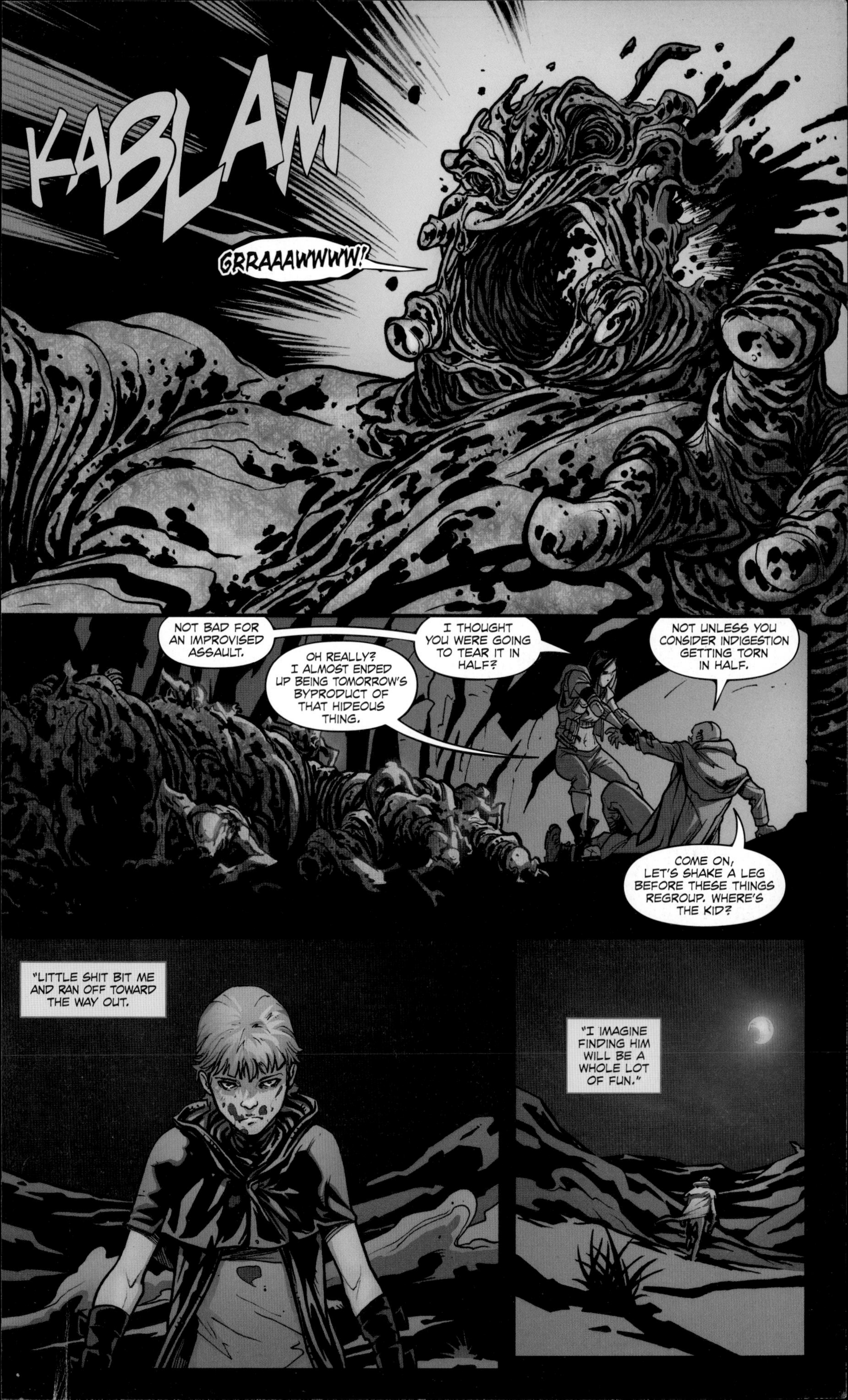
KABLAM
GRRAAAWWWW!
NOT BAD FOR AN IMPROVISED ASSAULT.
I THOUGHT YOU WERE GOING TO TEAR IT IN HALF?
OH REALLY? I ALMOST ENDED UP BEING TOMORROW'S BYPRODUCT OF THAT HIDEOUS THING.
NOT UNLESS YOU CONSIDER INDIGESTION GETTING TORN IN HALF.
COME ON, LET'S SHAKE A LEG BEFORE THESE THINGS REGROUP. WHERE'S THE KID?
"LITTLE SHIT BIT ME AND RAN OFF TOWARD THE WAY OUT.
"I IMAGINE FINDING HIM WILL BE A WHOLE LOT OF FUN."

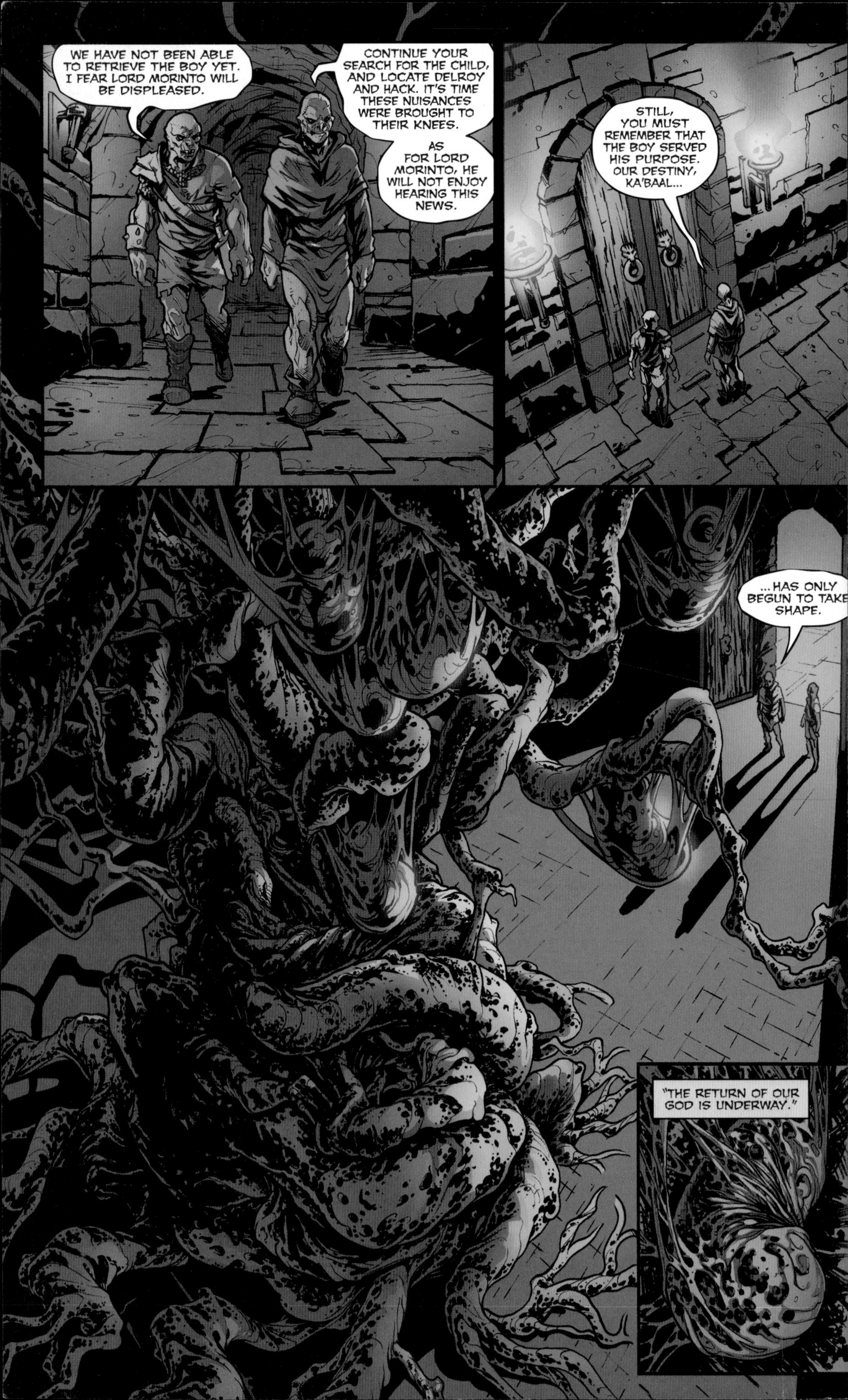
WE HAVE NOT BEEN ABLE TO RETRIEVE THE BOY YET. I FEAR LORD MORINTO WILL BE DISPLEASED.
CONTINUE YOUR SEARCH FOR THE CHILD, AND LOCATE DELROY AND HACK. IT'S TIME THESE NUISANCES WERE BROUGHT TO THEIR KNEES.
AS FOR LORD MORINTO, HE WILL NOT ENJOY HEARING THIS NEWS.
STILL, YOU MUST REMEMBER THAT THE BOY SERVED HIS PURPOSE. OUR DESTINY, KA'BAAL...
...HAS ONLY BEGUN TO TAKE SHAPE.
"THE RETURN OF OUR GOD IS UNDERWAY."

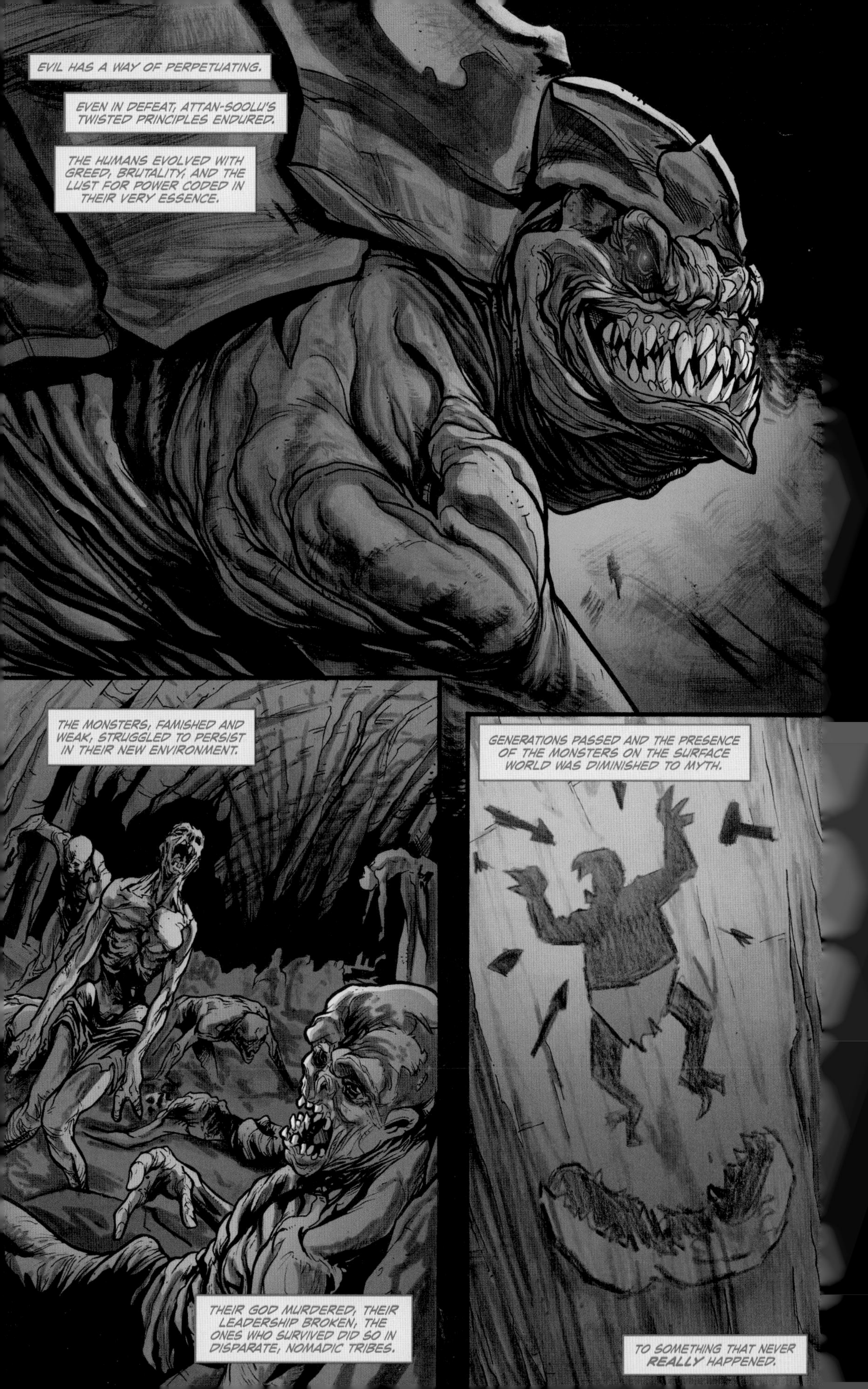
EVIL HAS A WAY OF PERPETUATING.
EVEN IN DEFEAT, ATTAN-SOOLU'S TWISTED PRINCIPLES ENDURED.
THE HUMANS EVOLVED WITH GREED, BRUTALITY, AND THE LUST FOR POWER CODED IN THEIR VERY ESSENCE.
THE MONSTERS, FAMISHED AND WEAK, STRUGGLED TO PERSIST IN THEIR NEW ENVIRONMENT.
THEIR GOD MURDERED, THEIR LEADERSHIP BROKEN, THE ONES WHO SURVIVED DID SO IN DISPARATE, NOMADIC TRIBES.
GENERATIONS PASSED AND THE PRESENCE OF THE MONSTERS ON THE SURFACE WORLD WAS DIMINISHED TO MYTH.
TO SOMETHING THAT NEVER REALLY HAPPENED.

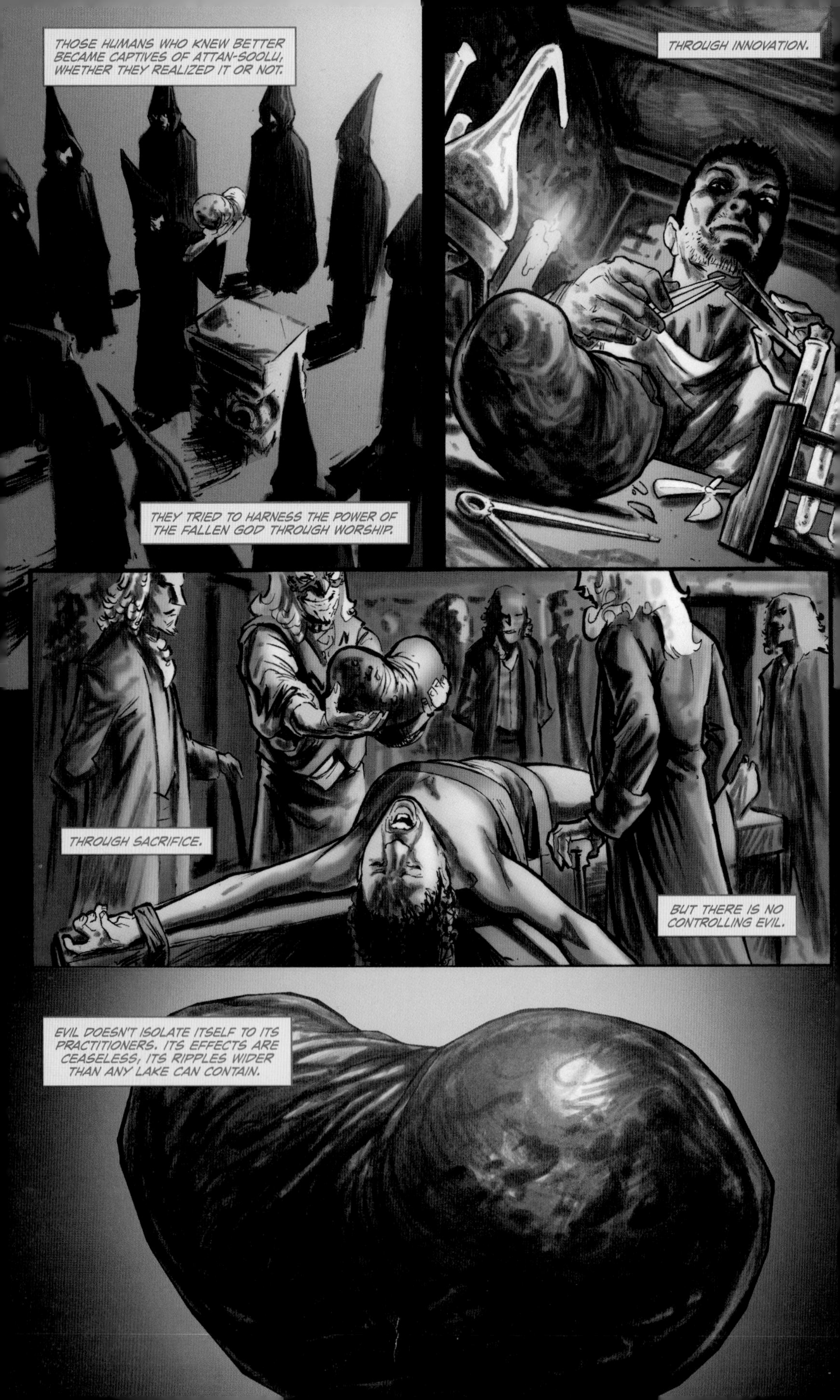
THOSE HUMANS WHO KNEW BETTER BECAME CAPTIVES OF ATTAN-SOOLU, WHETHER THEY REALIZED IT OR NOT.
THEY TRIED TO HARNESS THE POWER OF THE FALLEN GOD THROUGH WORSHIP.
THROUGH INNOVATION.
THROUGH SACRIFICE.
BUT THERE IS NO CONTROLLING EVIL.
EVIL DOESN'T ISOLATE ITSELF TO ITS PRACTITIONERS. ITS EFFECTS ARE CEASELESS, ITS RIPPLES WIDER THAN ANY LAKE CAN CONTAIN.

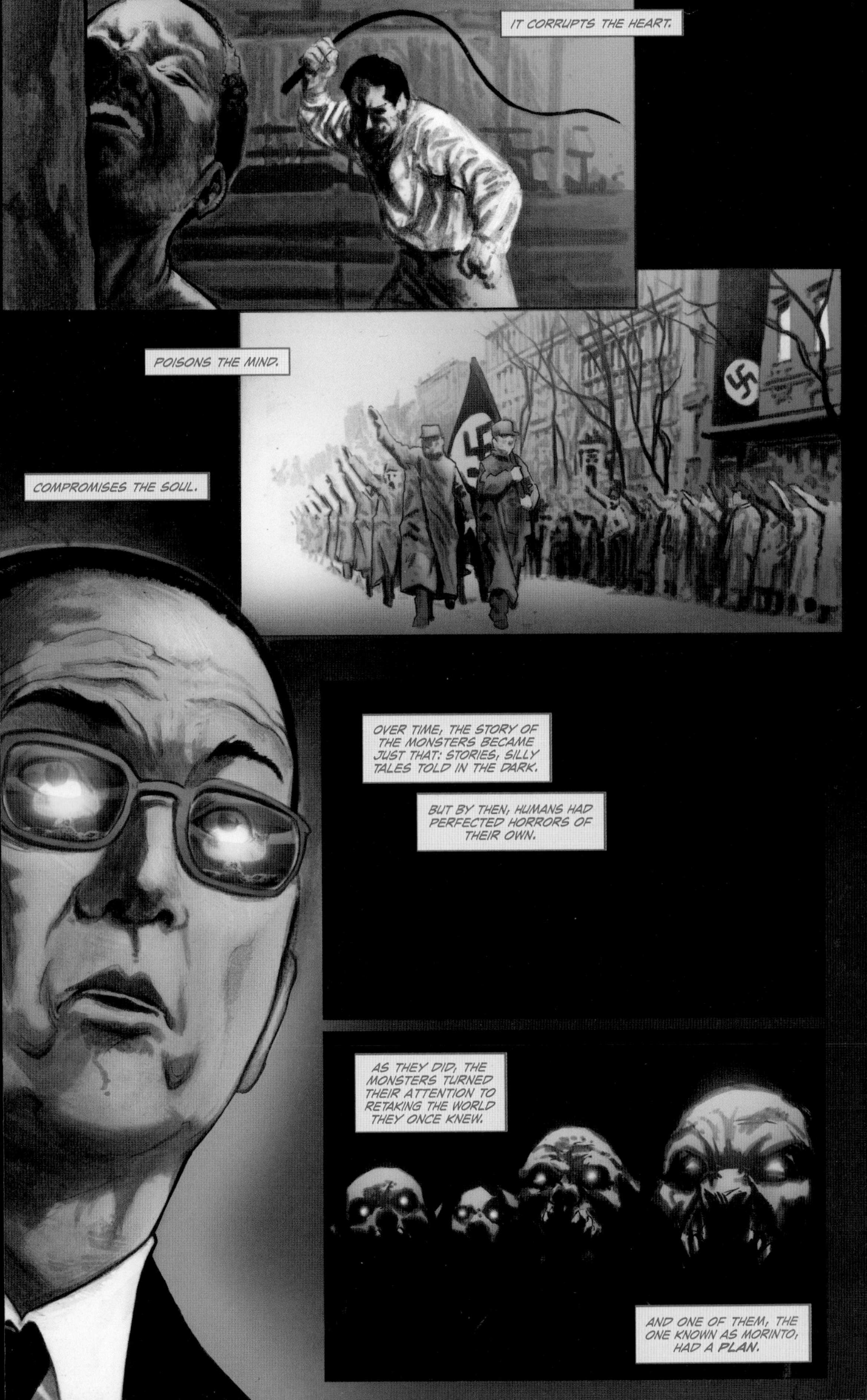
IT CORRUPTS THE HEART.
POISONS THE MIND.
COMPROMISES THE SOUL.
OVER TIME, THE STORY OF THE MONSTERS BECAME JUST THAT: STORIES, SILLY TALES TOLD IN THE DARK.
BUT BY THEN, HUMANS HAD PERFECTED HORRORS OF THEIR OWN.
AS THEY DID, THE MONSTERS TURNED THEIR ATTENTION TO RETAKING THE WORLD THEY ONCE KNEW.
AND ONE OF THEM, THE ONE KNOWN AS MORINTO, HAD A **PLAN**.

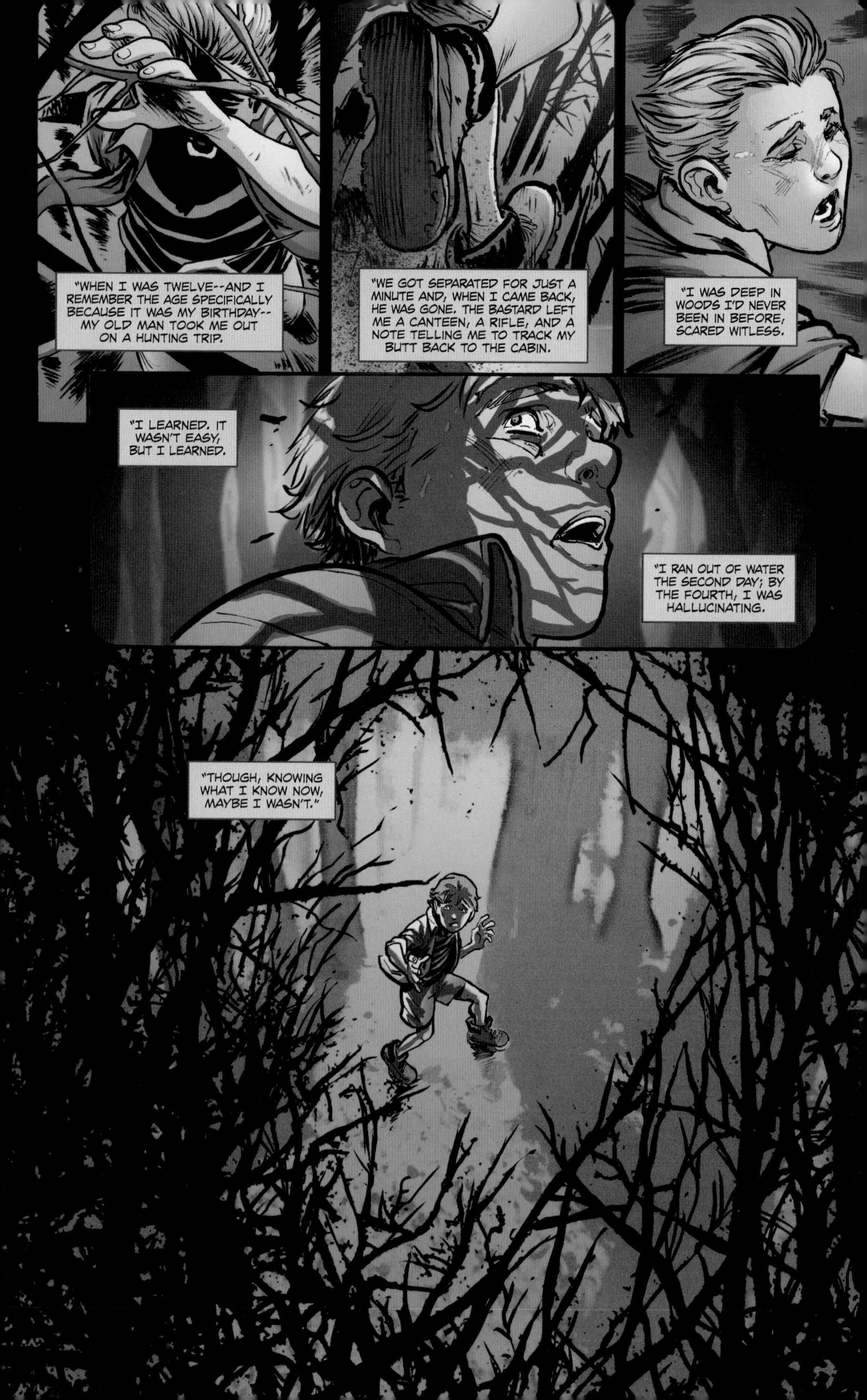
"WHEN I WAS TWELVE--AND I REMEMBER THE AGE SPECIFICALLY BECAUSE IT WAS MY BIRTHDAY--MY OLD MAN TOOK ME OUT ON A HUNTING TRIP.
"WE GOT SEPARATED FOR JUST A MINUTE AND, WHEN I CAME BACK, HE WAS GONE. THE BASTARD LEFT ME A CANTEEN, A RIFLE, AND A NOTE TELLING ME TO TRACK MY BUTT BACK TO THE CABIN.
"I WAS DEEP IN WOODS I'D NEVER BEEN IN BEFORE, SCARED WITLESS.
"I LEARNED. IT WASN'T EASY, BUT I LEARNED.
"I RAN OUT OF WATER THE SECOND DAY; BY THE FOURTH, I WAS HALLUCINATING.
"THOUGH, KNOWING WHAT I KNOW NOW, MAYBE I WASN'T."

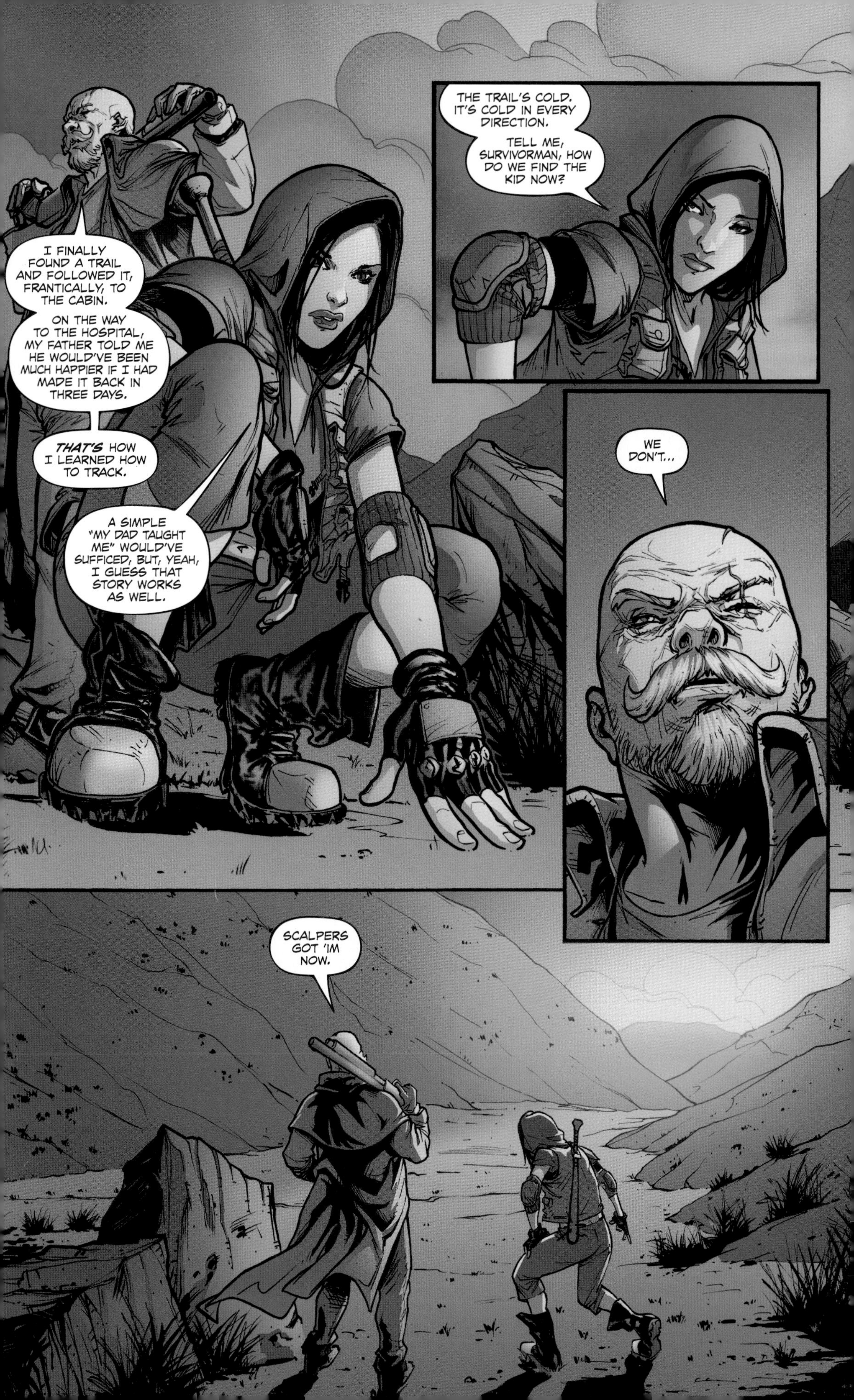
I FINALLY FOUND A TRAIL AND FOLLOWED IT, FRANTICALLY, TO THE CABIN.
ON THE WAY TO THE HOSPITAL, MY FATHER TOLD ME HE WOULD'VE BEEN MUCH HAPPIER IF I HAD MADE IT BACK IN THREE DAYS.
THAT'S HOW I LEARNED HOW TO TRACK.
A SIMPLE "MY DAD TAUGHT ME" WOULD'VE SUFFICED, BUT, YEAH, I GUESS THAT STORY WORKS AS WELL.
THE TRAIL'S COLD. IT'S COLD IN EVERY DIRECTION.
TELL ME, SURVIVORMAN, HOW DO WE FIND THE KID NOW?
WE DON'T...
SCALPERS GOT 'IM NOW.

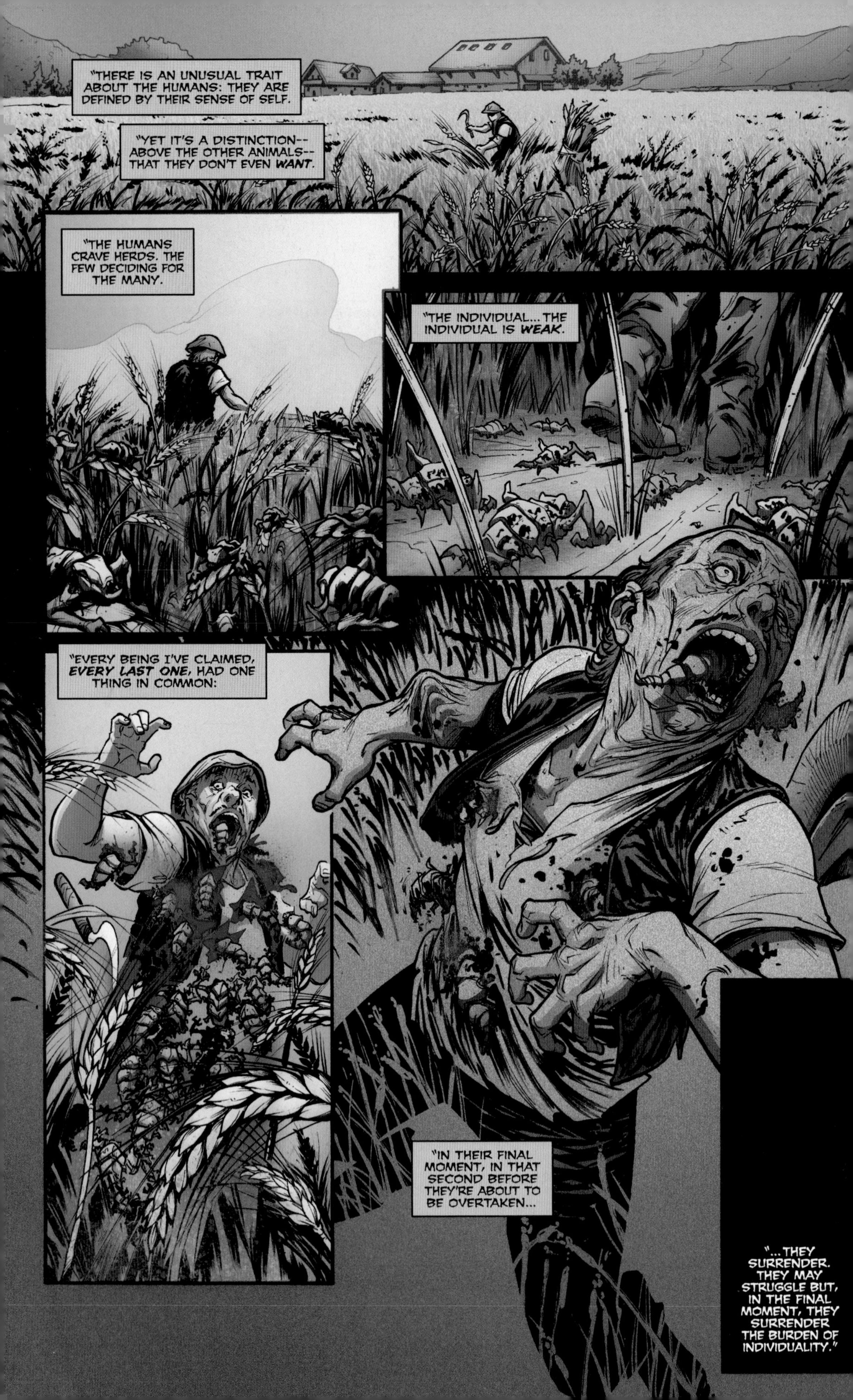
"THERE IS AN UNUSUAL TRAIT ABOUT THE HUMANS: THEY ARE DEFINED BY THEIR SENSE OF SELF.
"YET IT'S A DISTINCTION-- ABOVE THE OTHER ANIMALS-- THAT THEY DON'T EVEN WANT.
"THE HUMANS CRAVE HERDS. THE FEW DECIDING FOR THE MANY.
"THE INDIVIDUAL... THE INDIVIDUAL IS WEAK.
"EVERY BEING I'VE CLAIMED, EVERY LAST ONE, HAD ONE THING IN COMMON:
"IN THEIR FINAL MOMENT, IN THAT SECOND BEFORE THEY'RE ABOUT TO BE OVERTAKEN...
"...THEY SURRENDER. THEY MAY STRUGGLE BUT, IN THE FINAL MOMENT, THEY SURRENDER THE BURDEN OF INDIVIDUALITY."

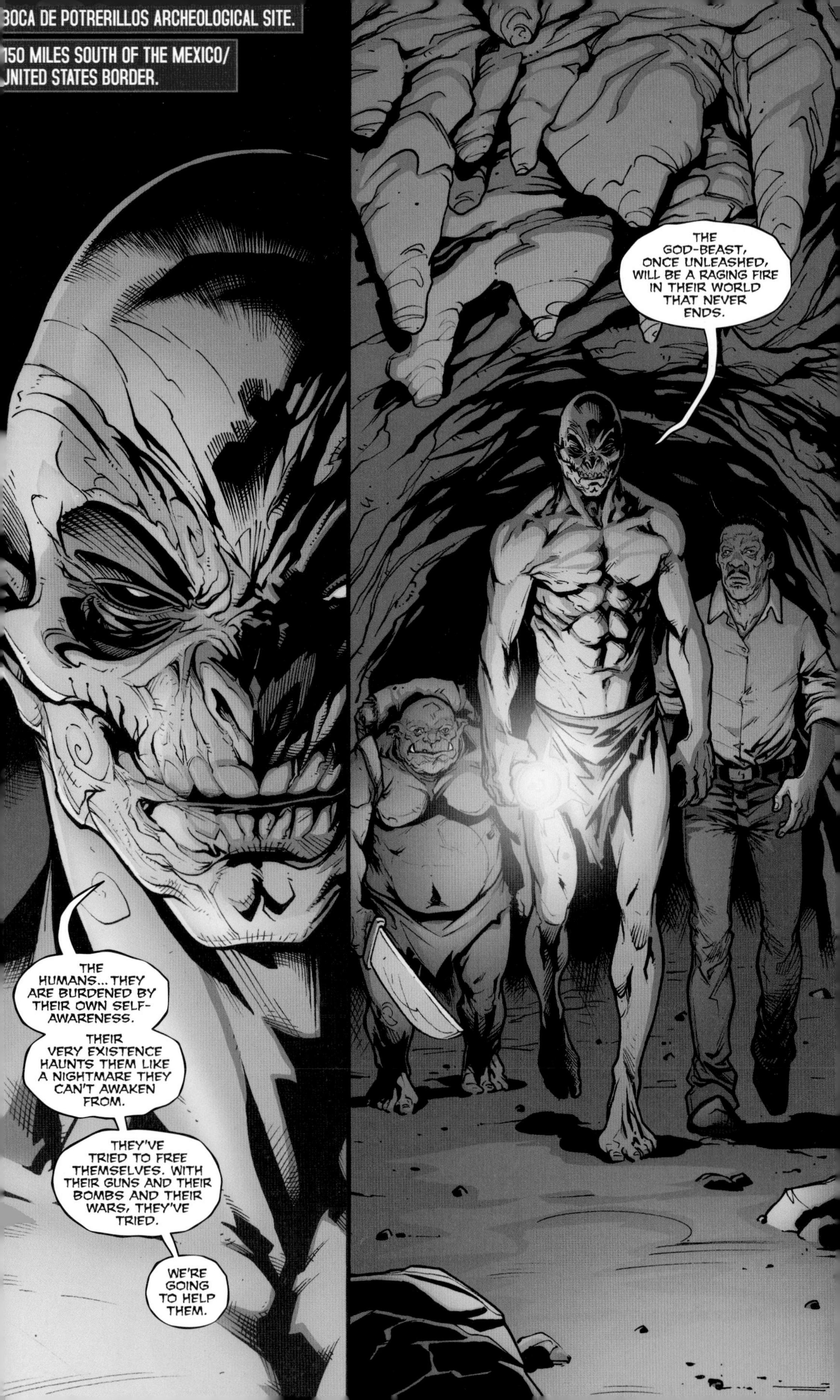

BOCA DE POTRERILLOS ARCHEOLOGICAL SITE.
150 MILES SOUTH OF THE MEXICO/ UNITED STATES BORDER.
THE HUMANS... THEY ARE BURDENED BY THEIR OWN SELF-AWARENESS.
THEIR VERY EXISTENCE HAUNTS THEM LIKE A NIGHTMARE THEY CAN'T AWAKEN FROM.
THEY'VE TRIED TO FREE THEMSELVES. WITH THEIR GUNS AND THEIR BOMBS AND THEIR WARS, THEY'VE TRIED.
WE'RE GOING TO HELP THEM.
THE GOD-BEAST, ONCE UNLEASHED, WILL BE A RAGING FIRE IN THEIR WORLD THAT NEVER ENDS.

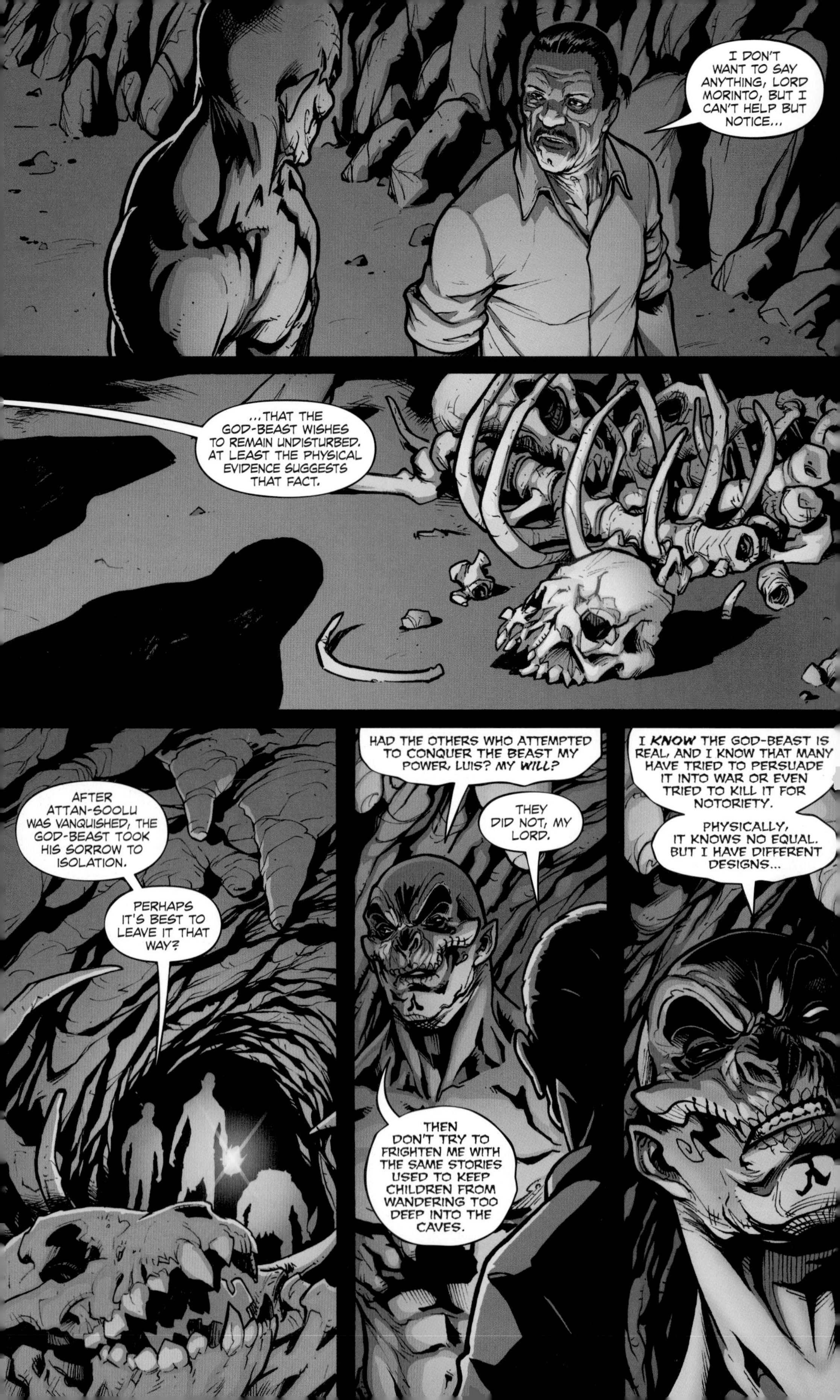
I DON'T WANT TO SAY ANYTHING, LORD MORINTO, BUT I CAN'T HELP BUT NOTICE...
...THAT THE GOD-BEAST WISHES TO REMAIN UNDISTURBED. AT LEAST THE PHYSICAL EVIDENCE SUGGESTS THAT FACT.
AFTER ATTAN-SOOLU WAS VANQUISHED, THE GOD-BEAST TOOK HIS SORROW TO ISOLATION.
PERHAPS IT'S BEST TO LEAVE IT THAT WAY?
HAD THE OTHERS WHO ATTEMPTED TO CONQUER THE BEAST MY POWER, LUIS? MY *WILL*?
THEY DID NOT, MY LORD.
THEN DON'T TRY TO FRIGHTEN ME WITH THE SAME STORIES USED TO KEEP CHILDREN FROM WANDERING TOO DEEP INTO THE CAVES.
I *KNOW* THE GOD-BEAST IS REAL, AND I KNOW THAT MANY HAVE TRIED TO PERSUADE IT INTO WAR OR EVEN TRIED TO KILL IT FOR NOTORIETY.
PHYSICALLY, IT KNOWS NO EQUAL. BUT I HAVE DIFFERENT DESIGNS...

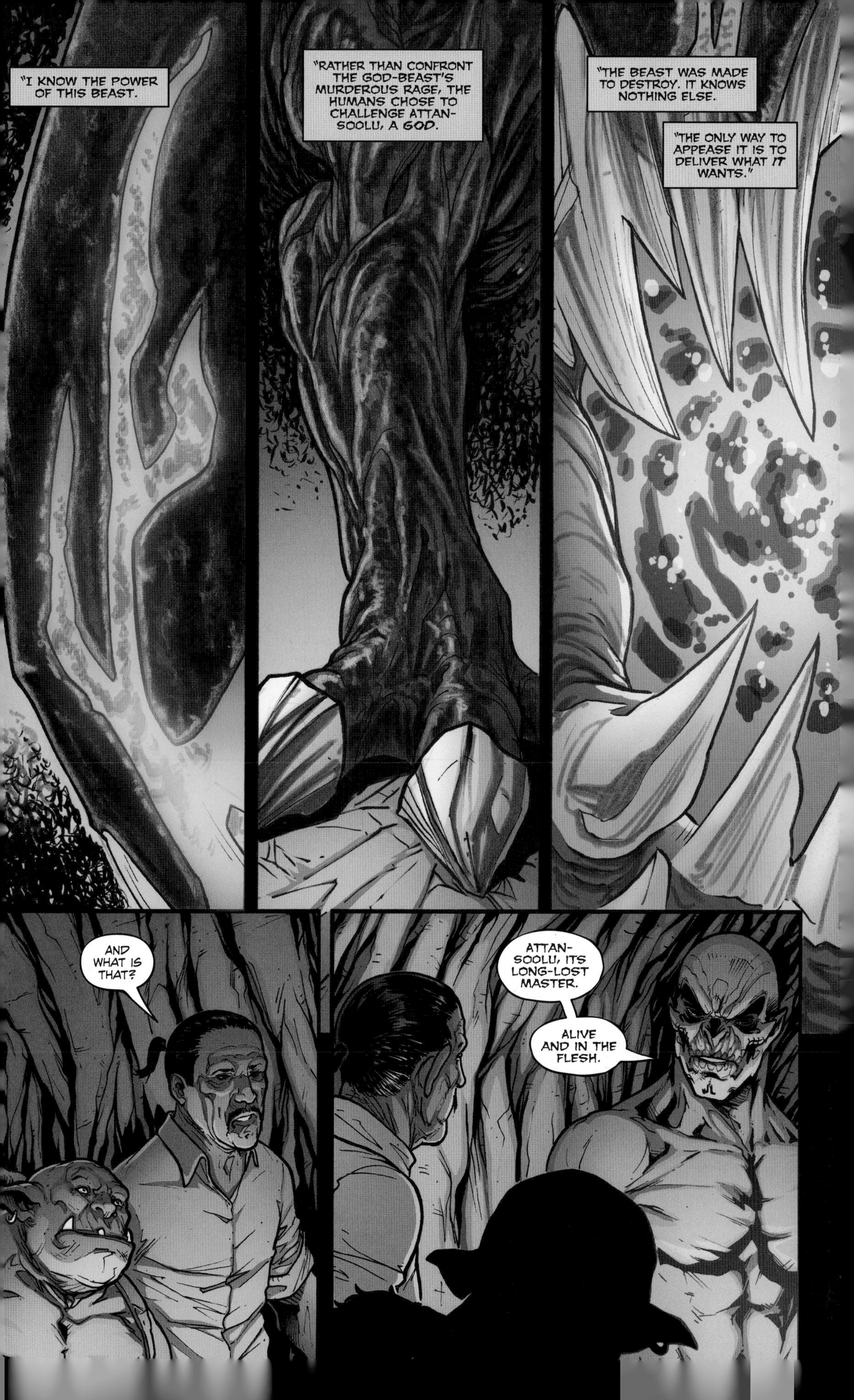
"I KNOW THE POWER OF THIS BEAST.
"RATHER THAN CONFRONT THE GOD-BEAST'S MURDEROUS RAGE, THE HUMANS CHOSE TO CHALLENGE ATTAN-SOOLU, A *GOD*.
"THE BEAST WAS MADE TO DESTROY. IT KNOWS NOTHING ELSE.
"THE ONLY WAY TO APPEASE IT IS TO DELIVER WHAT *IT* WANTS."
AND WHAT IS THAT?
ATTAN-SOOLU, ITS LONG-LOST MASTER.
ALIVE AND IN THE FLESH.

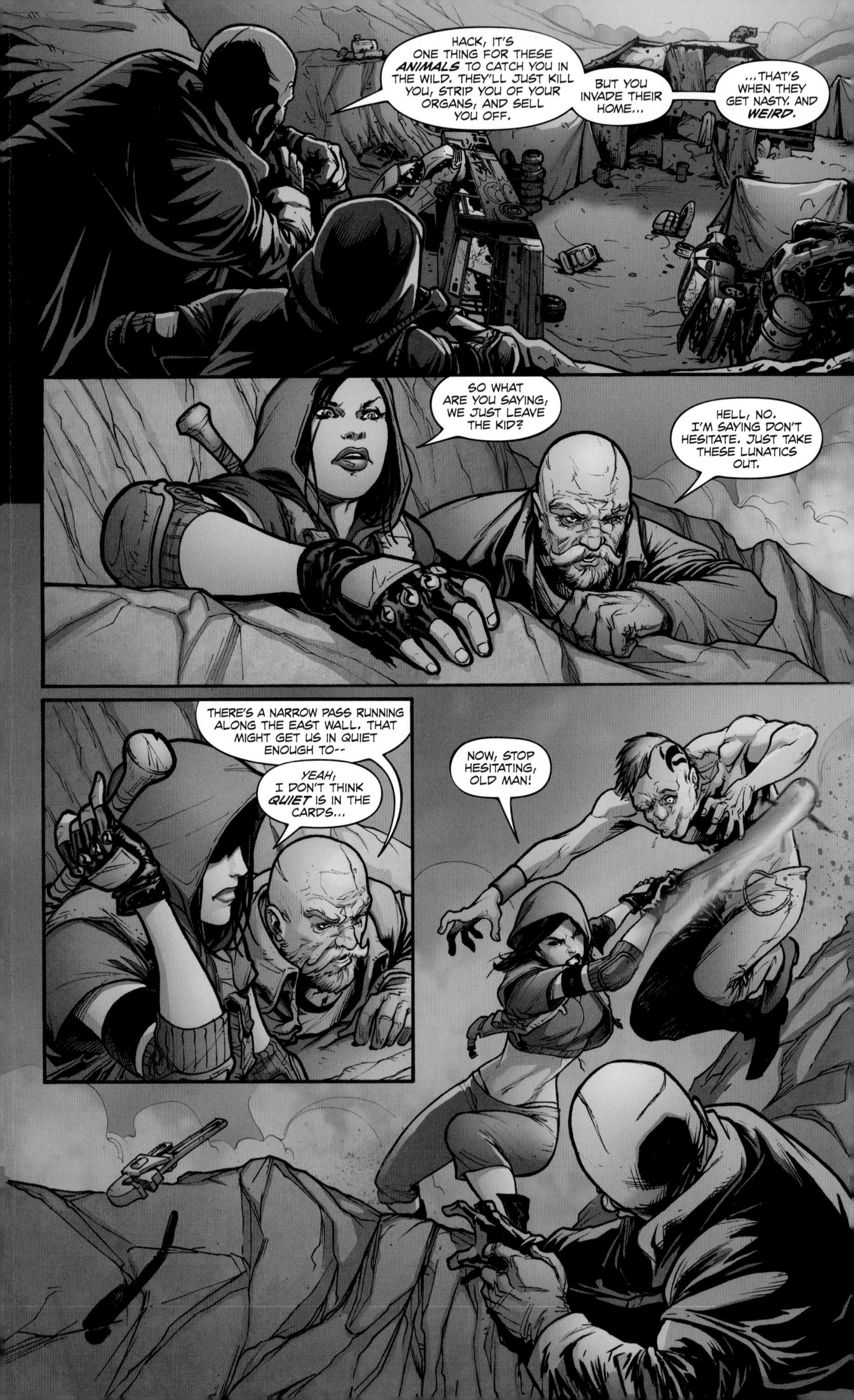
HACK, IT'S ONE THING FOR THESE ANIMALS TO CATCH YOU IN THE WILD. THEY'LL JUST KILL YOU, STRIP YOU OF YOUR ORGANS, AND SELL YOU OFF.
BUT YOU INVADE THEIR HOME...
...THAT'S WHEN THEY GET NASTY. AND WEIRD.
SO WHAT ARE YOU SAYING, WE JUST LEAVE THE KID?
HELL, NO. I'M SAYING DON'T HESITATE. JUST TAKE THESE LUNATICS OUT.
THERE'S A NARROW PASS RUNNING ALONG THE EAST WALL. THAT MIGHT GET US IN QUIET ENOUGH TO--
YEAH, I DON'T THINK QUIET IS IN THE CARDS...
NOW, STOP HESITATING, OLD MAN!

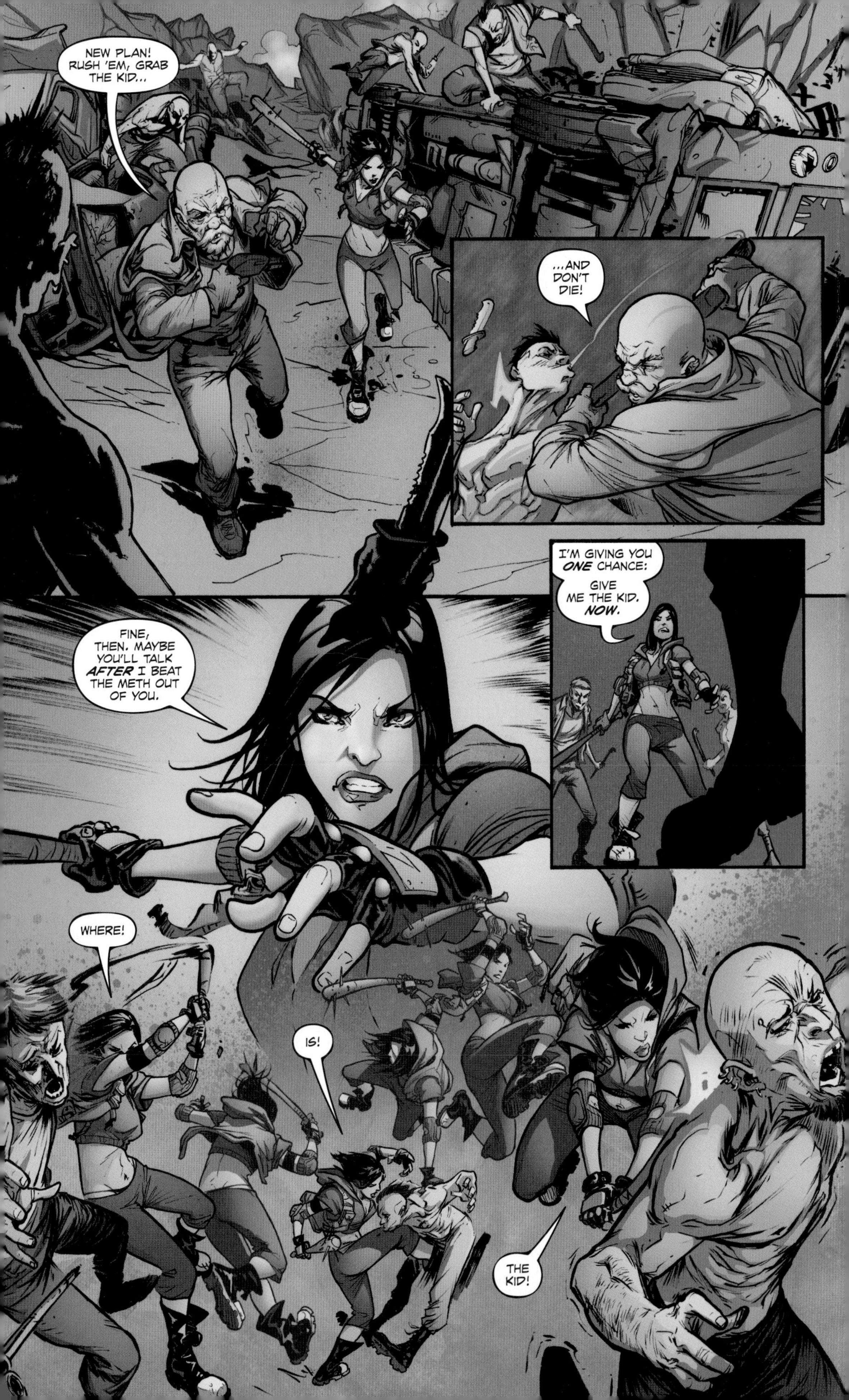
NEW PLAN! RUSH 'EM, GRAB THE KID...
...AND DON'T DIE!
I'M GIVING YOU ONE CHANCE:
GIVE ME THE KID. NOW.
FINE, THEN. MAYBE YOU'LL TALK AFTER I BEAT THE METH OUT OF YOU.
WHERE!
IS!
THE KID!

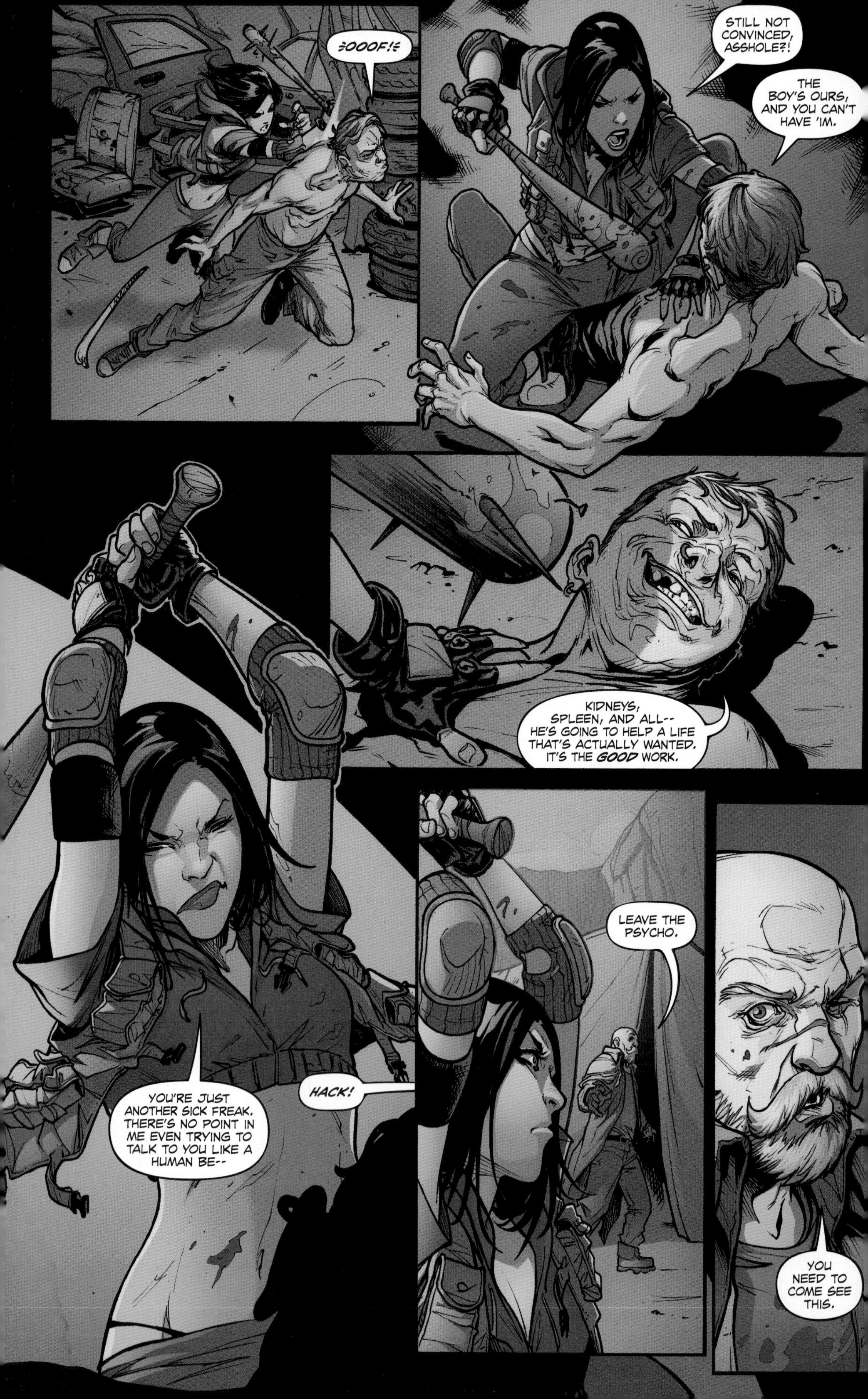
OOOF!
STILL NOT CONVINCED, ASSHOLE?!
THE BOY'S OURS, AND YOU CAN'T HAVE 'IM.
KIDNEYS, SPLEEN, AND ALL-- HE'S GOING TO HELP A LIFE THAT'S ACTUALLY WANTED. IT'S THE GOOD WORK.
YOU'RE JUST ANOTHER SICK FREAK. THERE'S NO POINT IN ME EVEN TRYING TO TALK TO YOU LIKE A HUMAN BE--
HACK!
LEAVE THE PSYCHO.
YOU NEED TO COME SEE THIS.

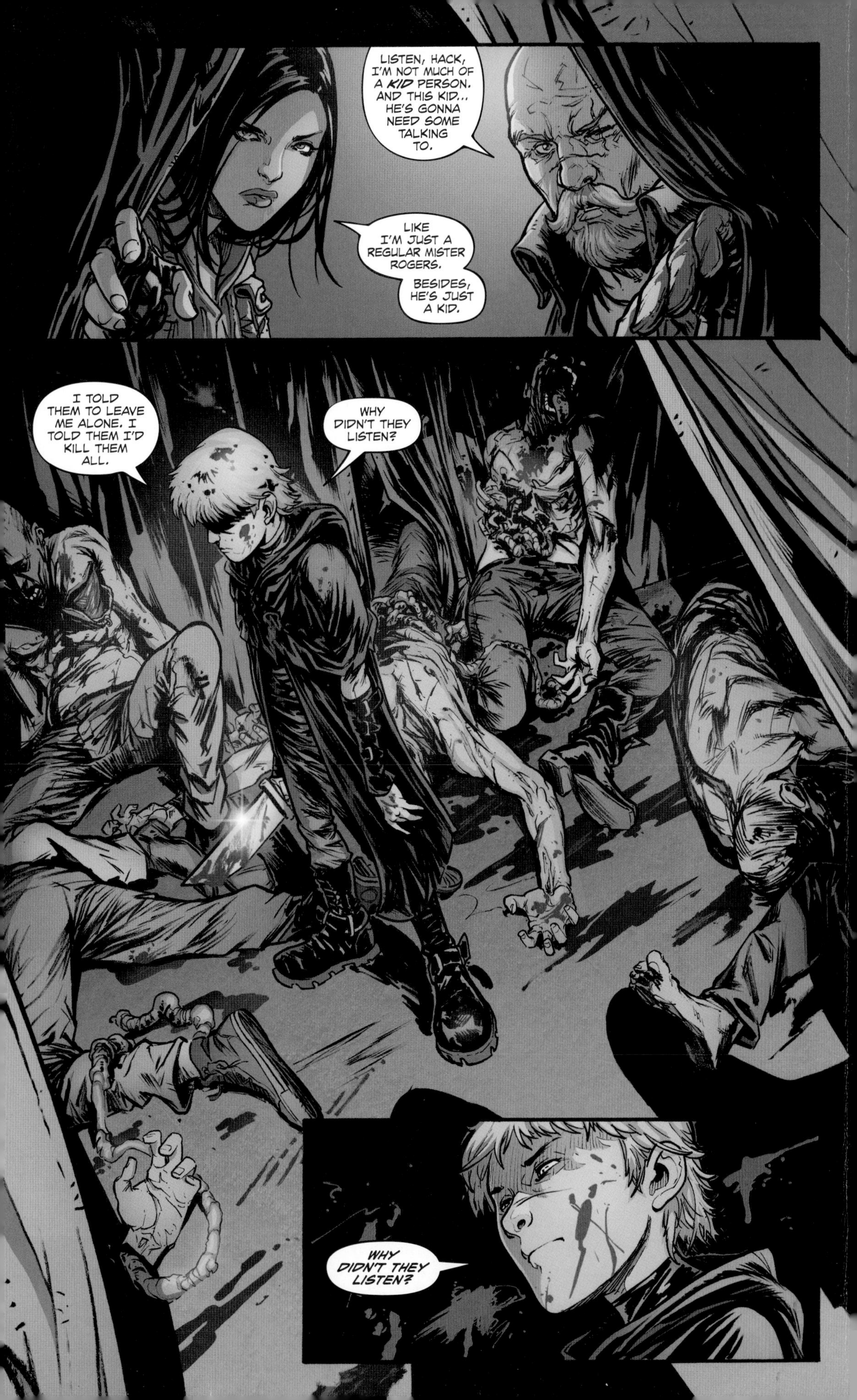
LISTEN, HACK, I'M NOT MUCH OF A *KID* PERSON. AND THIS KID... HE'S GONNA NEED SOME TALKING TO.
LIKE I'M JUST A REGULAR MISTER ROGERS.
BESIDES, HE'S JUST A KID.
I TOLD THEM TO LEAVE ME ALONE. I TOLD THEM I'D KILL THEM ALL.
WHY DIDN'T THEY LISTEN?
WHY DIDN'T THEY LISTEN?

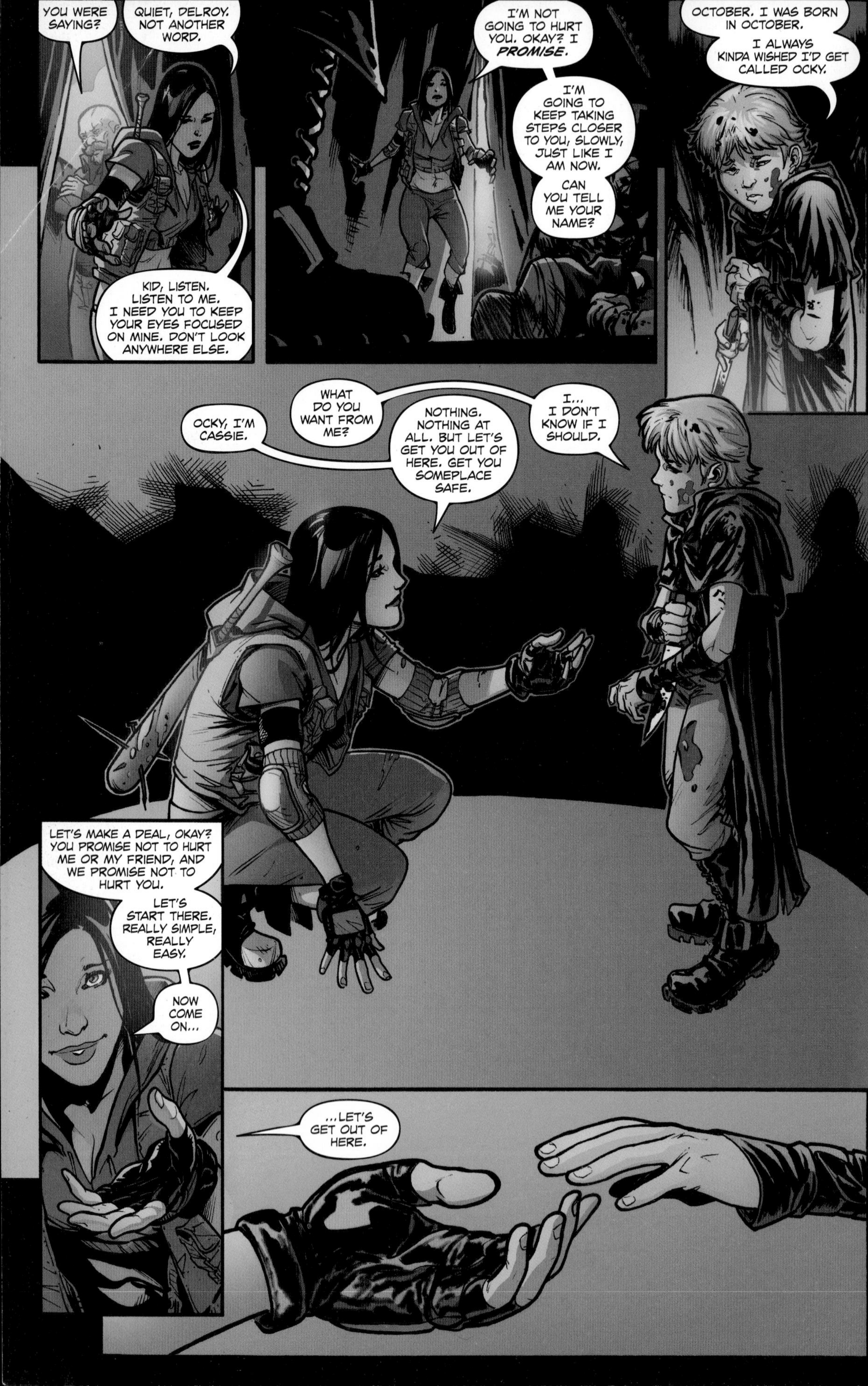
YOU WERE SAYING?
QUIET, DELROY. NOT ANOTHER WORD.
KID, LISTEN. LISTEN TO ME. I NEED YOU TO KEEP YOUR EYES FOCUSED ON MINE. DON'T LOOK ANYWHERE ELSE.
I'M NOT GOING TO HURT YOU. OKAY? I *PROMISE.*
I'M GOING TO KEEP TAKING STEPS CLOSER TO YOU, SLOWLY, JUST LIKE I AM NOW.
CAN YOU TELL ME YOUR NAME?
OCTOBER. I WAS BORN IN OCTOBER.
I ALWAYS KINDA WISHED I'D GET CALLED OCKY.
OCKY, I'M CASSIE.
WHAT DO YOU WANT FROM ME?
NOTHING. NOTHING AT ALL. BUT LET'S GET YOU OUT OF HERE. GET YOU SOMEPLACE SAFE.
I... I DON'T KNOW IF I SHOULD.
LET'S MAKE A DEAL, OKAY? YOU PROMISE NOT TO HURT ME OR MY FRIEND, AND WE PROMISE NOT TO HURT YOU.
LET'S START THERE. REALLY SIMPLE, REALLY EASY.
NOW COME ON...
...LET'S GET OUT OF HERE.

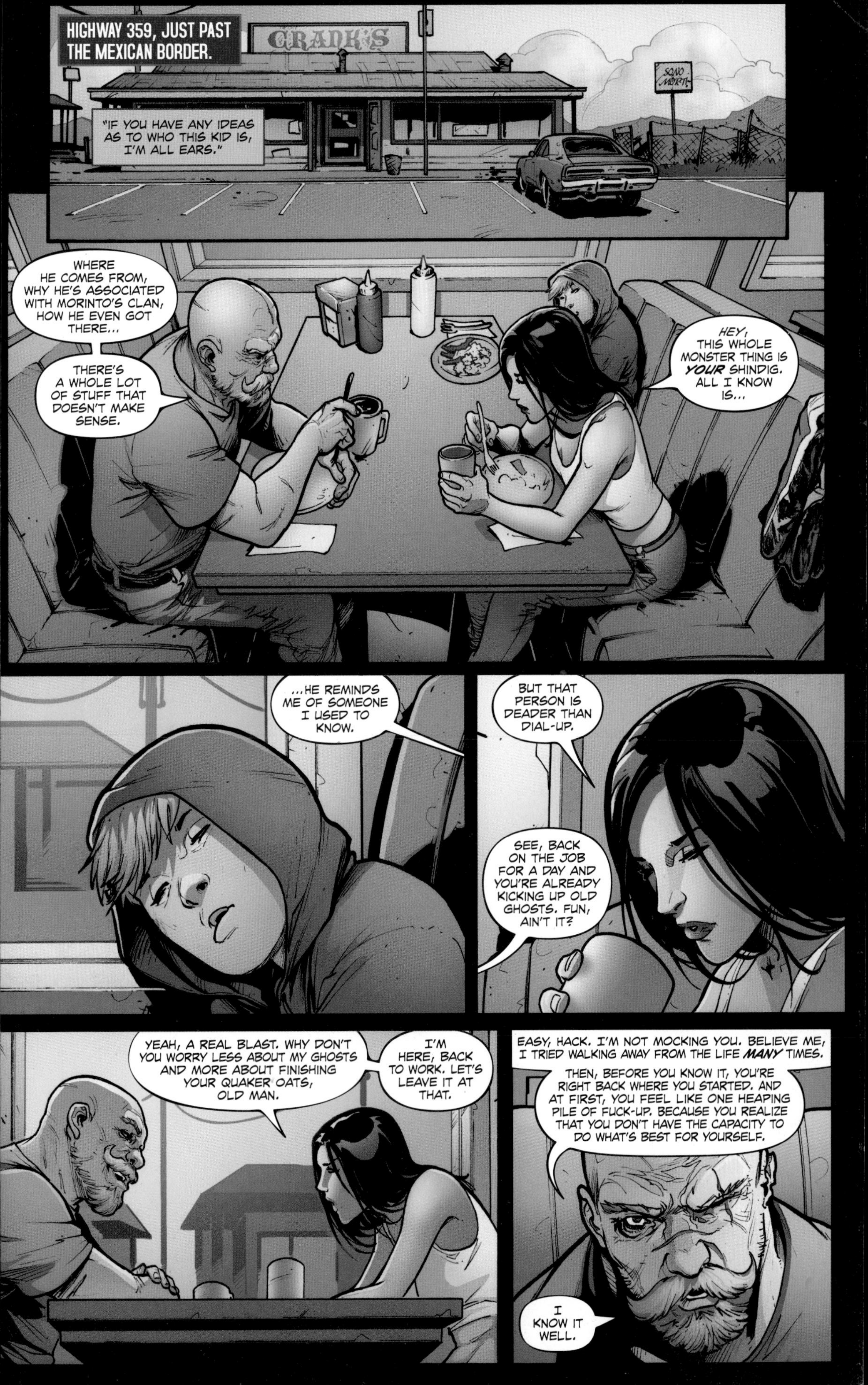
HIGHWAY 359, JUST PAST THE MEXICAN BORDER.
CRANK'S
"IF YOU HAVE ANY IDEAS AS TO WHO THIS KID IS, I'M ALL EARS."
WHERE HE COMES FROM, WHY HE'S ASSOCIATED WITH MORINTO'S CLAN, HOW HE EVEN GOT THERE...
THERE'S A WHOLE LOT OF STUFF THAT DOESN'T MAKE SENSE.
HEY, THIS WHOLE MONSTER THING IS YOUR SHINDIG. ALL I KNOW IS...
...HE REMINDS ME OF SOMEONE I USED TO KNOW.
BUT THAT PERSON IS DEADER THAN DIAL-UP.
SEE, BACK ON THE JOB FOR A DAY AND YOU'RE ALREADY KICKING UP OLD GHOSTS. FUN, AIN'T IT?
YEAH, A REAL BLAST. WHY DON'T YOU WORRY LESS ABOUT MY GHOSTS AND MORE ABOUT FINISHING YOUR QUAKER OATS, OLD MAN.
I'M HERE, BACK TO WORK. LET'S LEAVE IT AT THAT.
EASY, HACK. I'M NOT MOCKING YOU. BELIEVE ME, I TRIED WALKING AWAY FROM THE LIFE MANY TIMES.
THEN, BEFORE YOU KNOW IT, YOU'RE RIGHT BACK WHERE YOU STARTED. AND AT FIRST, YOU FEEL LIKE ONE HEAPING PILE OF FUCK-UP. BECAUSE YOU REALIZE THAT YOU DON'T HAVE THE CAPACITY TO DO WHAT'S BEST FOR YOURSELF.
I KNOW IT WELL.

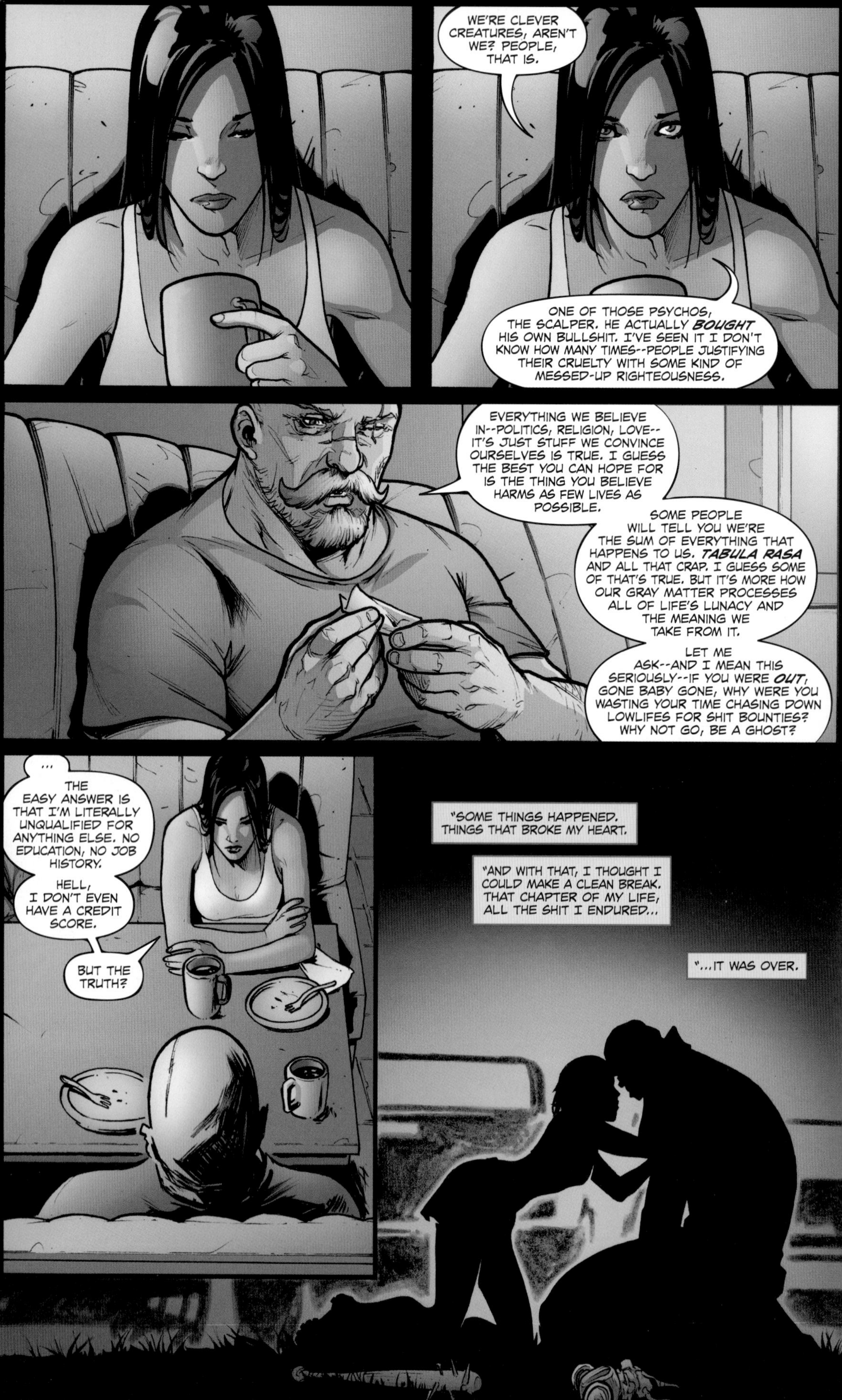
WE'RE CLEVER CREATURES, AREN'T WE? PEOPLE, THAT IS.
ONE OF THOSE PSYCHOS, THE SCALPER. HE ACTUALLY ***BOUGHT*** HIS OWN BULLSHIT. I'VE SEEN IT I DON'T KNOW HOW MANY TIMES--PEOPLE JUSTIFYING THEIR CRUELTY WITH SOME KIND OF MESSED-UP RIGHTEOUSNESS.
EVERYTHING WE BELIEVE IN--POLITICS, RELIGION, LOVE--IT'S JUST STUFF WE CONVINCE OURSELVES IS TRUE. I GUESS THE BEST YOU CAN HOPE FOR IS THE THING YOU BELIEVE HARMS AS FEW LIVES AS POSSIBLE.
SOME PEOPLE WILL TELL YOU WE'RE THE SUM OF EVERYTHING THAT HAPPENS TO US. ***TABULA RASA*** AND ALL THAT CRAP. I GUESS SOME OF THAT'S TRUE. BUT IT'S MORE HOW OUR GRAY MATTER PROCESSES ALL OF LIFE'S LUNACY AND THE MEANING WE TAKE FROM IT.
LET ME ASK--AND I MEAN THIS SERIOUSLY--IF YOU WERE ***OUT***, GONE BABY GONE, WHY WERE YOU WASTING YOUR TIME CHASING DOWN LOWLIFES FOR SHIT BOUNTIES? WHY NOT GO, BE A GHOST?
...
THE EASY ANSWER IS THAT I'M LITERALLY UNQUALIFIED FOR ANYTHING ELSE. NO EDUCATION, NO JOB HISTORY.
HELL, I DON'T EVEN HAVE A CREDIT SCORE.
BUT THE TRUTH?
"SOME THINGS HAPPENED. THINGS THAT BROKE MY HEART.
"AND WITH THAT, I THOUGHT I COULD MAKE A CLEAN BREAK. THAT CHAPTER OF MY LIFE, ALL THE SHIT I ENDURED...
"...IT WAS OVER.

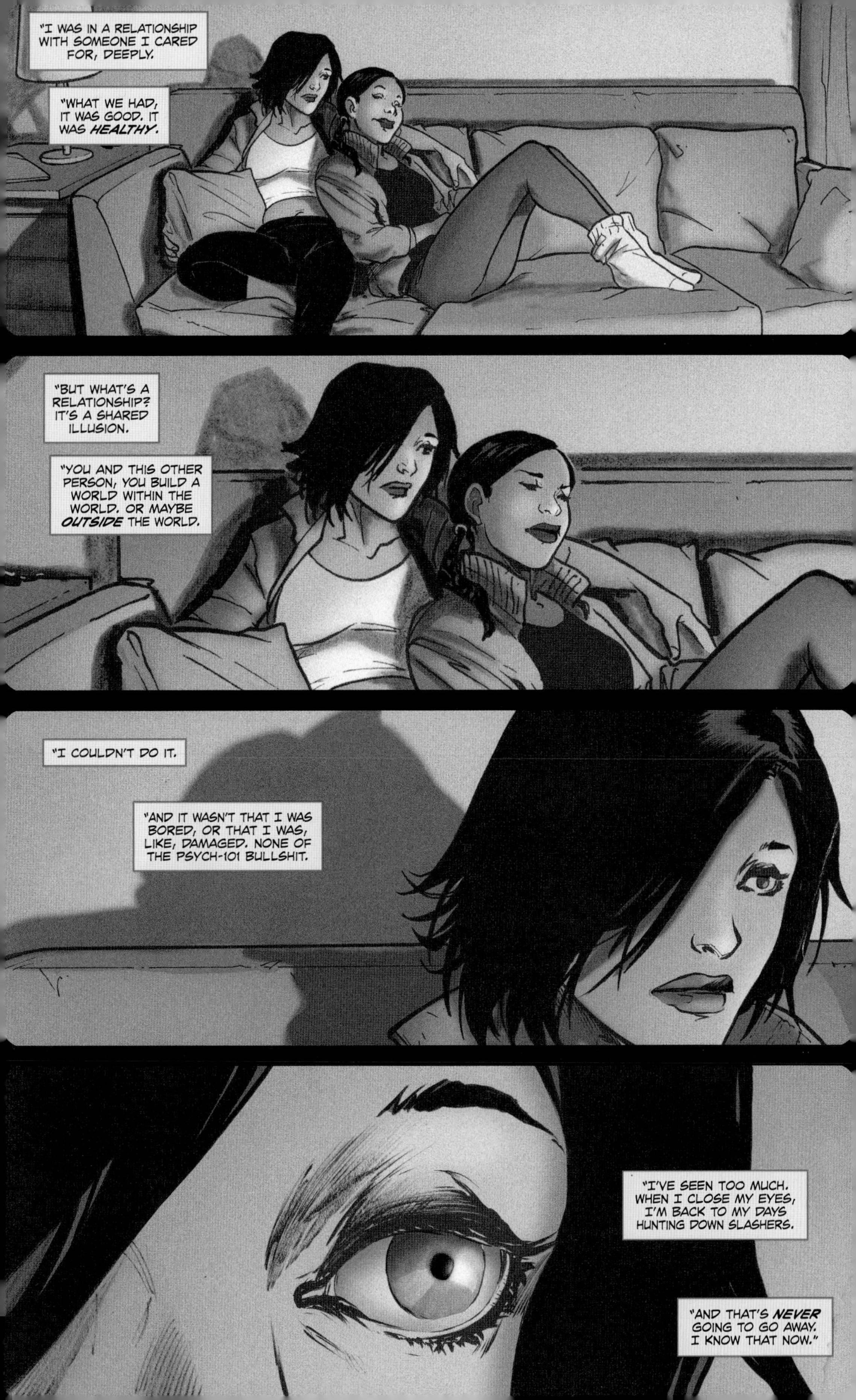
"I WAS IN A RELATIONSHIP WITH SOMEONE I CARED FOR, DEEPLY.
"WHAT WE HAD, IT WAS GOOD. IT WAS *HEALTHY*.
"BUT WHAT'S A RELATIONSHIP? IT'S A SHARED ILLUSION.
"YOU AND THIS OTHER PERSON, YOU BUILD A WORLD WITHIN THE WORLD. OR MAYBE *OUTSIDE* THE WORLD.
"I COULDN'T DO IT.
"AND IT WASN'T THAT I WAS BORED, OR THAT I WAS, LIKE, DAMAGED. NONE OF THE PSYCH-101 BULLSHIT.
"I'VE SEEN TOO MUCH. WHEN I CLOSE MY EYES, I'M BACK TO MY DAYS HUNTING DOWN SLASHERS.
"AND THAT'S *NEVER* GOING TO GO AWAY. I KNOW THAT NOW."

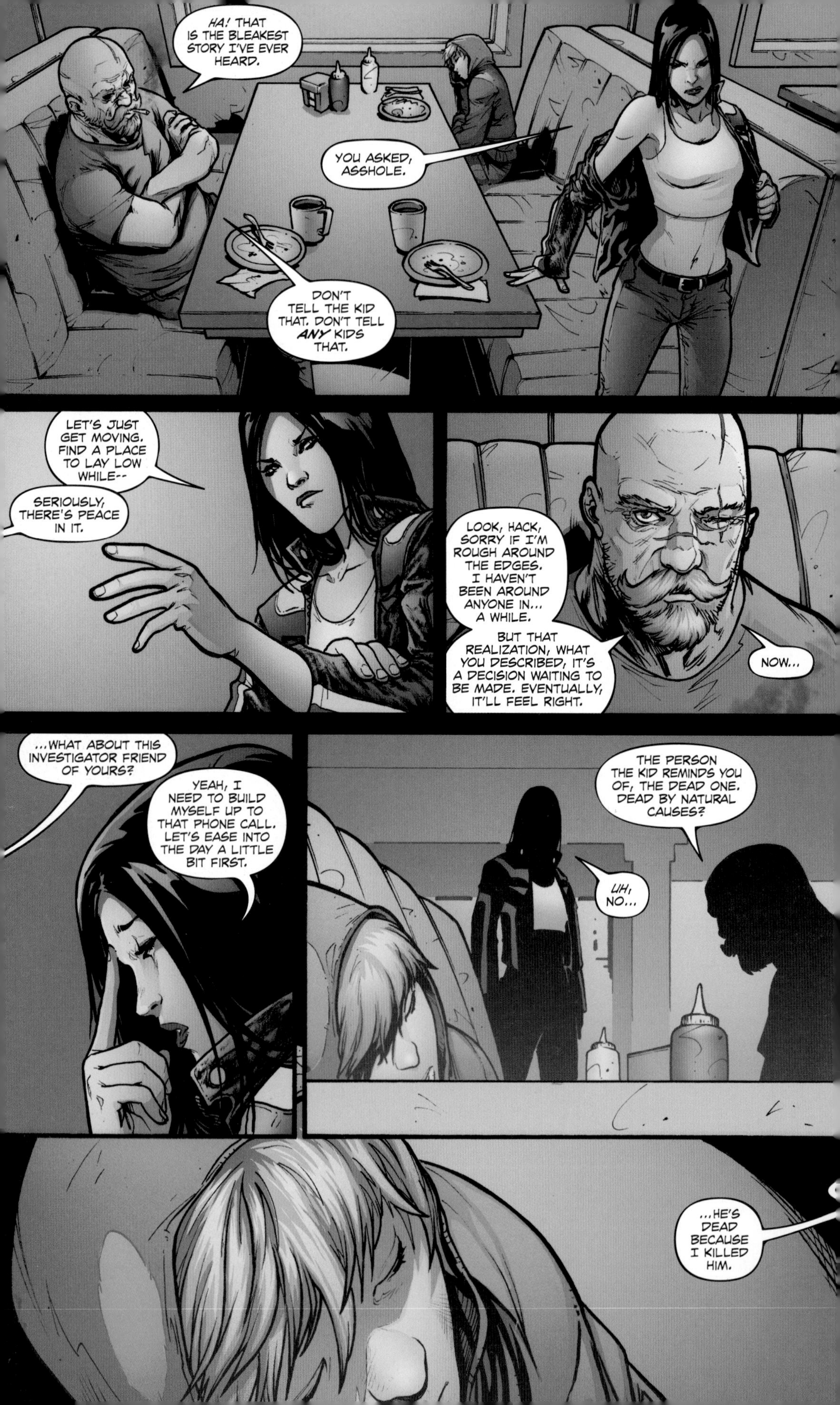

HA! THAT IS THE BLEAKEST STORY I'VE EVER HEARD.
YOU ASKED, ASSHOLE.
DON'T TELL THE KID THAT. DON'T TELL ANY KIDS THAT.
LET'S JUST GET MOVING. FIND A PLACE TO LAY LOW WHILE--
SERIOUSLY, THERE'S PEACE IN IT.
LOOK, HACK, SORRY IF I'M ROUGH AROUND THE EDGES. I HAVEN'T BEEN AROUND ANYONE IN... A WHILE.
BUT THAT REALIZATION, WHAT YOU DESCRIBED, IT'S A DECISION WAITING TO BE MADE. EVENTUALLY, IT'LL FEEL RIGHT.
NOW...
...WHAT ABOUT THIS INVESTIGATOR FRIEND OF YOURS?
YEAH, I NEED TO BUILD MYSELF UP TO THAT PHONE CALL. LET'S EASE INTO THE DAY A LITTLE BIT FIRST.
THE PERSON THE KID REMINDS YOU OF, THE DEAD ONE. DEAD BY NATURAL CAUSES?
UH, NO...
...HE'S DEAD BECAUSE I KILLED HIM.

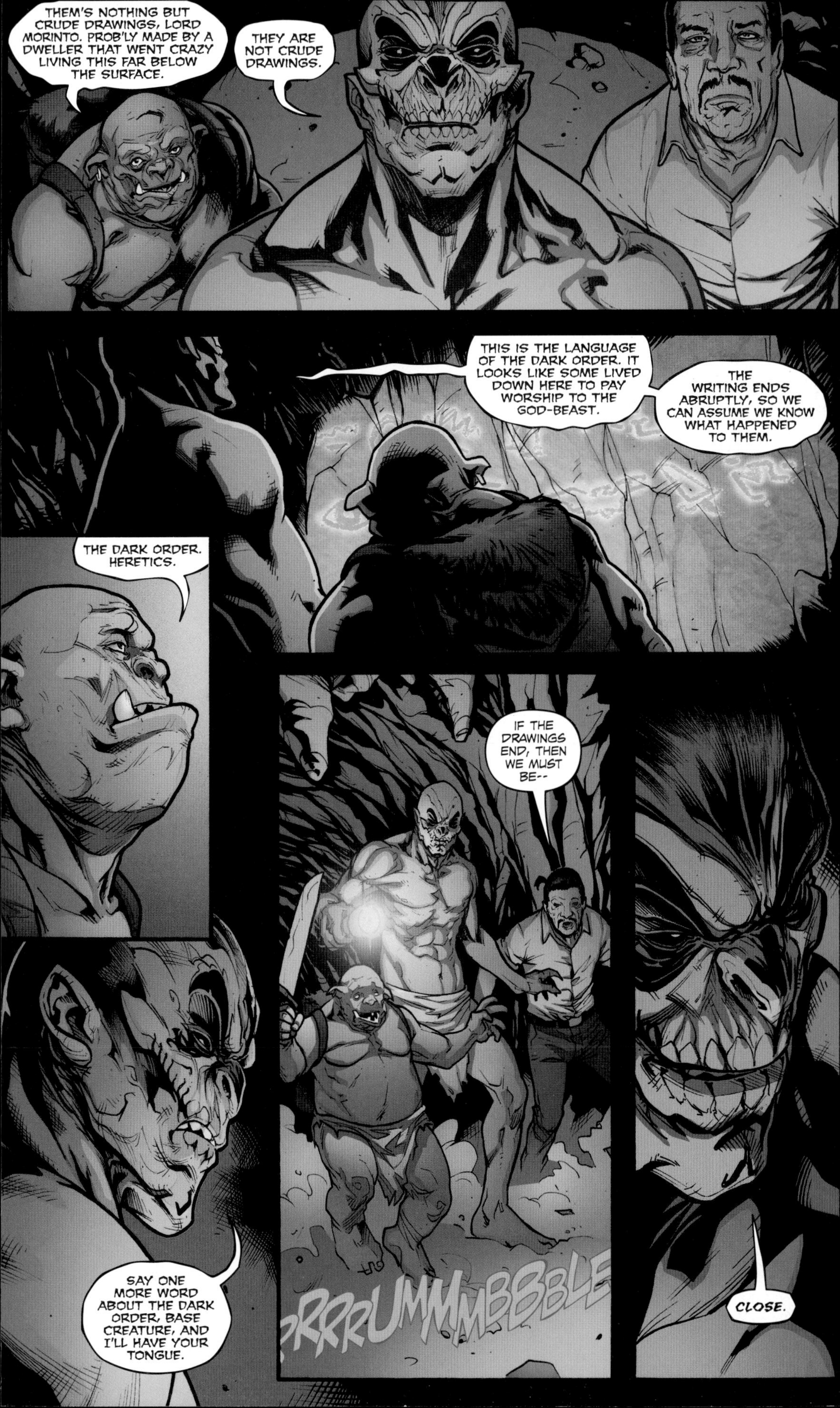
THEM'S NOTHING BUT CRUDE DRAWINGS, LORD MORINTO. PROB'LY MADE BY A DWELLER THAT WENT CRAZY LIVING THIS FAR BELOW THE SURFACE.
THEY ARE NOT CRUDE DRAWINGS.
THIS IS THE LANGUAGE OF THE DARK ORDER. IT LOOKS LIKE SOME LIVED DOWN HERE TO PAY WORSHIP TO THE GOD-BEAST.
THE WRITING ENDS ABRUPTLY, SO WE CAN ASSUME WE KNOW WHAT HAPPENED TO THEM.
THE DARK ORDER. HERETICS.
SAY ONE MORE WORD ABOUT THE DARK ORDER, BASE CREATURE, AND I'LL HAVE YOUR TONGUE.
IF THE DRAWINGS END, THEN WE MUST BE--
RRRRUMMMBBBLE
CLOSE.

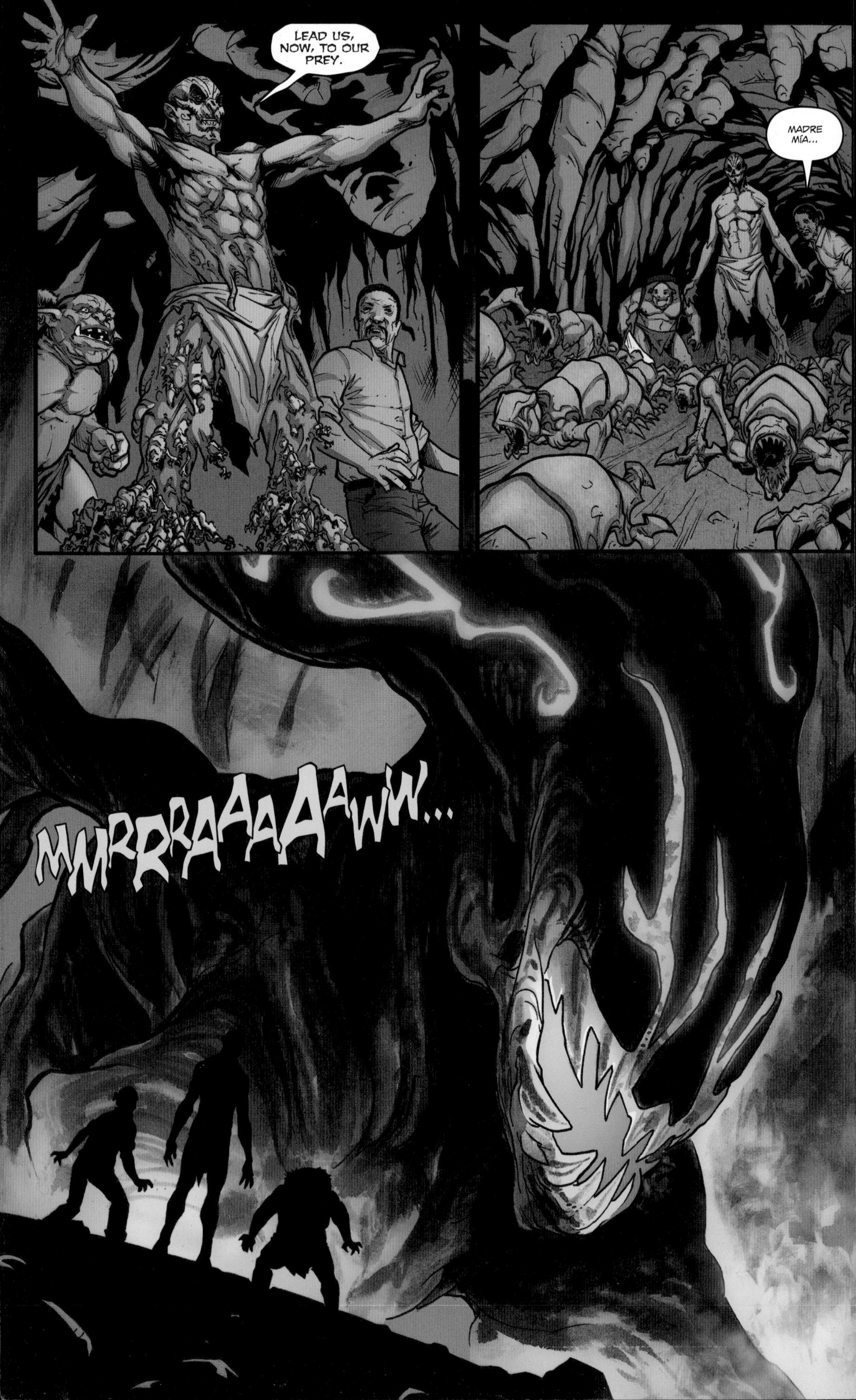
LEAD US, NOW, TO OUR PREY.
MADRE MÍA...
MNRRRAAAAAWW...

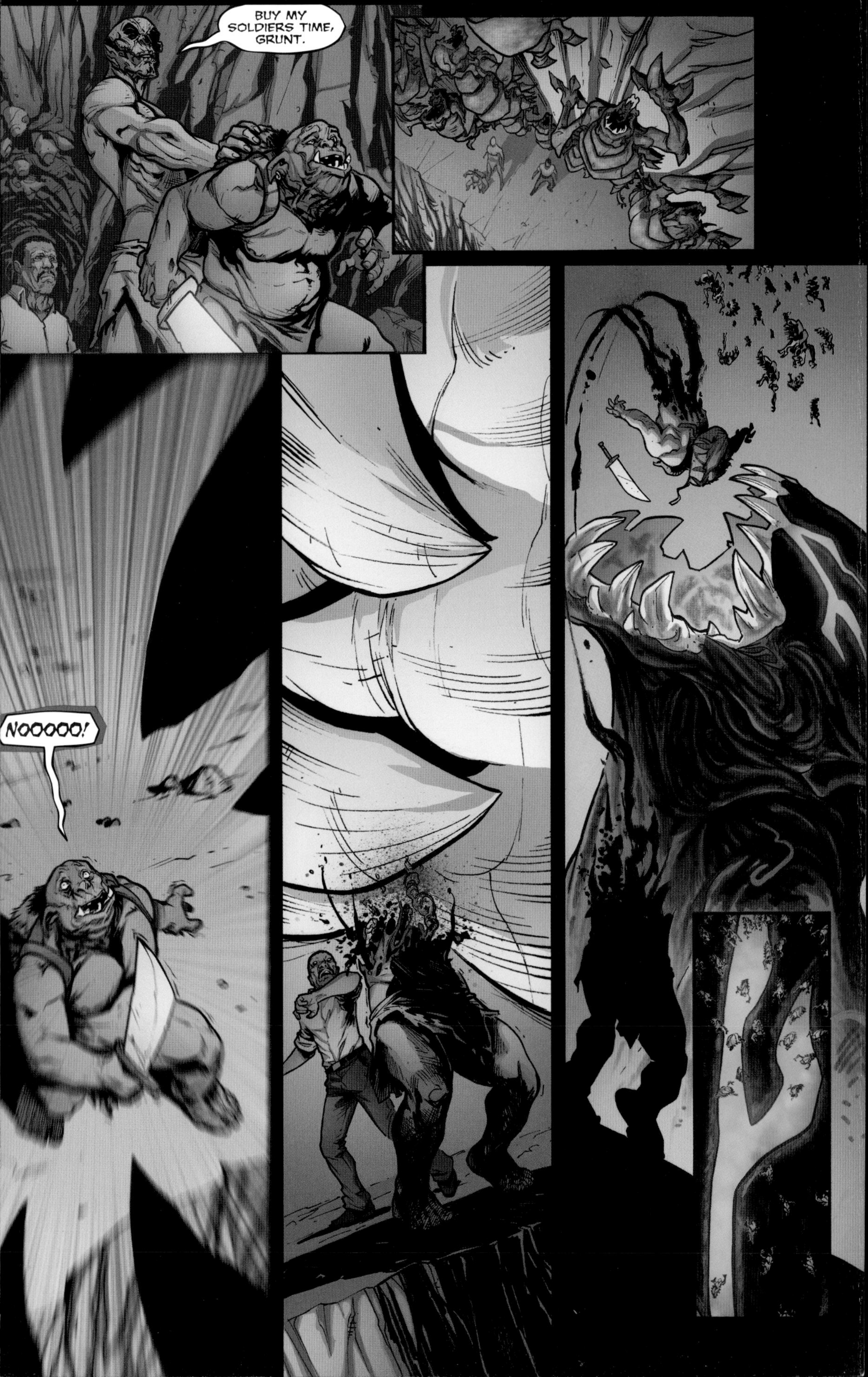
BUY MY SOLDIERS TIME, GRUNT.
NOOOOO!

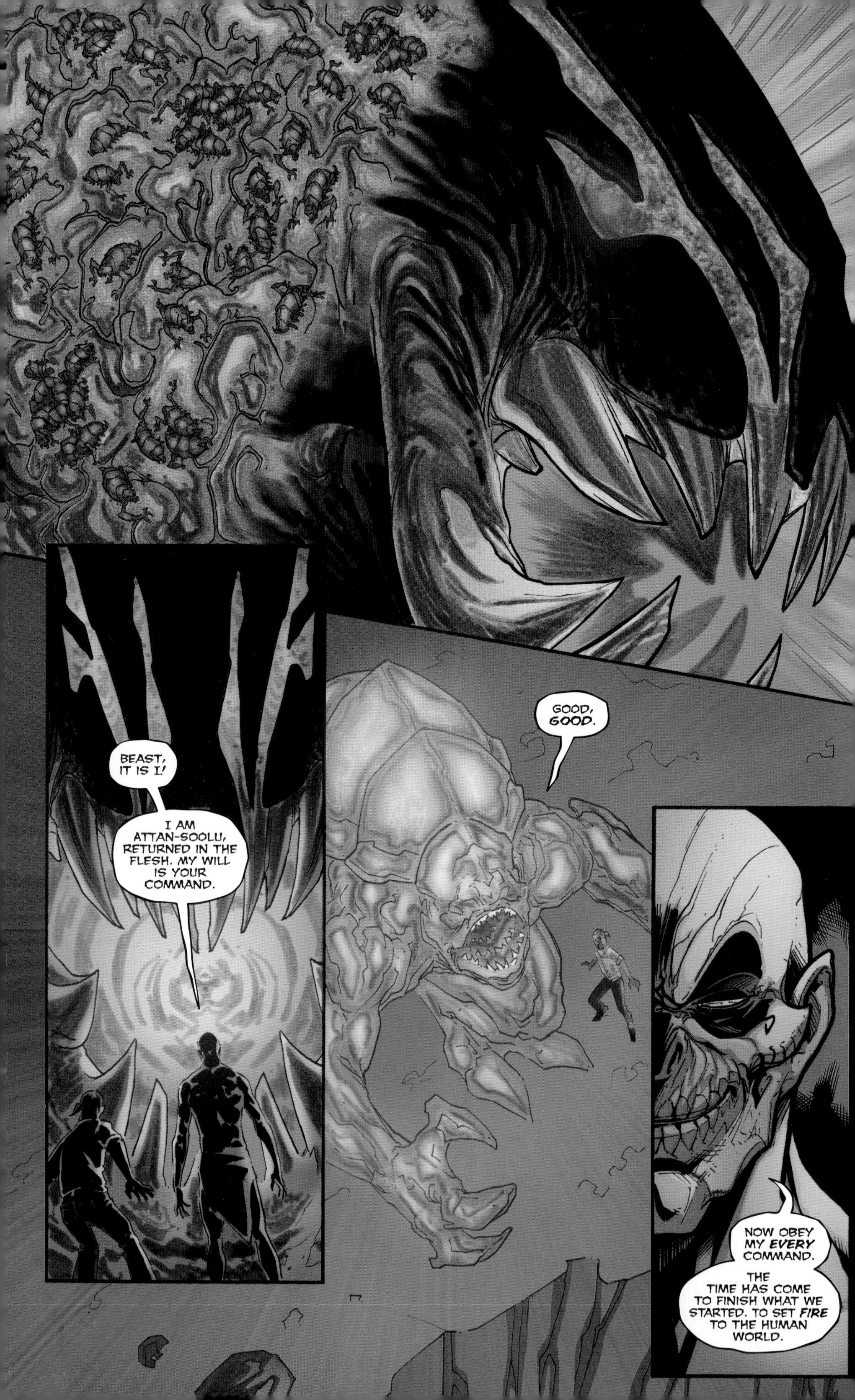
BEAST, IT IS I!
I AM ATTAN-SOOLU, RETURNED IN THE FLESH. MY WILL IS YOUR COMMAND.
GOOD, *GOOD*.
NOW OBEY MY *EVERY* COMMAND.
THE TIME HAS COME TO FINISH WHAT WE STARTED. TO SET *FIRE* TO THE HUMAN WORLD.

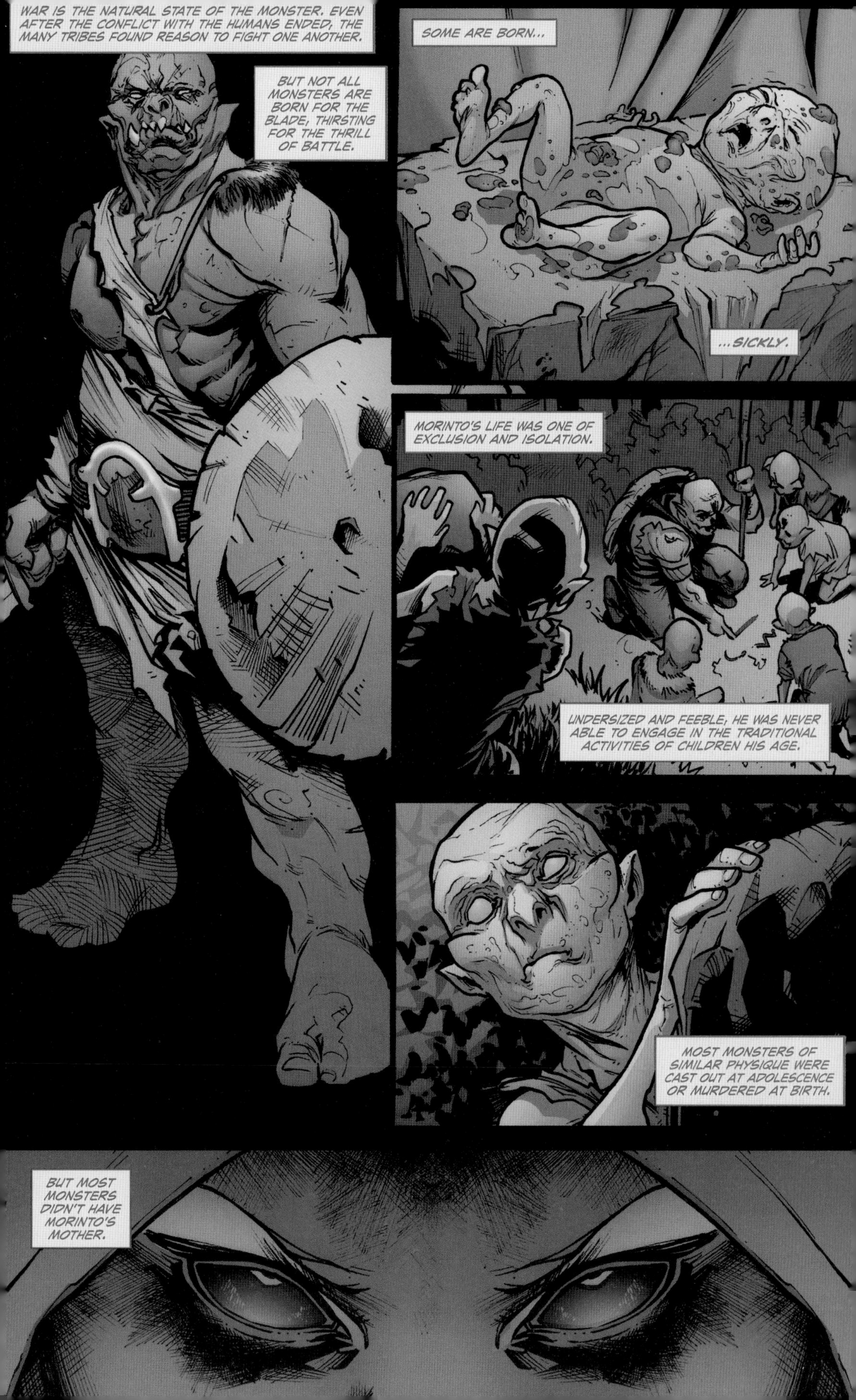
WAR IS THE NATURAL STATE OF THE MONSTER. EVEN AFTER THE CONFLICT WITH THE HUMANS ENDED, THE MANY TRIBES FOUND REASON TO FIGHT ONE ANOTHER.
BUT NOT ALL MONSTERS ARE BORN FOR THE BLADE, THIRSTING FOR THE THRILL OF BATTLE.
SOME ARE BORN...
...SICKLY.
MORINTO'S LIFE WAS ONE OF EXCLUSION AND ISOLATION.
UNDERSIZED AND FEEBLE, HE WAS NEVER ABLE TO ENGAGE IN THE TRADITIONAL ACTIVITIES OF CHILDREN HIS AGE.
MOST MONSTERS OF SIMILAR PHYSIQUE WERE CAST OUT AT ADOLESCENCE OR MURDERED AT BIRTH.
BUT MOST MONSTERS DIDN'T HAVE MORINTO'S MOTHER.

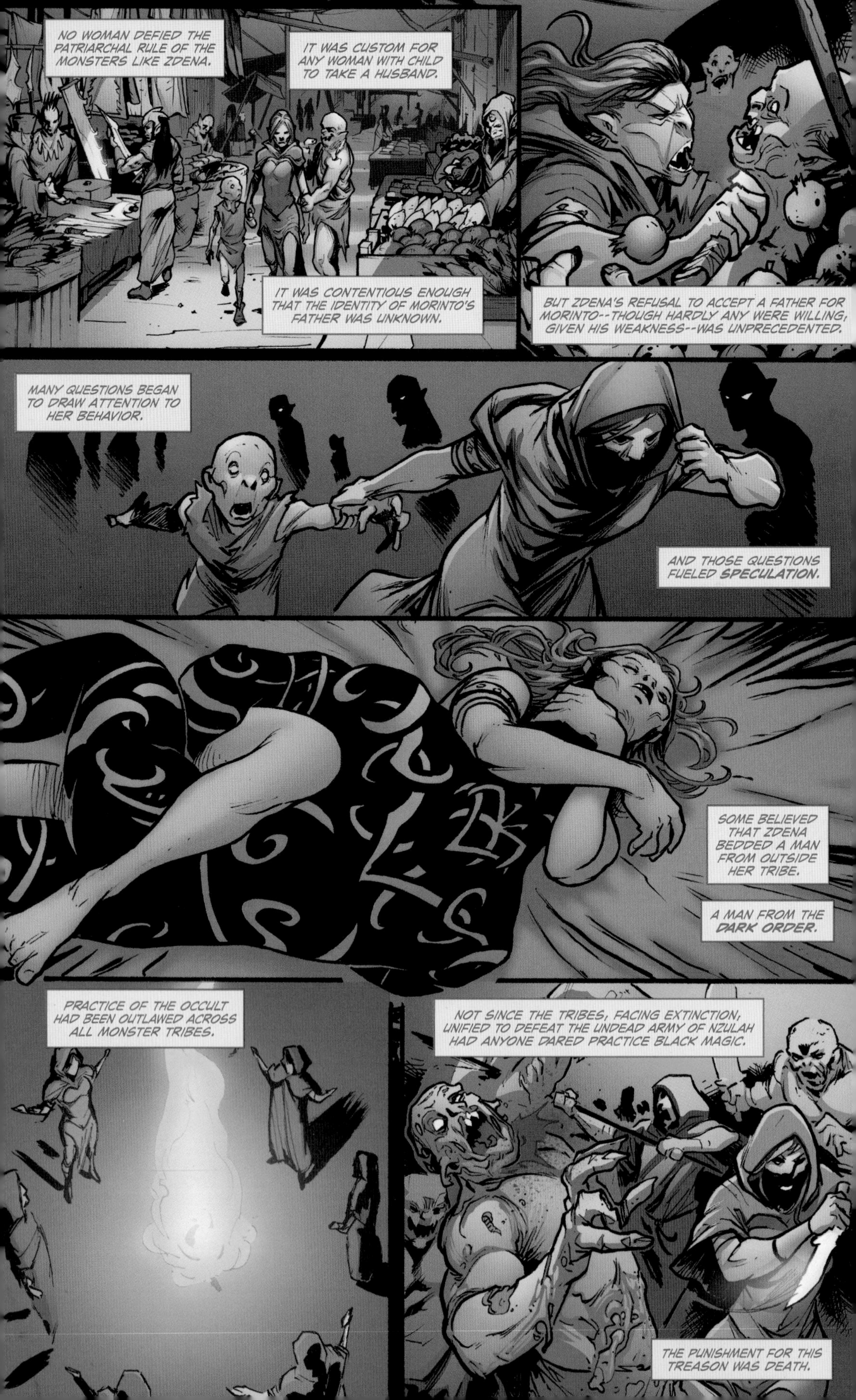
NO WOMAN DEFIED THE PATRIARCHAL RULE OF THE MONSTERS LIKE ZDENA.
IT WAS CUSTOM FOR ANY WOMAN WITH CHILD TO TAKE A HUSBAND.
IT WAS CONTENTIOUS ENOUGH THAT THE IDENTITY OF MORINTO'S FATHER WAS UNKNOWN.
BUT ZDENA'S REFUSAL TO ACCEPT A FATHER FOR MORINTO--THOUGH HARDLY ANY WERE WILLING, GIVEN HIS WEAKNESS--WAS UNPRECEDENTED.
MANY QUESTIONS BEGAN TO DRAW ATTENTION TO HER BEHAVIOR.
AND THOSE QUESTIONS FUELED SPECULATION.
SOME BELIEVED THAT ZDENA BEDDED A MAN FROM OUTSIDE HER TRIBE.
A MAN FROM THE DARK ORDER.
PRACTICE OF THE OCCULT HAD BEEN OUTLAWED ACROSS ALL MONSTER TRIBES.
NOT SINCE THE TRIBES, FACING EXTINCTION, UNIFIED TO DEFEAT THE UNDEAD ARMY OF NZULAH HAD ANYONE DARED PRACTICE BLACK MAGIC.
THE PUNISHMENT FOR THIS TREASON WAS DEATH.

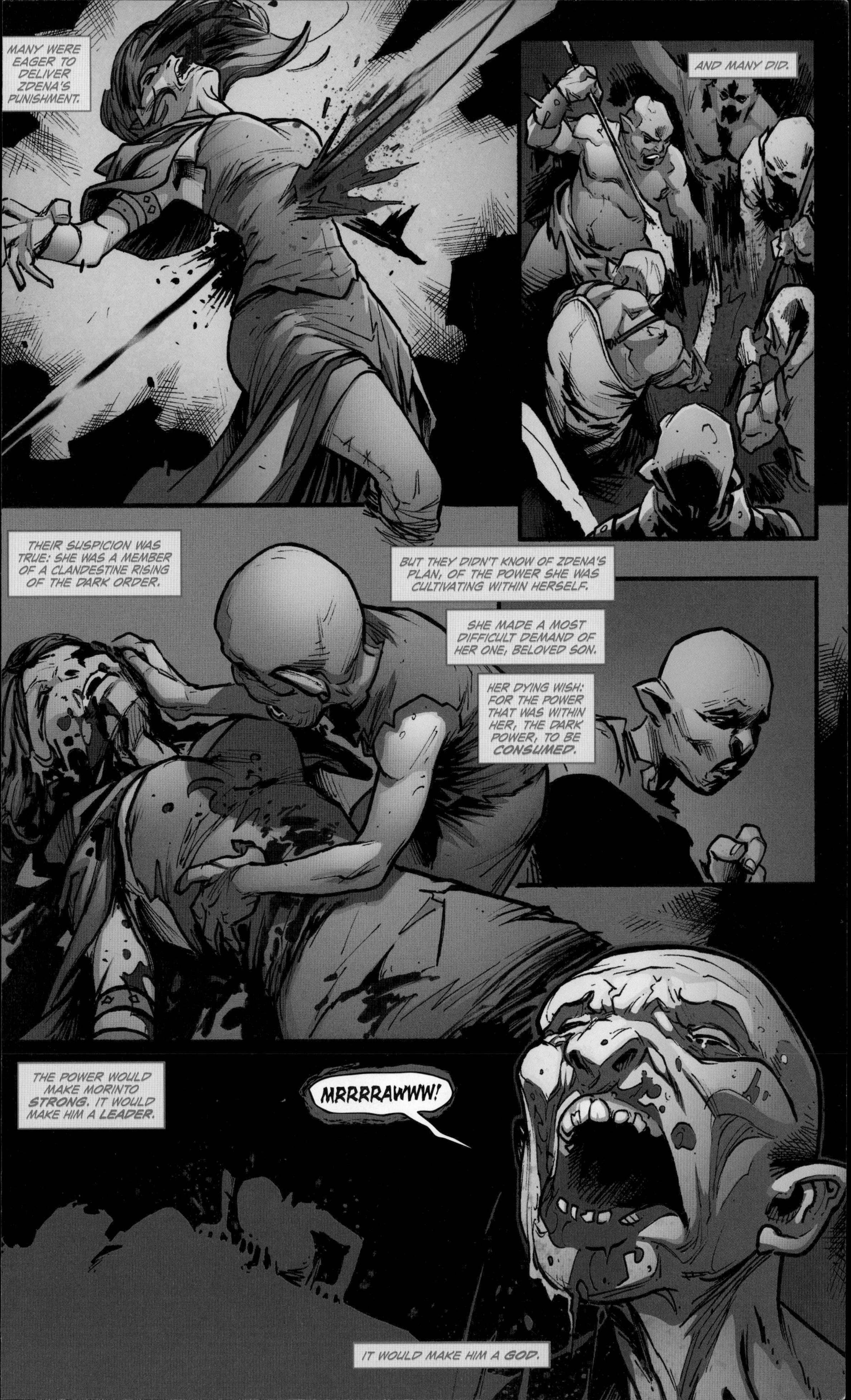
MANY WERE EAGER TO DELIVER ZDENA'S PUNISHMENT.
AND MANY DID.
THEIR SUSPICION WAS TRUE: SHE WAS A MEMBER OF A CLANDESTINE RISING OF THE DARK ORDER.
BUT THEY DIDN'T KNOW OF ZDENA'S PLAN, OF THE POWER SHE WAS CULTIVATING WITHIN HERSELF.
SHE MADE A MOST DIFFICULT DEMAND OF HER ONE, BELOVED SON.
HER DYING WISH: FOR THE POWER THAT WAS WITHIN HER, THE DARK POWER, TO BE CONSUMED.
THE POWER WOULD MAKE MORINTO STRONG. IT WOULD MAKE HIM A LEADER.
MRRRRAWWW!
IT WOULD MAKE HIM A GOD.

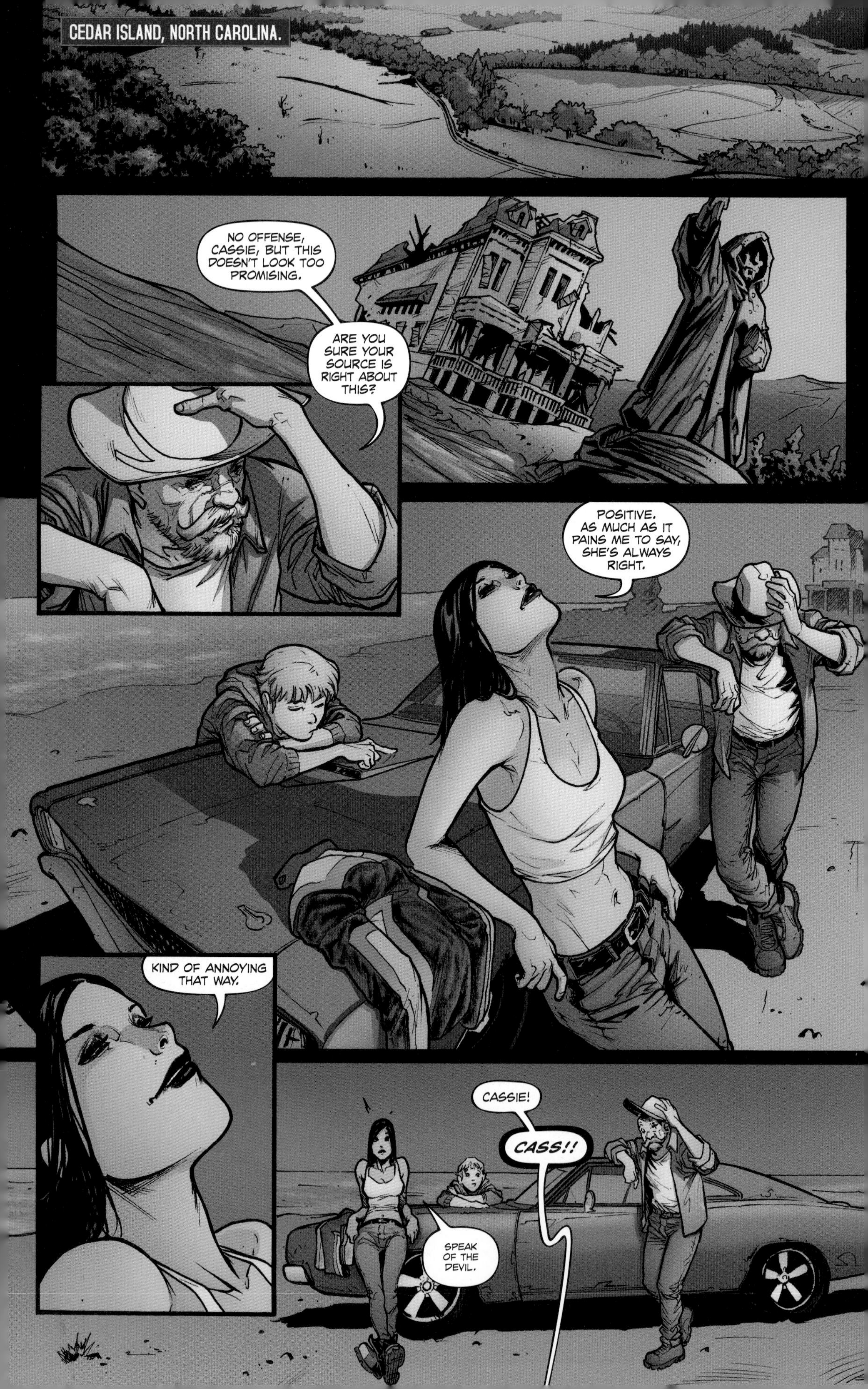
CEDAR ISLAND, NORTH CAROLINA.
NO OFFENSE, CASSIE, BUT THIS DOESN'T LOOK TOO PROMISING.
ARE YOU SURE YOUR SOURCE IS RIGHT ABOUT THIS?
POSITIVE. AS MUCH AS IT PAINS ME TO SAY, SHE'S ALWAYS RIGHT.
KIND OF ANNOYING THAT WAY.
CASSIE!
CASS!!
SPEAK OF THE DEVIL.

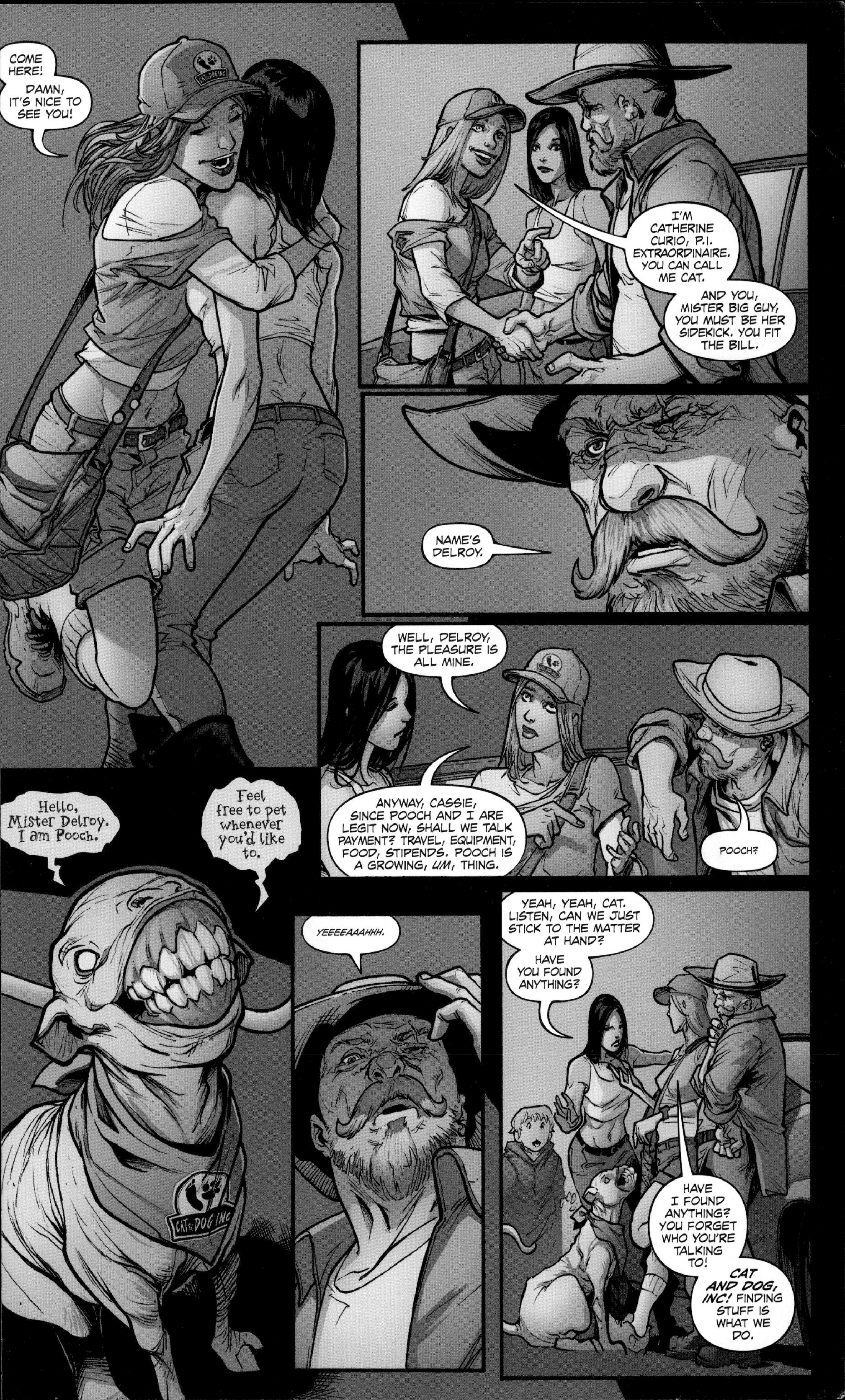
COME HERE!
DAMN, IT'S NICE TO SEE YOU!
I'M CATHERINE CURIO, P.I. EXTRAORDINAIRE. YOU CAN CALL ME CAT.
AND YOU, MISTER BIG GUY, YOU MUST BE HER SIDEKICK. YOU FIT THE BILL.
NAME'S DELROY.
WELL, DELROY, THE PLEASURE IS ALL MINE.
ANYWAY, CASSIE, SINCE POOCH AND I ARE LEGIT NOW, SHALL WE TALK PAYMENT? TRAVEL, EQUIPMENT, FOOD, STIPENDS. POOCH IS A GROWING, UM, THING.
POOCH?
Hello, Mister Delroy. I am Pooch.
Feel free to pet whenever you'd like to.
YEEEEAAAHHH.
YEAH, YEAH, CAT. LISTEN, CAN WE JUST STICK TO THE MATTER AT HAND?
HAVE YOU FOUND ANYTHING?
HAVE I FOUND ANYTHING? YOU FORGET WHO YOU'RE TALKING TO!
CAT AND DOG, INC! FINDING STUFF IS WHAT WE DO.

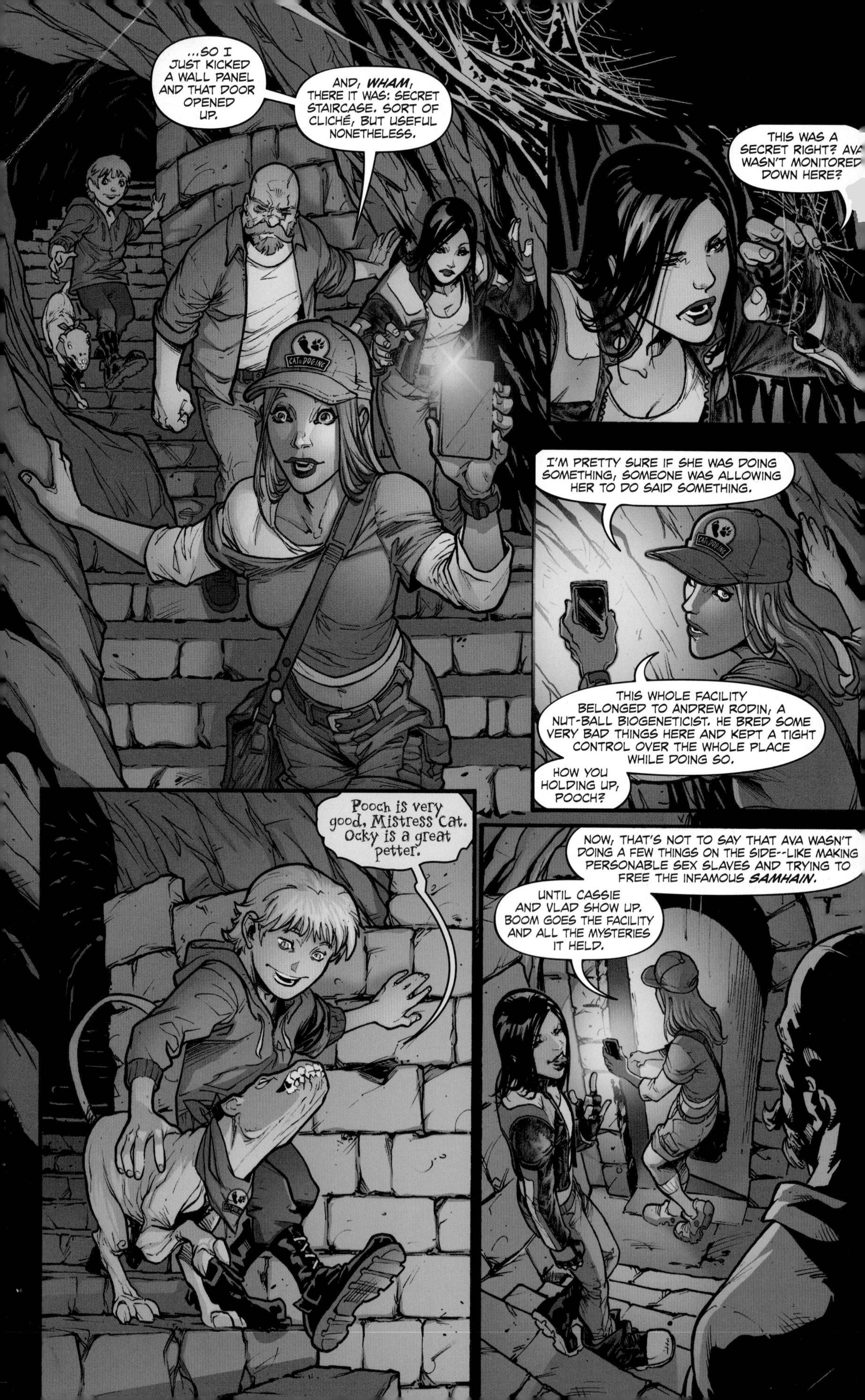
...SO I JUST KICKED A WALL PANEL AND THAT DOOR OPENED UP.
AND, **WHAM**, THERE IT WAS: SECRET STAIRCASE. SORT OF CLICHÉ, BUT USEFUL NONETHELESS.
CAT&DOGING
THIS WAS A SECRET RIGHT? AVA WASN'T MONITORED DOWN HERE?
I'M PRETTY SURE IF SHE WAS DOING SOMETHING, SOMEONE WAS ALLOWING HER TO DO SAID SOMETHING.
THIS WHOLE FACILITY BELONGED TO ANDREW RODIN, A NUT-BALL BIOGENETICIST. HE BRED SOME VERY BAD THINGS HERE AND KEPT A TIGHT CONTROL OVER THE WHOLE PLACE WHILE DOING SO.
HOW YOU HOLDING UP, POOCH?
Pooch is very good, Mistress Cat. Ocky is a great petter.
NOW, THAT'S NOT TO SAY THAT AVA WASN'T DOING A FEW THINGS ON THE SIDE--LIKE MAKING PERSONABLE SEX SLAVES AND TRYING TO FREE THE INFAMOUS ***SAMHAIN***.
UNTIL CASSIE AND VLAD SHOW UP. BOOM GOES THE FACILITY AND ALL THE MYSTERIES IT HELD.

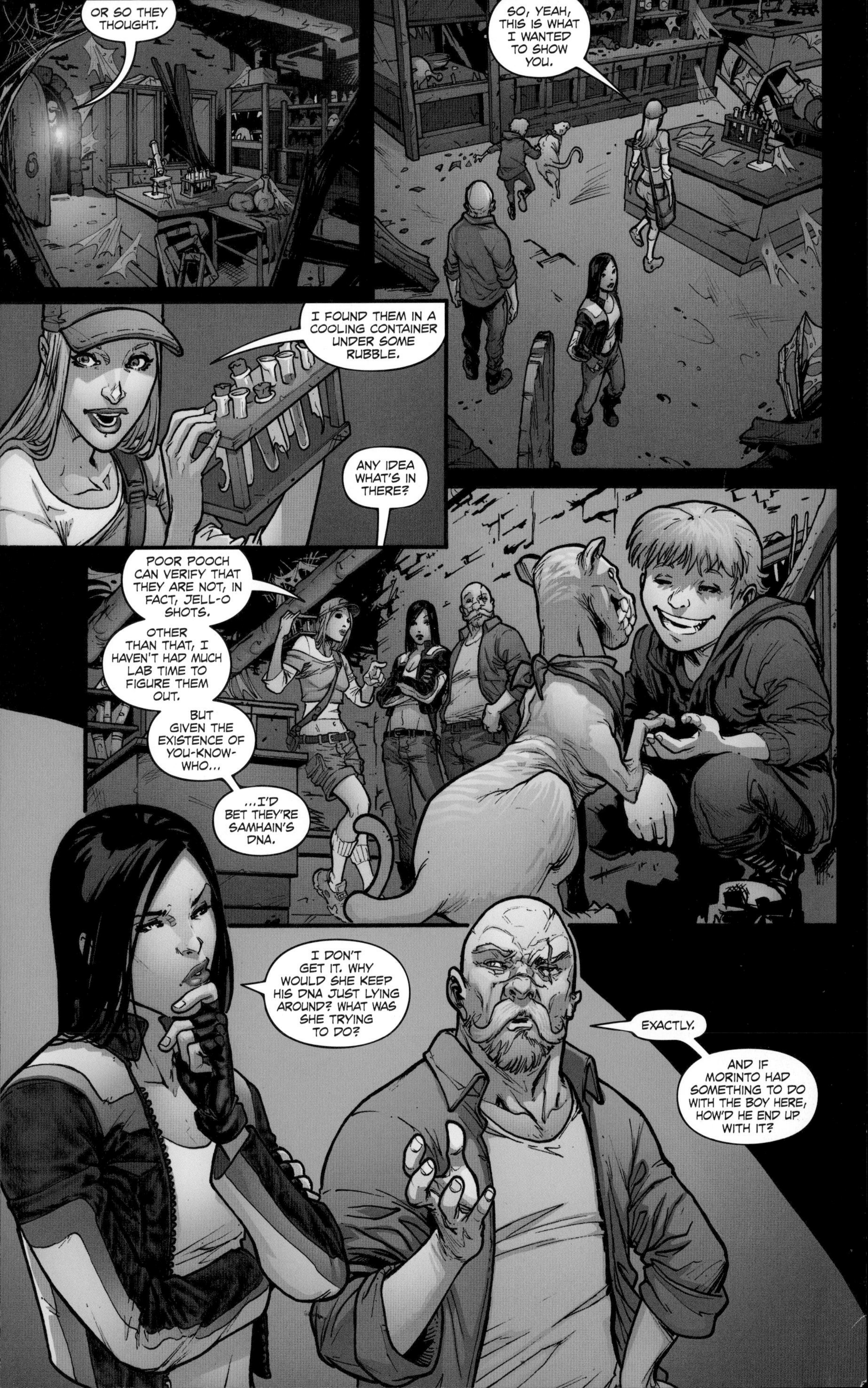

OR SO THEY THOUGHT.
SO, YEAH, THIS IS WHAT I WANTED TO SHOW YOU.
I FOUND THEM IN A COOLING CONTAINER UNDER SOME RUBBLE.
ANY IDEA WHAT'S IN THERE?
POOR POOCH CAN VERIFY THAT THEY ARE NOT, IN FACT, JELL-O SHOTS.
OTHER THAN THAT, I HAVEN'T HAD MUCH LAB TIME TO FIGURE THEM OUT.
BUT GIVEN THE EXISTENCE OF YOU-KNOW-WHO...
...I'D BET THEY'RE SAMHAIN'S DNA.
I DON'T GET IT. WHY WOULD SHE KEEP HIS DNA JUST LYING AROUND? WHAT WAS SHE TRYING TO DO?
EXACTLY.
AND IF MORINTO HAD SOMETHING TO DO WITH THE BOY HERE, HOW'D HE END UP WITH IT?

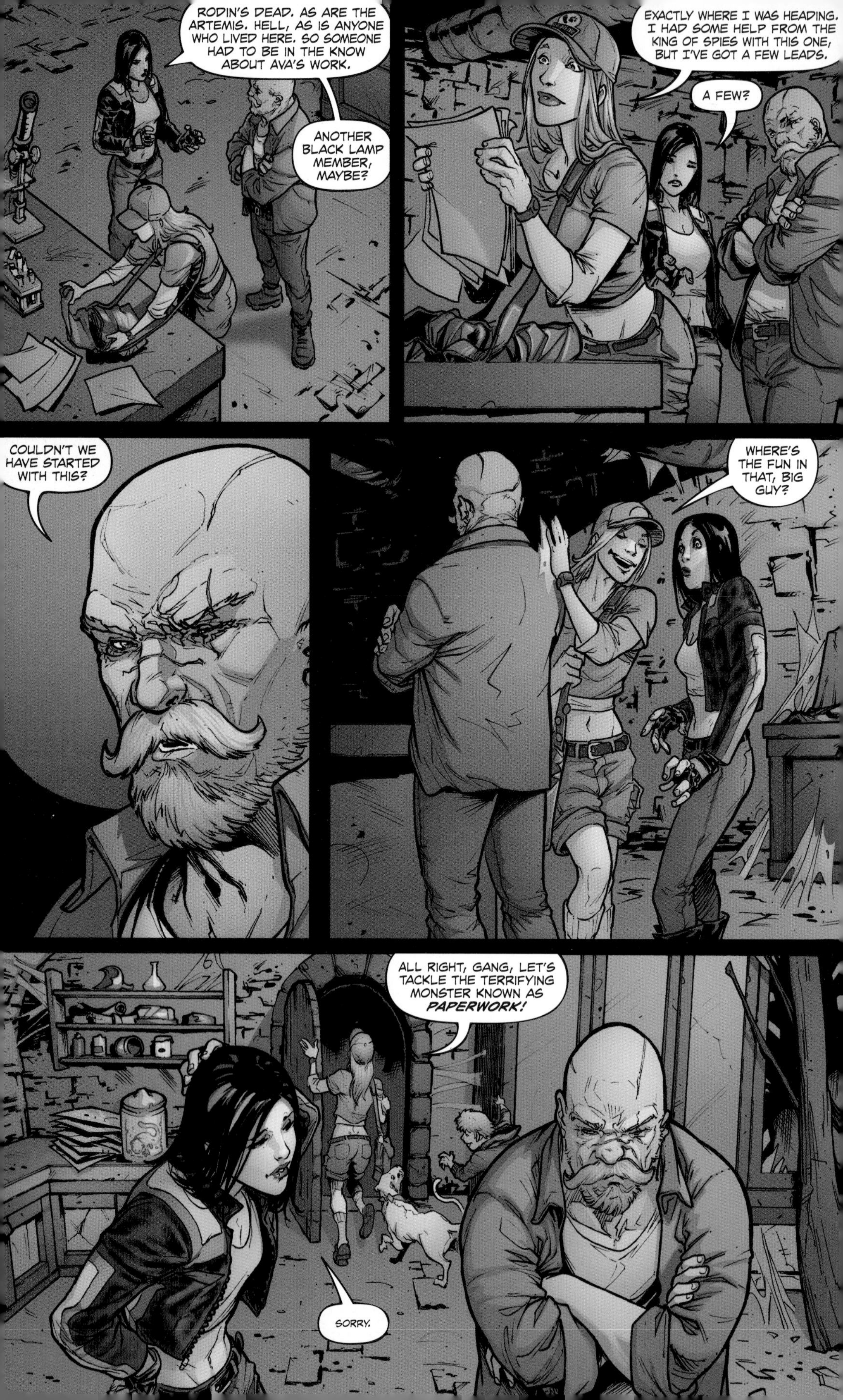
RODIN'S DEAD. AS ARE THE ARTEMIS. HELL, AS IS ANYONE WHO LIVED HERE. SO SOMEONE HAD TO BE IN THE KNOW ABOUT AVA'S WORK.
ANOTHER BLACK LAMP MEMBER, MAYBE?
EXACTLY WHERE I WAS HEADING. I HAD SOME HELP FROM THE KING OF SPIES WITH THIS ONE, BUT I'VE GOT A FEW LEADS.
A FEW?
COULDN'T WE HAVE STARTED WITH THIS?
WHERE'S THE FUN IN THAT, BIG GUY?
ALL RIGHT, GANG, LET'S TACKLE THE TERRIFYING MONSTER KNOWN AS *PAPERWORK!*
SORRY.

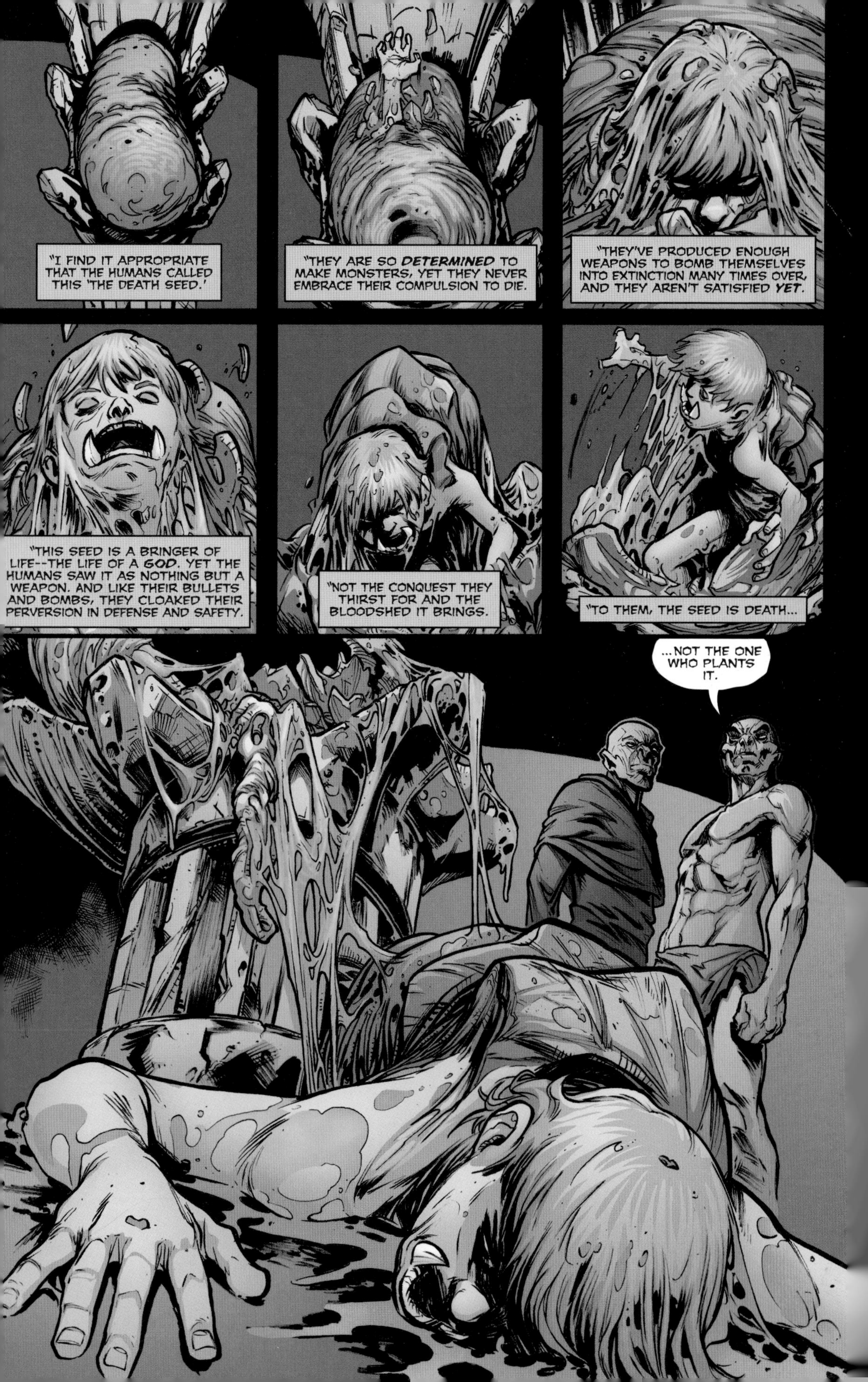
"I FIND IT APPROPRIATE THAT THE HUMANS CALLED THIS 'THE DEATH SEED.'
"THEY ARE SO DETERMINED TO MAKE MONSTERS, YET THEY NEVER EMBRACE THEIR COMPULSION TO DIE.
"THEY'VE PRODUCED ENOUGH WEAPONS TO BOMB THEMSELVES INTO EXTINCTION MANY TIMES OVER, AND THEY AREN'T SATISFIED YET.
"THIS SEED IS A BRINGER OF LIFE--THE LIFE OF A GOD. YET THE HUMANS SAW IT AS NOTHING BUT A WEAPON. AND LIKE THEIR BULLETS AND BOMBS, THEY CLOAKED THEIR PERVERSION IN DEFENSE AND SAFETY.
"NOT THE CONQUEST THEY THIRST FOR AND THE BLOODSHED IT BRINGS.
"TO THEM, THE SEED IS DEATH...
...NOT THE ONE WHO PLANTS IT.

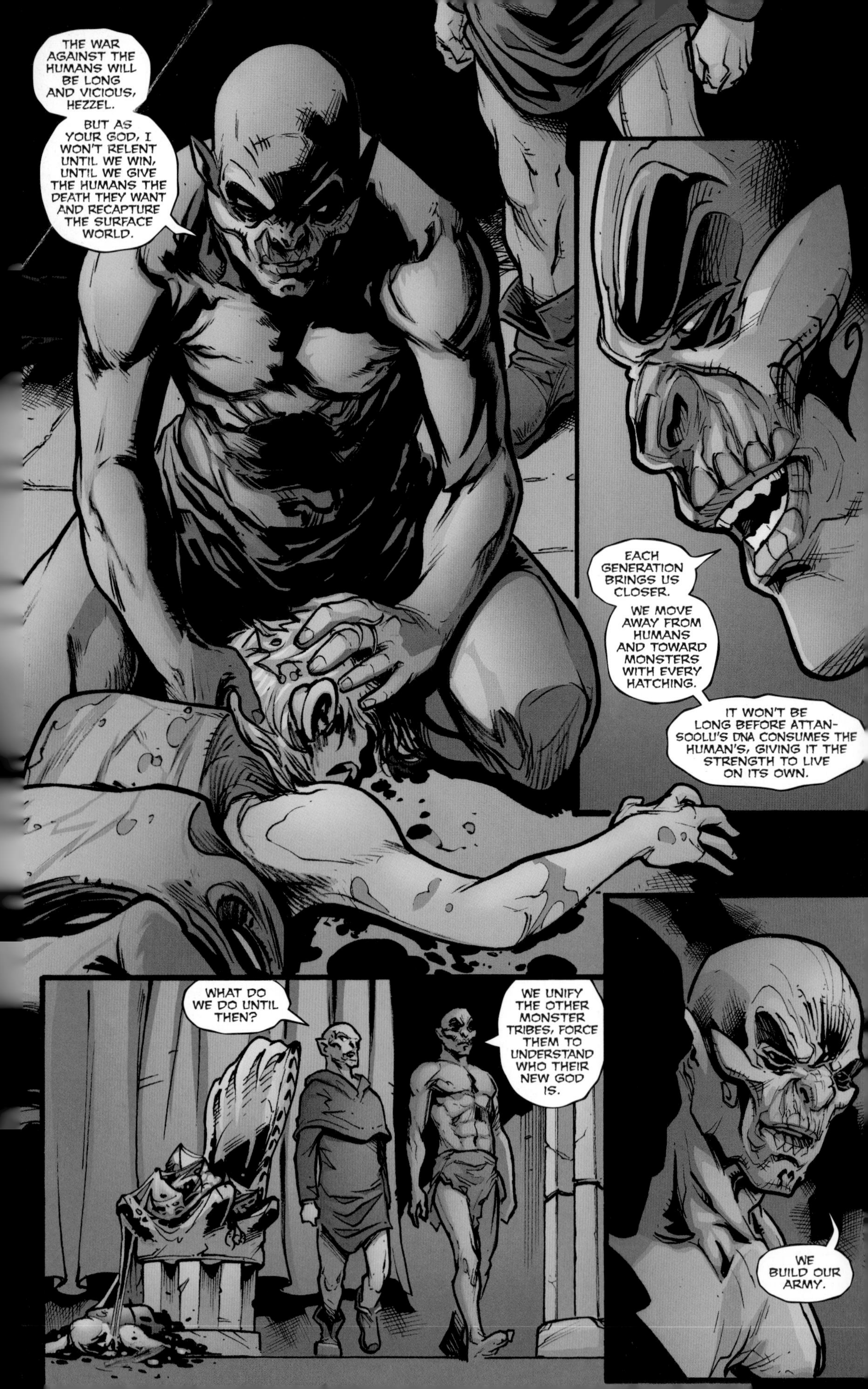
THE WAR AGAINST THE HUMANS WILL BE LONG AND VICIOUS, HEZZEL.
BUT AS YOUR GOD, I WON'T RELENT UNTIL WE WIN, UNTIL WE GIVE THE HUMANS THE DEATH THEY WANT AND RECAPTURE THE SURFACE WORLD.
EACH GENERATION BRINGS US CLOSER.
WE MOVE AWAY FROM HUMANS AND TOWARD MONSTERS WITH EVERY HATCHING.
IT WON'T BE LONG BEFORE ATTAN-SOOLU'S DNA CONSUMES THE HUMAN'S, GIVING IT THE STRENGTH TO LIVE ON ITS OWN.
WHAT DO WE DO UNTIL THEN?
WE UNIFY THE OTHER MONSTER TRIBES, FORCE THEM TO UNDERSTAND WHO THEIR NEW GOD IS.
WE BUILD OUR ARMY.

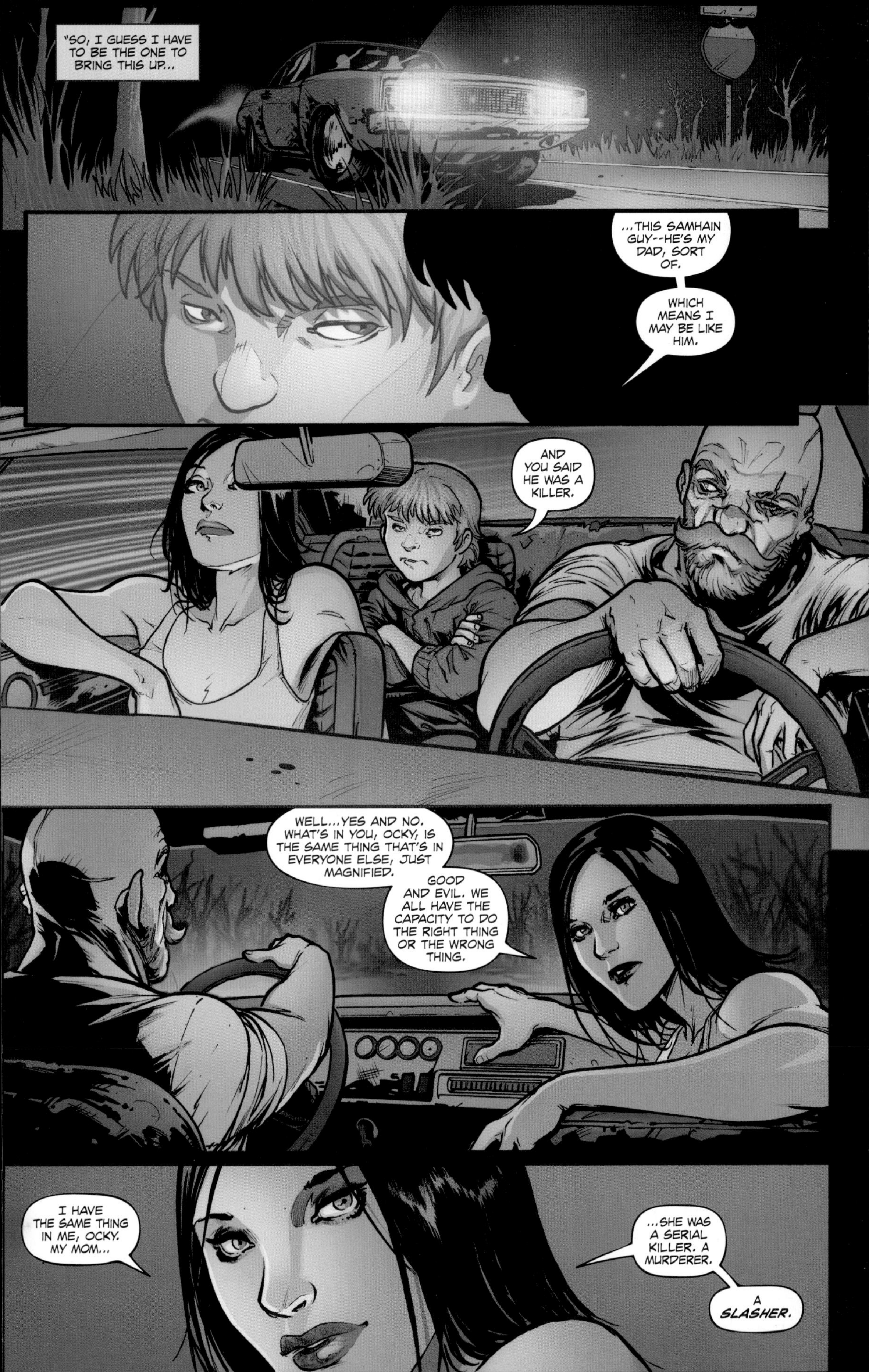
"SO, I GUESS I HAVE TO BE THE ONE TO BRING THIS UP...
...THIS SAMHAIN GUY--HE'S MY DAD, SORT OF.
WHICH MEANS I MAY BE LIKE HIM.
AND YOU SAID HE WAS A KILLER.
WELL...YES AND NO. WHAT'S IN YOU, OCKY, IS THE SAME THING THAT'S IN EVERYONE ELSE, JUST MAGNIFIED.
GOOD AND EVIL. WE ALL HAVE THE CAPACITY TO DO THE RIGHT THING OR THE WRONG THING.
I HAVE THE SAME THING IN ME, OCKY. MY MOM...
...SHE WAS A SERIAL KILLER. A MURDERER.
A SLASHER.

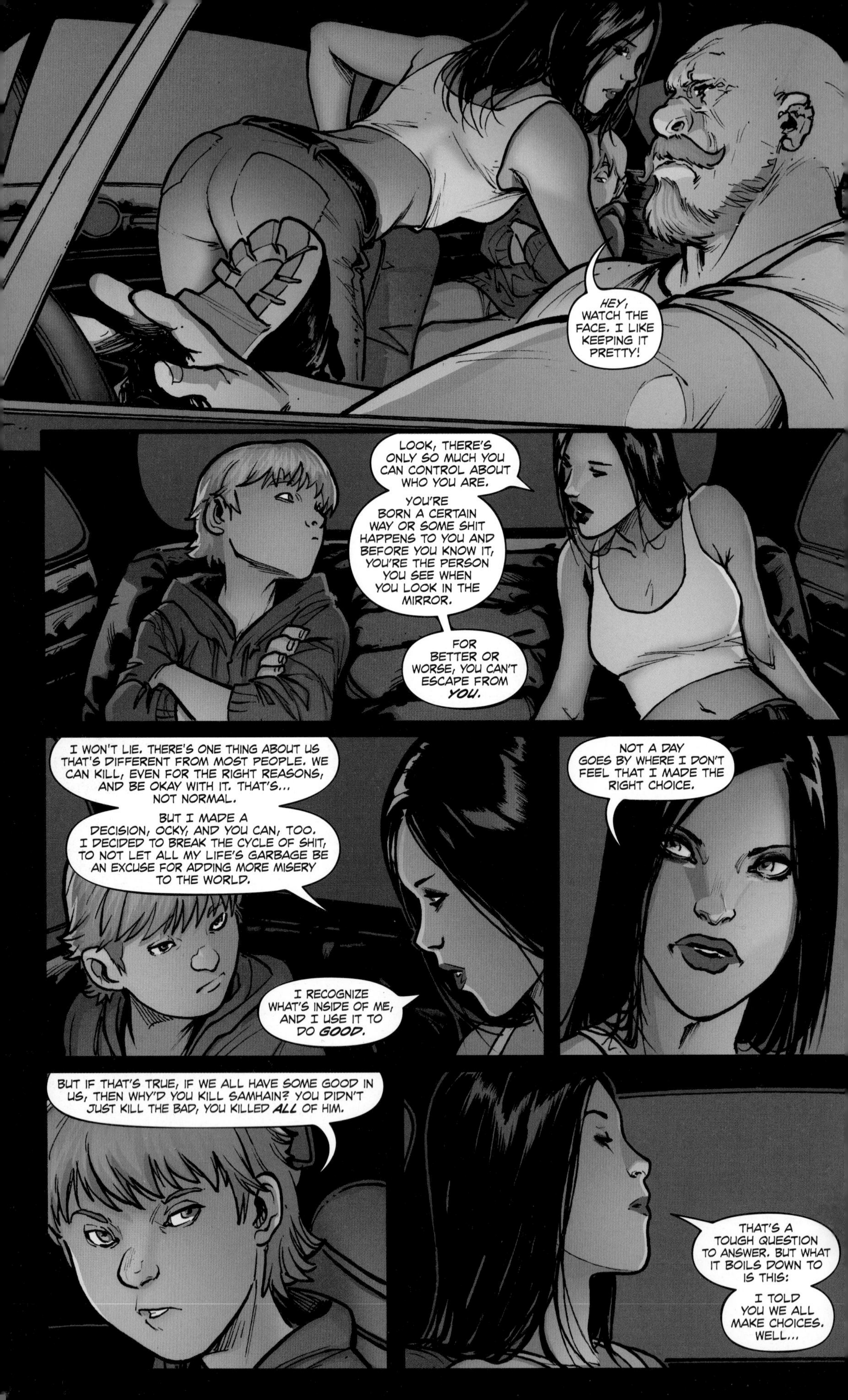
HEY, WATCH THE FACE. I LIKE KEEPING IT PRETTY!
LOOK, THERE'S ONLY SO MUCH YOU CAN CONTROL ABOUT WHO YOU ARE.
YOU'RE BORN A CERTAIN WAY OR SOME SHIT HAPPENS TO YOU AND BEFORE YOU KNOW IT, YOU'RE THE PERSON YOU SEE WHEN YOU LOOK IN THE MIRROR.
FOR BETTER OR WORSE, YOU CAN'T ESCAPE FROM YOU.
I WON'T LIE. THERE'S ONE THING ABOUT US THAT'S DIFFERENT FROM MOST PEOPLE. WE CAN KILL, EVEN FOR THE RIGHT REASONS, AND BE OKAY WITH IT. THAT'S... NOT NORMAL.
BUT I MADE A DECISION, OCKY, AND YOU CAN, TOO. I DECIDED TO BREAK THE CYCLE OF SHIT, TO NOT LET ALL MY LIFE'S GARBAGE BE AN EXCUSE FOR ADDING MORE MISERY TO THE WORLD.
I RECOGNIZE WHAT'S INSIDE OF ME, AND I USE IT TO DO GOOD.
NOT A DAY GOES BY WHERE I DON'T FEEL THAT I MADE THE RIGHT CHOICE.
BUT IF THAT'S TRUE, IF WE ALL HAVE SOME GOOD IN US, THEN WHY'D YOU KILL SAMHAIN? YOU DIDN'T JUST KILL THE BAD, YOU KILLED ALL OF HIM.
THAT'S A TOUGH QUESTION TO ANSWER. BUT WHAT IT BOILS DOWN TO IS THIS:
I TOLD YOU WE ALL MAKE CHOICES. WELL...

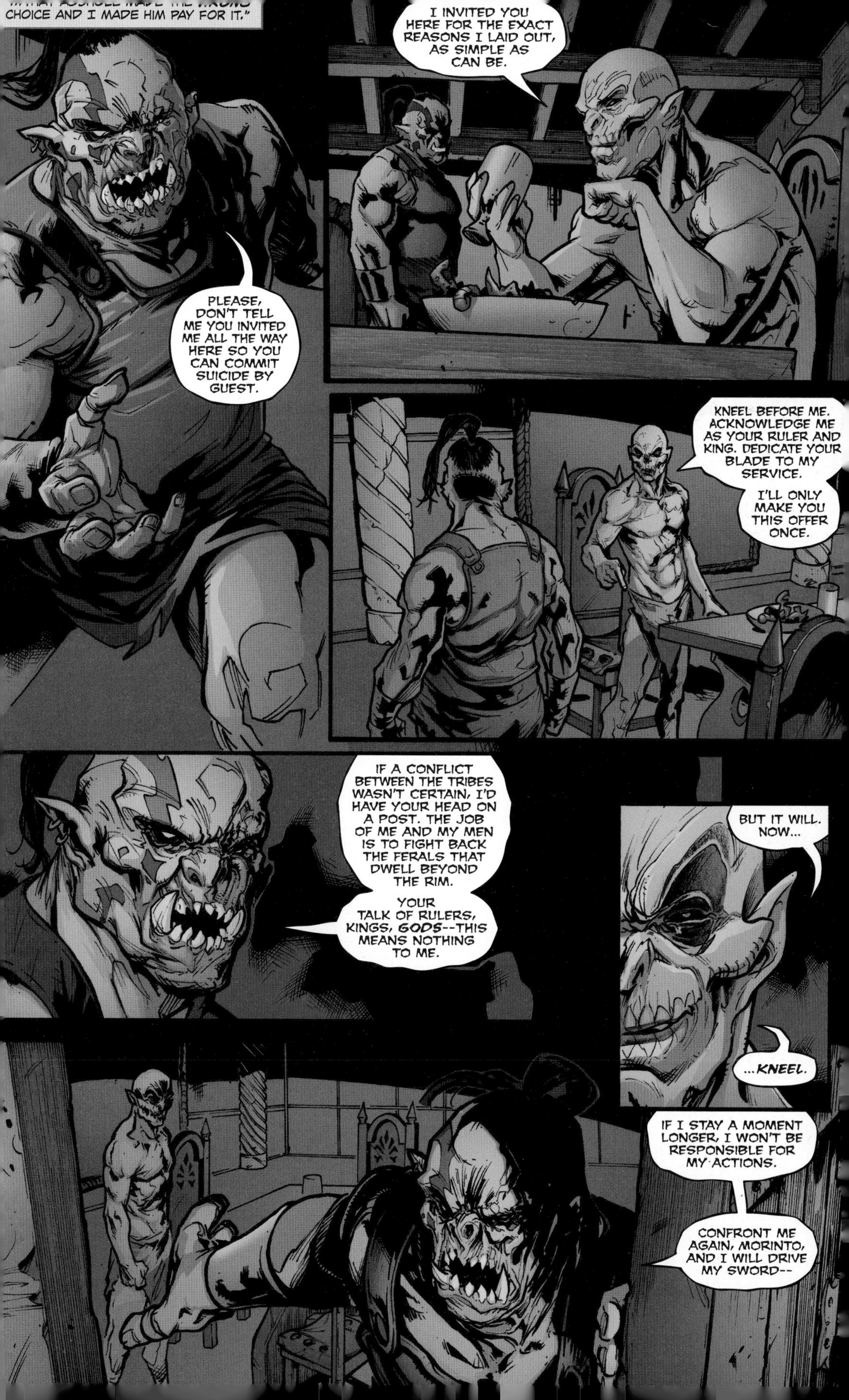

CHOICE AND I MADE HIM PAY FOR IT."
I INVITED YOU HERE FOR THE EXACT REASONS I LAID OUT, AS SIMPLE AS CAN BE.
PLEASE, DON'T TELL ME YOU INVITED ME ALL THE WAY HERE SO YOU CAN COMMIT SUICIDE BY GUEST.
KNEEL BEFORE ME. ACKNOWLEDGE ME AS YOUR RULER AND KING. DEDICATE YOUR BLADE TO MY SERVICE.
I'LL ONLY MAKE YOU THIS OFFER ONCE.
IF A CONFLICT BETWEEN THE TRIBES WASN'T CERTAIN, I'D HAVE YOUR HEAD ON A POST. THE JOB OF ME AND MY MEN IS TO FIGHT BACK THE FERALS THAT DWELL BEYOND THE RIM.
YOUR TALK OF RULERS, KINGS, GODS--THIS MEANS NOTHING TO ME.
BUT IT WILL. NOW...
...KNEEL.
IF I STAY A MOMENT LONGER, I WON'T BE RESPONSIBLE FOR MY ACTIONS.
CONFRONT ME AGAIN, MORINTO, AND I WILL DRIVE MY SWORD--

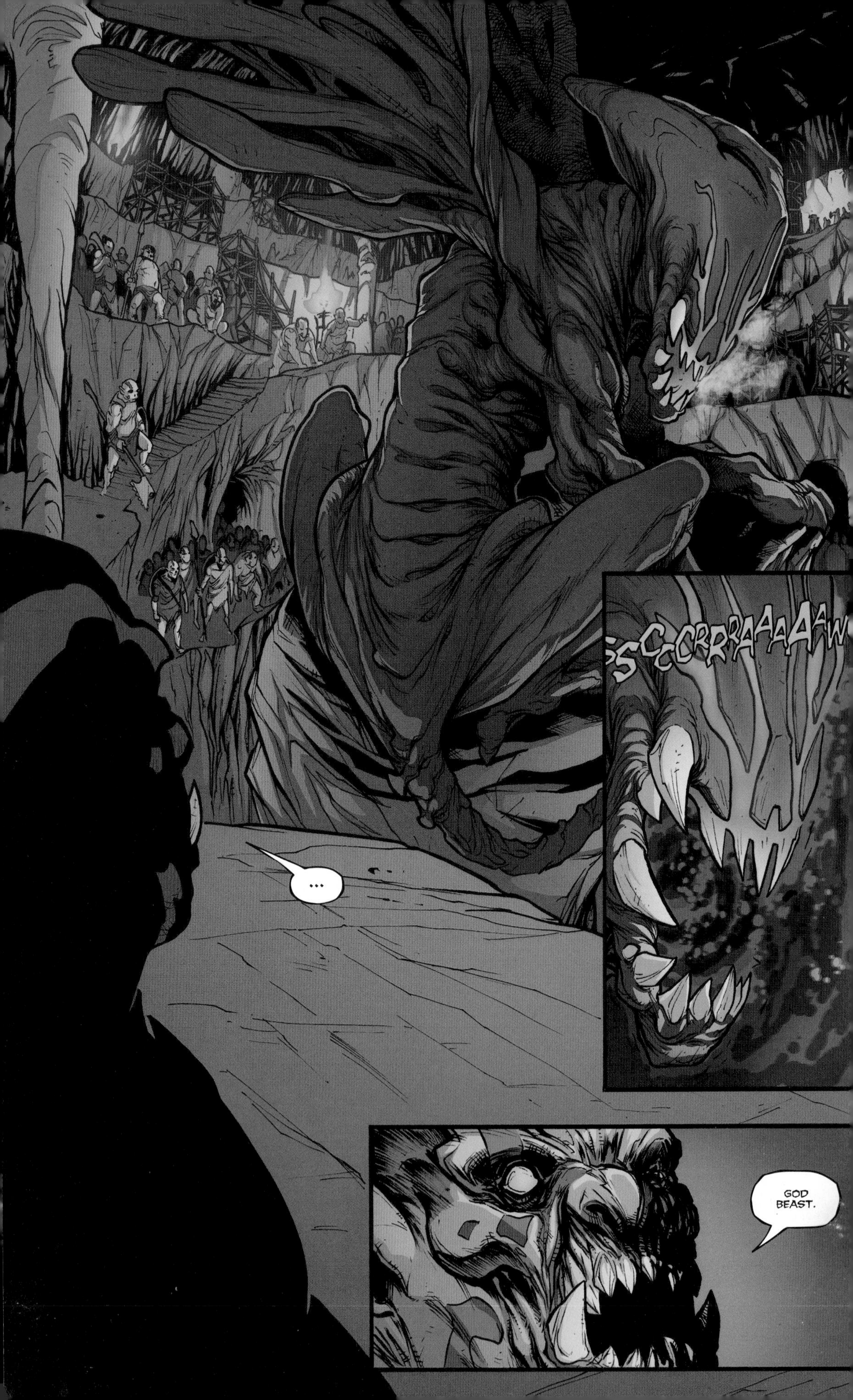
...
SSCCCRRRAAAAAW
GOD BEAST.

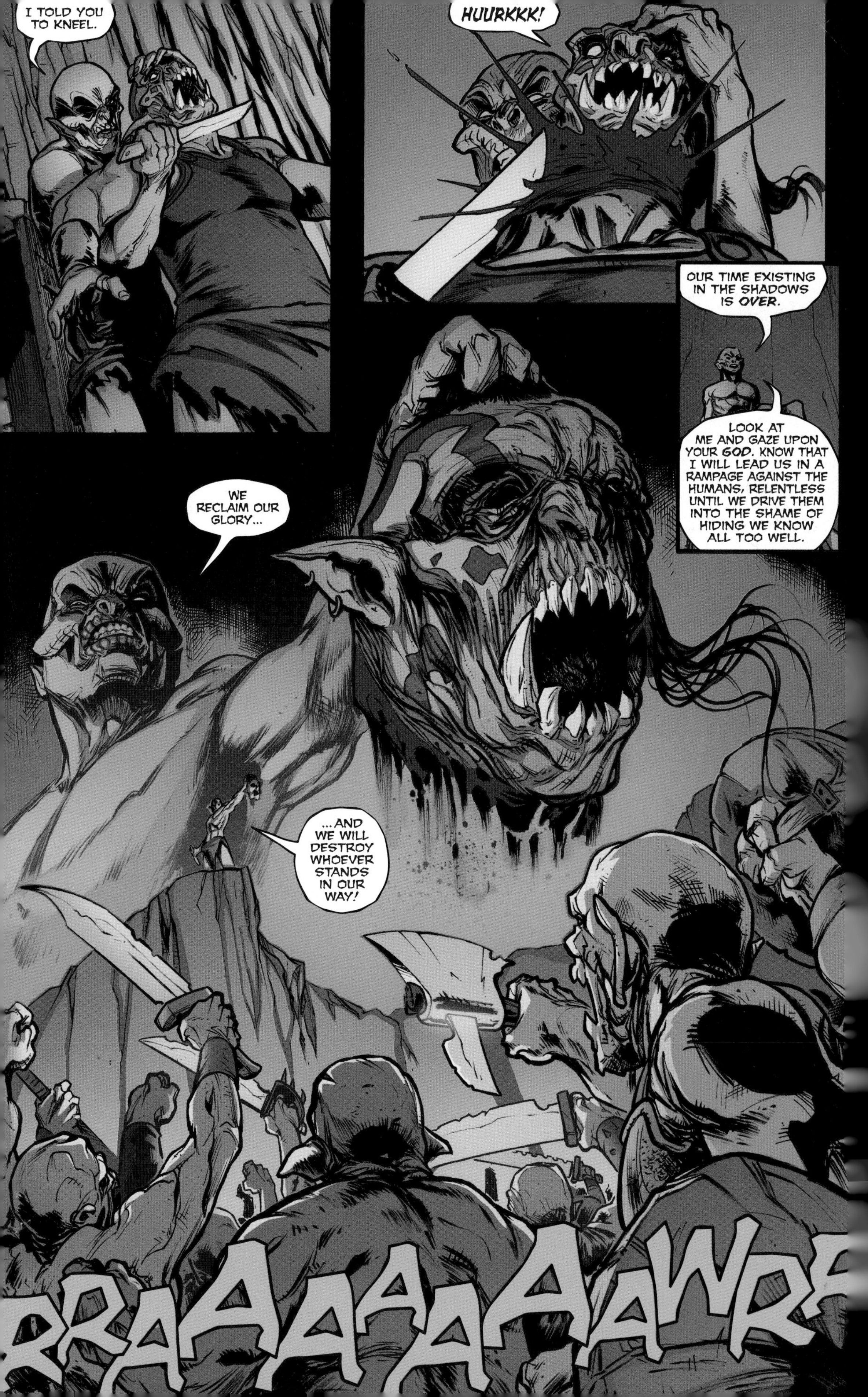
I TOLD YOU TO KNEEL.
HUURKKK!
OUR TIME EXISTING IN THE SHADOWS IS OVER.
LOOK AT ME AND GAZE UPON YOUR GOD. KNOW THAT I WILL LEAD US IN A RAMPAGE AGAINST THE HUMANS, RELENTLESS UNTIL WE DRIVE THEM INTO THE SHAME OF HIDING WE KNOW ALL TOO WELL.
WE RECLAIM OUR GLORY...
...AND WE WILL DESTROY WHOEVER STANDS IN OUR WAY!
RRAAAAAAAWRR

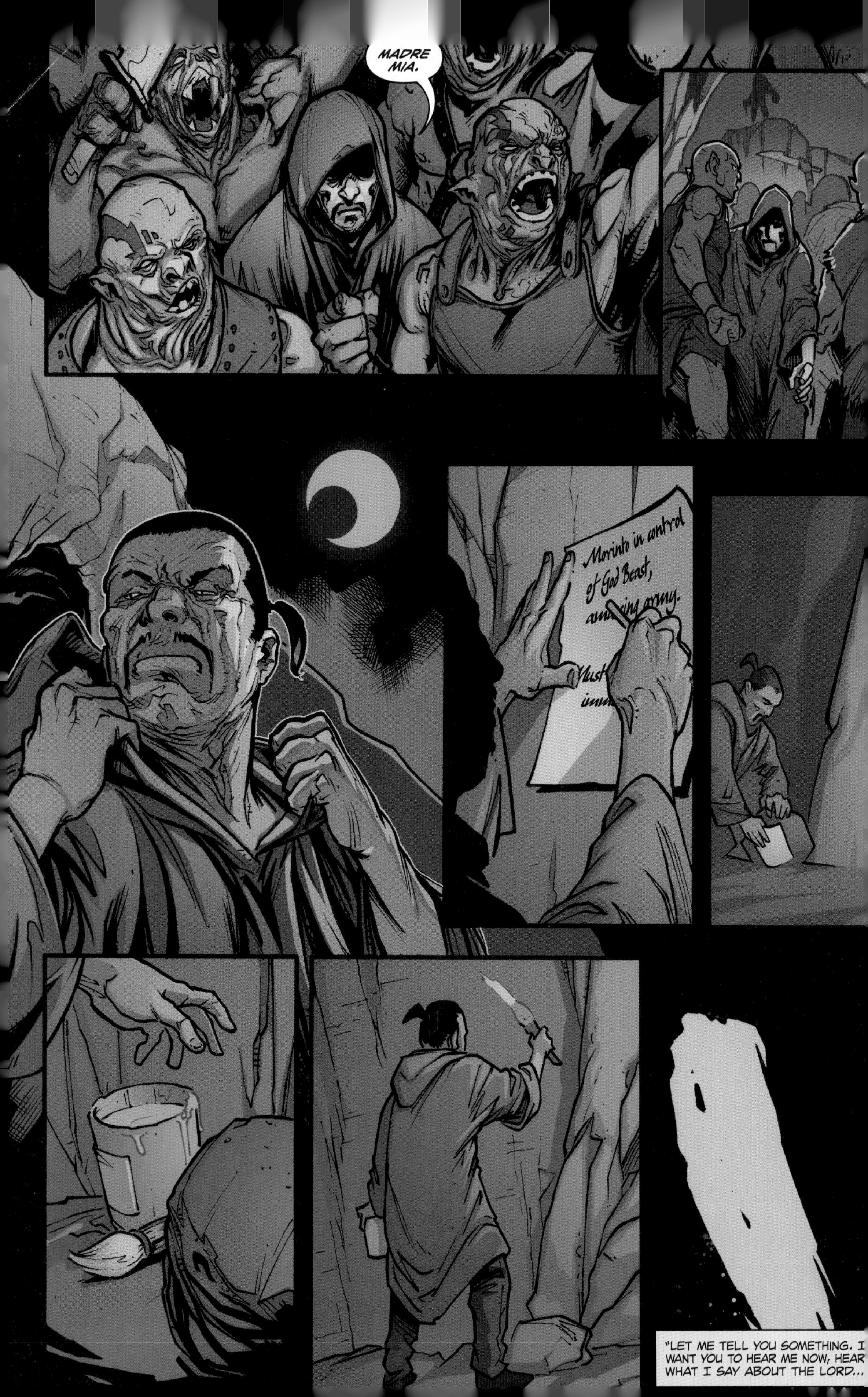
MADRE MIA.
Morinto in control of God Beast,
"LET ME TELL YOU SOMETHING. I WANT YOU TO HEAR ME NOW, HEAR WHAT I SAY ABOUT THE LORD...

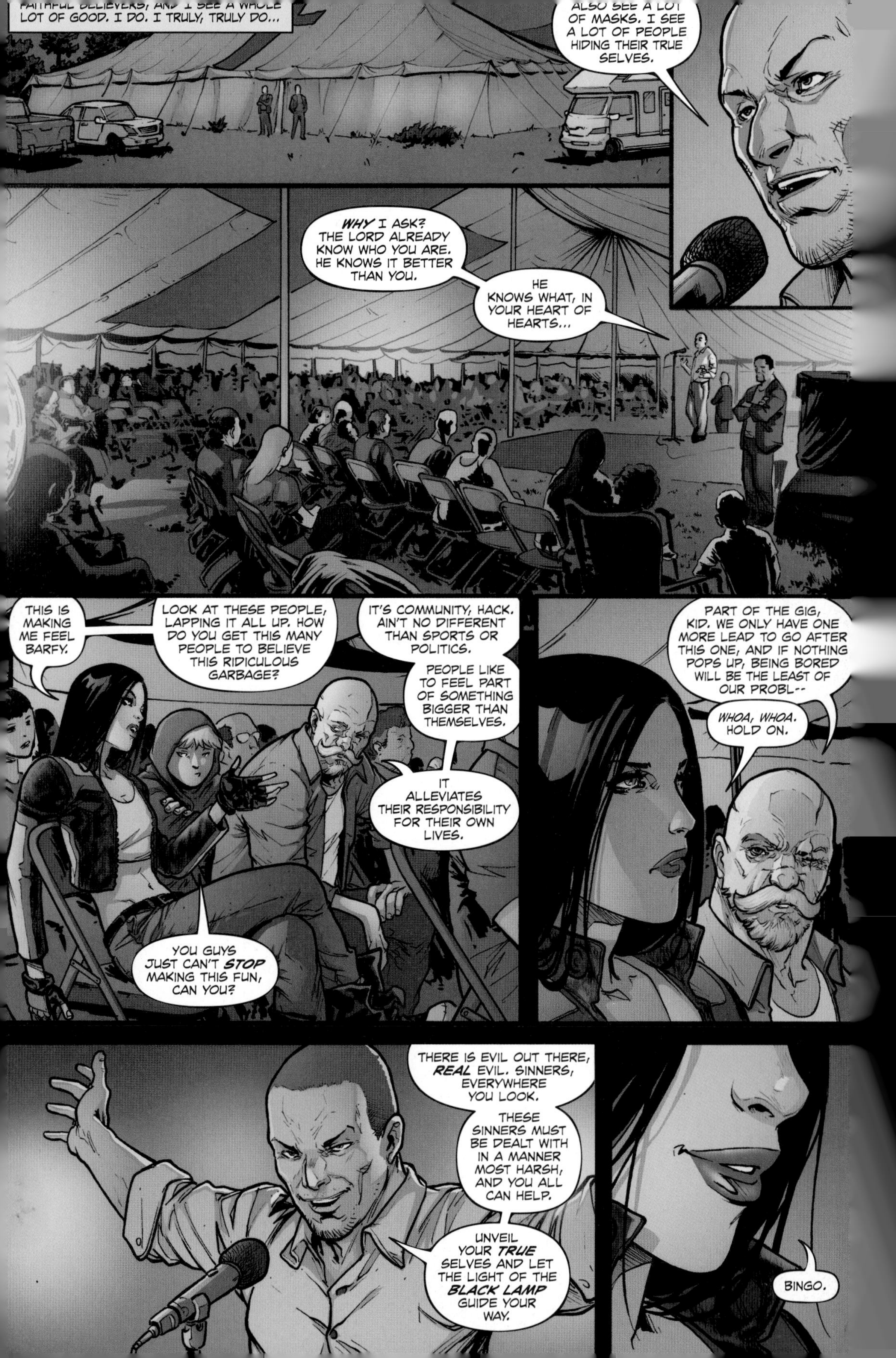
FAITHFUL BELIEVERS, AND I SEE A WHOLE LOT OF GOOD. I DO. I TRULY, TRULY DO...
ALSO SEE A LOT OF MASKS. I SEE A LOT OF PEOPLE HIDING THEIR TRUE SELVES.
WHY I ASK? THE LORD ALREADY KNOW WHO YOU ARE. HE KNOWS IT BETTER THAN YOU.
HE KNOWS WHAT, IN YOUR HEART OF HEARTS...
THIS IS MAKING ME FEEL BARFY.
LOOK AT THESE PEOPLE, LAPPING IT ALL UP. HOW DO YOU GET THIS MANY PEOPLE TO BELIEVE THIS RIDICULOUS GARBAGE?
IT'S COMMUNITY, HACK. AIN'T NO DIFFERENT THAN SPORTS OR POLITICS.
PEOPLE LIKE TO FEEL PART OF SOMETHING BIGGER THAN THEMSELVES.
IT ALLEVIATES THEIR RESPONSIBILITY FOR THEIR OWN LIVES.
YOU GUYS JUST CAN'T STOP MAKING THIS FUN, CAN YOU?
PART OF THE GIG, KID. WE ONLY HAVE ONE MORE LEAD TO GO AFTER THIS ONE, AND IF NOTHING POPS UP, BEING BORED WILL BE THE LEAST OF OUR PROBL--
WHOA, WHOA. HOLD ON.
THERE IS EVIL OUT THERE, REAL EVIL. SINNERS, EVERYWHERE YOU LOOK.
THESE SINNERS MUST BE DEALT WITH IN A MANNER MOST HARSH, AND YOU ALL CAN HELP.
UNVEIL YOUR TRUE SELVES AND LET THE LIGHT OF THE BLACK LAMP GUIDE YOUR WAY.
BINGO.

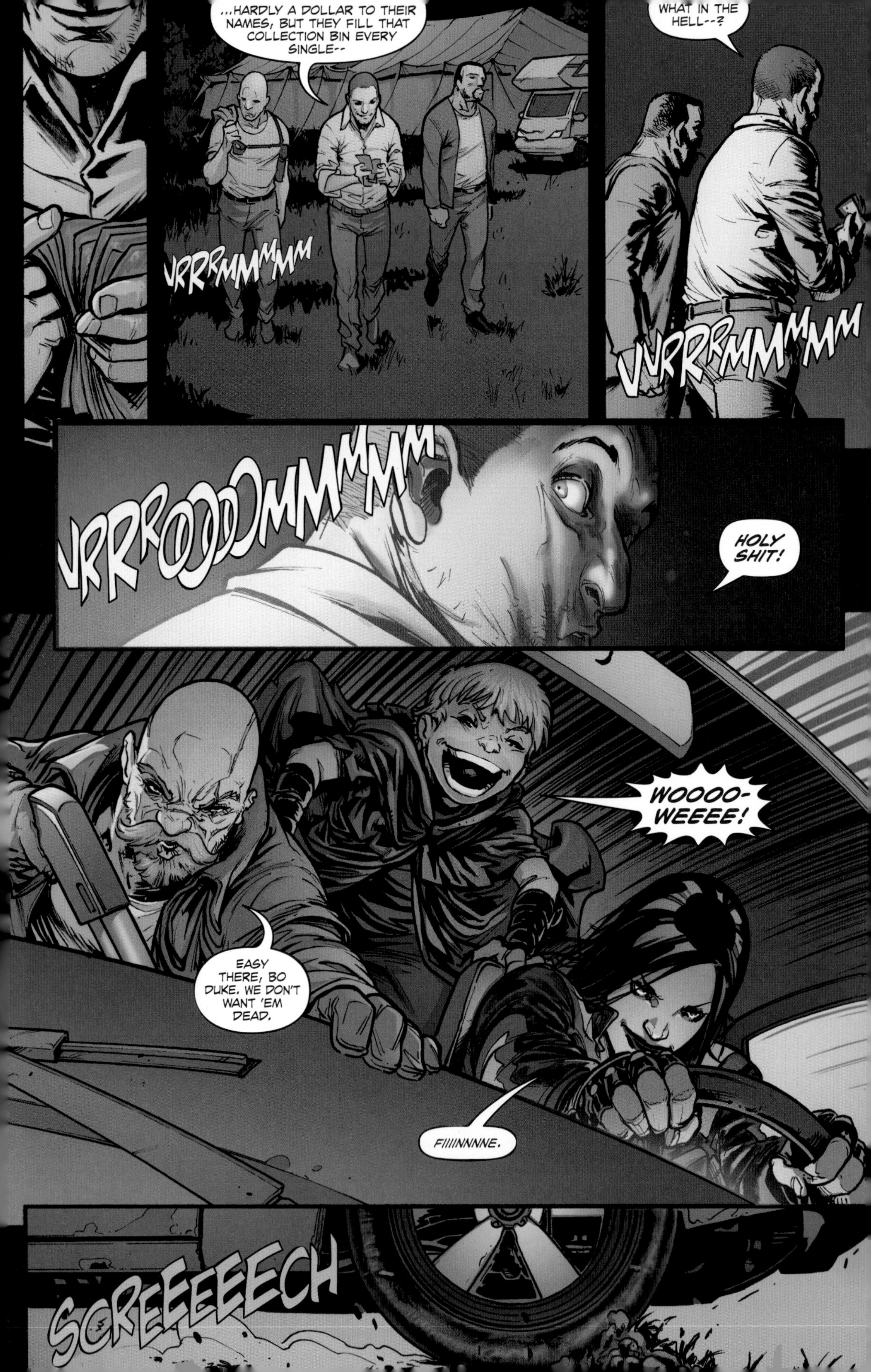
...HARDLY A DOLLAR TO THEIR NAMES, BUT THEY FILL THAT COLLECTION BIN EVERY SINGLE--
VRRRMMMMM
WHAT IN THE HELL--?
VVRRRMMMMMM
VRRROOOOMMMMMM
HOLY SHIT!
WOOOO-WEEEE!
EASY THERE, BO DUKE. WE DON'T WANT 'EM DEAD.
FIIIINNNNE.
SCREEEEECH

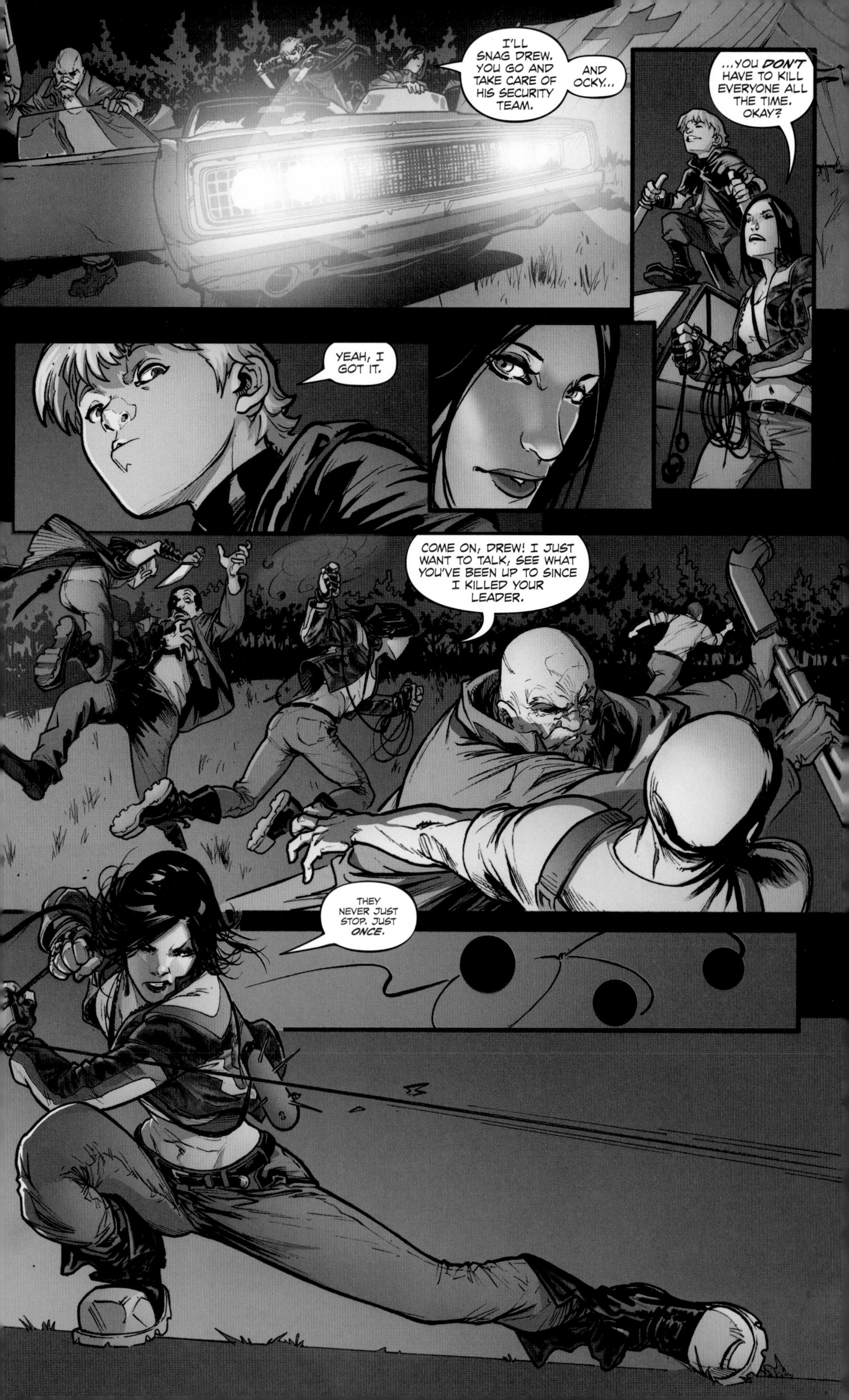
I'LL SNAG DREW. YOU GO AND TAKE CARE OF HIS SECURITY TEAM.
AND OCKY...
...YOU DON'T HAVE TO KILL EVERYONE ALL THE TIME. OKAY?
YEAH, I GOT IT.
COME ON, DREW! I JUST WANT TO TALK, SEE WHAT YOU'VE BEEN UP TO SINCE I KILLED YOUR LEADER.
THEY NEVER JUST STOP. JUST ONCE.

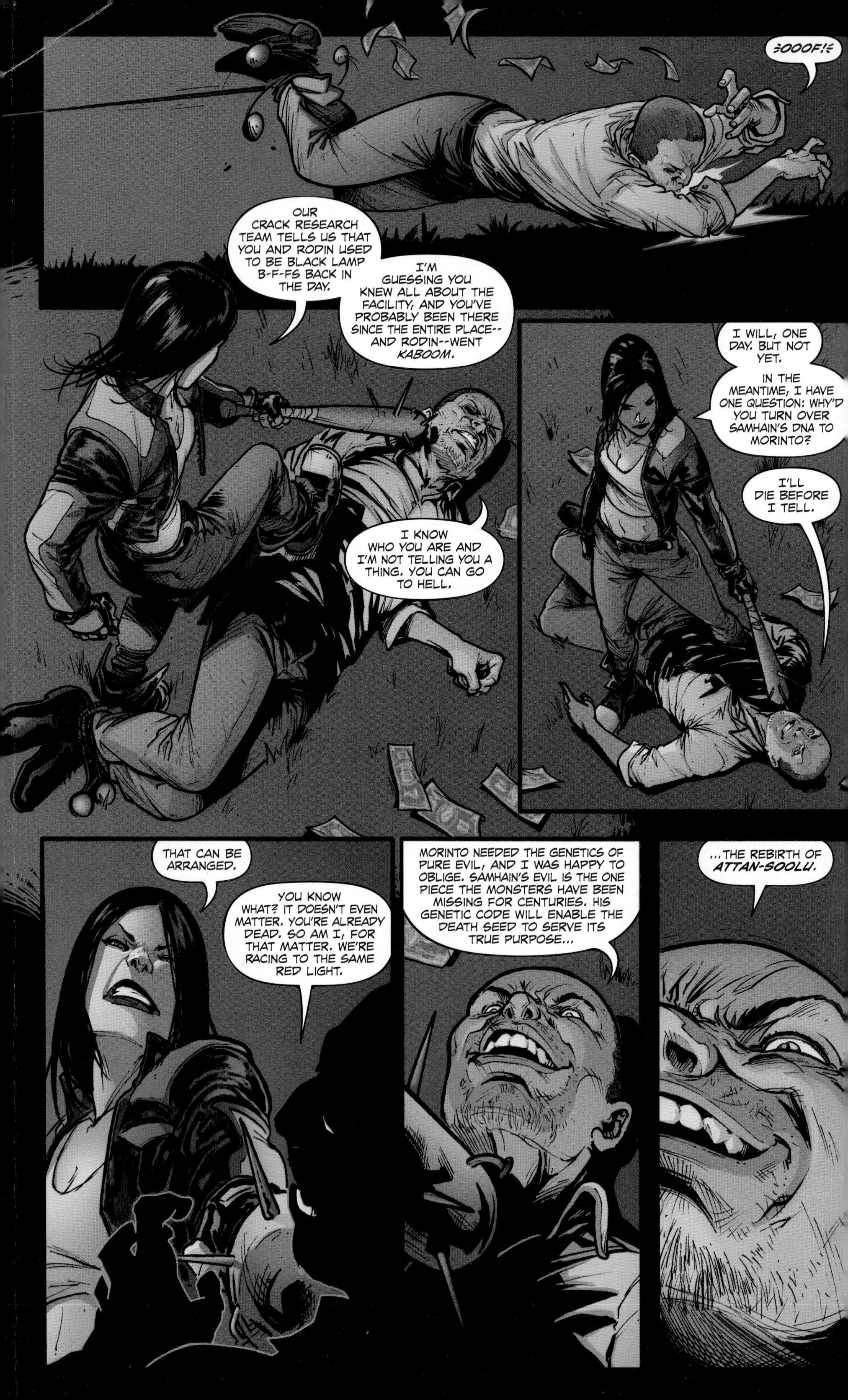
OOOF!
OUR CRACK RESEARCH TEAM TELLS US THAT YOU AND RODIN USED TO BE BLACK LAMP B-F-FS BACK IN THE DAY.
I'M GUESSING YOU KNEW ALL ABOUT THE FACILITY, AND YOU'VE PROBABLY BEEN THERE SINCE THE ENTIRE PLACE-- AND RODIN--WENT KABOOM.
I KNOW WHO YOU ARE AND I'M NOT TELLING YOU A THING. YOU CAN GO TO HELL.
I WILL, ONE DAY. BUT NOT YET.
IN THE MEANTIME, I HAVE ONE QUESTION: WHY'D YOU TURN OVER SAMHAIN'S DNA TO MORINTO?
I'LL DIE BEFORE I TELL.
THAT CAN BE ARRANGED.
YOU KNOW WHAT? IT DOESN'T EVEN MATTER. YOU'RE ALREADY DEAD. SO AM I, FOR THAT MATTER. WE'RE RACING TO THE SAME RED LIGHT.
MORINTO NEEDED THE GENETICS OF PURE EVIL, AND I WAS HAPPY TO OBLIGE. SAMHAIN'S EVIL IS THE ONE PIECE THE MONSTERS HAVE BEEN MISSING FOR CENTURIES. HIS GENETIC CODE WILL ENABLE THE DEATH SEED TO SERVE ITS TRUE PURPOSE...
...THE REBIRTH OF ATTAN-SOOLU.

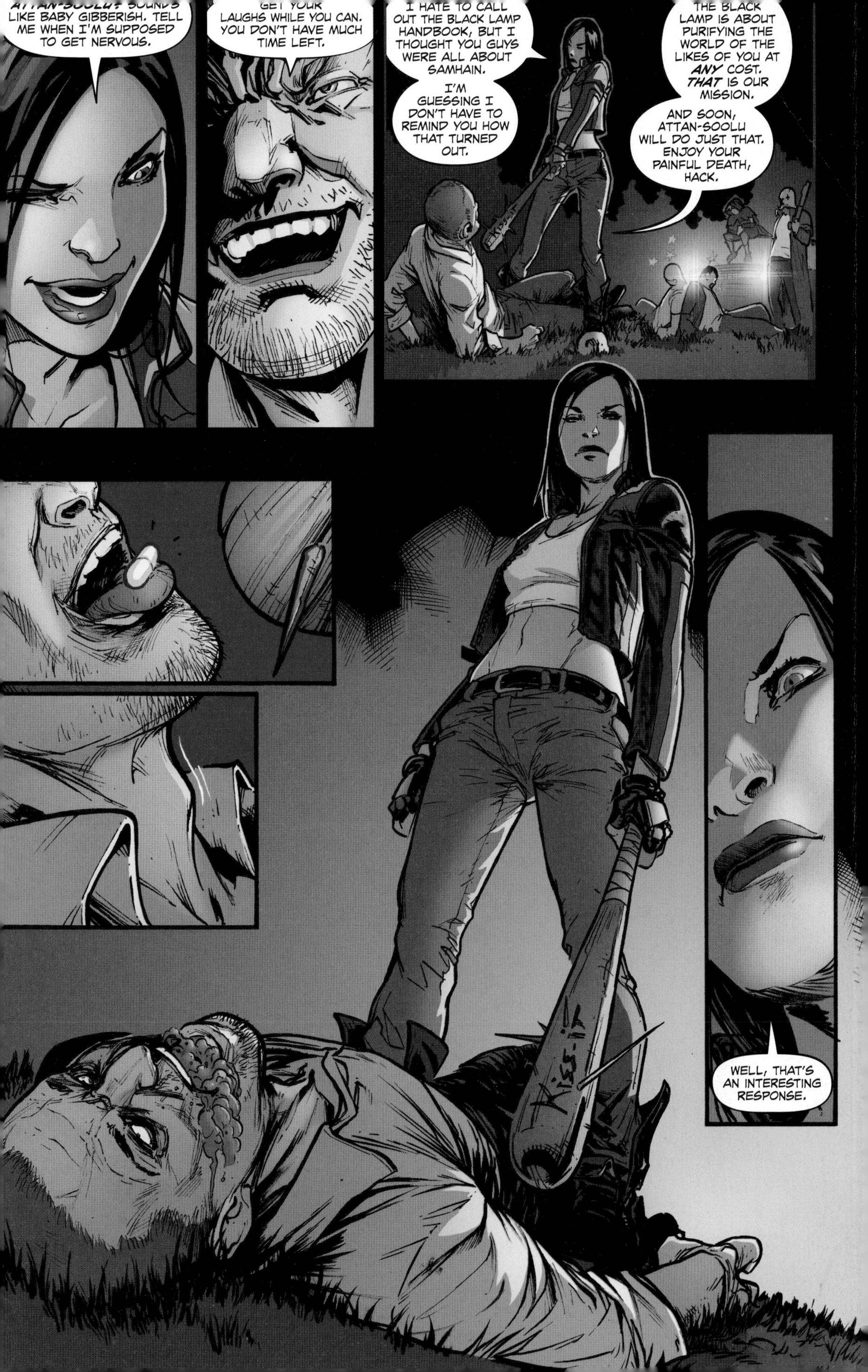
LIKE BABY GIBBERISH. TELL ME WHEN I'M SUPPOSED TO GET NERVOUS.
LAUGHS WHILE YOU CAN. YOU DON'T HAVE MUCH TIME LEFT.
I HATE TO CALL OUT THE BLACK LAMP HANDBOOK, BUT I THOUGHT YOU GUYS WERE ALL ABOUT SAMHAIN.
I'M GUESSING I DON'T HAVE TO REMIND YOU HOW THAT TURNED OUT.
THE BLACK LAMP IS ABOUT PURIFYING THE WORLD OF THE LIKES OF YOU AT ANY COST. THAT IS OUR MISSION.
AND SOON, ATTAN-SOOLU WILL DO JUST THAT. ENJOY YOUR PAINFUL DEATH, HACK.
WELL, THAT'S AN INTERESTING RESPONSE.

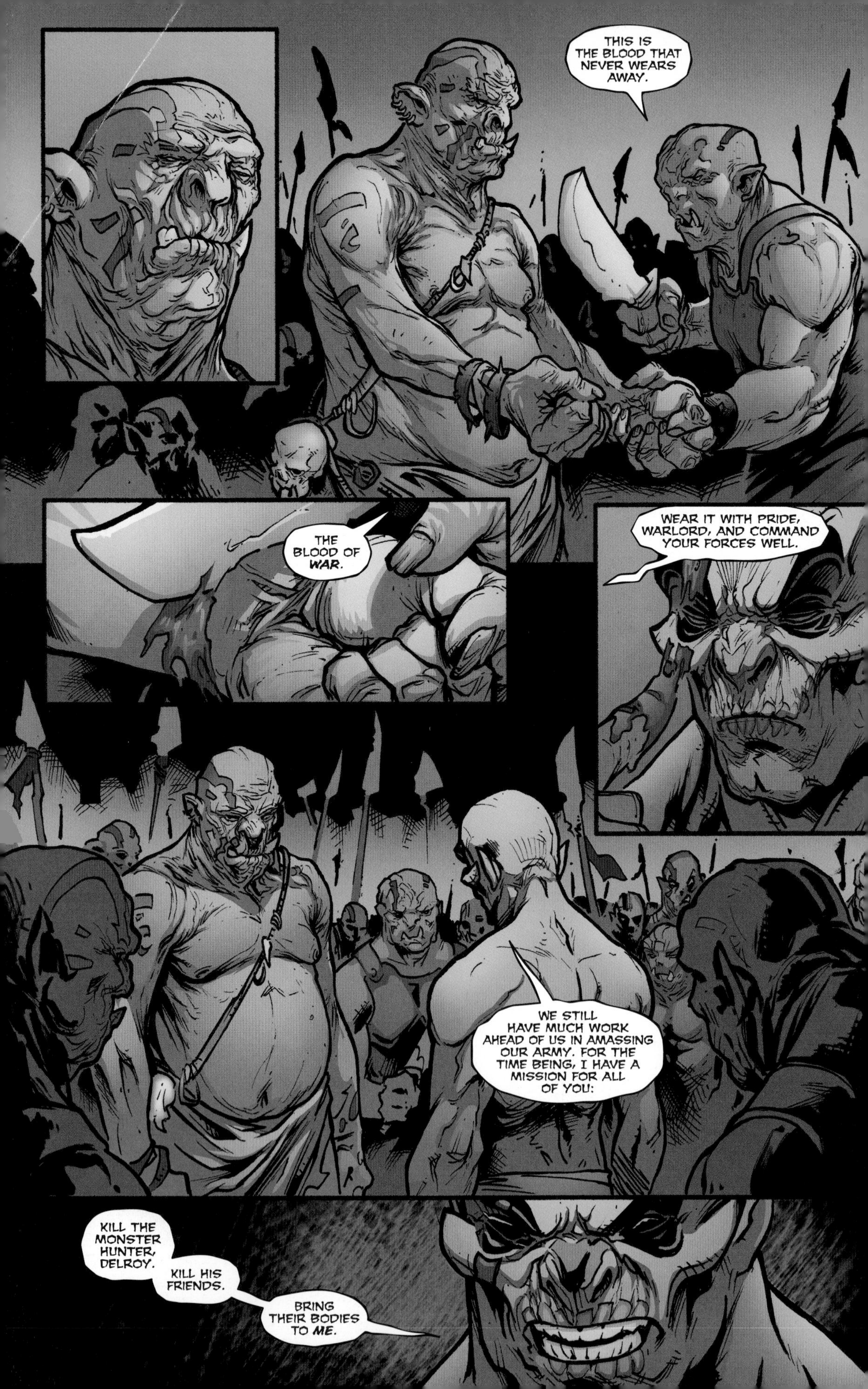
THIS IS THE BLOOD THAT NEVER WEARS AWAY.
THE BLOOD OF *WAR*.
WEAR IT WITH PRIDE, WARLORD, AND COMMAND YOUR FORCES WELL.
WE STILL HAVE MUCH WORK AHEAD OF US IN AMASSING OUR ARMY. FOR THE TIME BEING, I HAVE A MISSION FOR ALL OF YOU:
KILL THE MONSTER HUNTER, DELROY.
KILL HIS FRIENDS.
BRING THEIR BODIES TO *ME*.

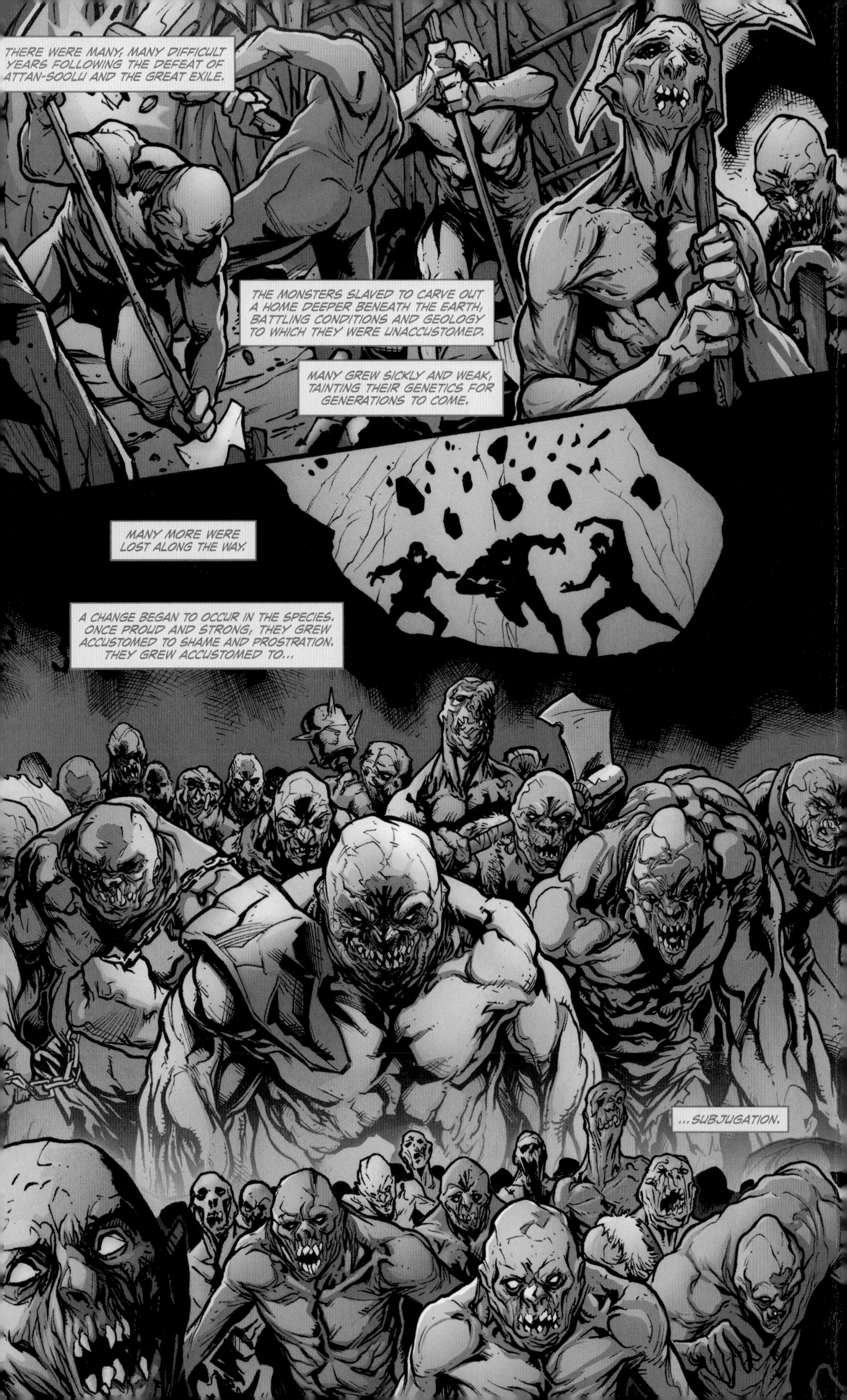
THERE WERE MANY, MANY DIFFICULT YEARS FOLLOWING THE DEFEAT OF ATTAN-SOOLU AND THE GREAT EXILE.
THE MONSTERS SLAVED TO CARVE OUT A HOME DEEPER BENEATH THE EARTH, BATTLING CONDITIONS AND GEOLOGY TO WHICH THEY WERE UNACCUSTOMED.
MANY GREW SICKLY AND WEAK, TAINTING THEIR GENETICS FOR GENERATIONS TO COME.
MANY MORE WERE LOST ALONG THE WAY.
A CHANGE BEGAN TO OCCUR IN THE SPECIES. ONCE PROUD AND STRONG, THEY GREW ACCUSTOMED TO SHAME AND PROSTRATION. THEY GREW ACCUSTOMED TO...
...SUBJUGATION.

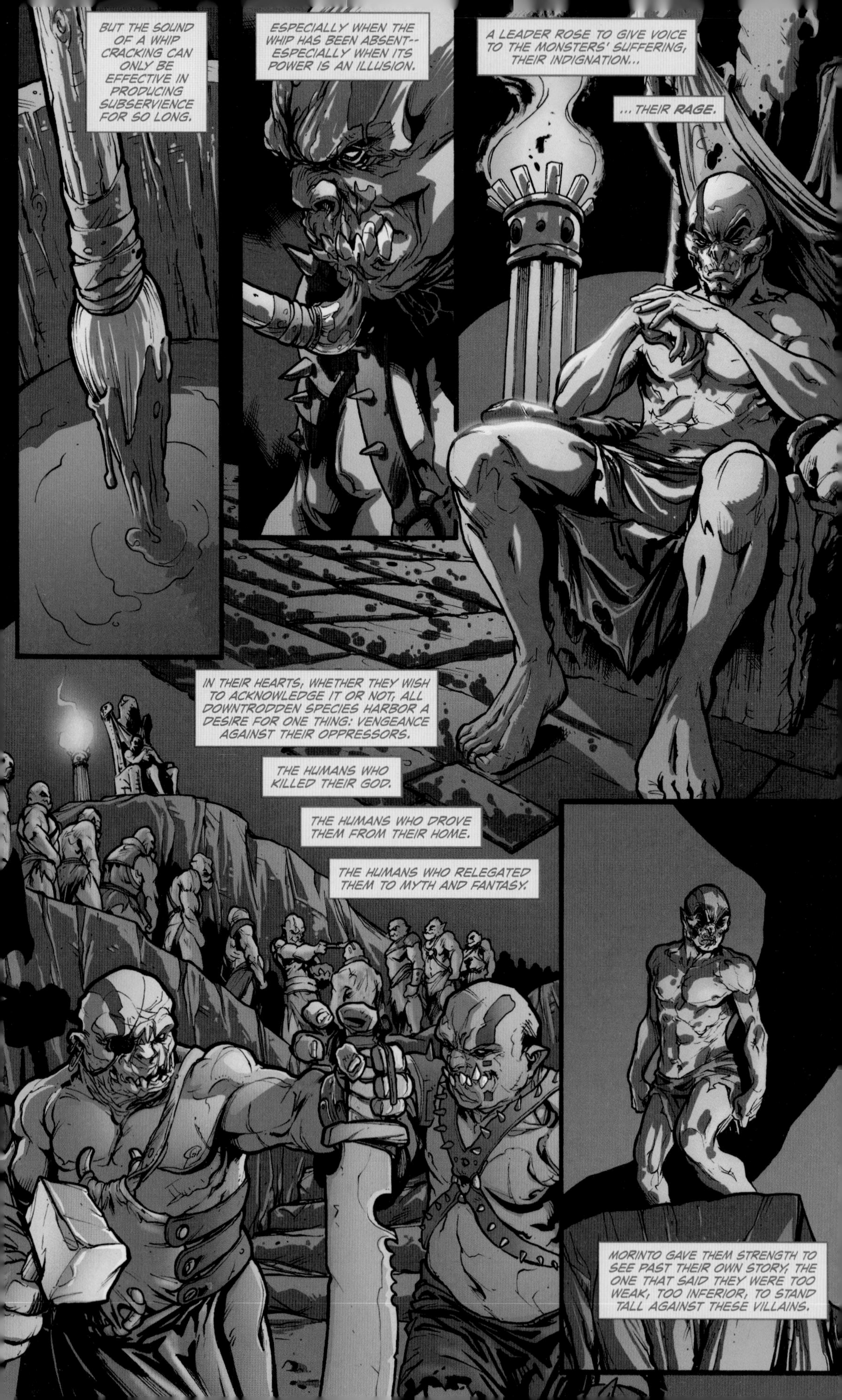
BUT THE SOUND OF A WHIP CRACKING CAN ONLY BE EFFECTIVE IN PRODUCING SUBSERVIENCE FOR SO LONG.
ESPECIALLY WHEN THE WHIP HAS BEEN ABSENT-- ESPECIALLY WHEN ITS POWER IS AN ILLUSION.
A LEADER ROSE TO GIVE VOICE TO THE MONSTERS' SUFFERING, THEIR INDIGNATION...
...THEIR RAGE.
IN THEIR HEARTS, WHETHER THEY WISH TO ACKNOWLEDGE IT OR NOT, ALL DOWNTRODDEN SPECIES HARBOR A DESIRE FOR ONE THING: VENGEANCE AGAINST THEIR OPPRESSORS.
THE HUMANS WHO KILLED THEIR GOD.
THE HUMANS WHO DROVE THEM FROM THEIR HOME.
THE HUMANS WHO RELEGATED THEM TO MYTH AND FANTASY.
MORINTO GAVE THEM STRENGTH TO SEE PAST THEIR OWN STORY, THE ONE THAT SAID THEY WERE TOO WEAK, TOO INFERIOR, TO STAND TALL AGAINST THESE VILLAINS.

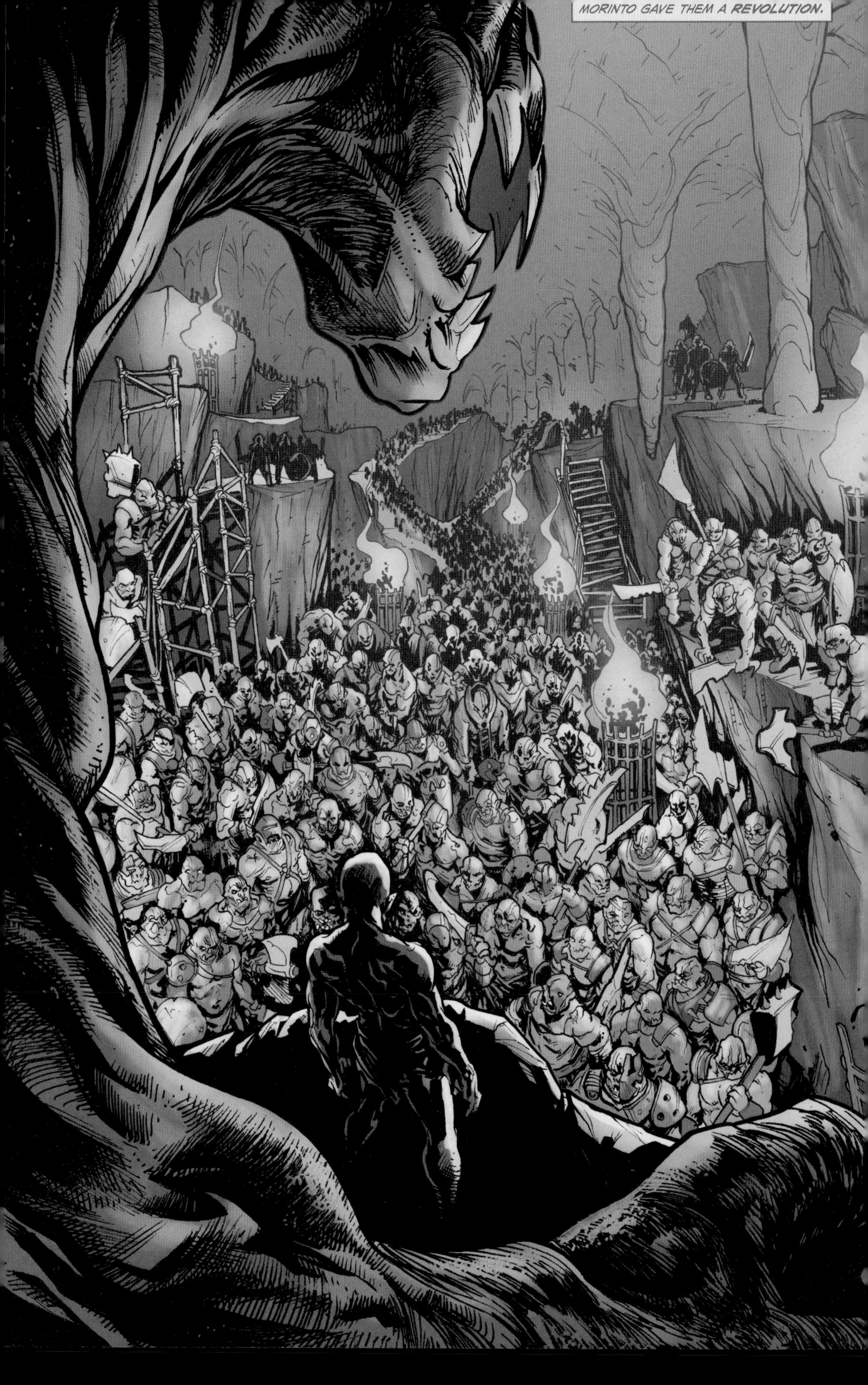
MORINTO GAVE THEM A REVOLUTION.

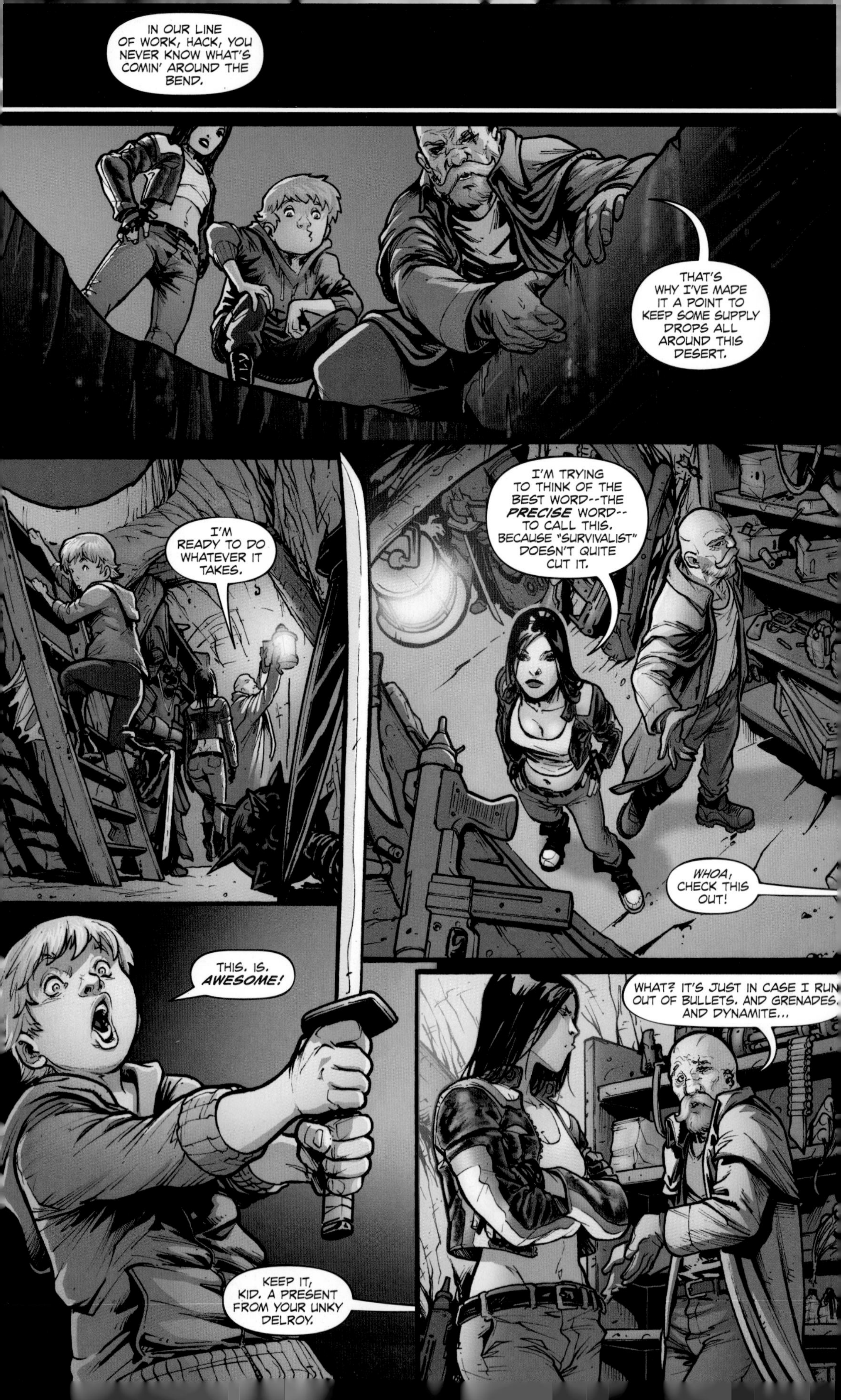
IN OUR LINE OF WORK, HACK, YOU NEVER KNOW WHAT'S COMIN' AROUND THE BEND.
THAT'S WHY I'VE MADE IT A POINT TO KEEP SOME SUPPLY DROPS ALL AROUND THIS DESERT.
I'M READY TO DO WHATEVER IT TAKES.
I'M TRYING TO THINK OF THE BEST WORD--THE *PRECISE* WORD--TO CALL THIS. BECAUSE "SURVIVALIST" DOESN'T QUITE CUT IT.
WHOA, CHECK THIS OUT!
THIS. IS. ***AWESOME!***
KEEP IT, KID. A PRESENT FROM YOUR UNKY DELROY.
WHAT? IT'S JUST IN CASE I RUN OUT OF BULLETS. AND GRENADES. AND DYNAMITE...

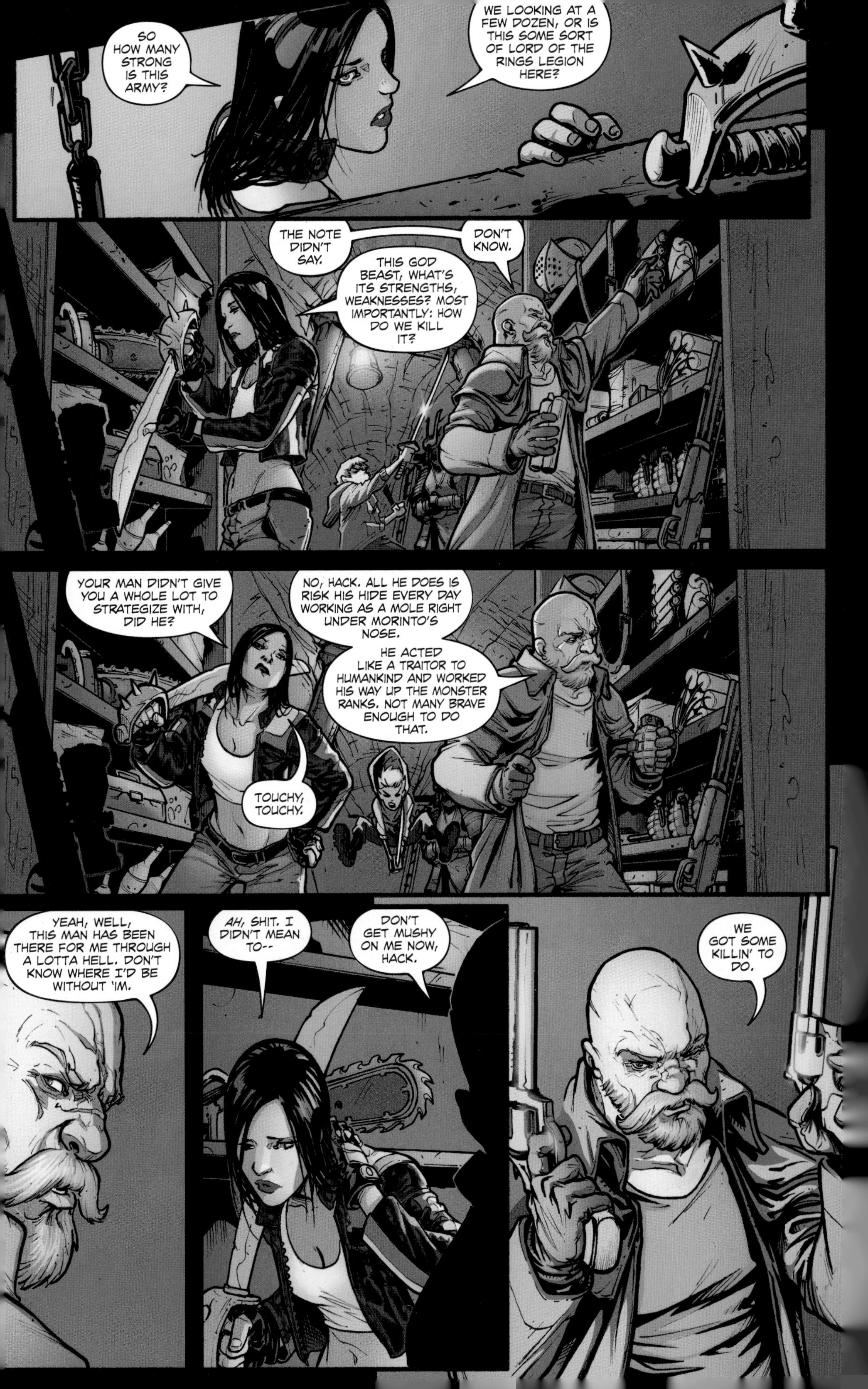

SO HOW MANY STRONG IS THIS ARMY?
WE LOOKING AT A FEW DOZEN, OR IS THIS SOME SORT OF LORD OF THE RINGS LEGION HERE?
THE NOTE DIDN'T SAY.
DON'T KNOW.
THIS GOD BEAST, WHAT'S ITS STRENGTHS, WEAKNESSES? MOST IMPORTANTLY: HOW DO WE KILL IT?
YOUR MAN DIDN'T GIVE YOU A WHOLE LOT TO STRATEGIZE WITH, DID HE?
NO, HACK. ALL HE DOES IS RISK HIS HIDE EVERY DAY WORKING AS A MOLE RIGHT UNDER MORINTO'S NOSE.
HE ACTED LIKE A TRAITOR TO HUMANKIND AND WORKED HIS WAY UP THE MONSTER RANKS. NOT MANY BRAVE ENOUGH TO DO THAT.
TOUCHY, TOUCHY.
YEAH, WELL, THIS MAN HAS BEEN THERE FOR ME THROUGH A LOTTA HELL. DON'T KNOW WHERE I'D BE WITHOUT 'IM.
AH, SHIT. I DIDN'T MEAN TO--
DON'T GET MUSHY ON ME NOW, HACK.
WE GOT SOME KILLIN' TO DO.

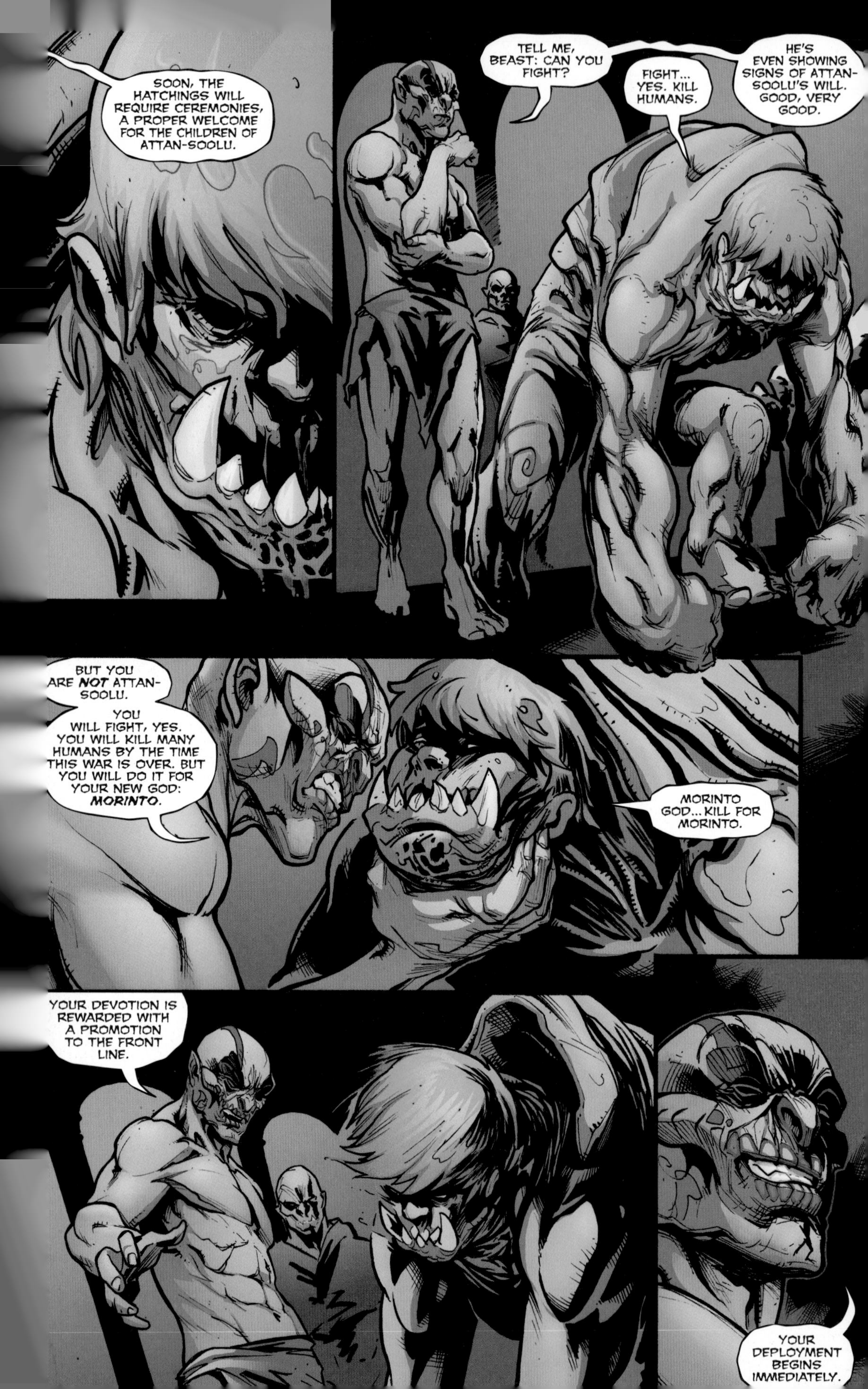
SOON, THE HATCHINGS WILL REQUIRE CEREMONIES, A PROPER WELCOME FOR THE CHILDREN OF ATTAN-SOOLU.
TELL ME, BEAST: CAN YOU FIGHT?
FIGHT... YES. KILL HUMANS.
HE'S EVEN SHOWING SIGNS OF ATTAN-SOOLU'S WILL. GOOD, VERY GOOD.
BUT YOU ARE NOT ATTAN-SOOLU.
YOU WILL FIGHT, YES. YOU WILL KILL MANY HUMANS BY THE TIME THIS WAR IS OVER. BUT YOU WILL DO IT FOR YOUR NEW GOD: MORINTO.
MORINTO GOD... KILL FOR MORINTO.
YOUR DEVOTION IS REWARDED WITH A PROMOTION TO THE FRONT LINE.
YOUR DEPLOYMENT BEGINS IMMEDIATELY.

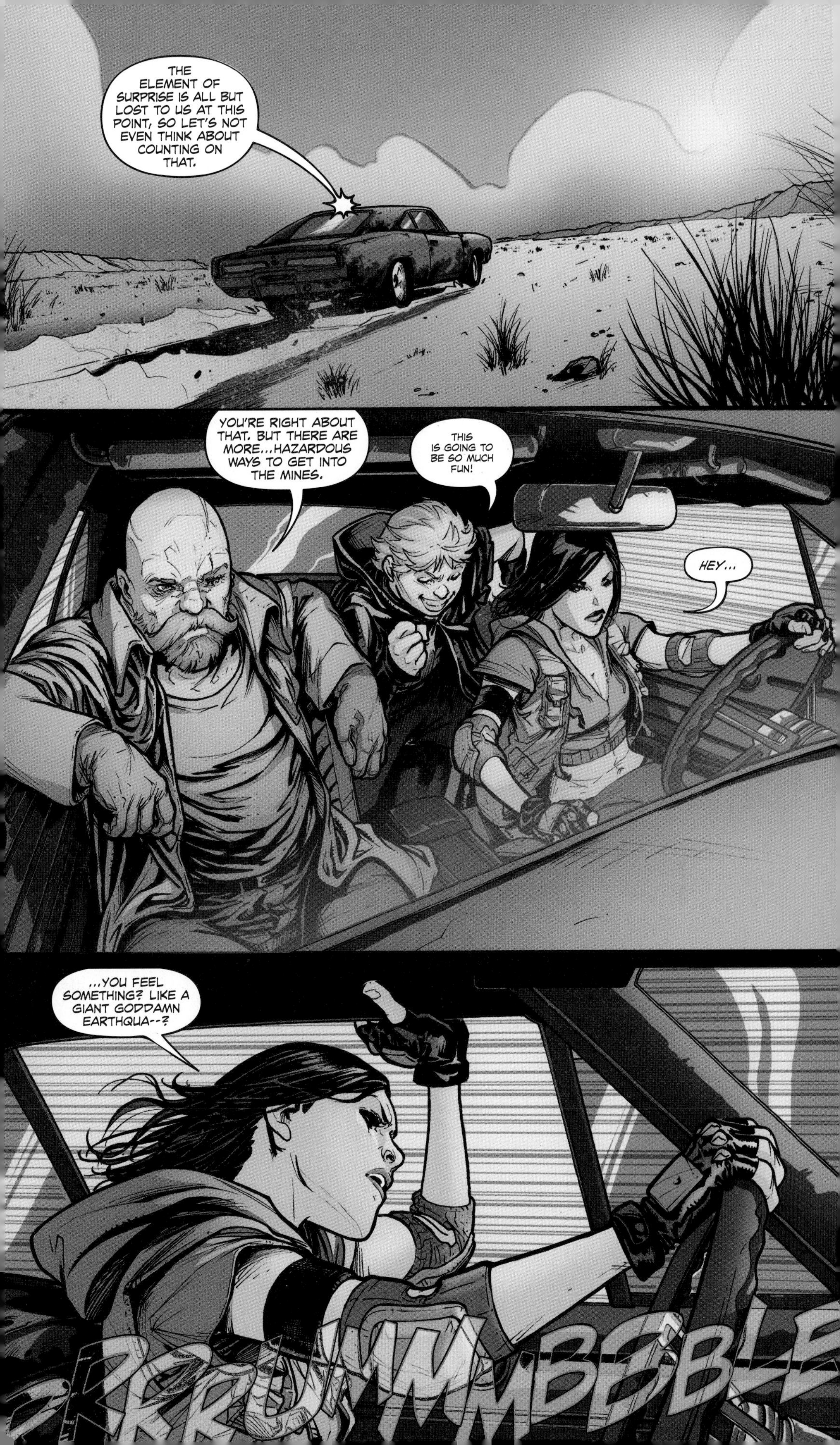
THE ELEMENT OF SURPRISE IS ALL BUT LOST TO US AT THIS POINT, SO LET'S NOT EVEN THINK ABOUT COUNTING ON THAT.
YOU'RE RIGHT ABOUT THAT. BUT THERE ARE MORE...HAZARDOUS WAYS TO GET INTO THE MINES.
THIS IS GOING TO BE SO MUCH FUN!
HEY...
...YOU FEEL SOMETHING? LIKE A GIANT GODDAMN EARTHQUA--?
KRRUMMMBBBLE

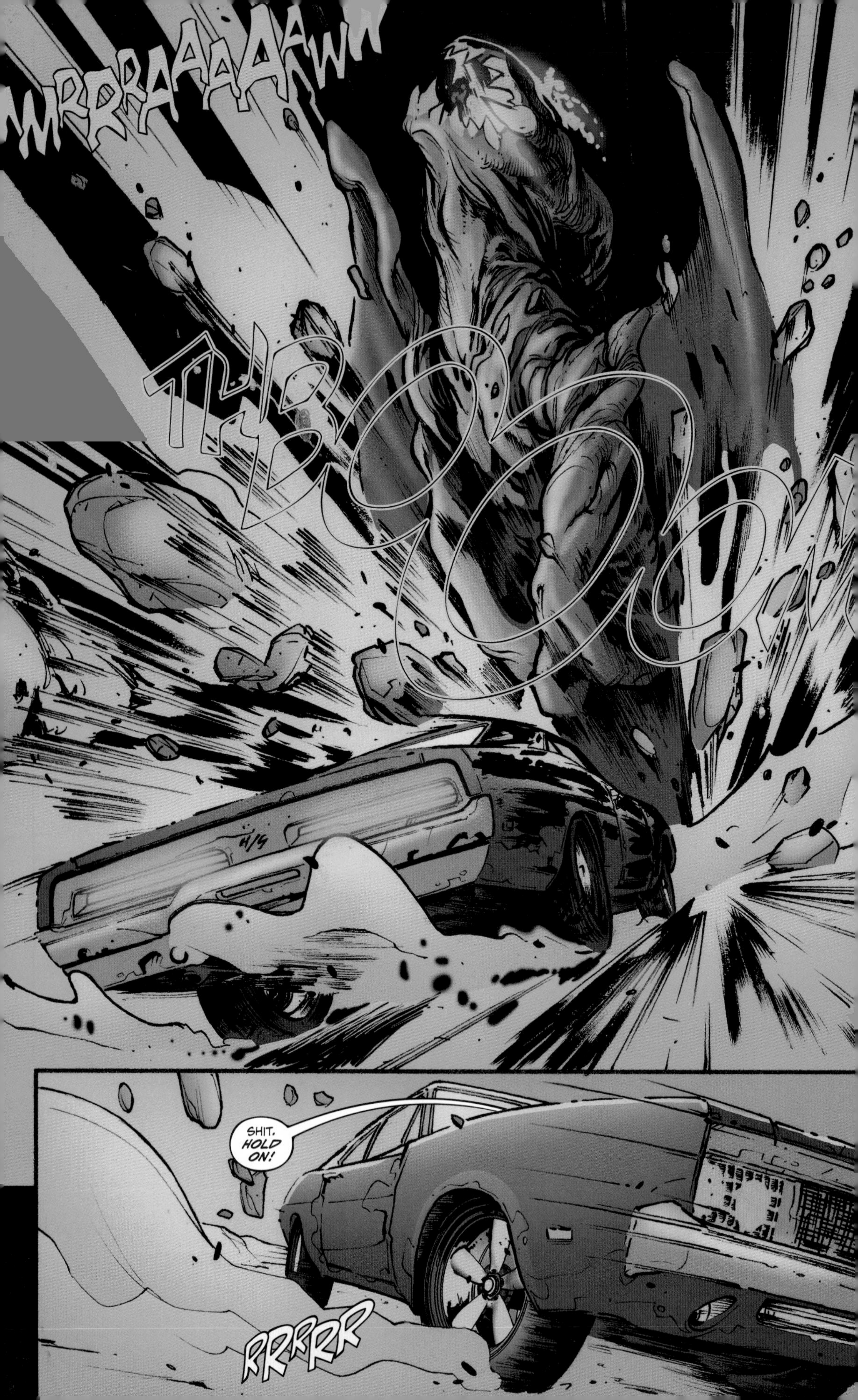

WRRRAAAAAAWN
THBOOOOM
SHIT. HOLD ON!
RRRRR

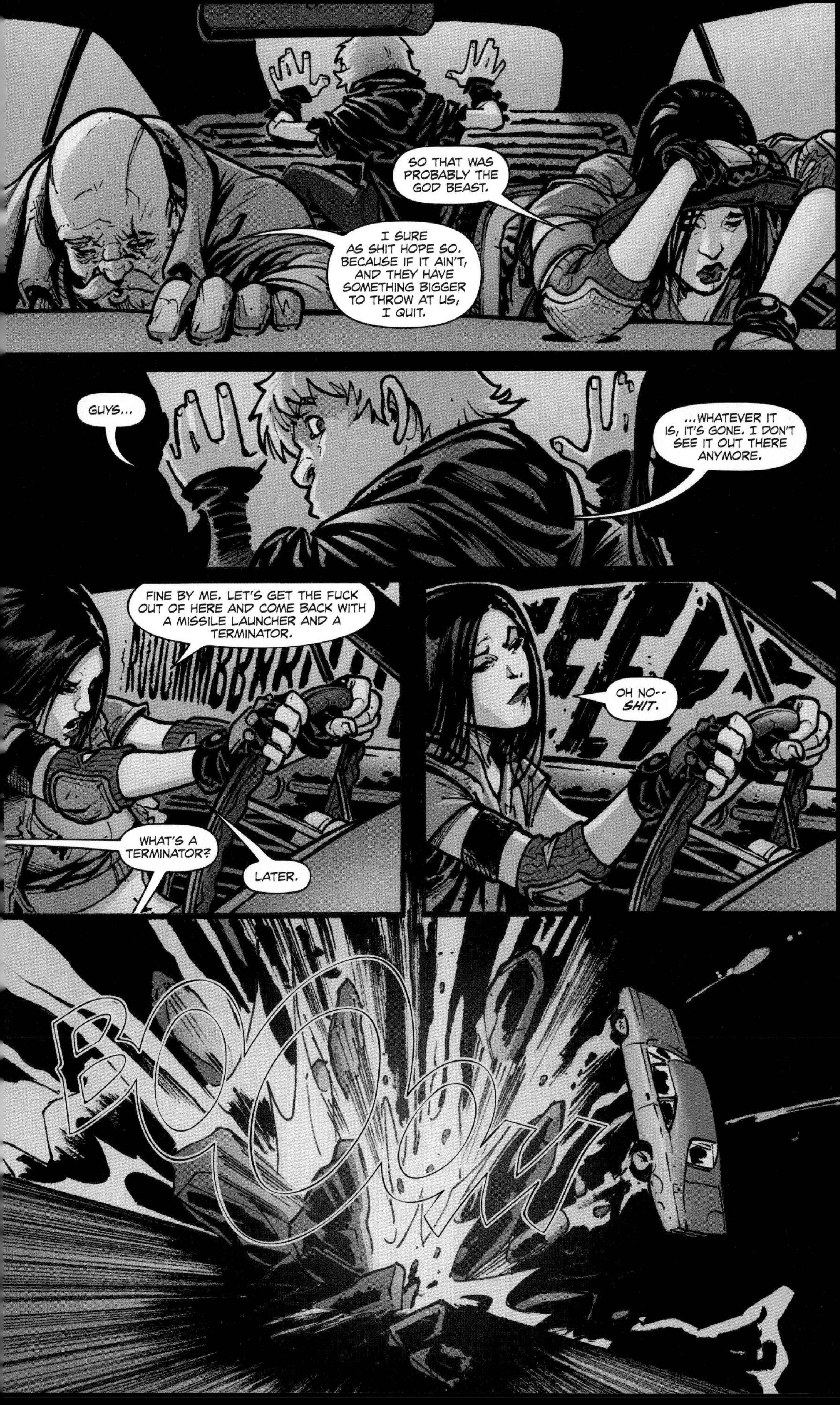
SO THAT WAS PROBABLY THE GOD BEAST.
I SURE AS SHIT HOPE SO. BECAUSE IF IT AIN'T, AND THEY HAVE SOMETHING BIGGER TO THROW AT US, I QUIT.
GUYS...
...WHATEVER IT IS, IT'S GONE. I DON'T SEE IT OUT THERE ANYMORE.
FINE BY ME. LET'S GET THE FUCK OUT OF HERE AND COME BACK WITH A MISSILE LAUNCHER AND A TERMINATOR.
RRUUMMBBARR
WHAT'S A TERMINATOR?
LATER.
OH NO-- *SHIT*.
BOOOM

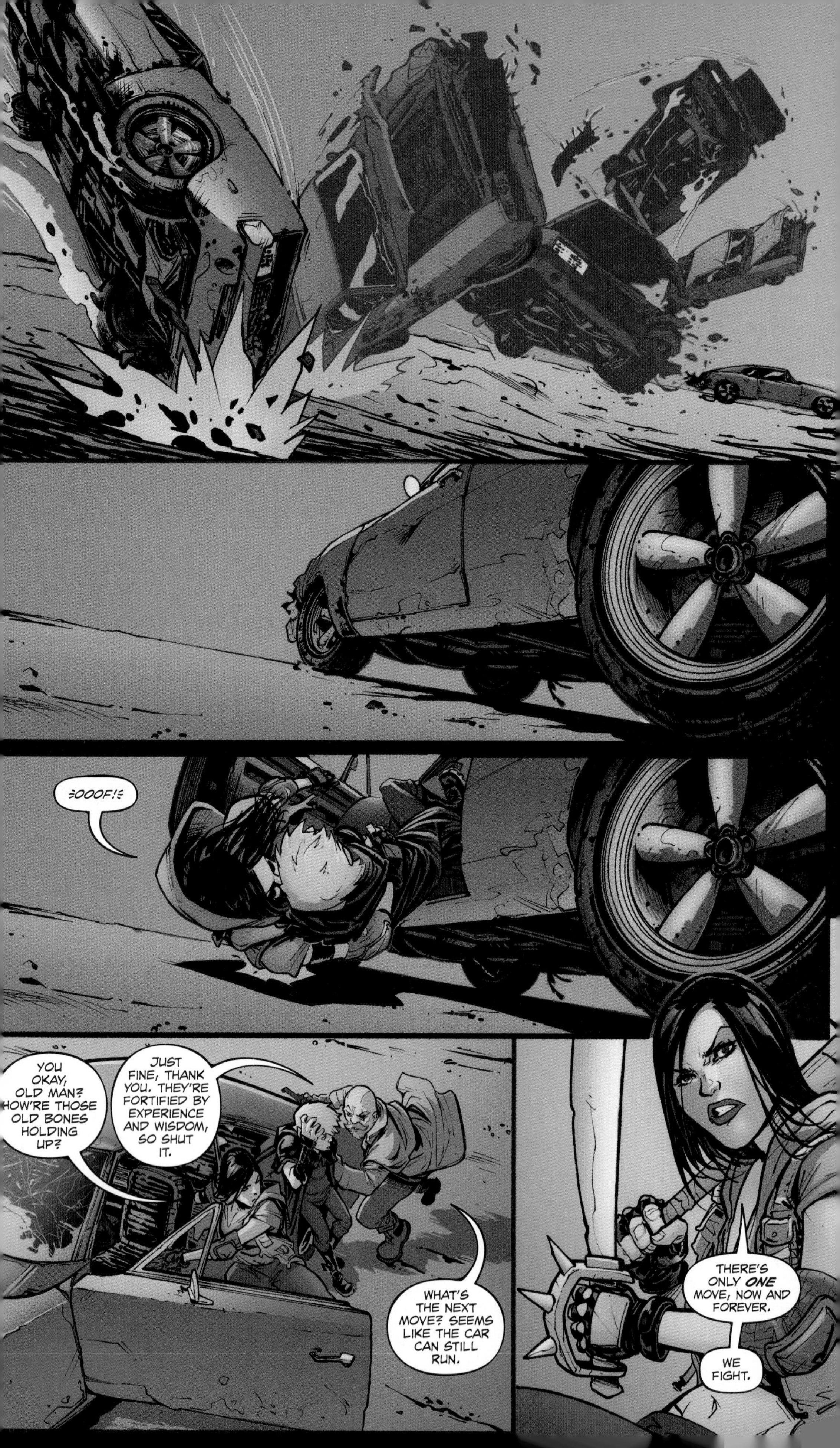
OOOF!
YOU OKAY, OLD MAN? HOW'RE THOSE OLD BONES HOLDING UP?
JUST FINE, THANK YOU. THEY'RE FORTIFIED BY EXPERIENCE AND WISDOM, SO SHUT IT.
WHAT'S THE NEXT MOVE? SEEMS LIKE THE CAR CAN STILL RUN.
THERE'S ONLY ONE MOVE, NOW AND FOREVER.
WE FIGHT.

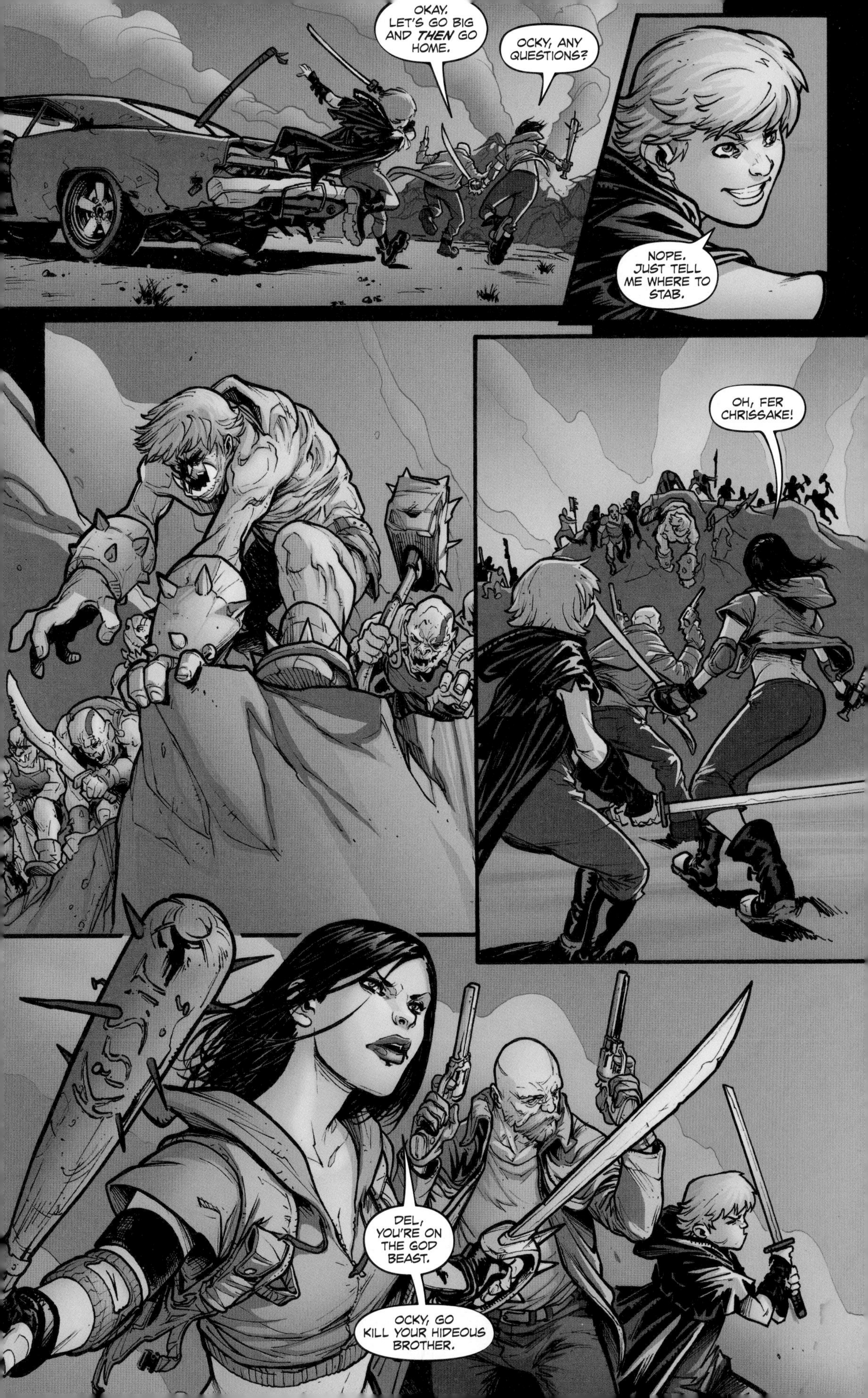
OKAY. LET'S GO BIG AND *THEN* GO HOME.
OCKY, ANY QUESTIONS?
NOPE. JUST TELL ME WHERE TO STAB.
OH, FER CHRISSAKE!
DEL, YOU'RE ON THE GOD BEAST.
OCKY, GO KILL YOUR HIDEOUS BROTHER.

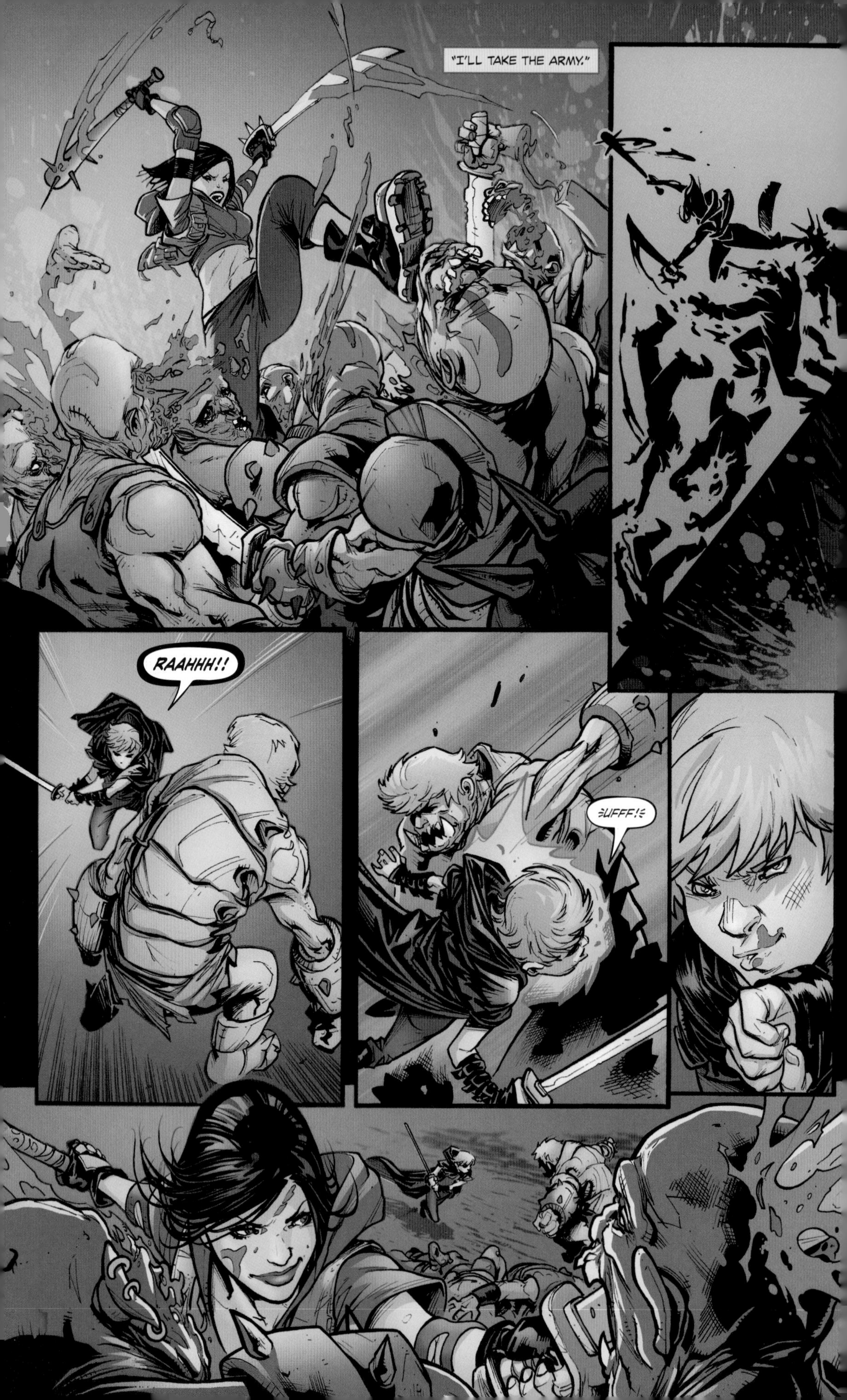
"I'LL TAKE THE ARMY."
RAAHHH!!
UFFF!

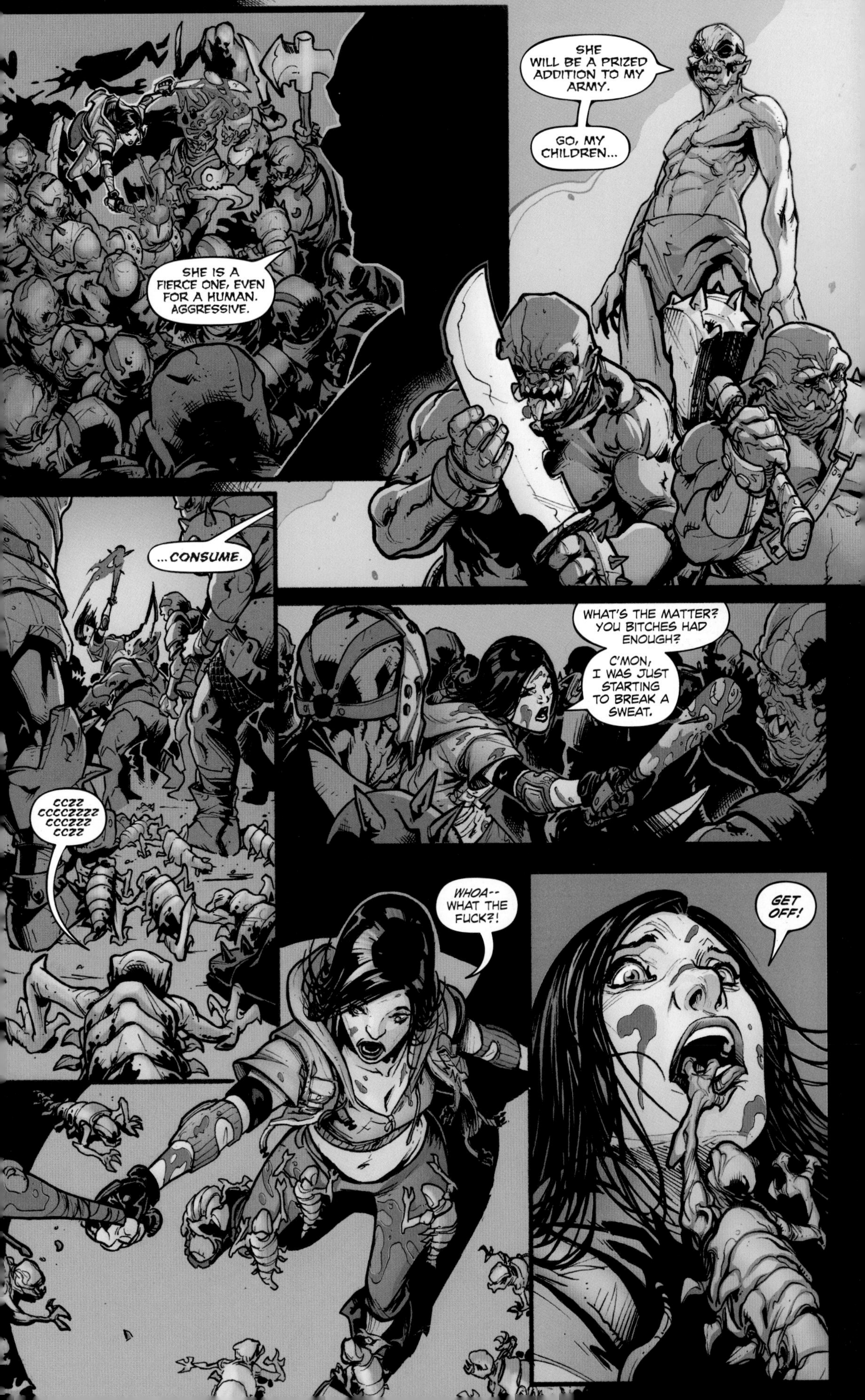
SHE IS A FIERCE ONE, EVEN FOR A HUMAN. AGGRESSIVE.
SHE WILL BE A PRIZED ADDITION TO MY ARMY.
GO, MY CHILDREN...
...CONSUME.
CCZZ CCCCZZZZ CCCZZZ CCZZ
WHAT'S THE MATTER? YOU BITCHES HAD ENOUGH?
C'MON, I WAS JUST STARTING TO BREAK A SWEAT.
WHOA-- WHAT THE FUCK?!
GET OFF!

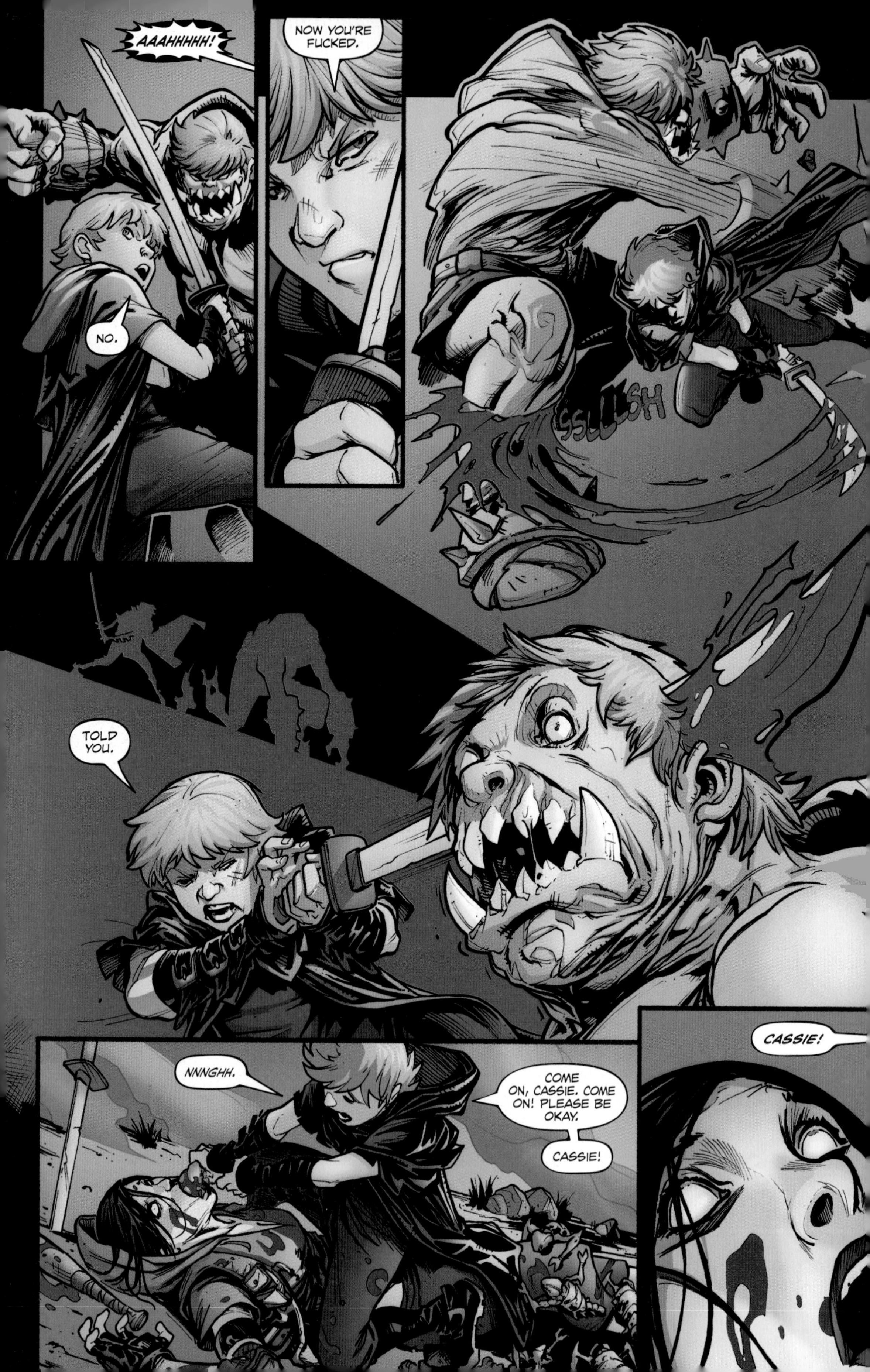
AAAHHHHH!
NO.
NOW YOU'RE FUCKED.
SSLLLISH
TOLD YOU.
NNNGHH.
COME ON, CASSIE. COME ON! PLEASE BE OKAY.
CASSIE!
CASSIE!

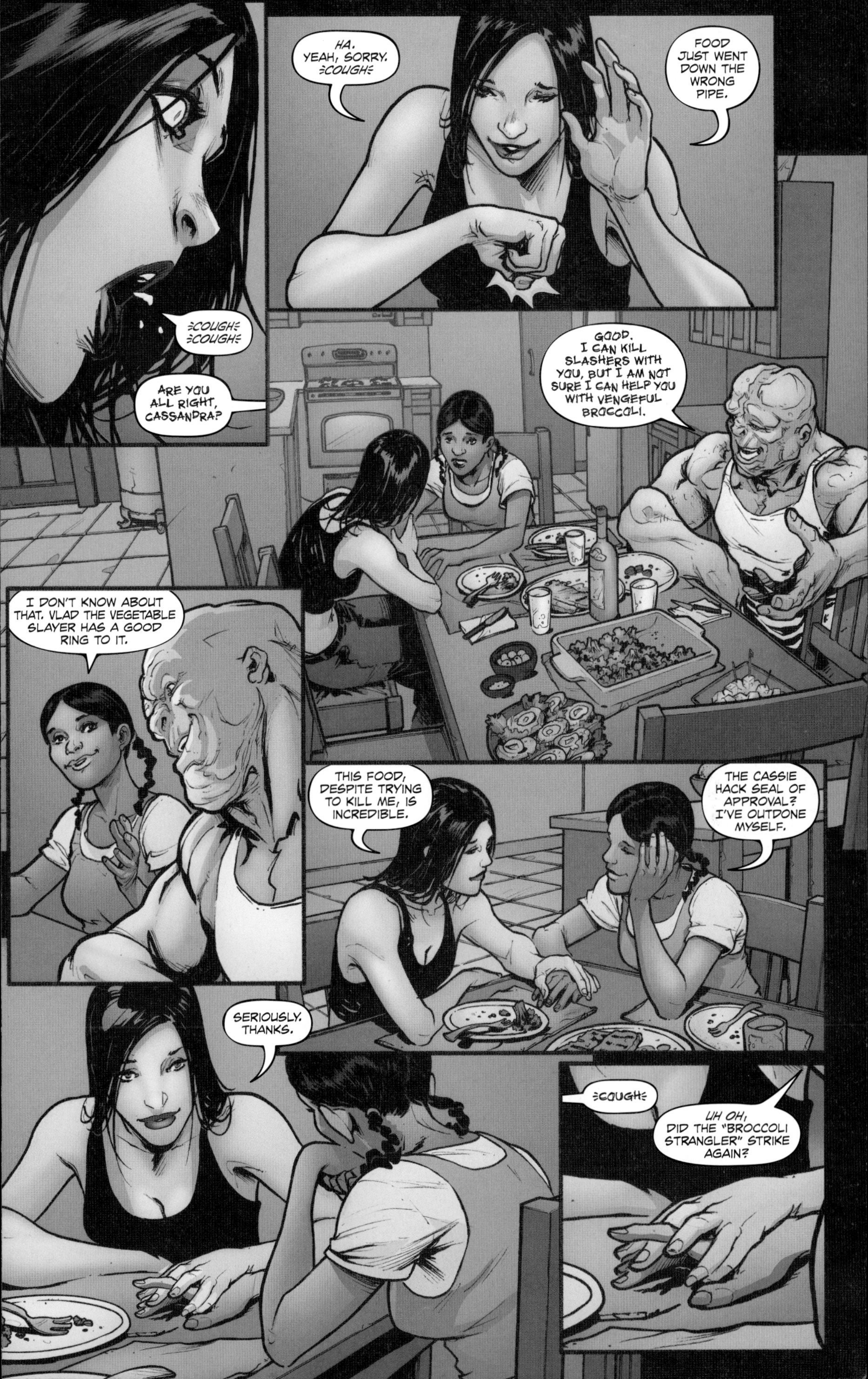
HA. YEAH, SORRY. *COUGH*
FOOD JUST WENT DOWN THE WRONG PIPE.
COUGH *COUGH*
ARE YOU ALL RIGHT, CASSANDRA?
GOOD. I CAN KILL SLASHERS WITH YOU, BUT I AM NOT SURE I CAN HELP YOU WITH VENGEFUL BROCCOLI.
I DON'T KNOW ABOUT THAT. VLAD THE VEGETABLE SLAYER HAS A GOOD RING TO IT.
THIS FOOD, DESPITE TRYING TO KILL ME, IS INCREDIBLE.
THE CASSIE HACK SEAL OF APPROVAL? I'VE OUTDONE MYSELF.
SERIOUSLY. THANKS.
COUGH
UH OH, DID THE "BROCCOLI STRANGLER" STRIKE AGAIN?

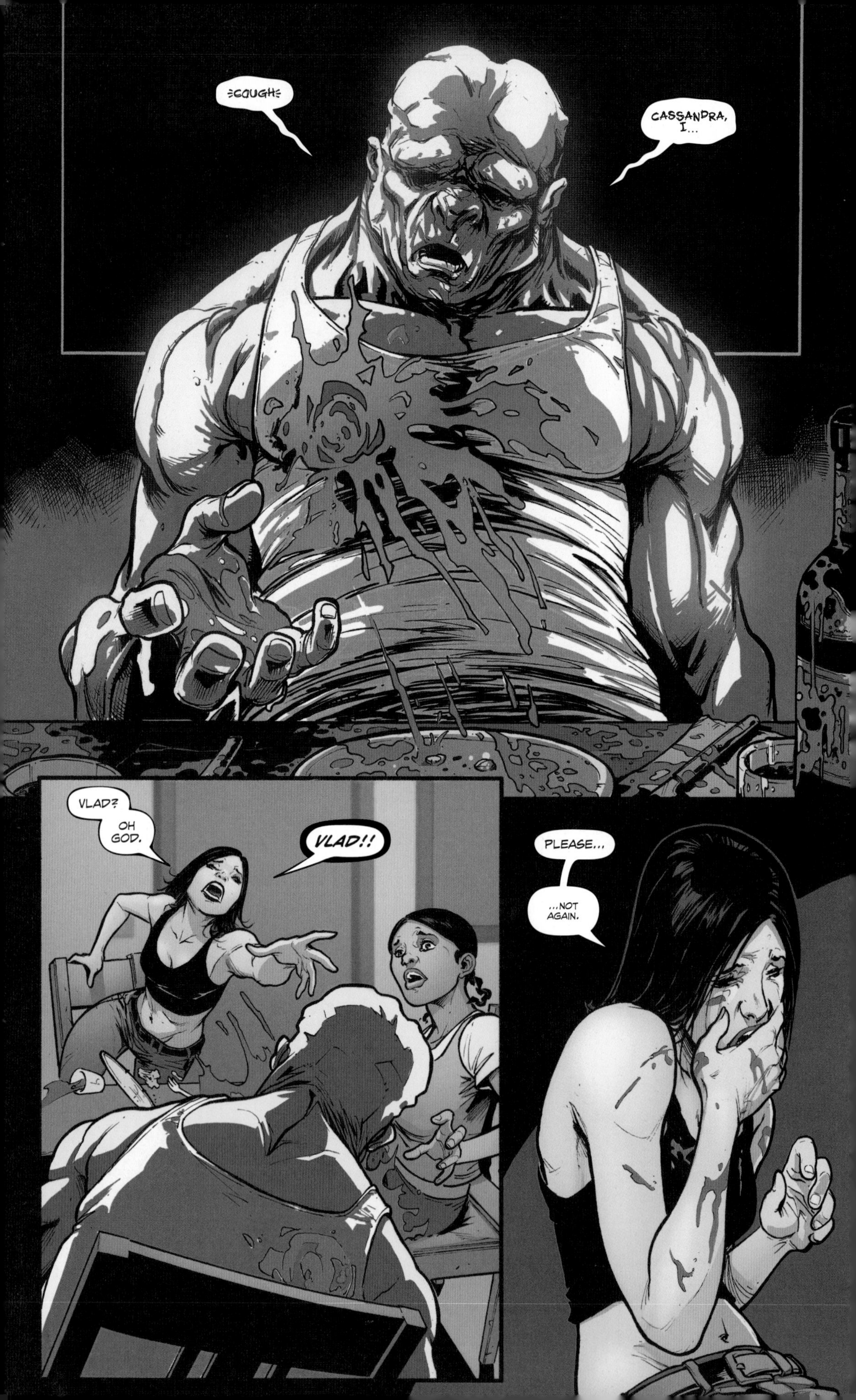

COUGH
CASSANDRA, I...
VLAD? OH GOD.
VLAD!!
PLEASE...
...NOT AGAIN.

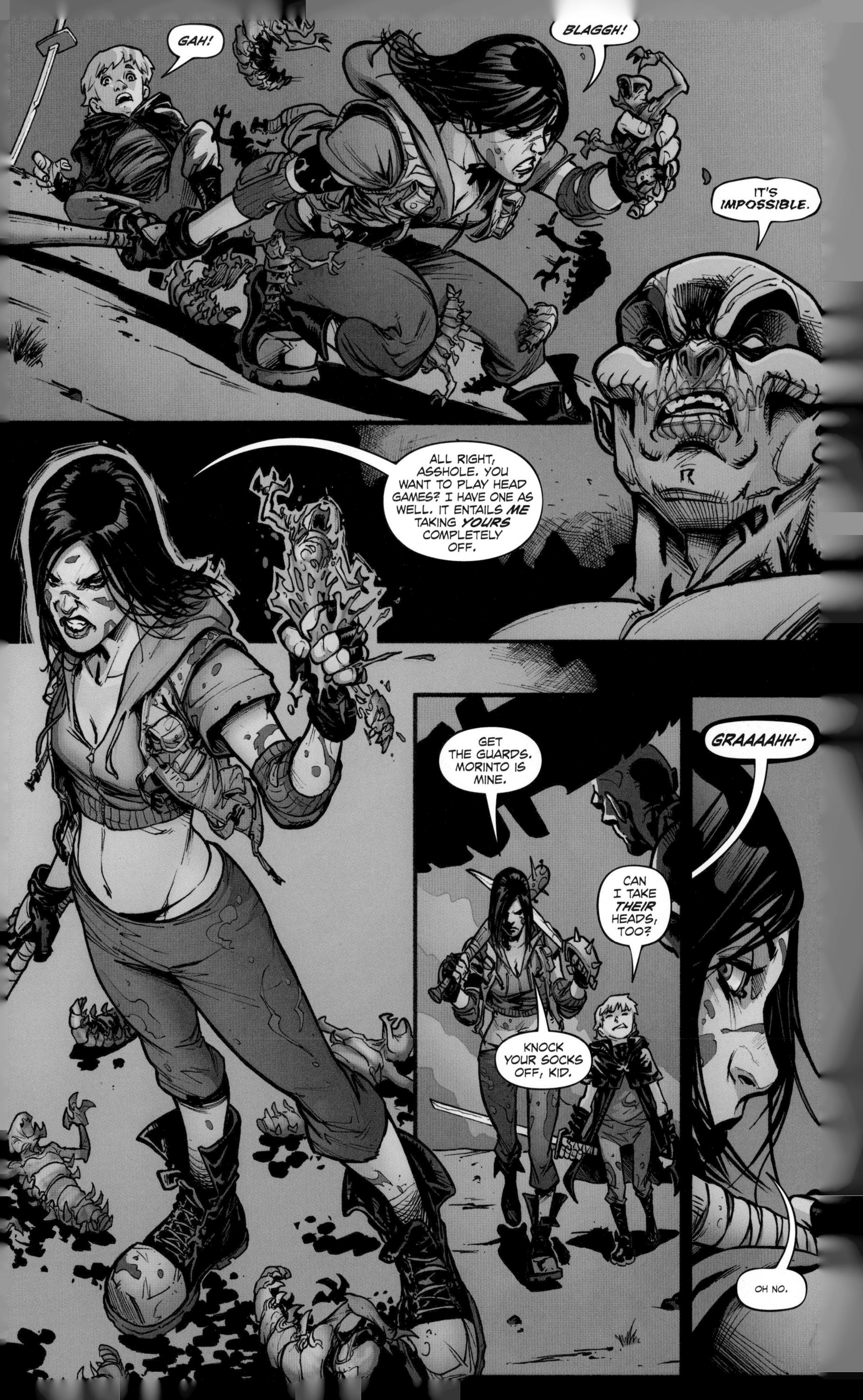
GAH!
BLAGGH!
IT'S IMPOSSIBLE.
ALL RIGHT, ASSHOLE. YOU WANT TO PLAY HEAD GAMES? I HAVE ONE AS WELL. IT ENTAILS ME TAKING YOURS COMPLETELY OFF.
GET THE GUARDS. MORINTO IS MINE.
CAN I TAKE THEIR HEADS, TOO?
KNOCK YOUR SOCKS OFF, KID.
GRAAAAHH--
OH NO.

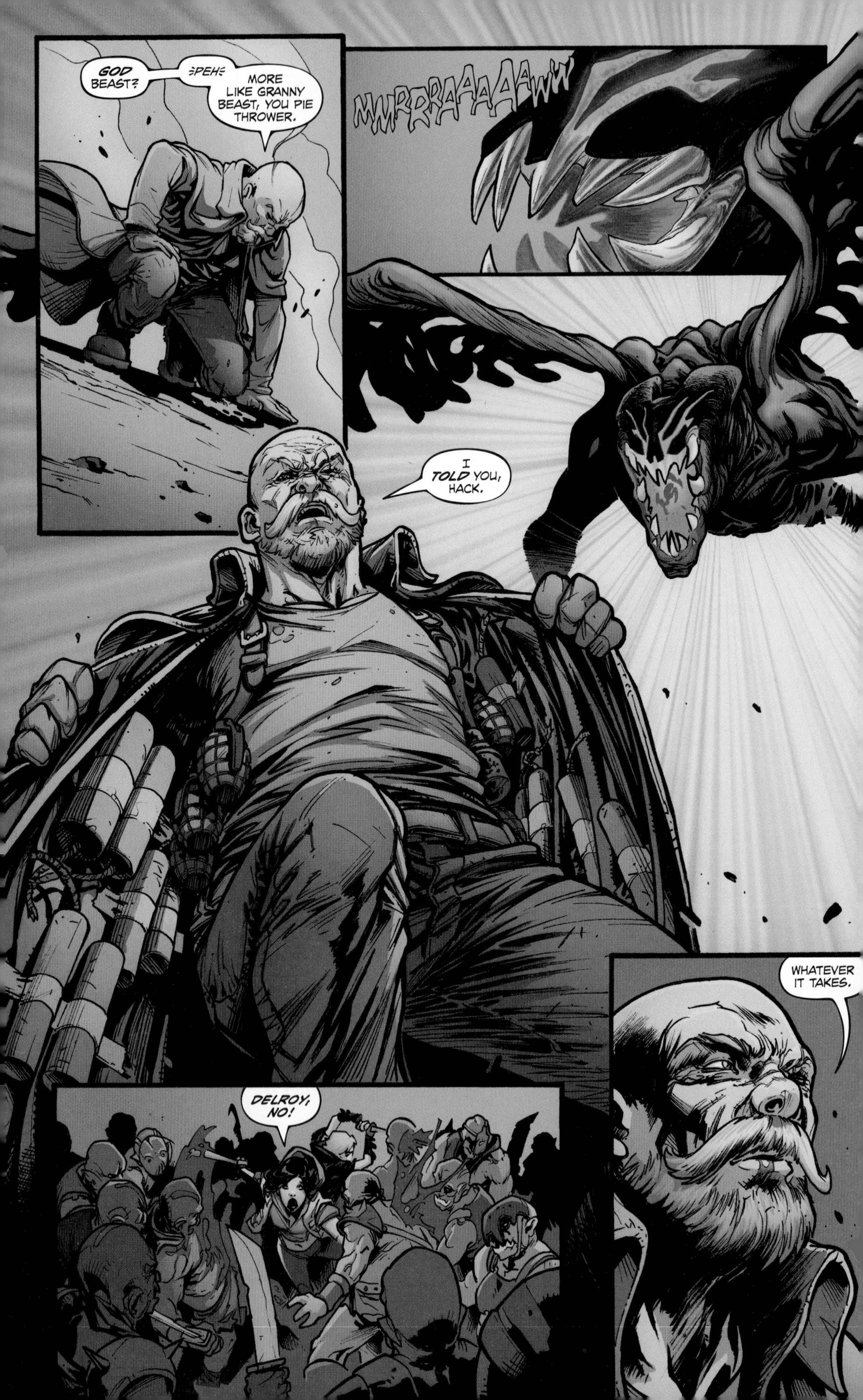
GOD BEAST?
PEH
MORE LIKE GRANNY BEAST, YOU PIE THROWER.
MMRRRAAAAAAWW
I TOLD YOU, HACK.
WHATEVER IT TAKES.
DELROY, NO!

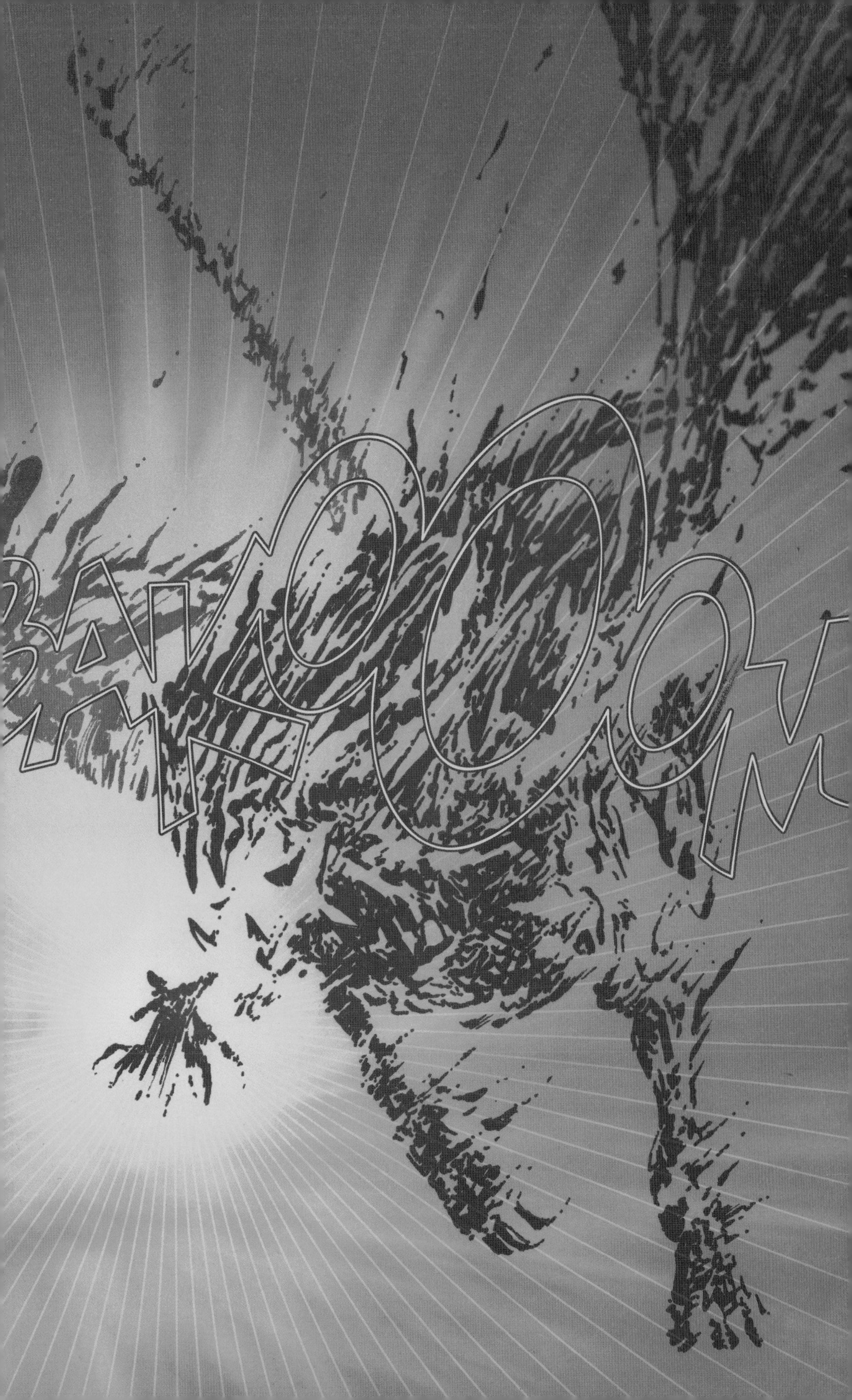
BAROOOOM

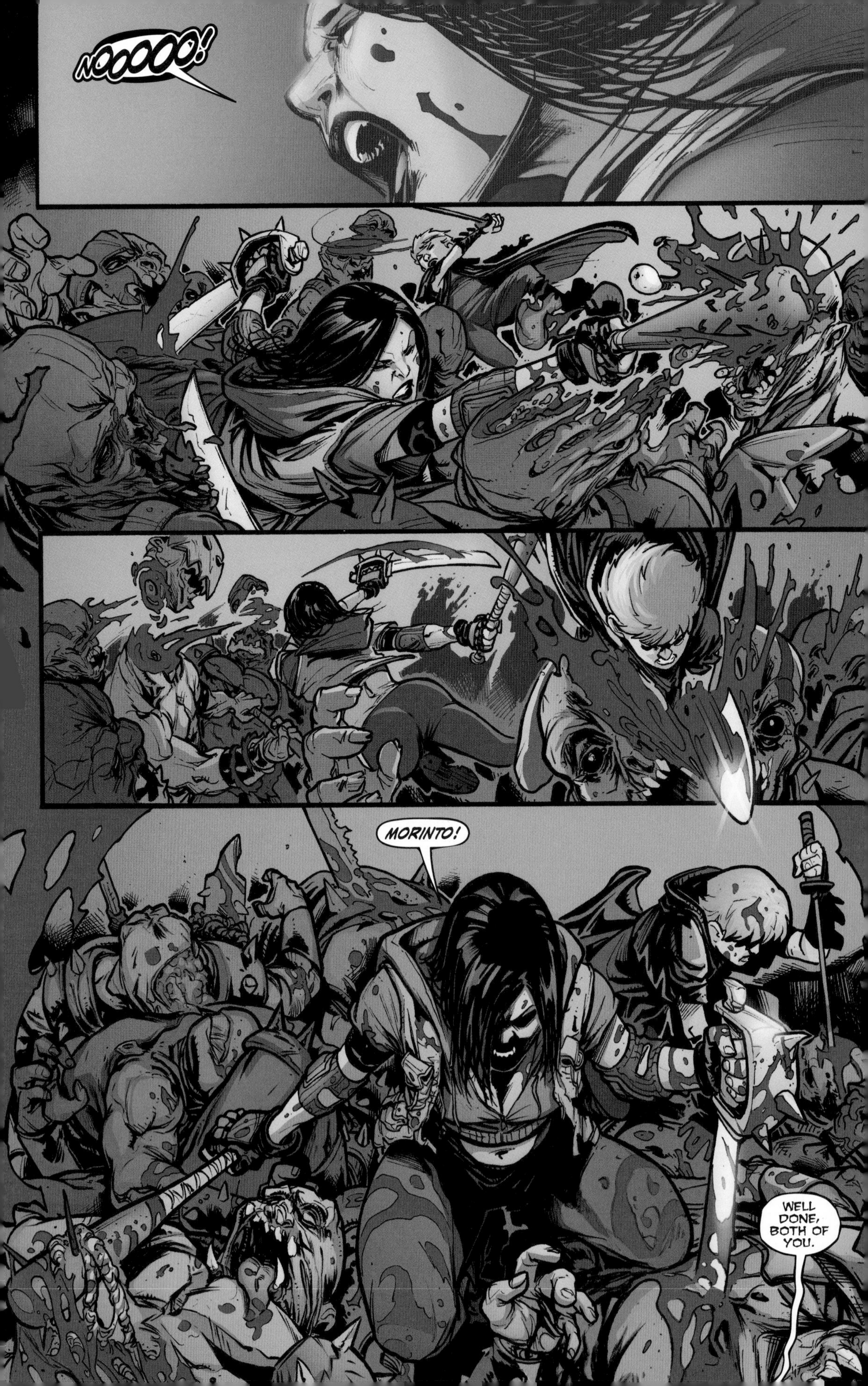
NOOOOO!
MORINTO!
WELL DONE, BOTH OF YOU.

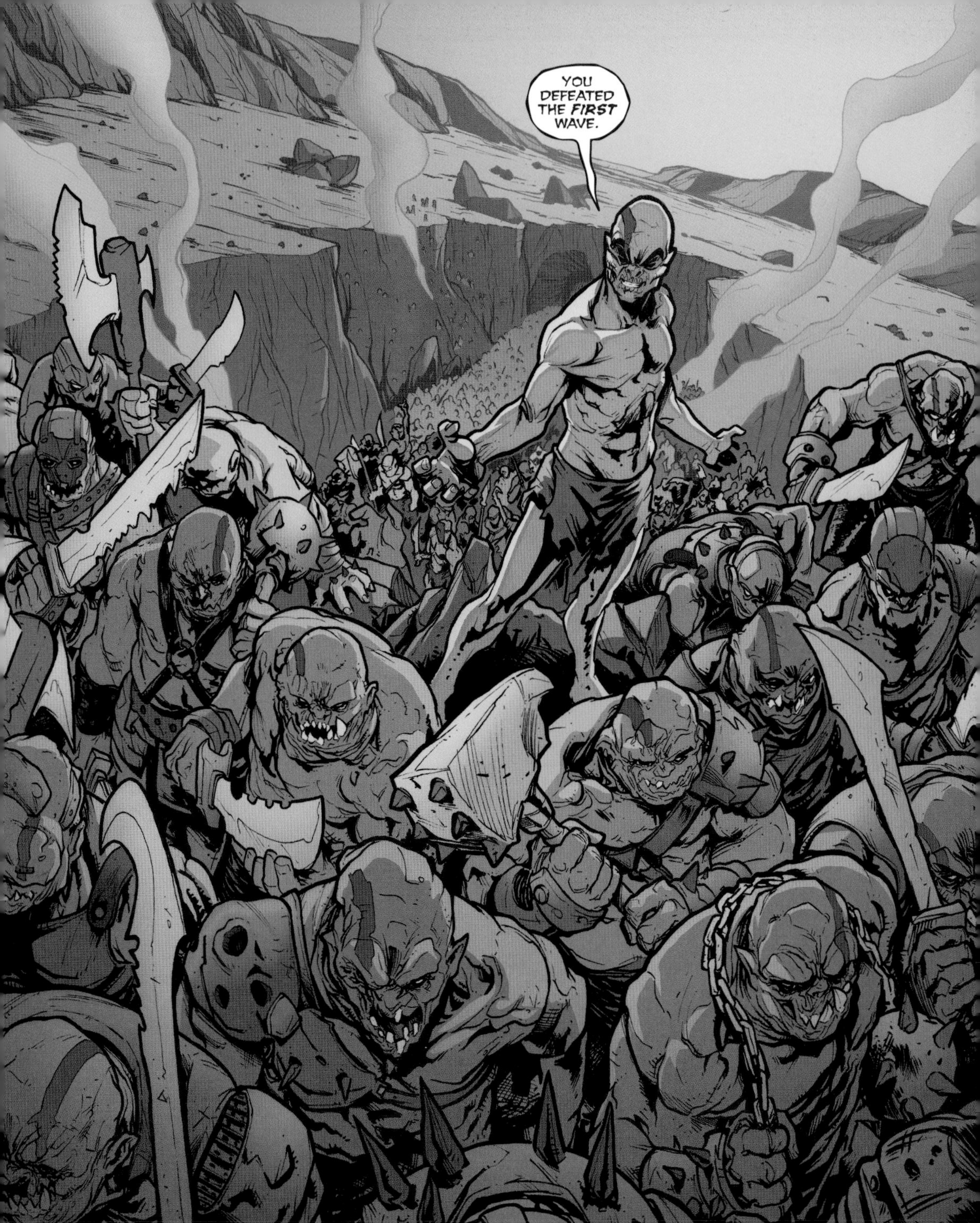
YOU DEFEATED THE FIRST WAVE.

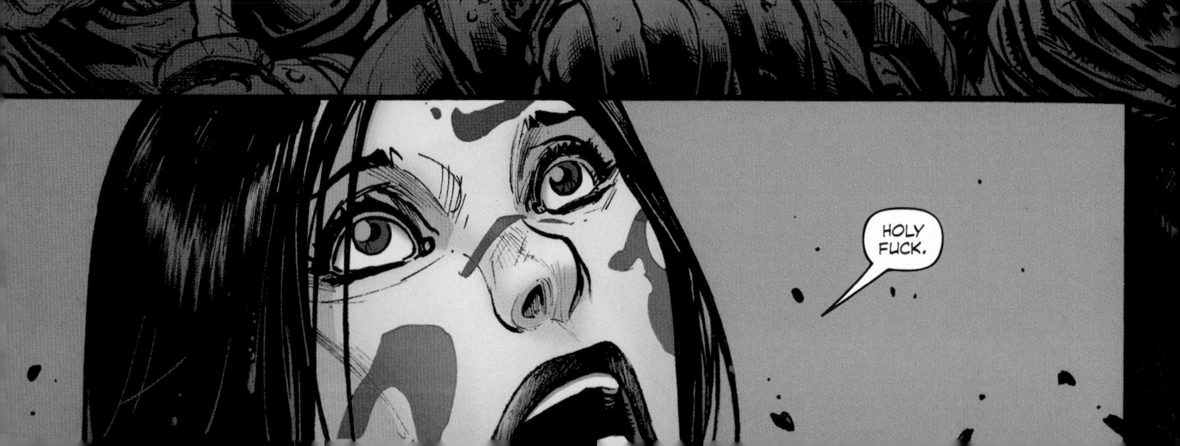
HOLY FUCK.

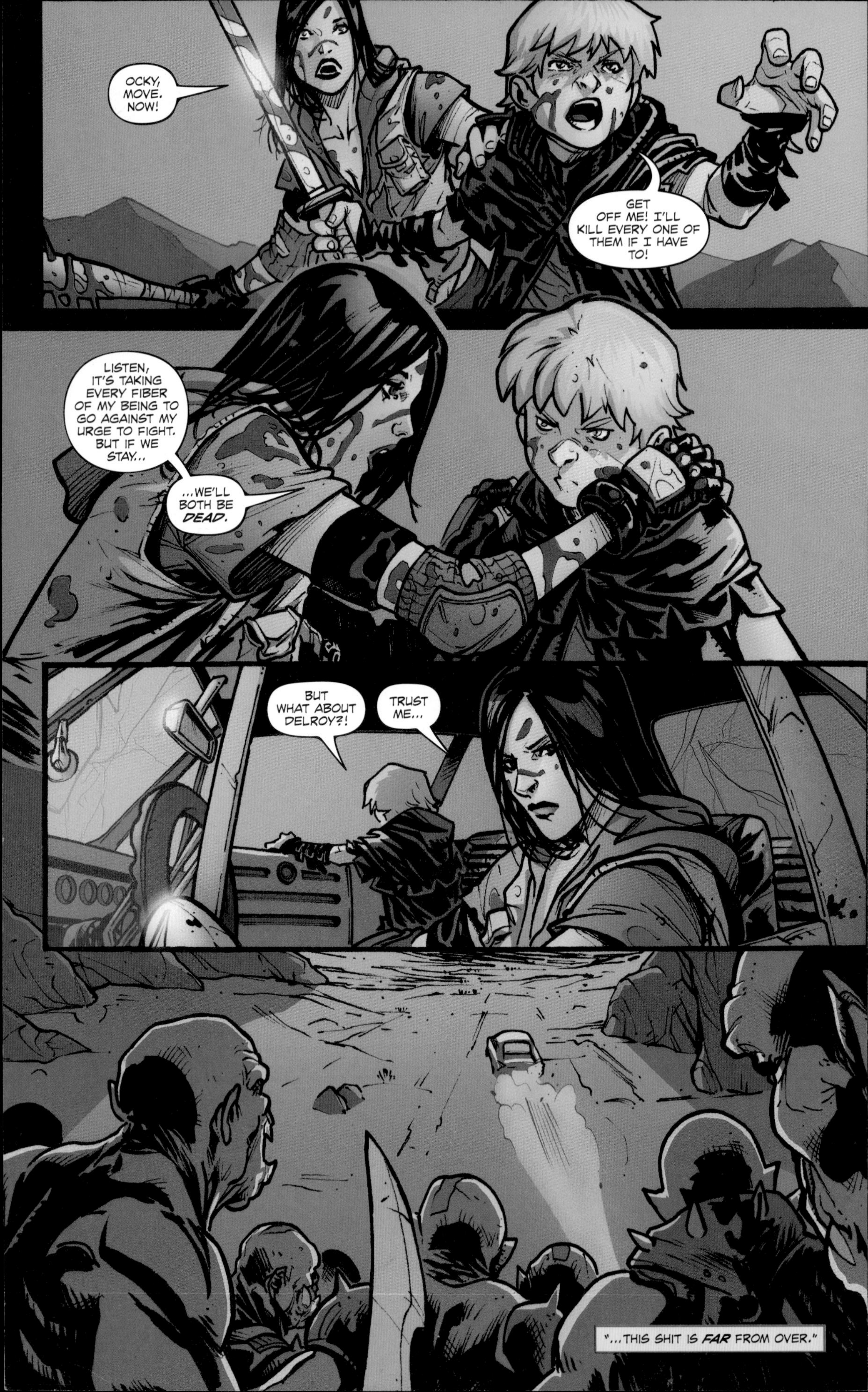
OCKY, MOVE. NOW!
GET OFF ME! I'LL KILL EVERY ONE OF THEM IF I HAVE TO!
LISTEN, IT'S TAKING EVERY FIBER OF MY BEING TO GO AGAINST MY URGE TO FIGHT. BUT IF WE STAY...
...WE'LL BOTH BE *DEAD*.
BUT WHAT ABOUT DELROY?!
TRUST ME...
"...THIS SHIT IS *FAR* FROM OVER."

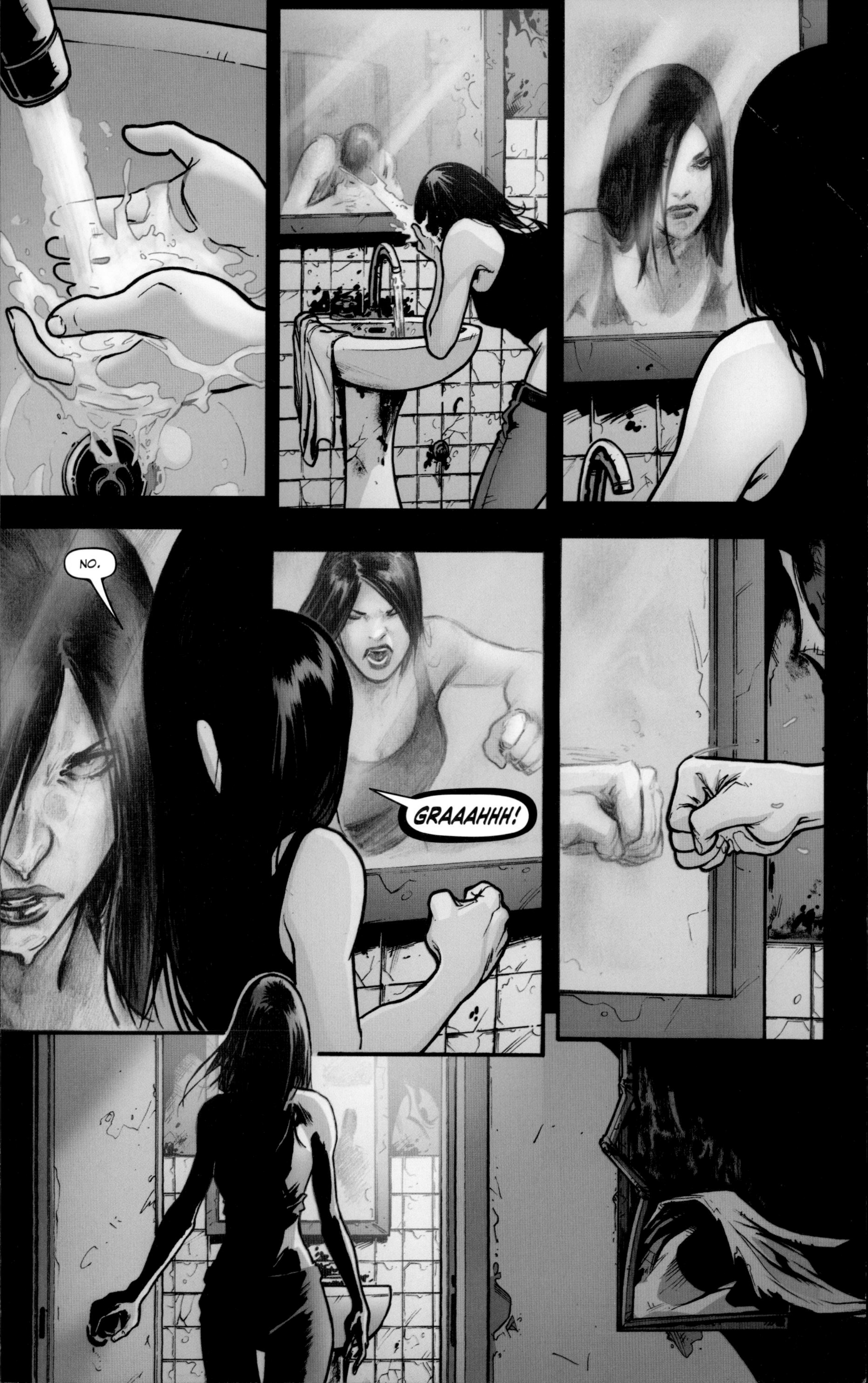
NO.
GRAAAHHH!

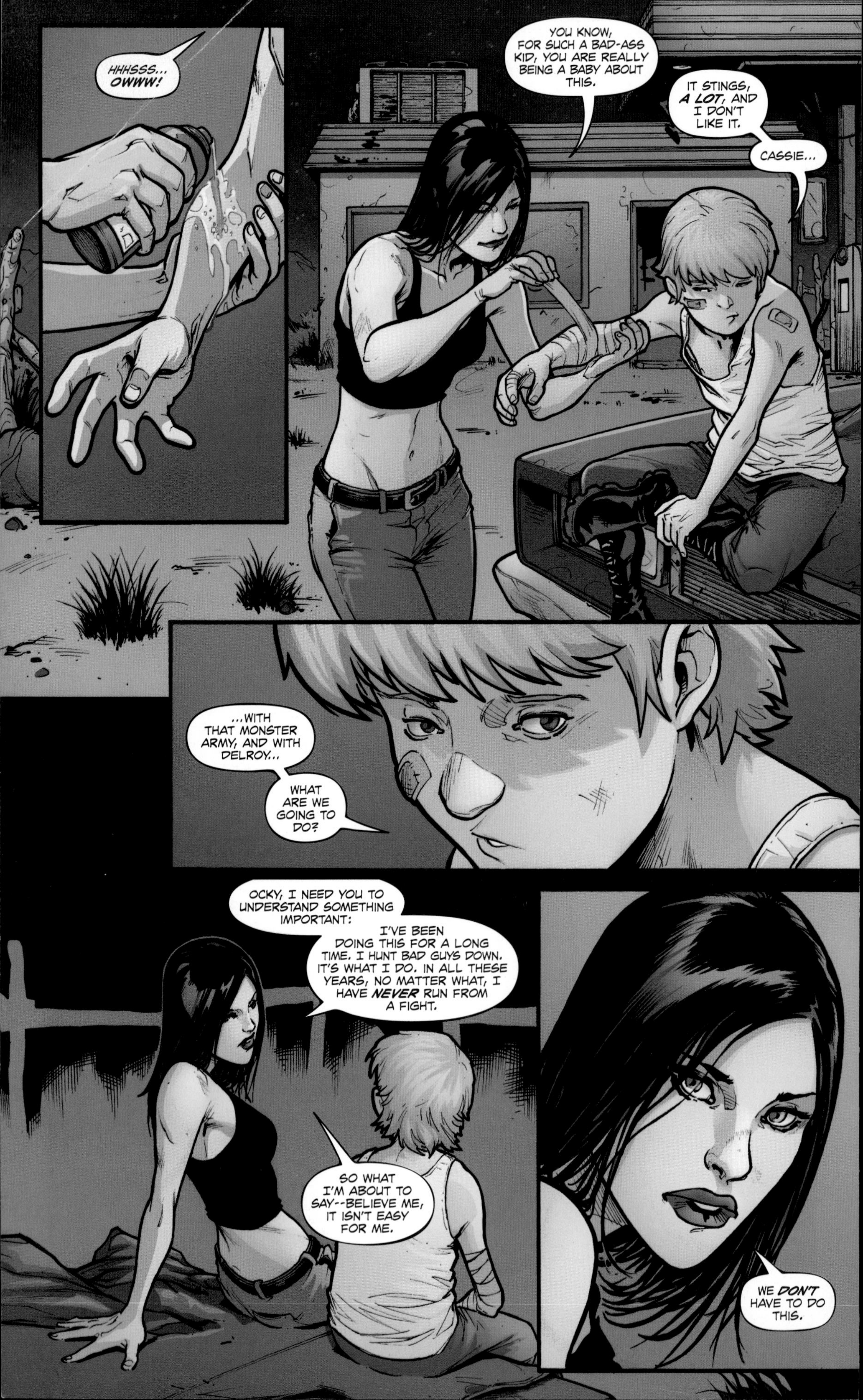
HHHSSS... OWWW!
YOU KNOW, FOR SUCH A BAD-ASS KID, YOU ARE REALLY BEING A BABY ABOUT THIS.
IT STINGS, A LOT, AND I DON'T LIKE IT.
CASSIE...
...WITH THAT MONSTER ARMY, AND WITH DELROY...
WHAT ARE WE GOING TO DO?
OCKY, I NEED YOU TO UNDERSTAND SOMETHING IMPORTANT:
I'VE BEEN DOING THIS FOR A LONG TIME. I HUNT BAD GUYS DOWN. IT'S WHAT I DO. IN ALL THESE YEARS, NO MATTER WHAT, I HAVE NEVER RUN FROM A FIGHT.
SO WHAT I'M ABOUT TO SAY--BELIEVE ME, IT ISN'T EASY FOR ME.
WE DON'T HAVE TO DO THIS.

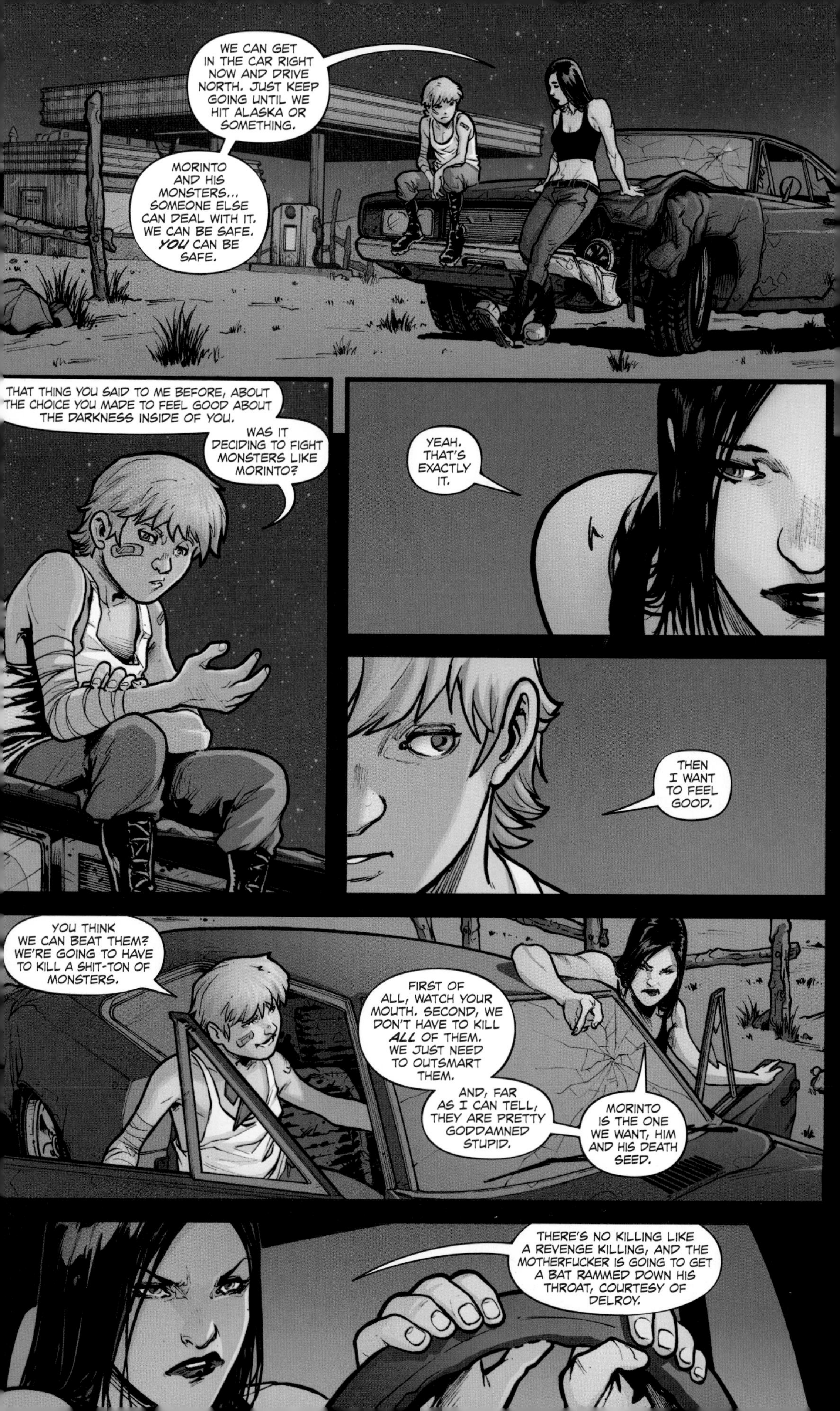

WE CAN GET IN THE CAR RIGHT NOW AND DRIVE NORTH. JUST KEEP GOING UNTIL WE HIT ALASKA OR SOMETHING.
MORINTO AND HIS MONSTERS... SOMEONE ELSE CAN DEAL WITH IT. WE CAN BE SAFE. YOU CAN BE SAFE.
THAT THING YOU SAID TO ME BEFORE, ABOUT THE CHOICE YOU MADE TO FEEL GOOD ABOUT THE DARKNESS INSIDE OF YOU.
WAS IT DECIDING TO FIGHT MONSTERS LIKE MORINTO?
YEAH. THAT'S EXACTLY IT.
THEN I WANT TO FEEL GOOD.
YOU THINK WE CAN BEAT THEM? WE'RE GOING TO HAVE TO KILL A SHIT-TON OF MONSTERS.
FIRST OF ALL, WATCH YOUR MOUTH. SECOND, WE DON'T HAVE TO KILL ALL OF THEM. WE JUST NEED TO OUTSMART THEM.
AND, FAR AS I CAN TELL, THEY ARE PRETTY GODDAMNED STUPID.
MORINTO IS THE ONE WE WANT, HIM AND HIS DEATH SEED.
THERE'S NO KILLING LIKE A REVENGE KILLING, AND THE MOTHERFUCKER IS GOING TO GET A BAT RAMMED DOWN HIS THROAT, COURTESY OF DELROY.

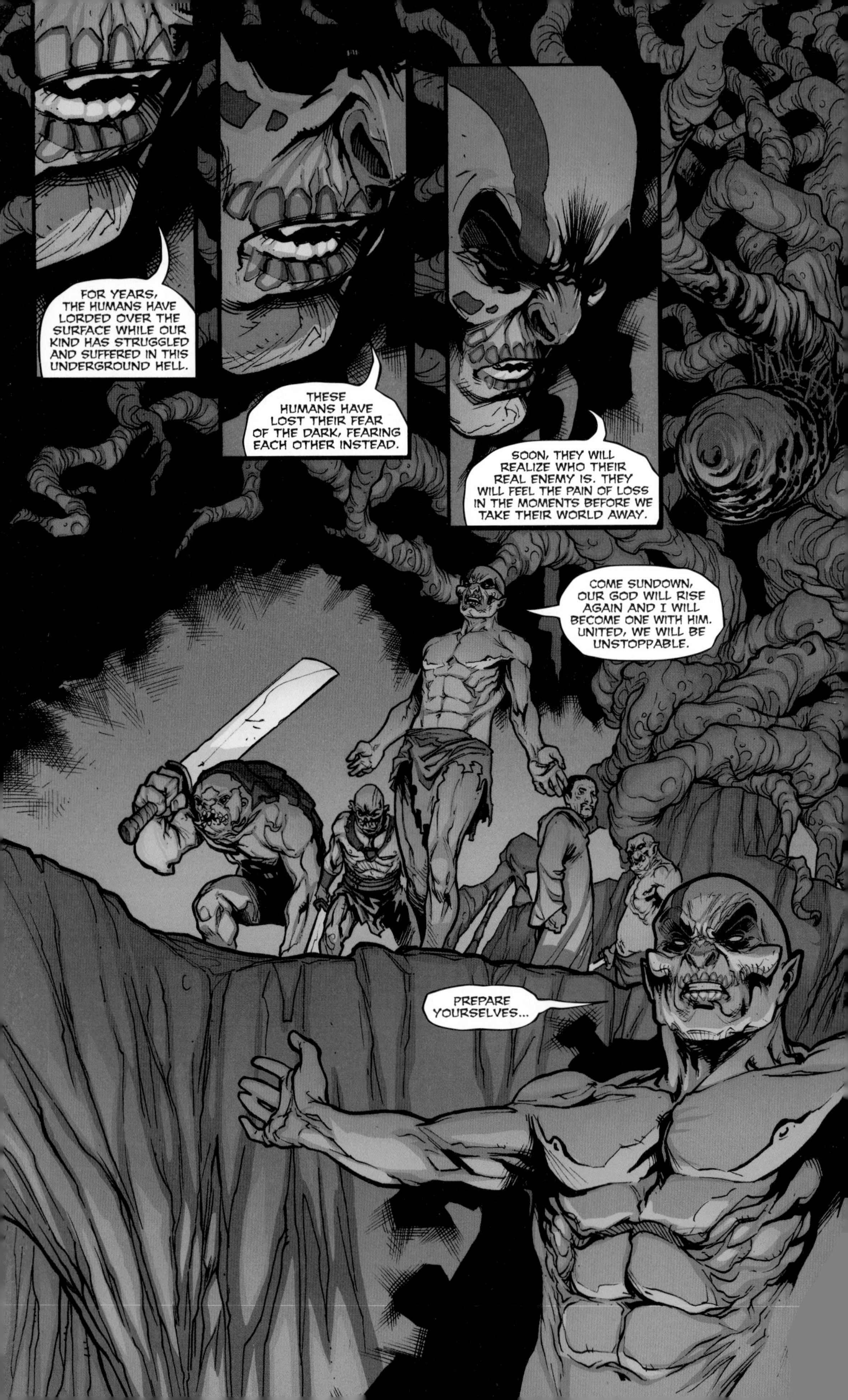
FOR YEARS, THE HUMANS HAVE LORDED OVER THE SURFACE WHILE OUR KIND HAS STRUGGLED AND SUFFERED IN THIS UNDERGROUND HELL.
THESE HUMANS HAVE LOST THEIR FEAR OF THE DARK, FEARING EACH OTHER INSTEAD.
SOON, THEY WILL REALIZE WHO THEIR REAL ENEMY IS. THEY WILL FEEL THE PAIN OF LOSS IN THE MOMENTS BEFORE WE TAKE THEIR WORLD AWAY.
COME SUNDOWN, OUR GOD WILL RISE AGAIN AND I WILL BECOME ONE WITH HIM. UNITED, WE WILL BE UNSTOPPABLE.
PREPARE YOURSELVES...

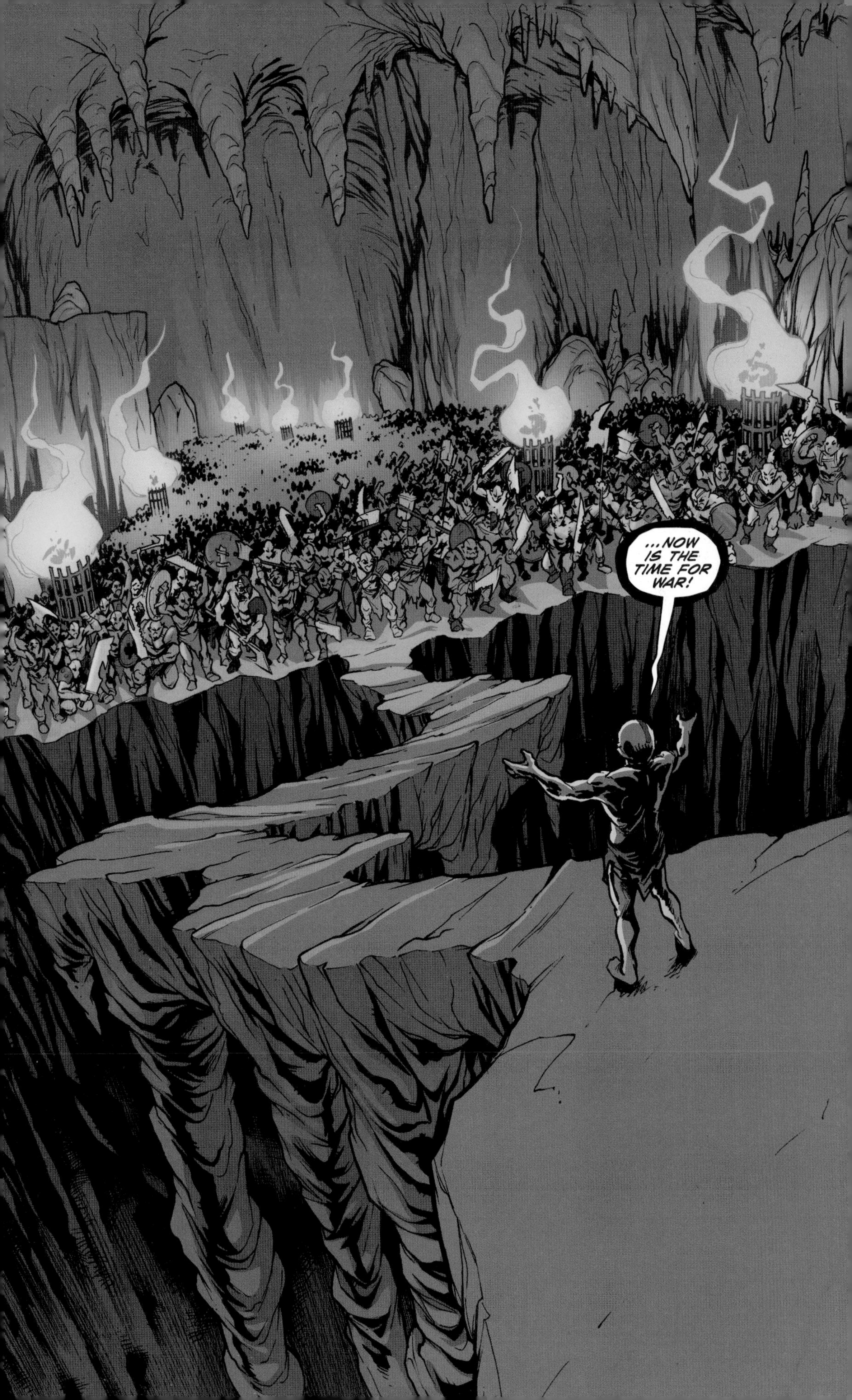
...NOW IS THE TIME FOR WAR!

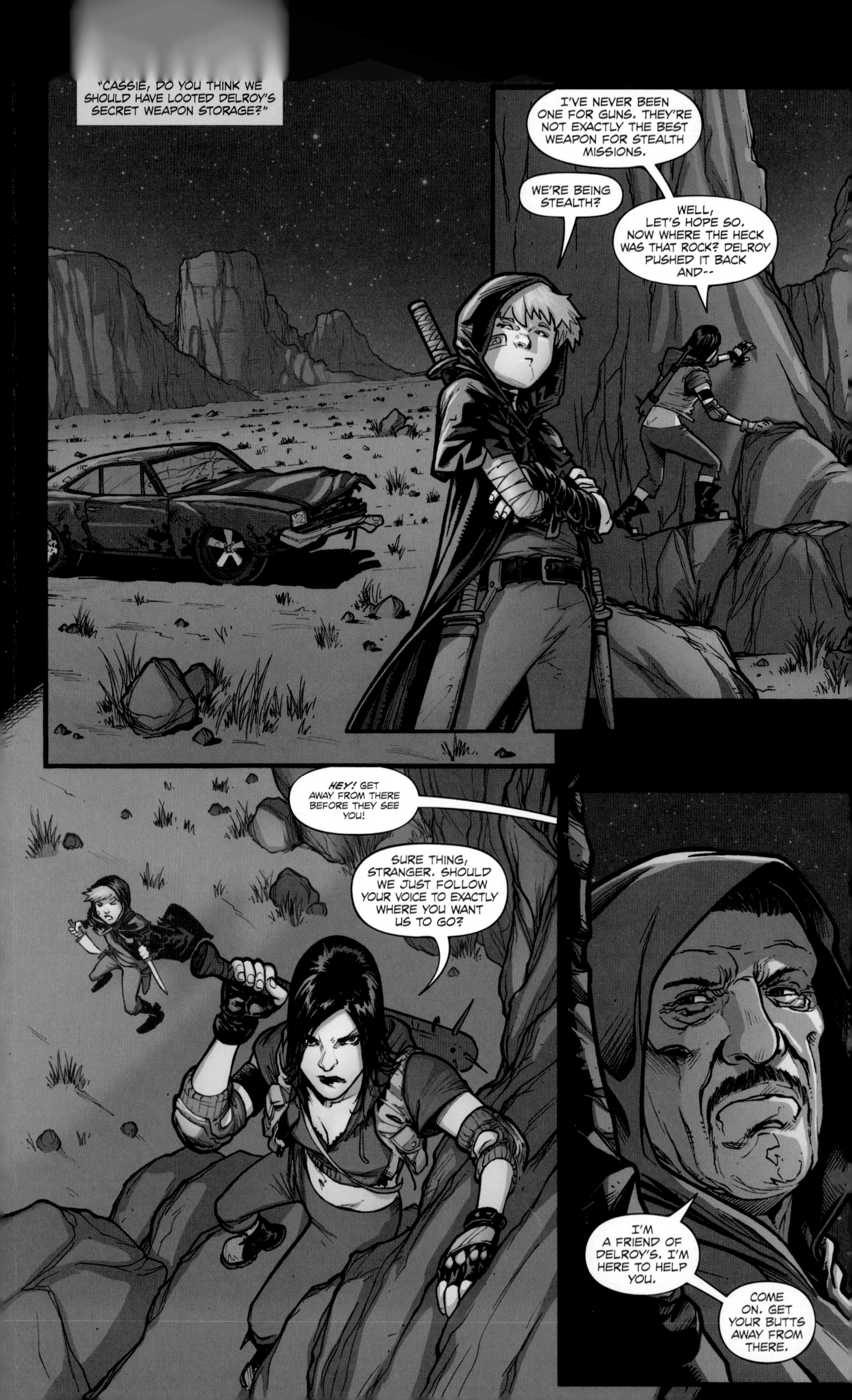
"CASSIE, DO YOU THINK WE SHOULD HAVE LOOTED DELROY'S SECRET WEAPON STORAGE?"
I'VE NEVER BEEN ONE FOR GUNS. THEY'RE NOT EXACTLY THE BEST WEAPON FOR STEALTH MISSIONS.
WE'RE BEING STEALTH?
WELL, LET'S HOPE SO. NOW WHERE THE HECK WAS THAT ROCK? DELROY PUSHED IT BACK AND--
HEY! GET AWAY FROM THERE BEFORE THEY SEE YOU!
SURE THING, STRANGER. SHOULD WE JUST FOLLOW YOUR VOICE TO EXACTLY WHERE YOU WANT US TO GO?
I'M A FRIEND OF DELROY'S. I'M HERE TO HELP YOU.
COME ON. GET YOUR BUTTS AWAY FROM THERE.

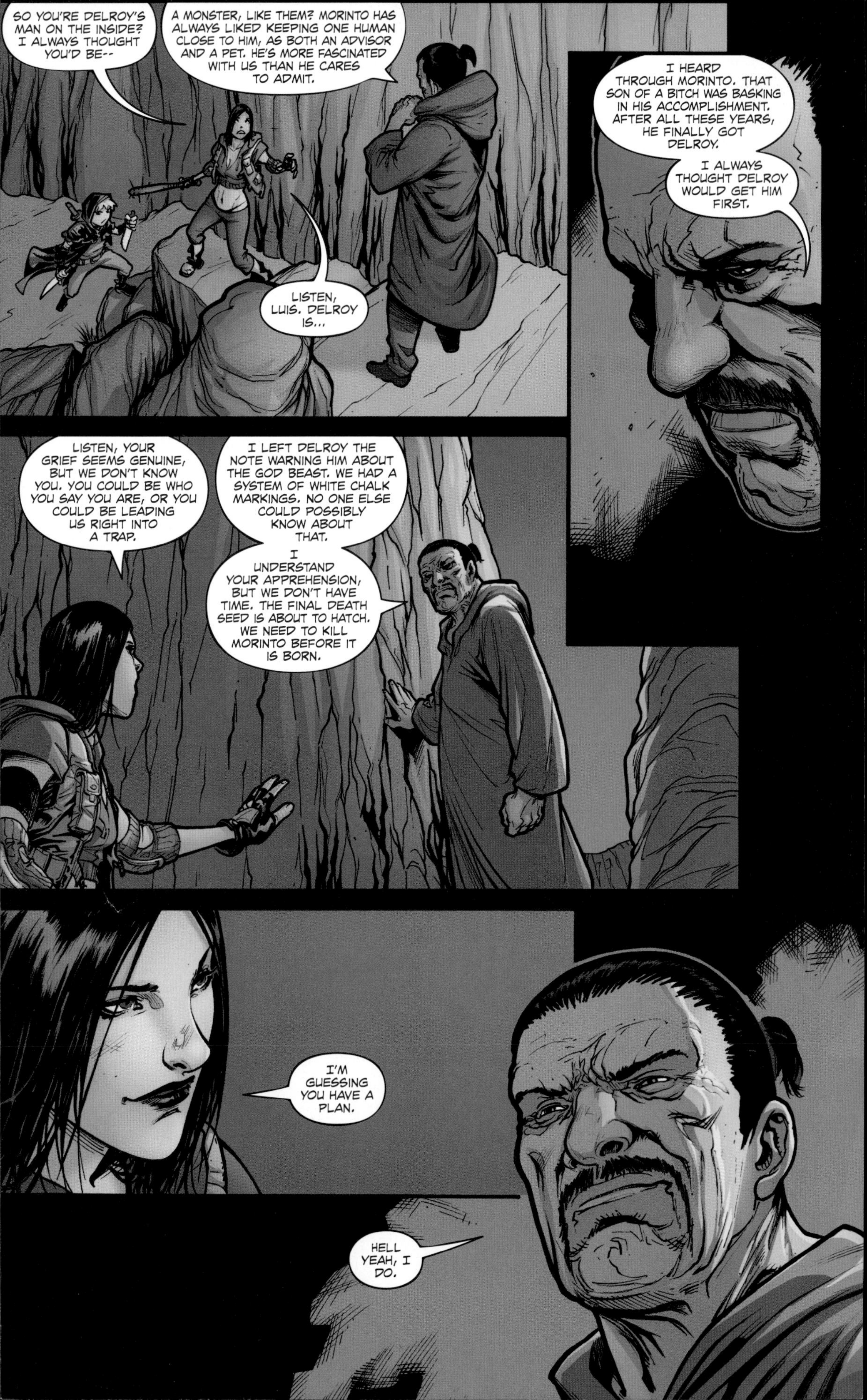
SO YOU'RE DELROY'S MAN ON THE INSIDE? I ALWAYS THOUGHT YOU'D BE--
A MONSTER, LIKE THEM? MORINTO HAS ALWAYS LIKED KEEPING ONE HUMAN CLOSE TO HIM, AS BOTH AN ADVISOR AND A PET. HE'S MORE FASCINATED WITH US THAN HE CARES TO ADMIT.
LISTEN, LUIS. DELROY IS...
I HEARD THROUGH MORINTO. THAT SON OF A BITCH WAS BASKING IN HIS ACCOMPLISHMENT. AFTER ALL THESE YEARS, HE FINALLY GOT DELROY.
I ALWAYS THOUGHT DELROY WOULD GET HIM FIRST.
LISTEN, YOUR GRIEF SEEMS GENUINE, BUT WE DON'T KNOW YOU. YOU COULD BE WHO YOU SAY YOU ARE, OR YOU COULD BE LEADING US RIGHT INTO A TRAP.
I LEFT DELROY THE NOTE WARNING HIM ABOUT THE GOD BEAST. WE HAD A SYSTEM OF WHITE CHALK MARKINGS. NO ONE ELSE COULD POSSIBLY KNOW ABOUT THAT.
I UNDERSTAND YOUR APPREHENSION, BUT WE DON'T HAVE TIME. THE FINAL DEATH SEED IS ABOUT TO HATCH. WE NEED TO KILL MORINTO BEFORE IT IS BORN.
I'M GUESSING YOU HAVE A PLAN.
HELL YEAH, I DO.

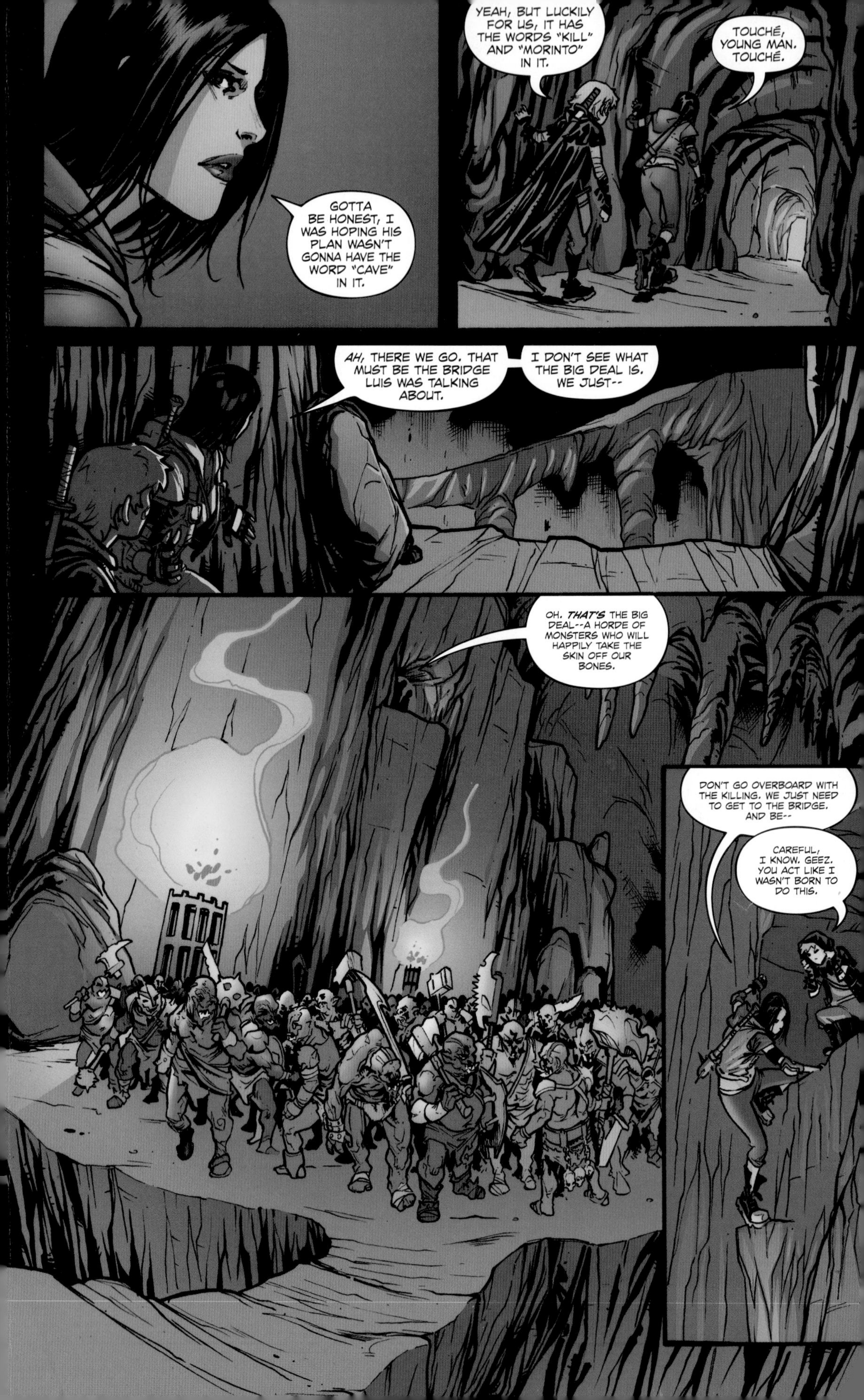
GOTTA BE HONEST, I WAS HOPING HIS PLAN WASN'T GONNA HAVE THE WORD "CAVE" IN IT.
YEAH, BUT LUCKILY FOR US, IT HAS THE WORDS "KILL" AND "MORINTO" IN IT.
TOUCHÉ, YOUNG MAN. TOUCHÉ.
AH, THERE WE GO. THAT MUST BE THE BRIDGE LUIS WAS TALKING ABOUT.
I DON'T SEE WHAT THE BIG DEAL IS. WE JUST--
OH. THAT'S THE BIG DEAL--A HORDE OF MONSTERS WHO WILL HAPPILY TAKE THE SKIN OFF OUR BONES.
DON'T GO OVERBOARD WITH THE KILLING. WE JUST NEED TO GET TO THE BRIDGE. AND BE--
CAREFUL, I KNOW. GEEZ. YOU ACT LIKE I WASN'T BORN TO DO THIS.

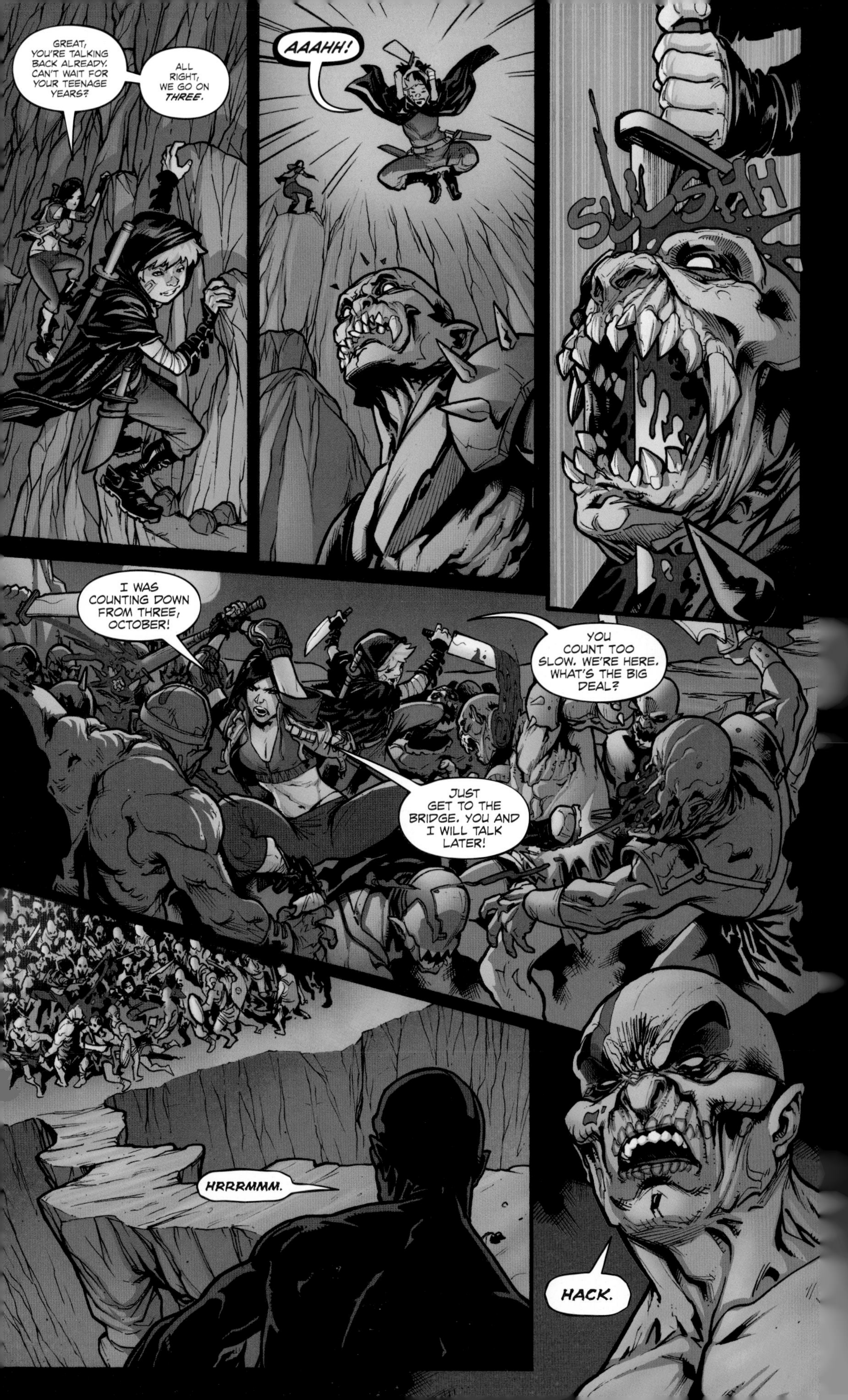
GREAT, YOU'RE TALKING BACK ALREADY. CAN'T WAIT FOR YOUR TEENAGE YEARS?
ALL RIGHT, WE GO ON THREE.
AAAHH!
SLUSHH
I WAS COUNTING DOWN FROM THREE, OCTOBER!
YOU COUNT TOO SLOW. WE'RE HERE. WHAT'S THE BIG DEAL?
JUST GET TO THE BRIDGE. YOU AND I WILL TALK LATER!
HRRRMMM.
HACK.

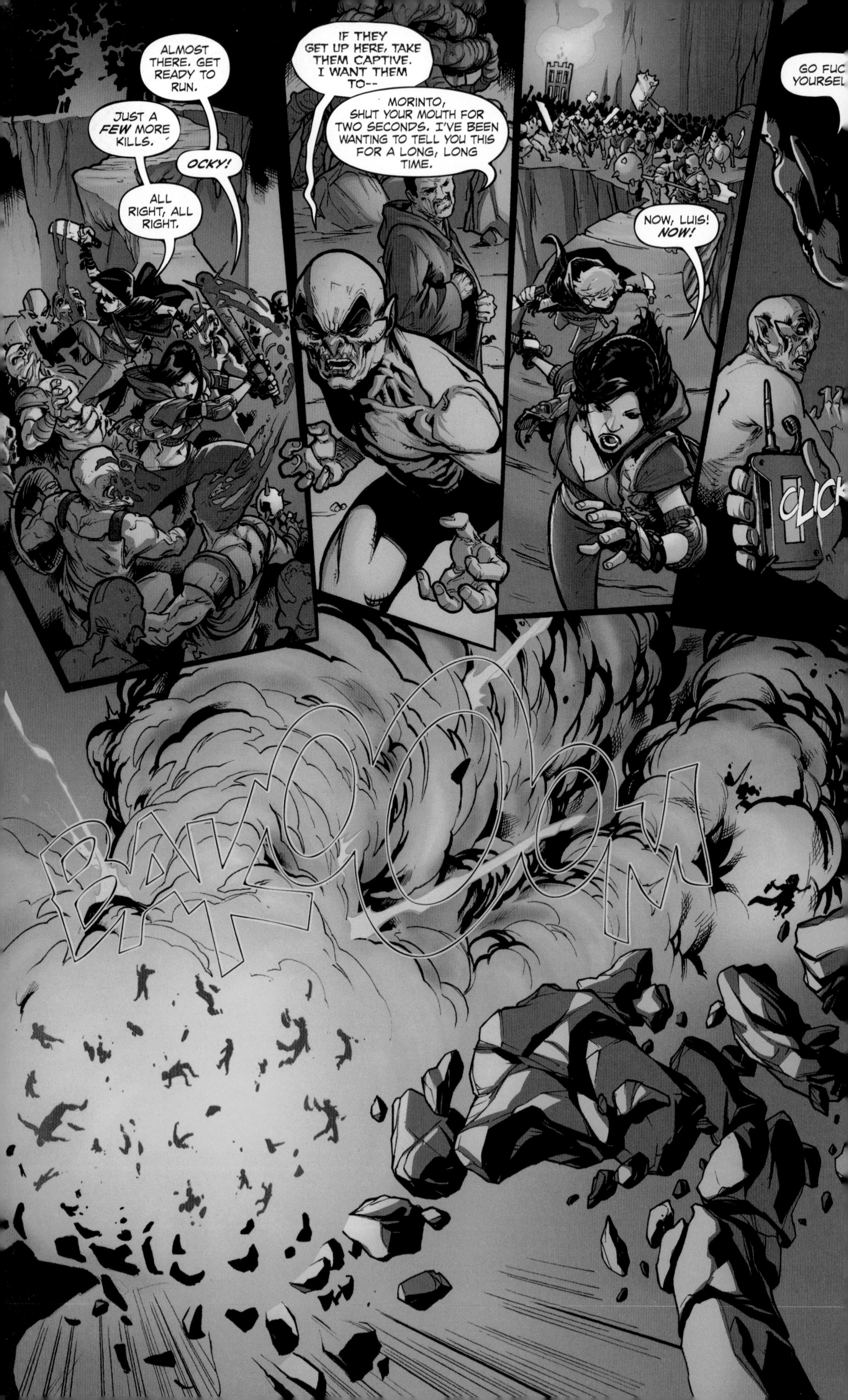
ALMOST THERE. GET READY TO RUN.
JUST A *FEW* MORE KILLS.
OCKY!
ALL RIGHT, ALL RIGHT.
IF THEY GET UP HERE, TAKE THEM CAPTIVE. I WANT THEM TO--
MORINTO, SHUT YOUR MOUTH FOR TWO SECONDS. I'VE BEEN WANTING TO TELL YOU THIS FOR A LONG, LONG TIME.
NOW, LUIS! *NOW!*
GO FUC YOURSEL
CLICK
BAKOOOOM

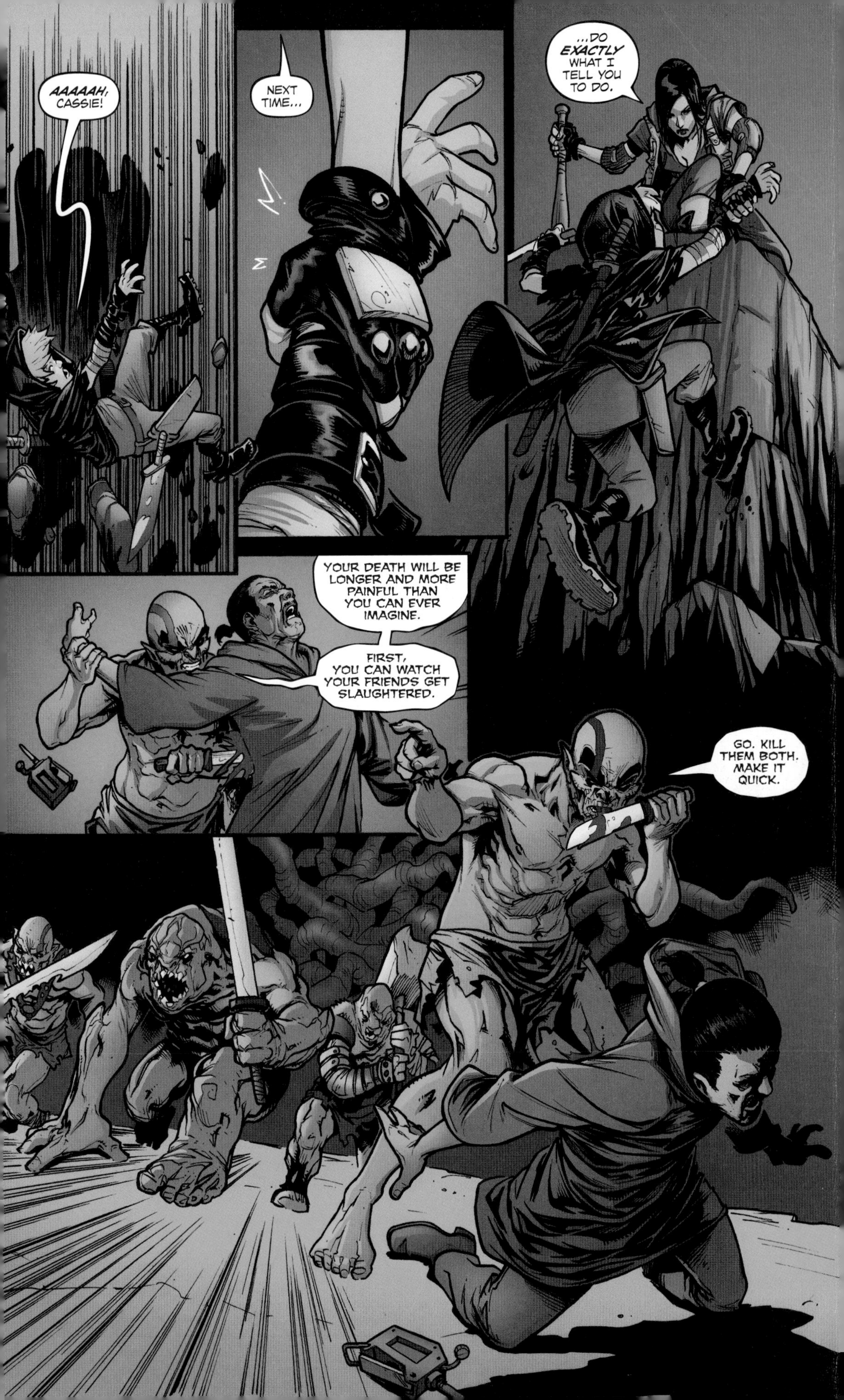
AAAAAH, CASSIE!
NEXT TIME...
...DO EXACTLY WHAT I TELL YOU TO DO.
YOUR DEATH WILL BE LONGER AND MORE PAINFUL THAN YOU CAN EVER IMAGINE.
FIRST, YOU CAN WATCH YOUR FRIENDS GET SLAUGHTERED.
GO. KILL THEM BOTH. MAKE IT QUICK.

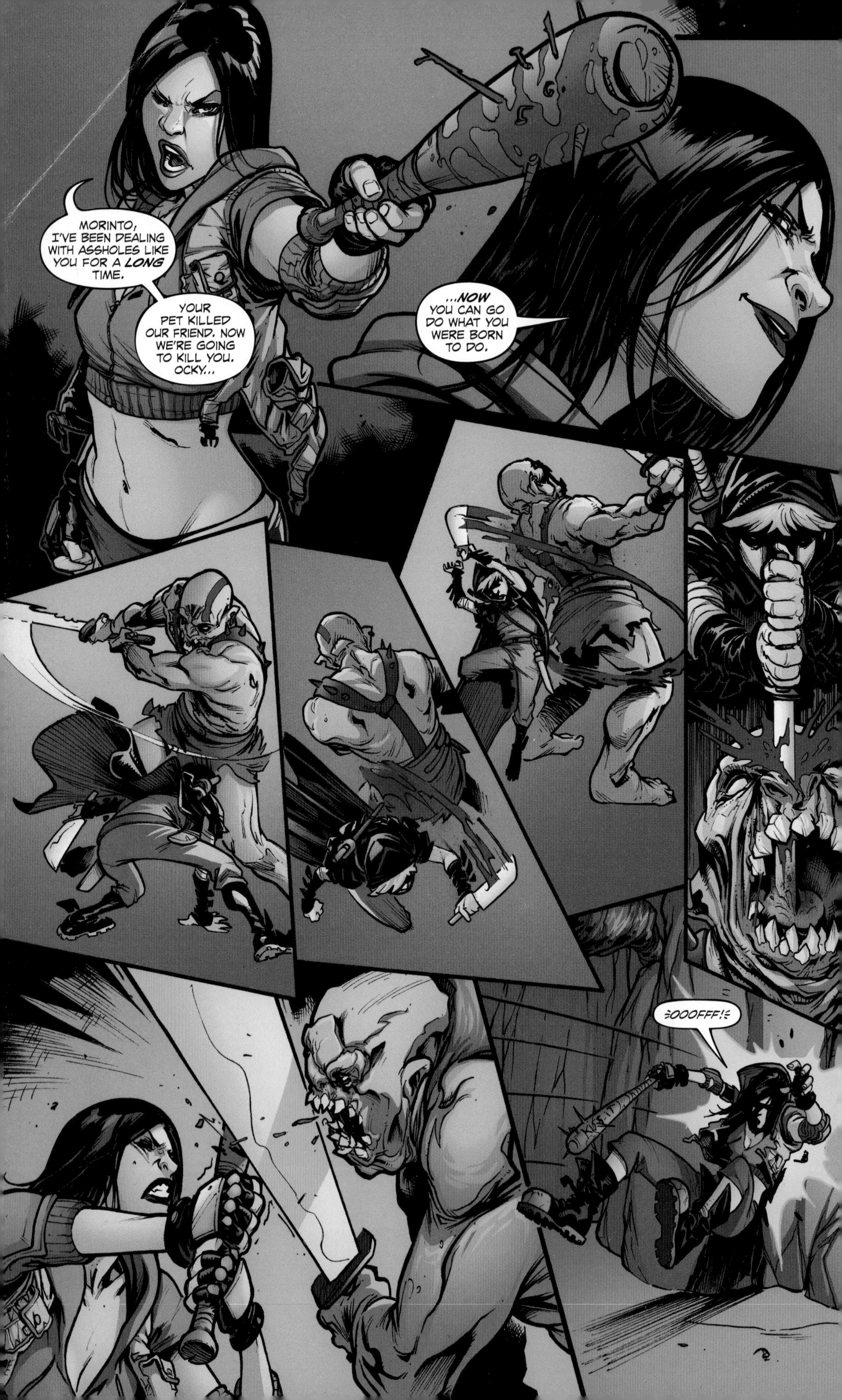
MORINTO, I'VE BEEN DEALING WITH ASSHOLES LIKE YOU FOR A *LONG* TIME.
YOUR PET KILLED OUR FRIEND. NOW WE'RE GOING TO KILL YOU. OCKY...
...*NOW* YOU CAN GO DO WHAT YOU WERE BORN TO DO.
OOOFFF!

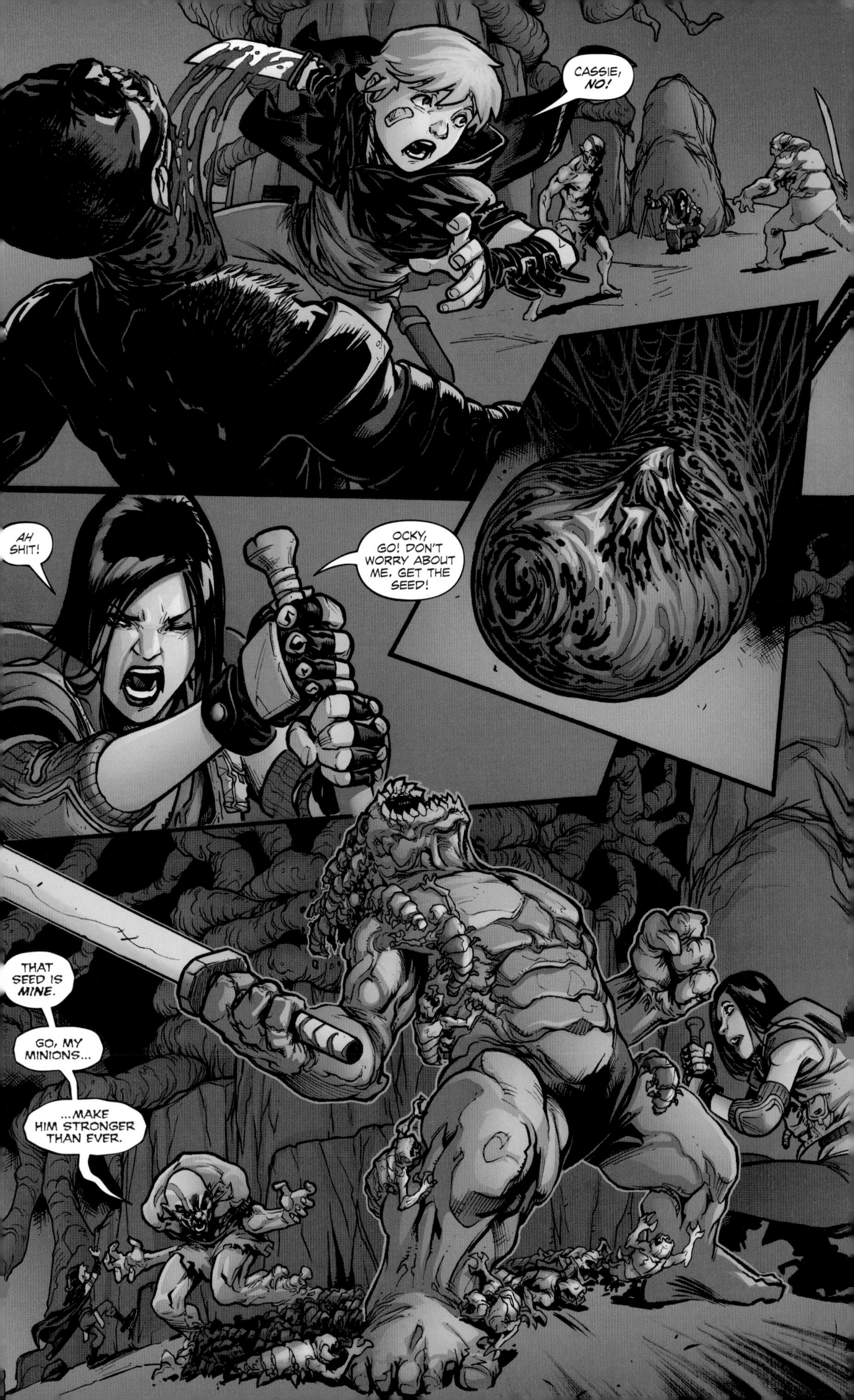
CASSIE, NO!
AH SHIT!
OCKY, GO! DON'T WORRY ABOUT ME. GET THE SEED!
THAT SEED IS MINE.
GO, MY MINIONS...
...MAKE HIM STRONGER THAN EVER.

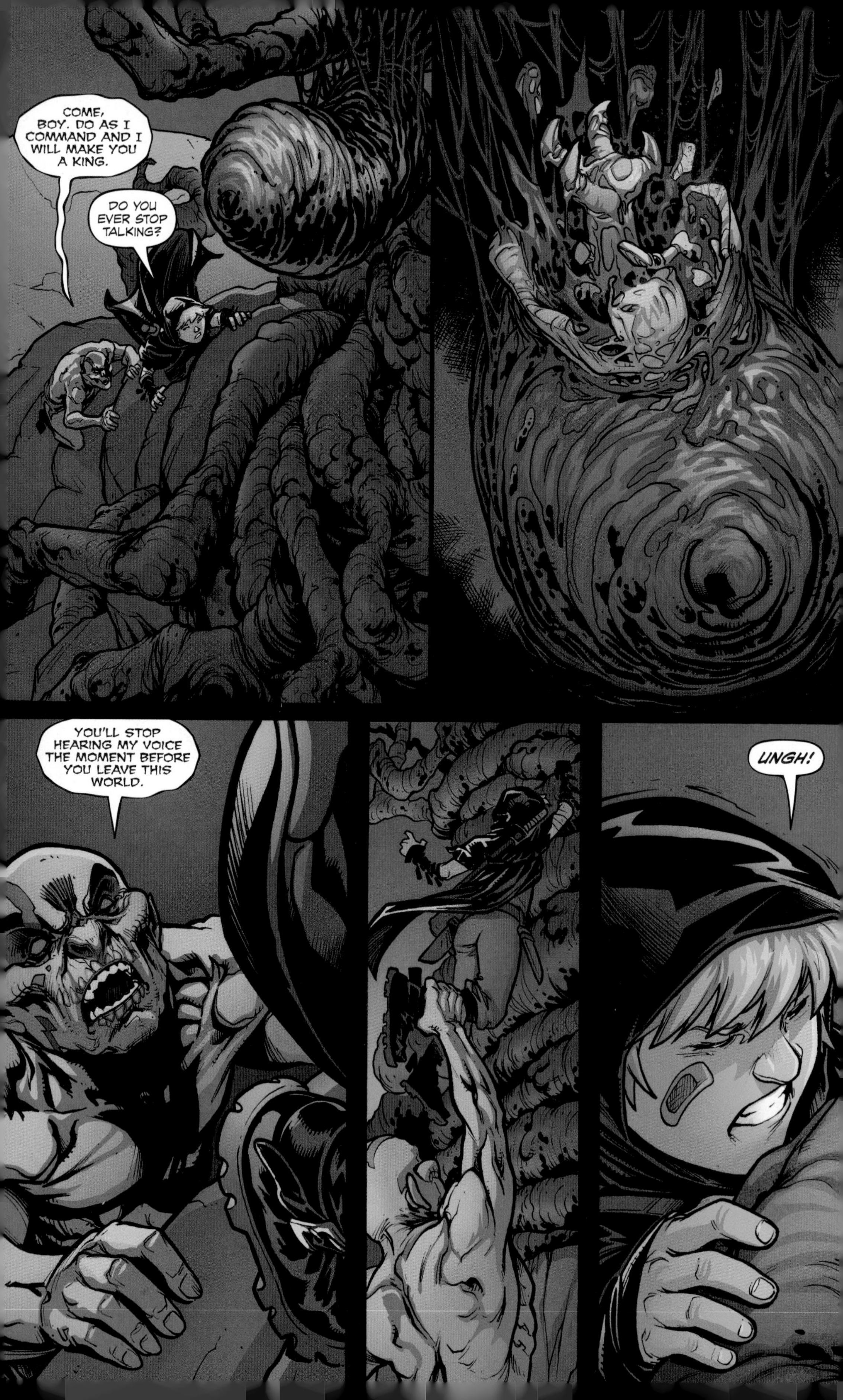
COME, BOY. DO AS I COMMAND AND I WILL MAKE YOU A KING.
DO YOU EVER STOP TALKING?
YOU'LL STOP HEARING MY VOICE THE MOMENT BEFORE YOU LEAVE THIS WORLD.
UNGH!

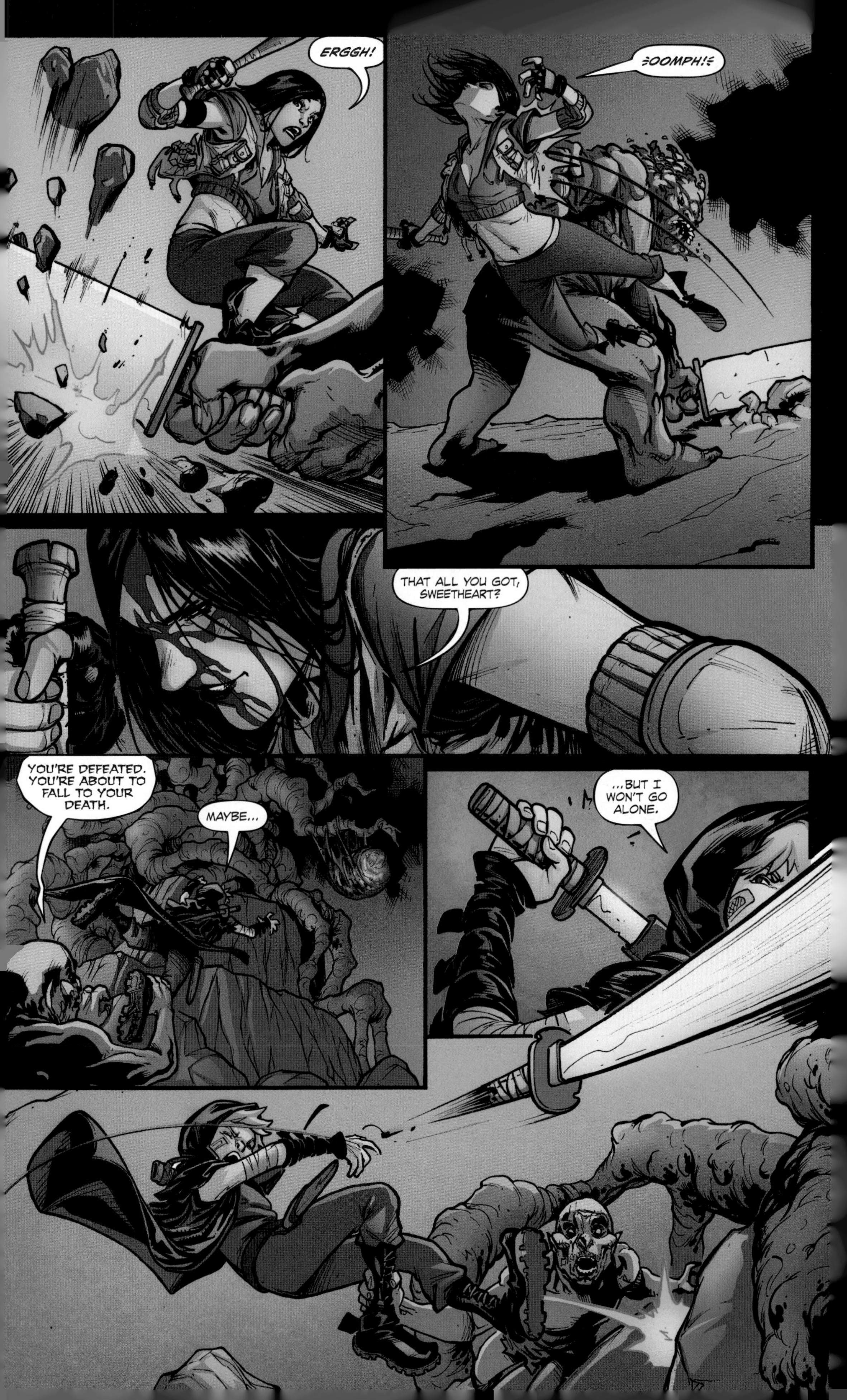
ERGGH!
OOMPH!
THAT ALL YOU GOT, SWEETHEART?
YOU'RE DEFEATED. YOU'RE ABOUT TO FALL TO YOUR DEATH.
MAYBE...
...BUT I WON'T GO ALONE.

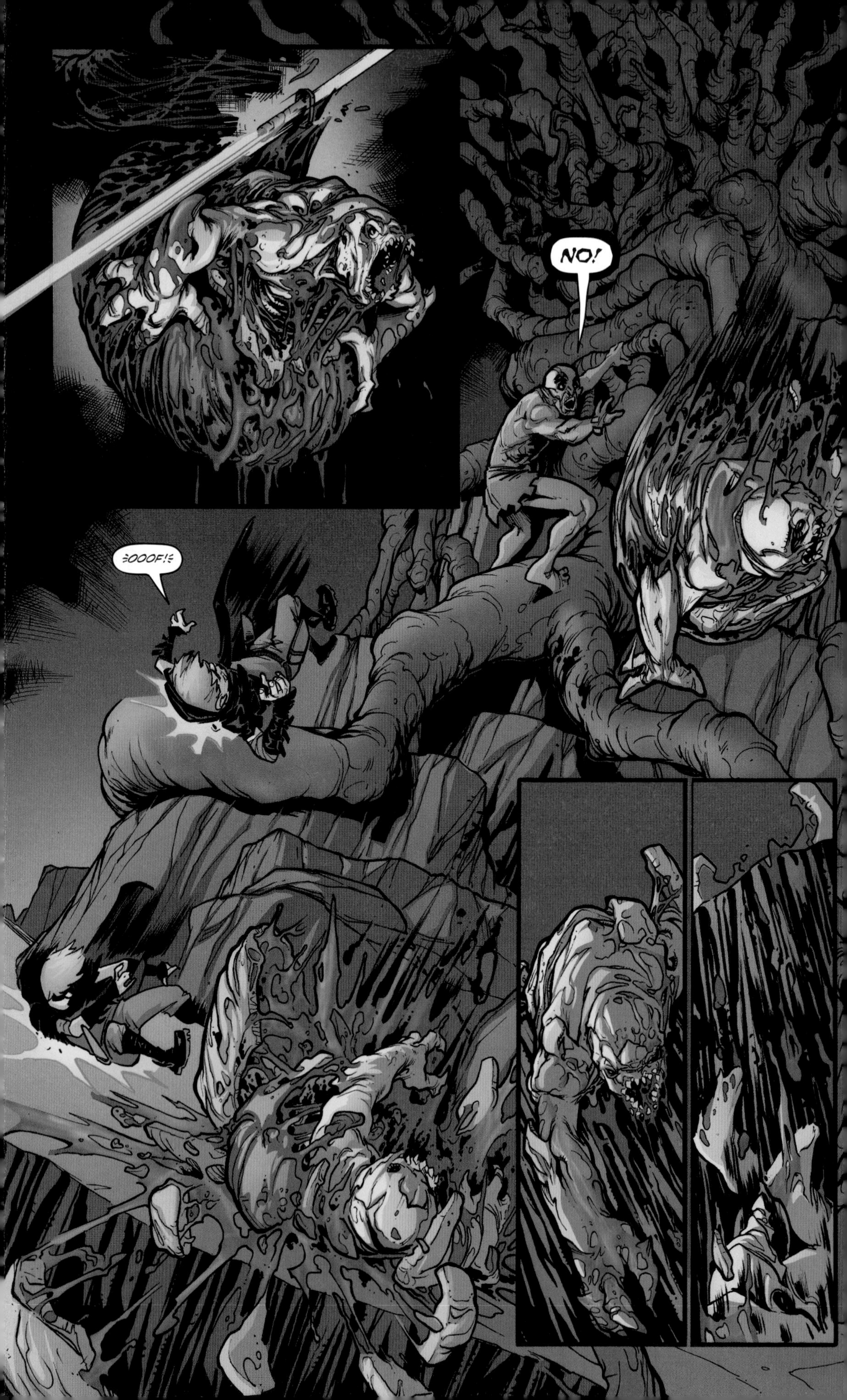
NO!
OOOF!

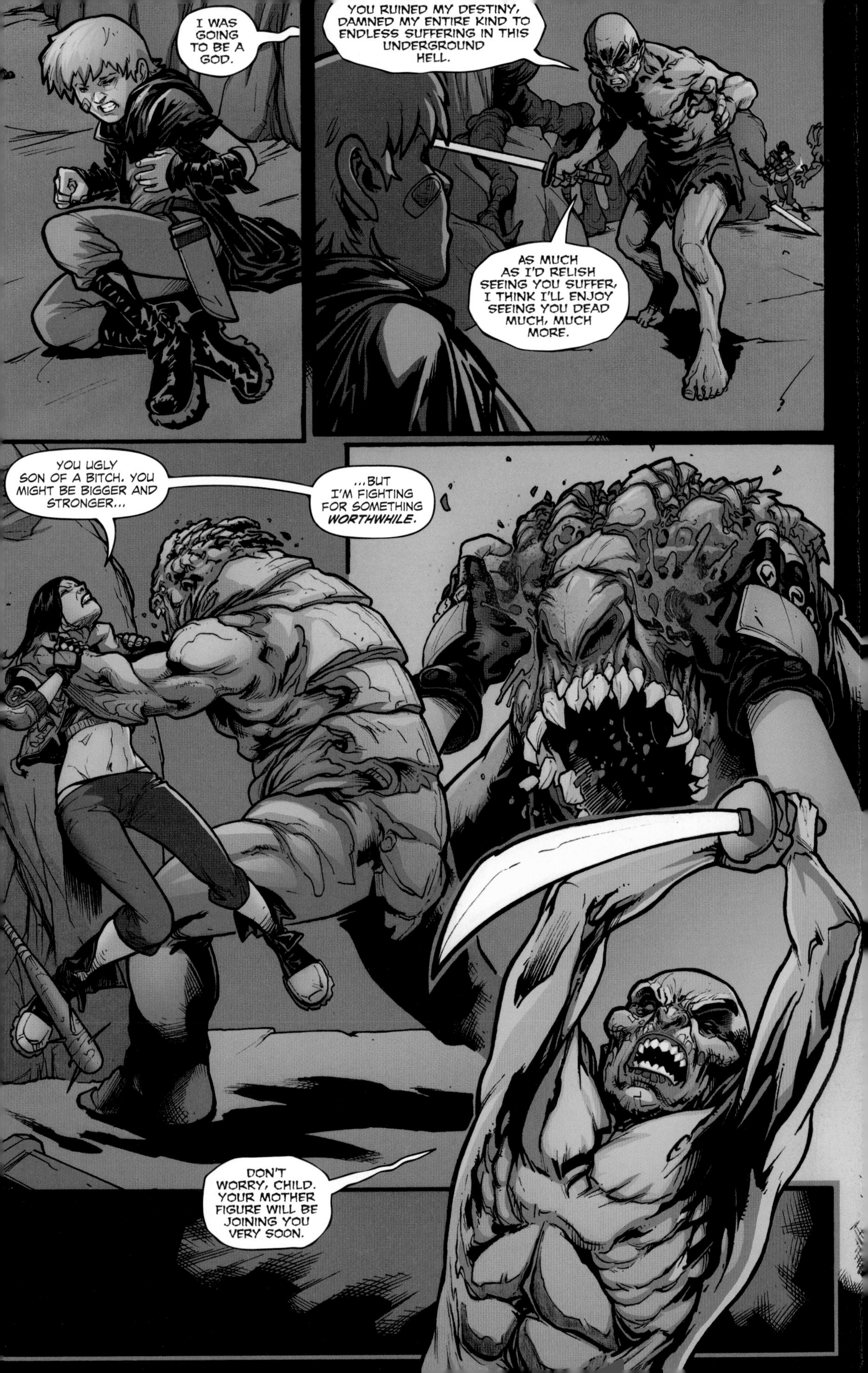
I WAS GOING TO BE A GOD.
YOU RUINED MY DESTINY, DAMNED MY ENTIRE KIND TO ENDLESS SUFFERING IN THIS UNDERGROUND HELL.
AS MUCH AS I'D RELISH SEEING YOU SUFFER, I THINK I'LL ENJOY SEEING YOU DEAD MUCH, MUCH MORE.
YOU UGLY SON OF A BITCH. YOU MIGHT BE BIGGER AND STRONGER...
...BUT I'M FIGHTING FOR SOMETHING *WORTHWHILE*.
DON'T WORRY, CHILD. YOUR MOTHER FIGURE WILL BE JOINING YOU VERY SOON.

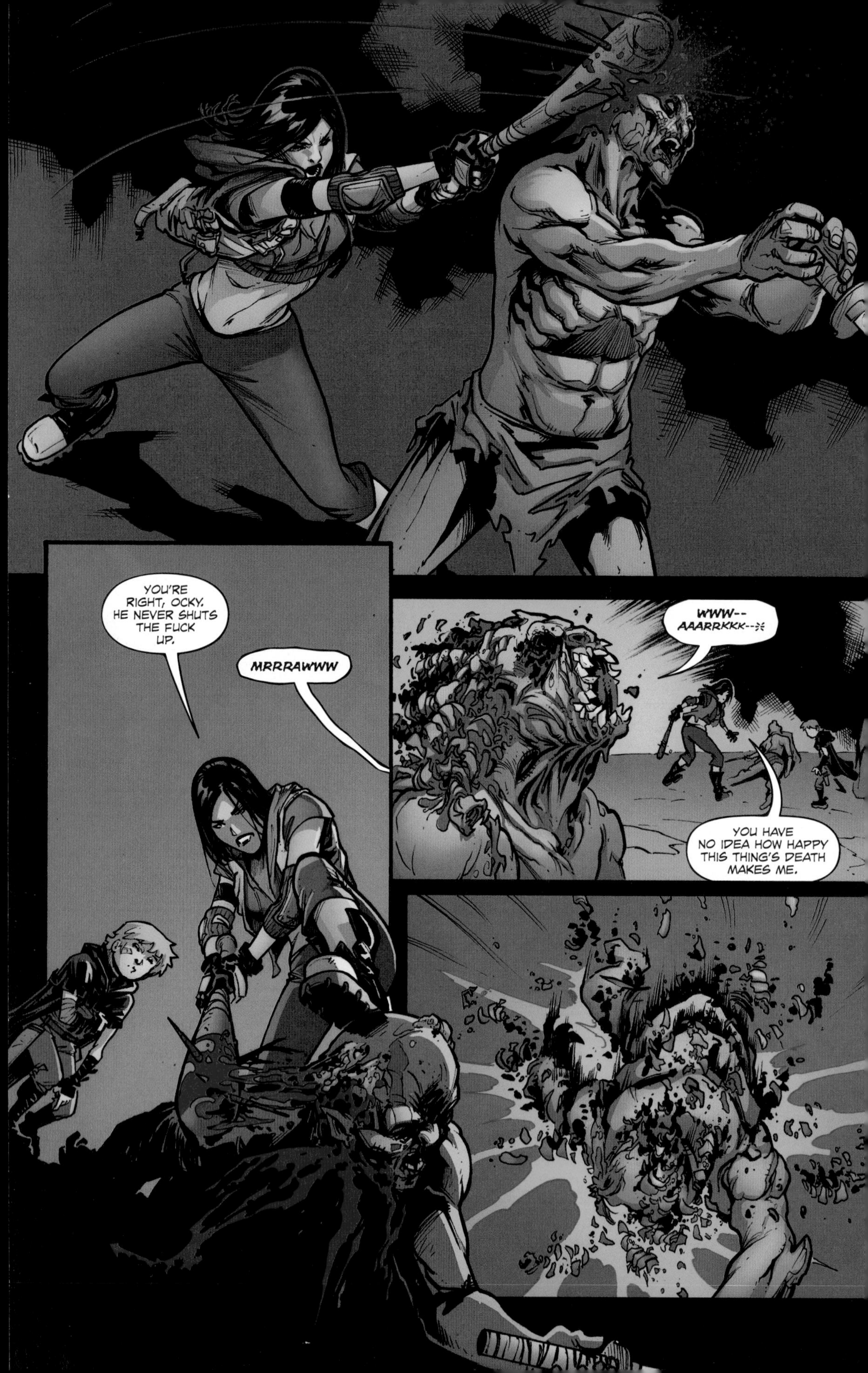
YOU'RE RIGHT, OCKY. HE NEVER SHUTS THE FUCK UP.
MRRRAWWW
WWW-- AAARRKKK--
YOU HAVE NO IDEA HOW HAPPY THIS THING'S DEATH MAKES ME.

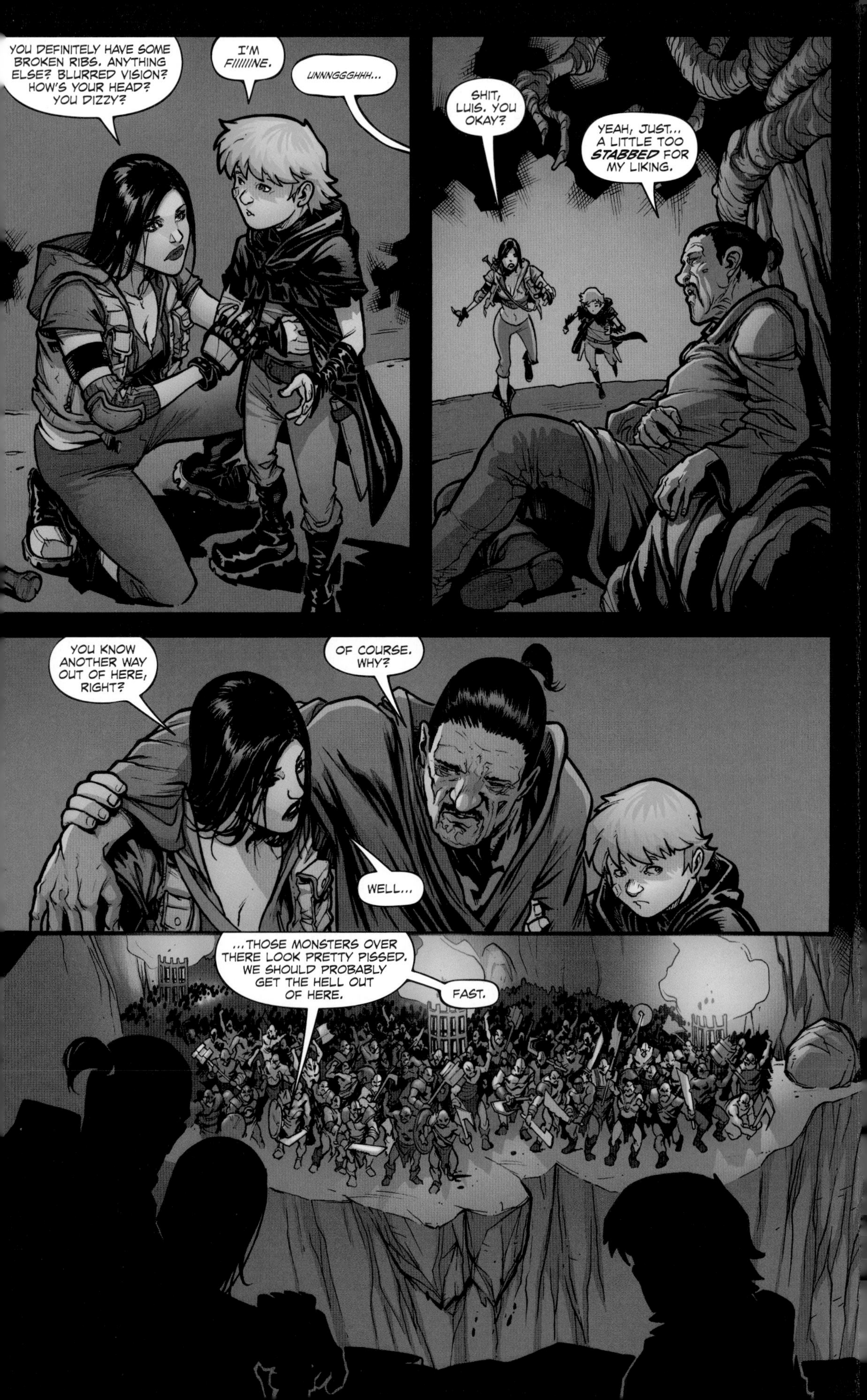
YOU DEFINITELY HAVE SOME BROKEN RIBS. ANYTHING ELSE? BLURRED VISION? HOW'S YOUR HEAD? YOU DIZZY?
I'M FIIIIIINE.
UNNNGGGHHH...
SHIT, LUIS. YOU OKAY?
YEAH, JUST... A LITTLE TOO STABBED FOR MY LIKING.
YOU KNOW ANOTHER WAY OUT OF HERE, RIGHT?
OF COURSE. WHY?
WELL...
...THOSE MONSTERS OVER THERE LOOK PRETTY PISSED. WE SHOULD PROBABLY GET THE HELL OUT OF HERE.
FAST.

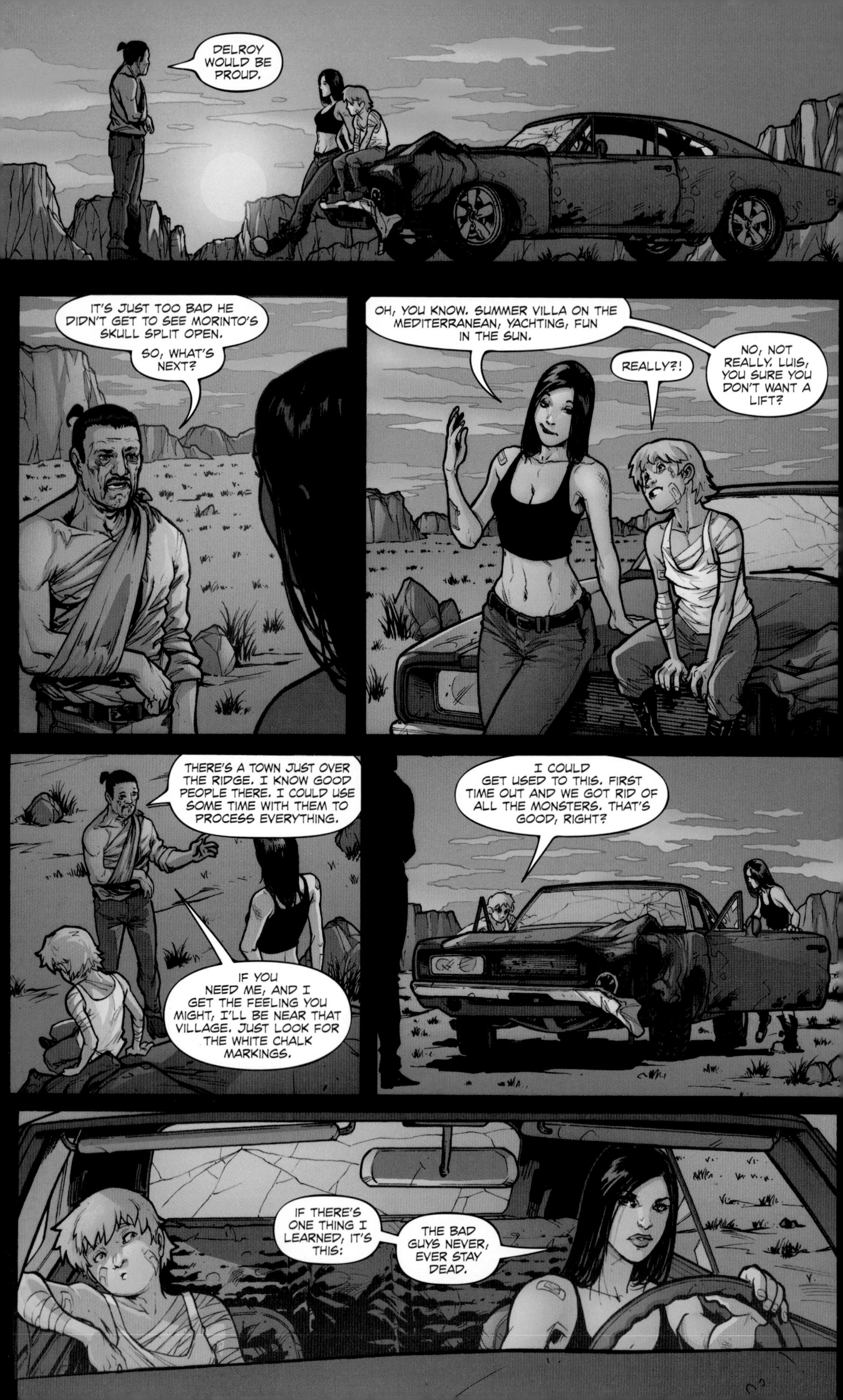
DELROY WOULD BE PROUD.
IT'S JUST TOO BAD HE DIDN'T GET TO SEE MORINTO'S SKULL SPLIT OPEN.
SO, WHAT'S NEXT?
OH, YOU KNOW. SUMMER VILLA ON THE MEDITERRANEAN, YACHTING, FUN IN THE SUN.
REALLY?!
NO, NOT REALLY. LUIS, YOU SURE YOU DON'T WANT A LIFT?
THERE'S A TOWN JUST OVER THE RIDGE. I KNOW GOOD PEOPLE THERE. I COULD USE SOME TIME WITH THEM TO PROCESS EVERYTHING.
IF YOU NEED ME, AND I GET THE FEELING YOU MIGHT, I'LL BE NEAR THAT VILLAGE. JUST LOOK FOR THE WHITE CHALK MARKINGS.
I COULD GET USED TO THIS. FIRST TIME OUT AND WE GOT RID OF ALL THE MONSTERS. THAT'S GOOD, RIGHT?
IF THERE'S ONE THING I LEARNED, IT'S THIS:
THE BAD GUYS NEVER, EVER STAY DEAD.

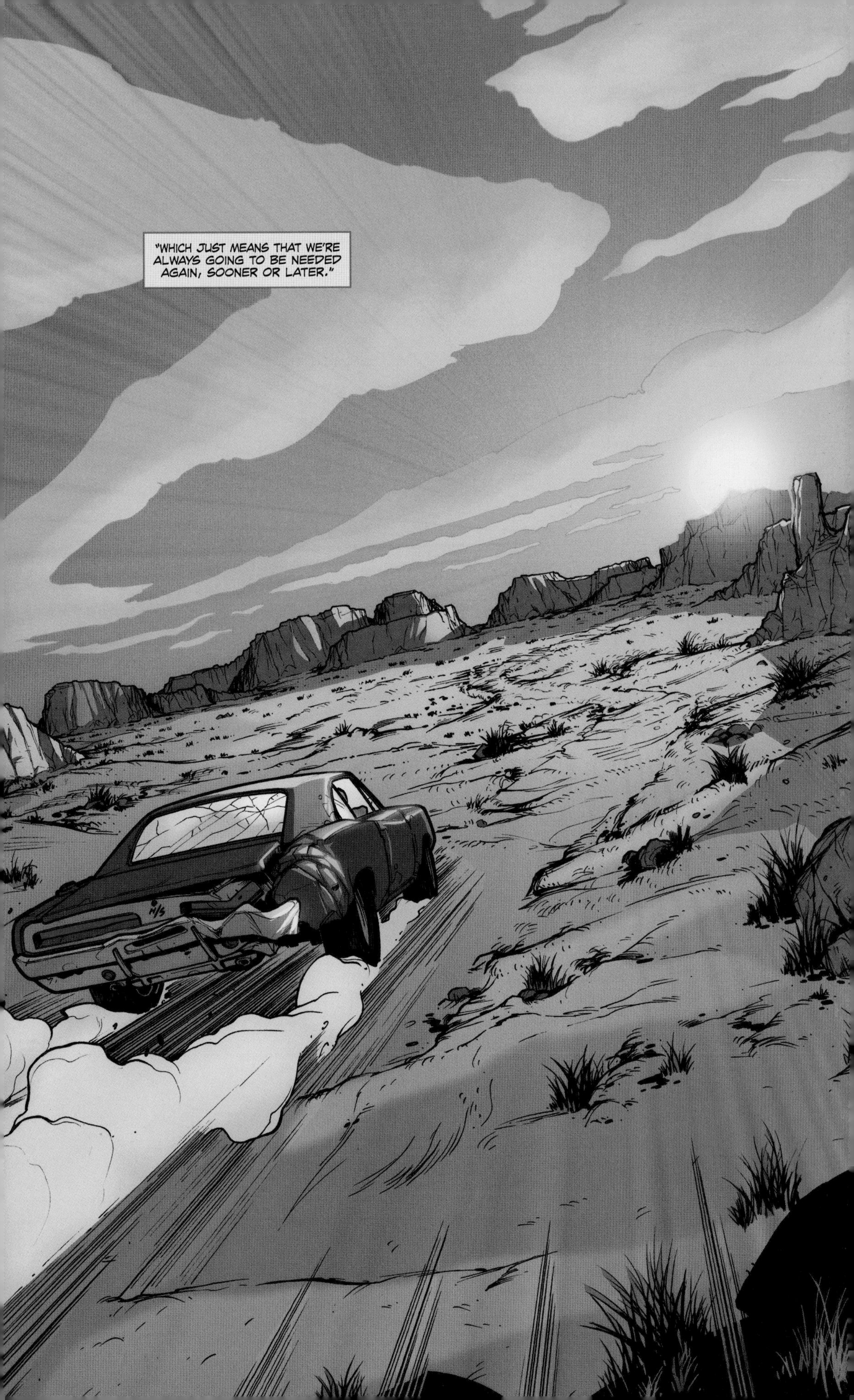
"WHICH JUST MEANS THAT WE'RE ALWAYS GOING TO BE NEEDED AGAIN, SOONER OR LATER."

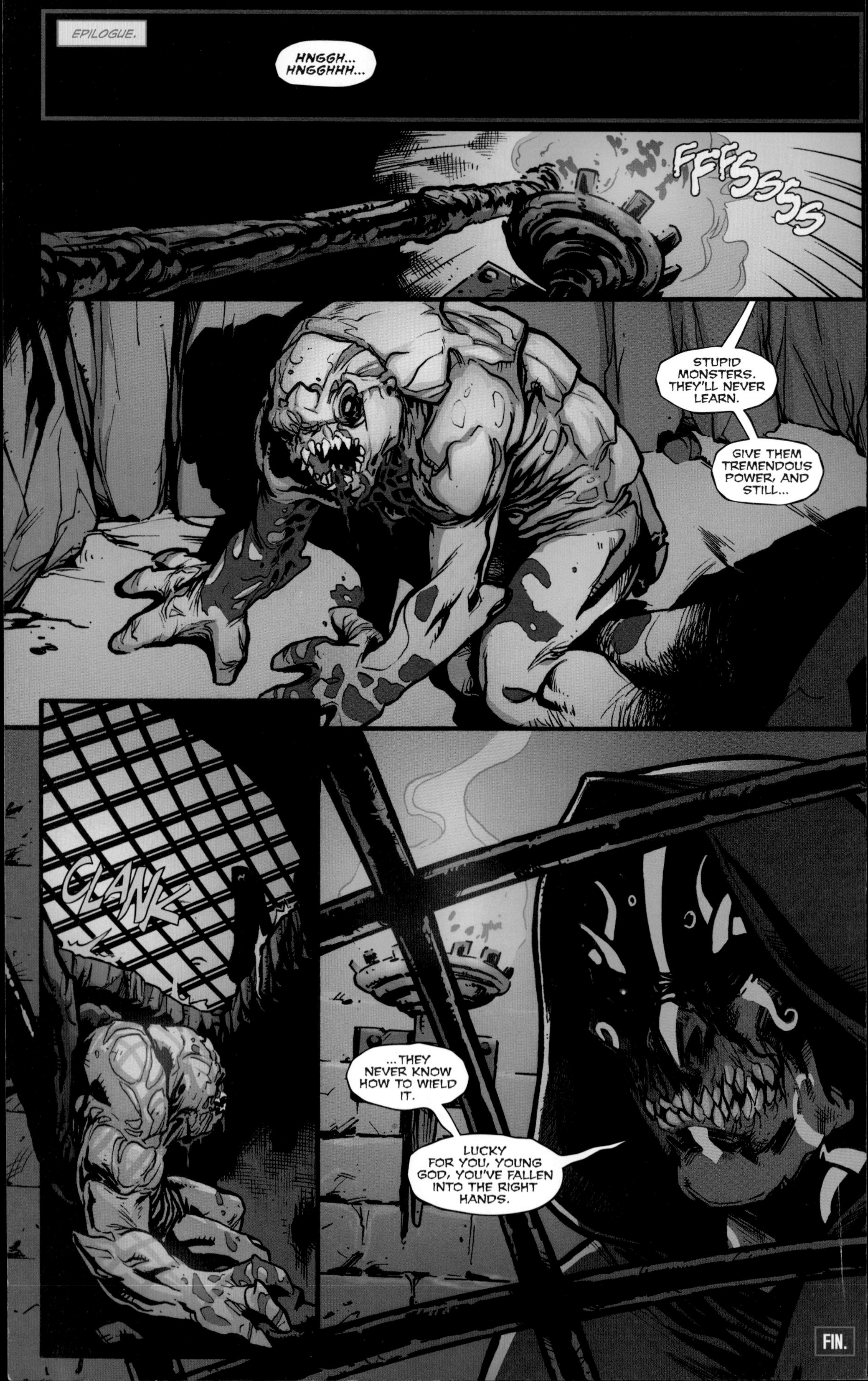
EPILOGUE.
HNGGH... HNGGHHH...
FFFSSSSS
STUPID MONSTERS. THEY'LL NEVER LEARN.
GIVE THEM TREMENDOUS POWER, AND STILL...
CLANK
...THEY NEVER KNOW HOW TO WIELD IT.
LUCKY FOR YOU, YOUNG GOD, YOU'VE FALLEN INTO THE RIGHT HANDS.
FIN.

COVER GALLERY

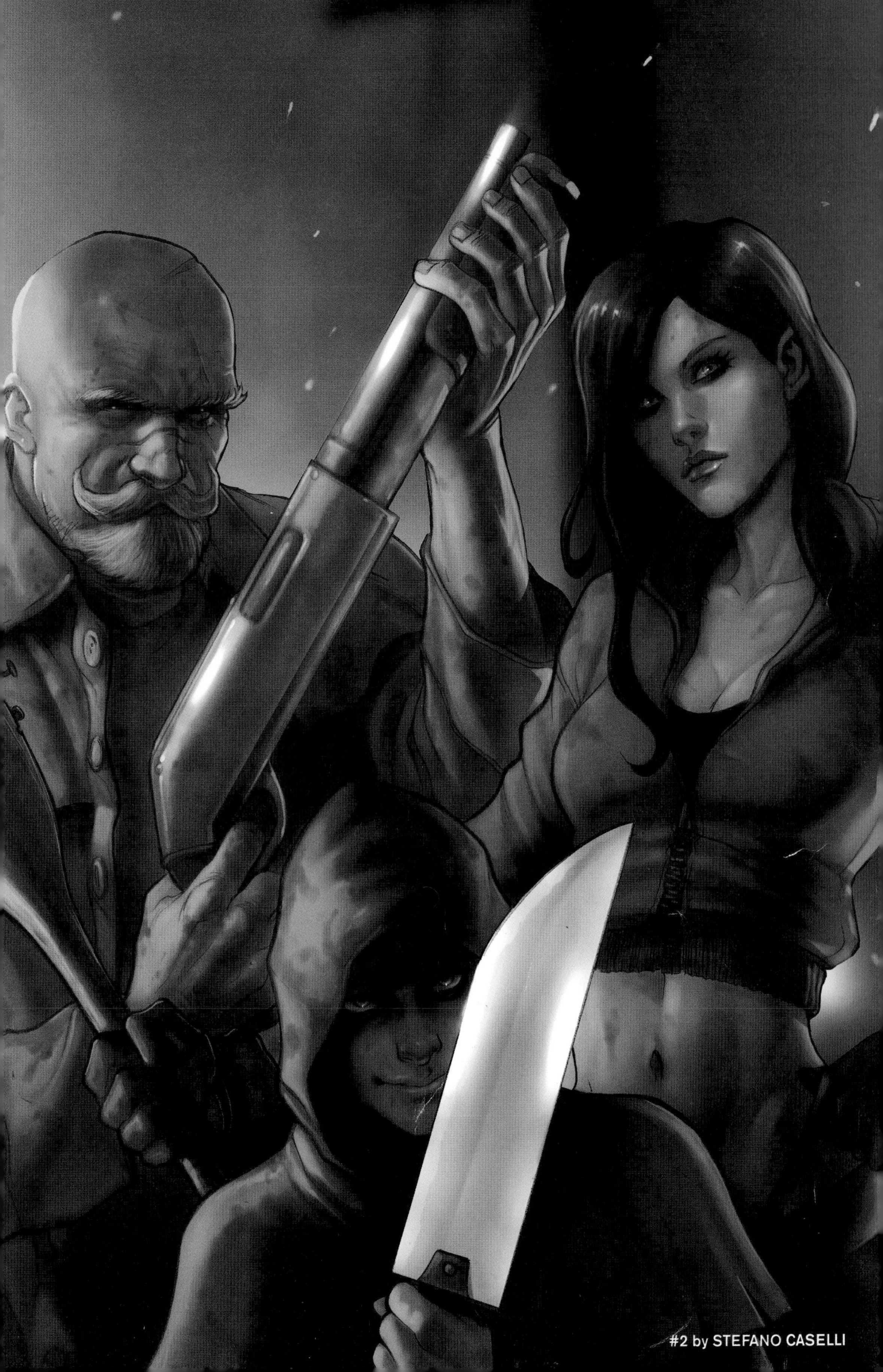

#2 by STEFANO CASELLI

#1B by CAMERON STEWART & RICO RENZI

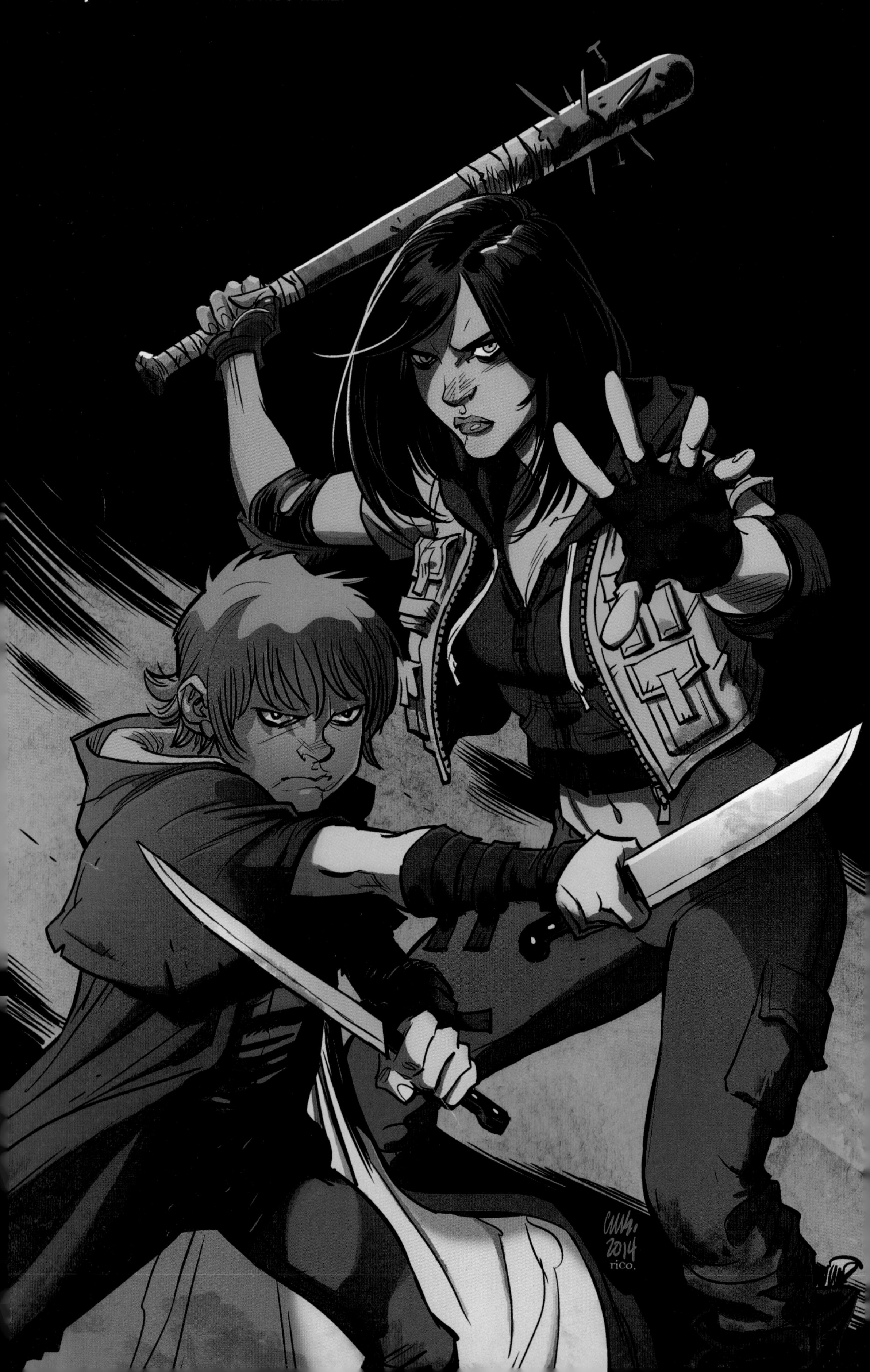

2014
rico.

#1 Reprint by TIM SEELEY

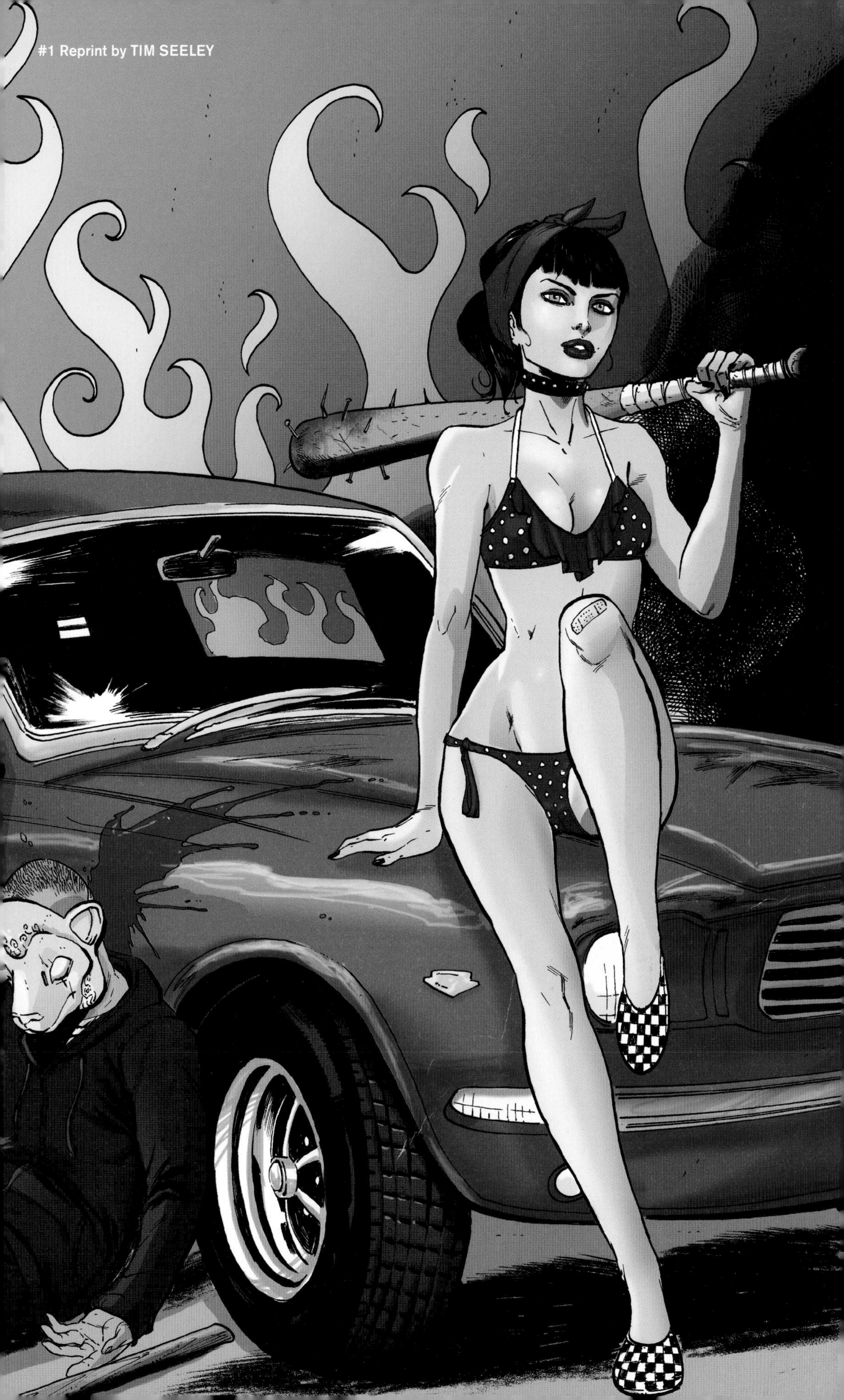

#4 by STEFANO CASELLI & EMILIO LAISO

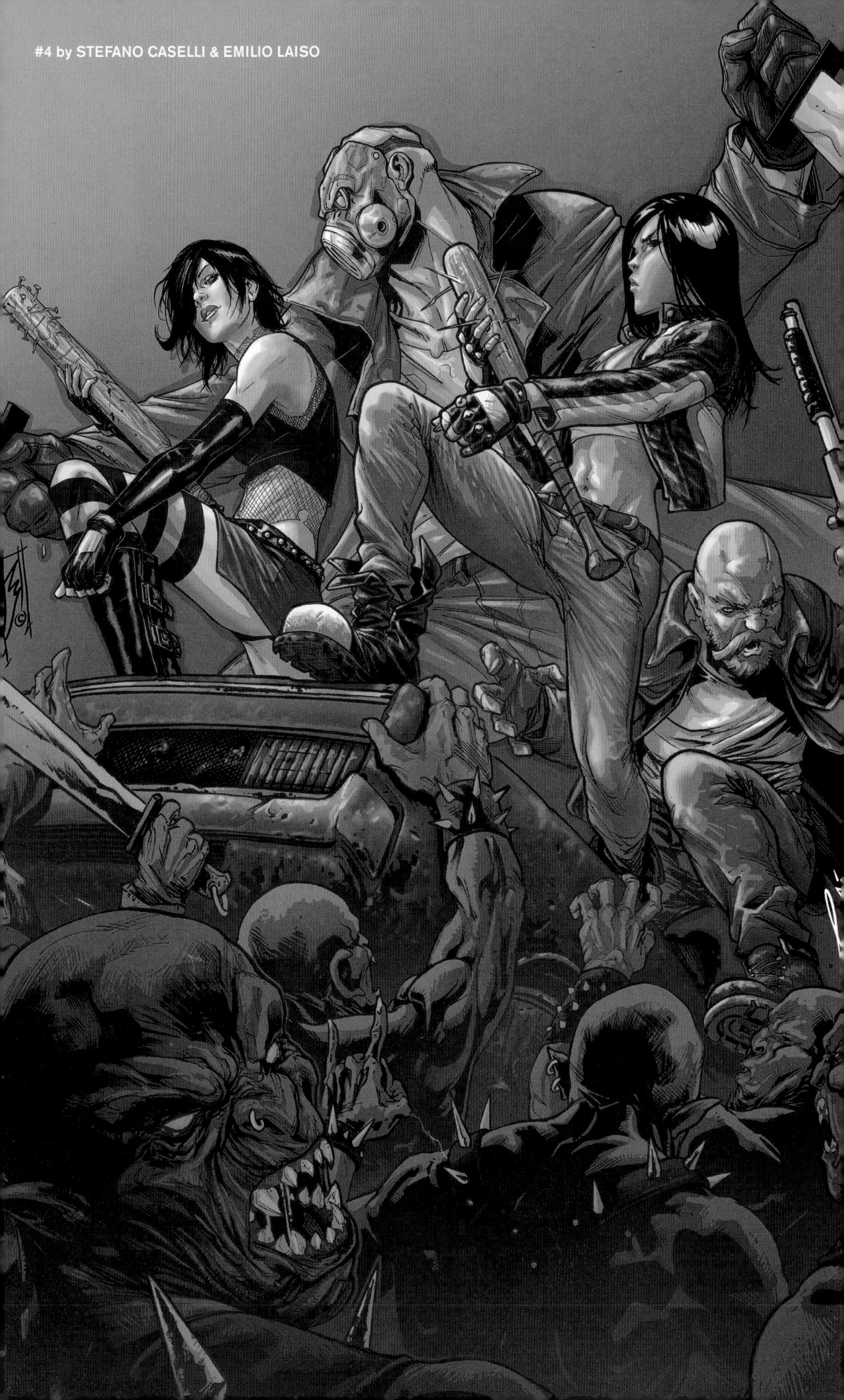

#1 Phantom Variant by ALE GARZA & K. MICHAEL RUSSELL

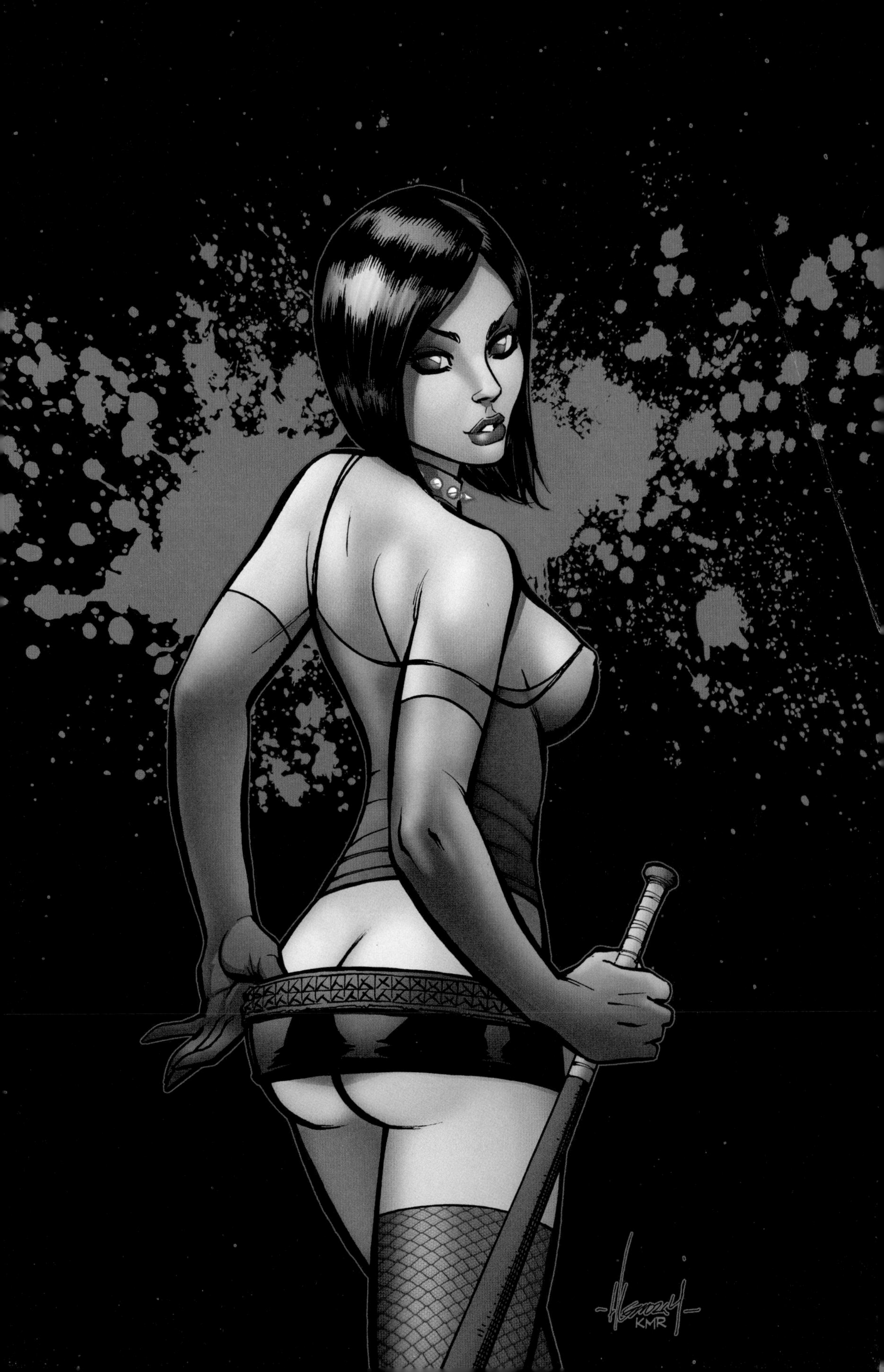
KMR

#3 by STEFANO CASELLI

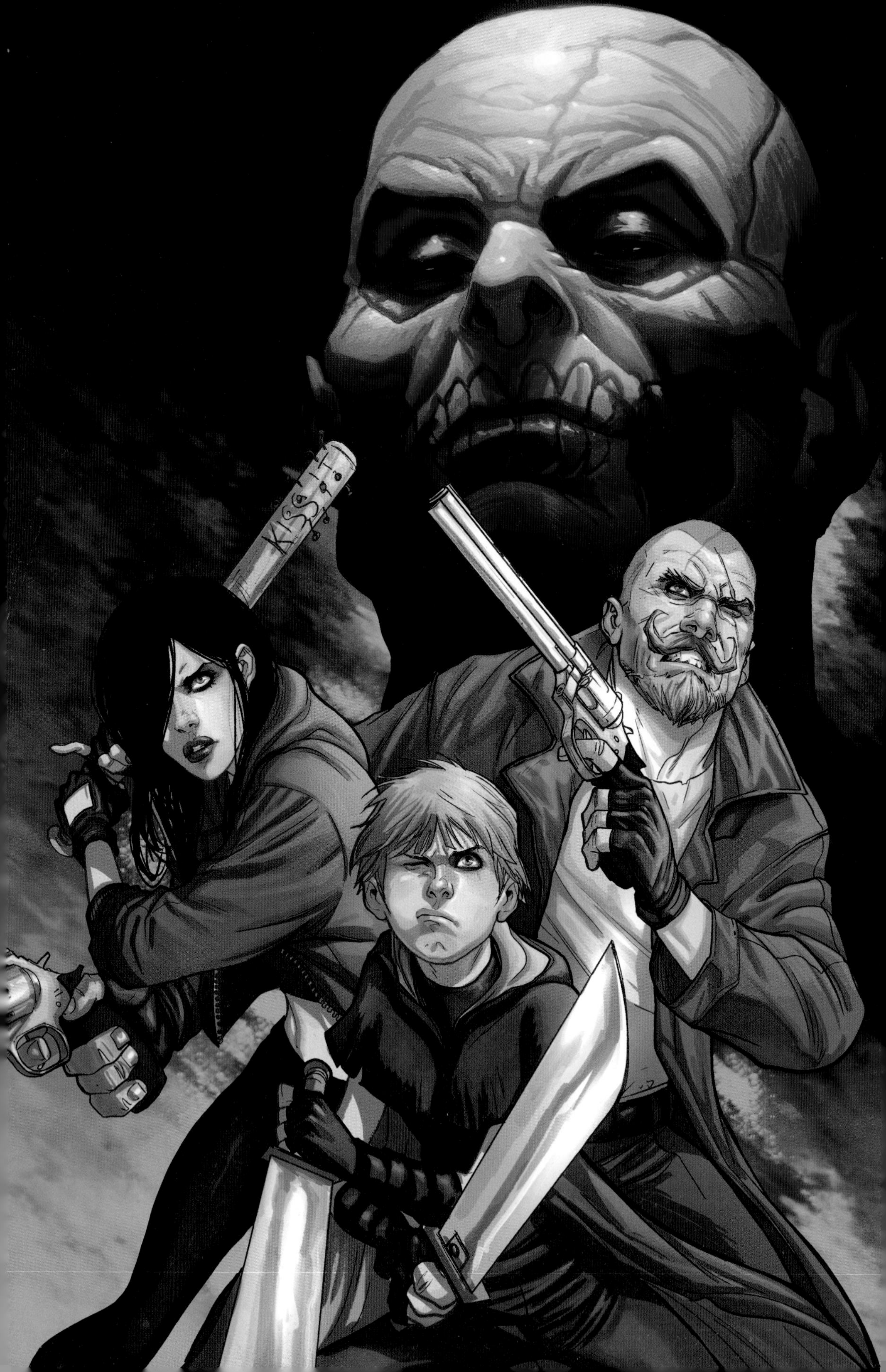

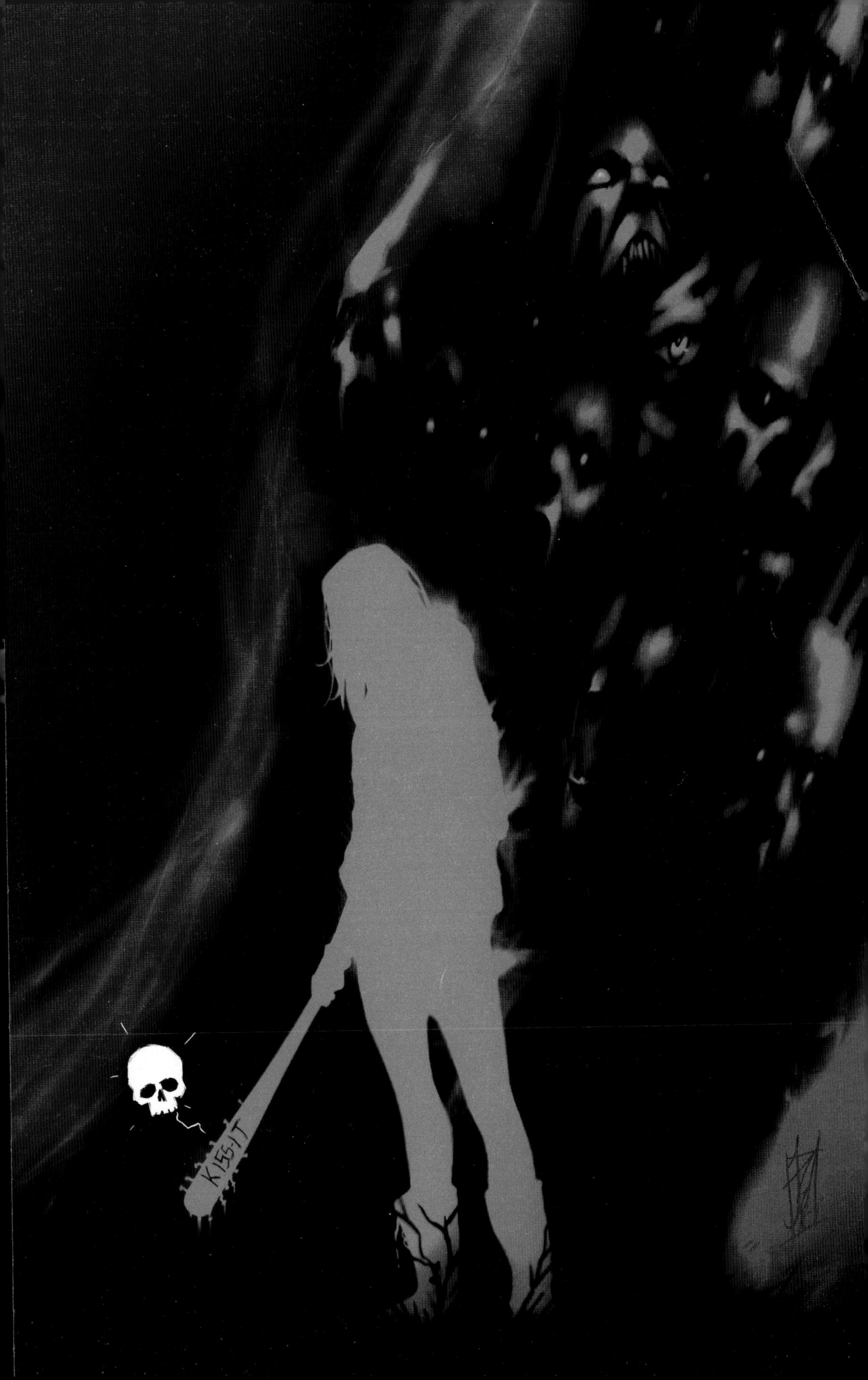
KISS-IT

SKETCHBOOK

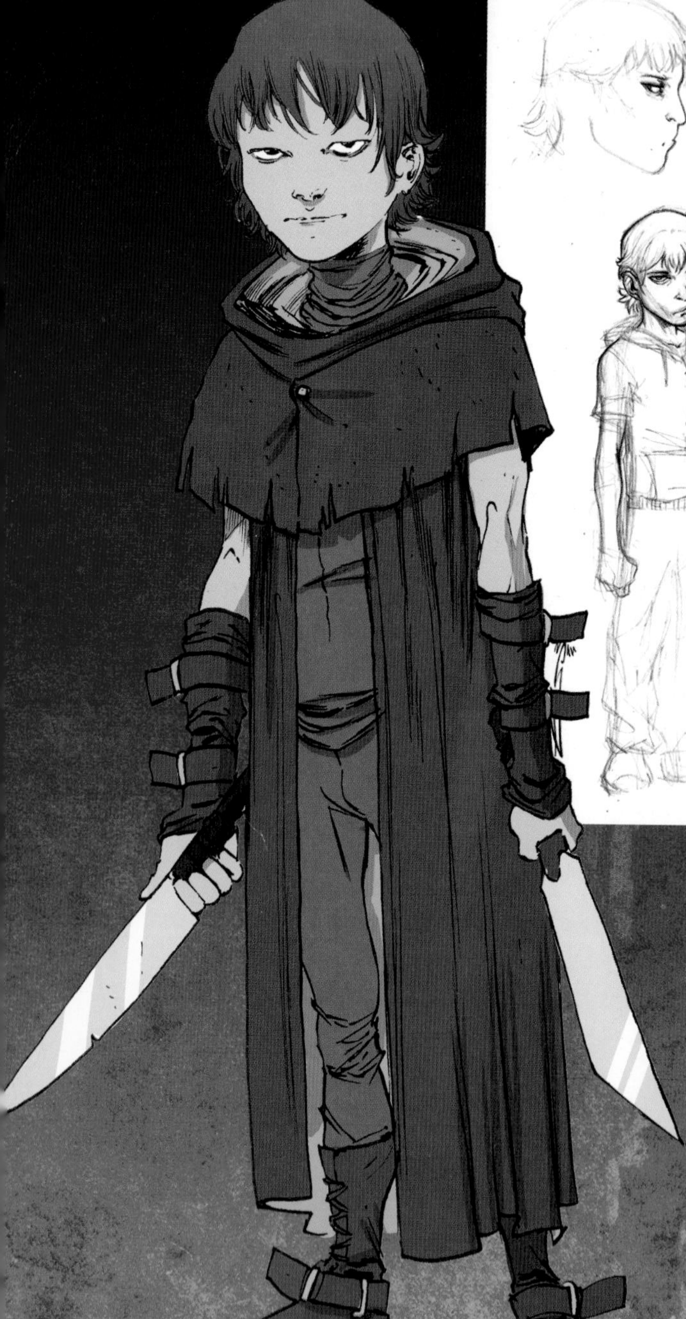

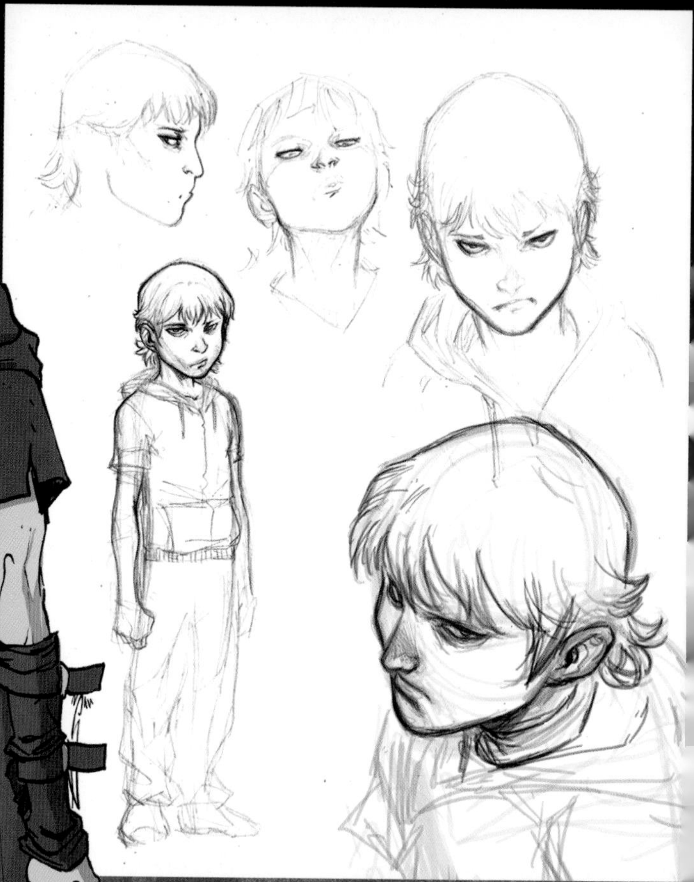

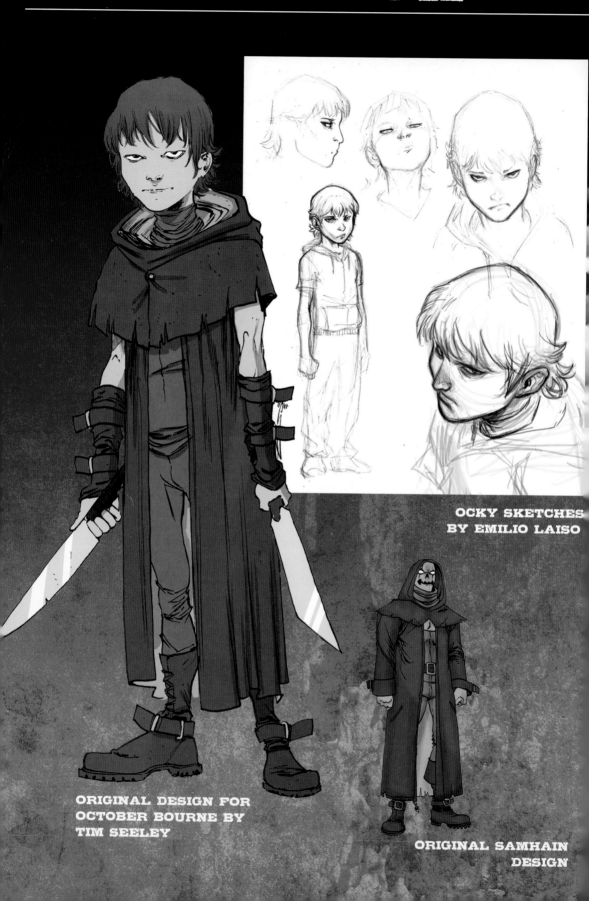

OCKY SKETCHES BY EMILIO LAISO

ORIGINAL DESIGN FOR OCTOBER BOURNE BY TIM SEELEY

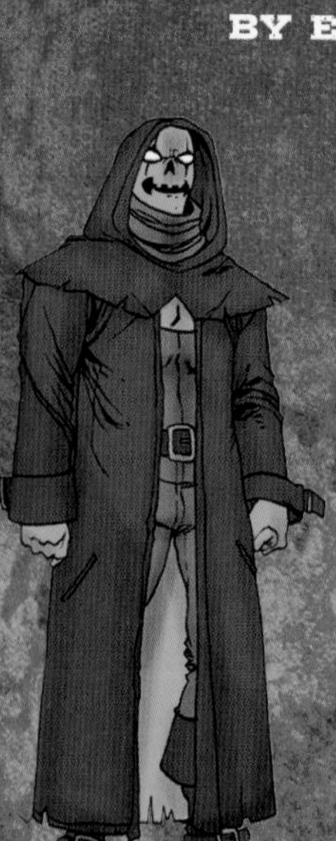

ORIGINAL SAMHAIN DESIGN

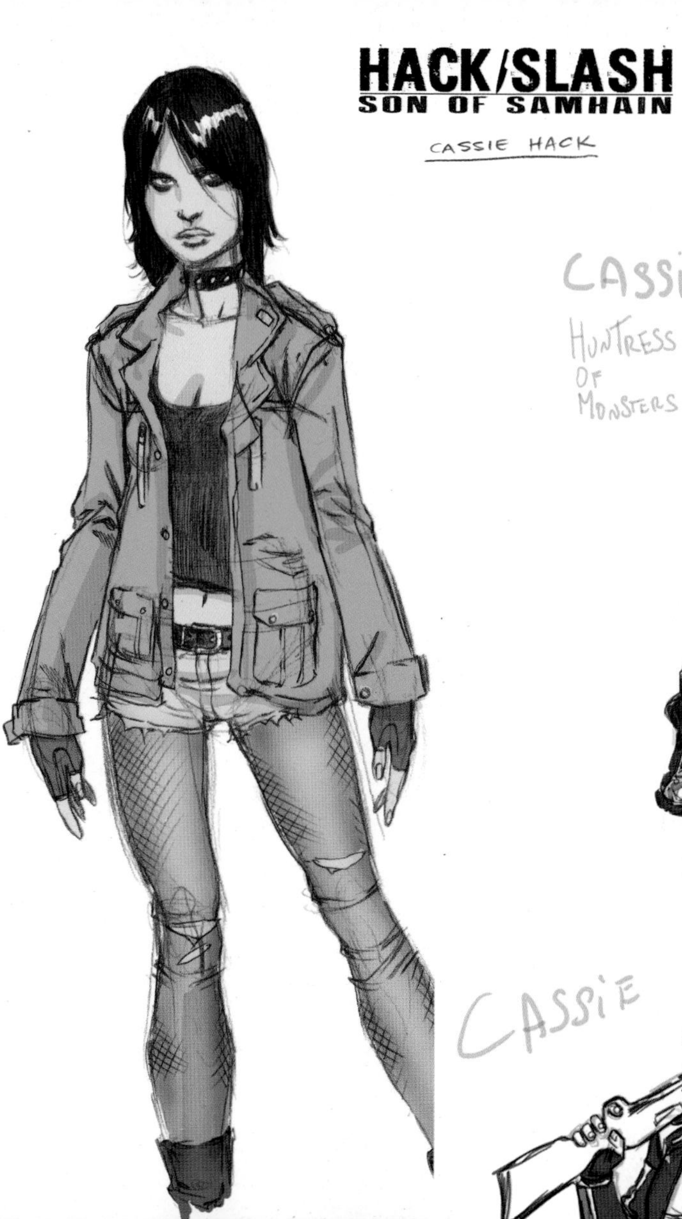
HACK/SLASH
SON OF SAMHAIN
CASSIE HACK

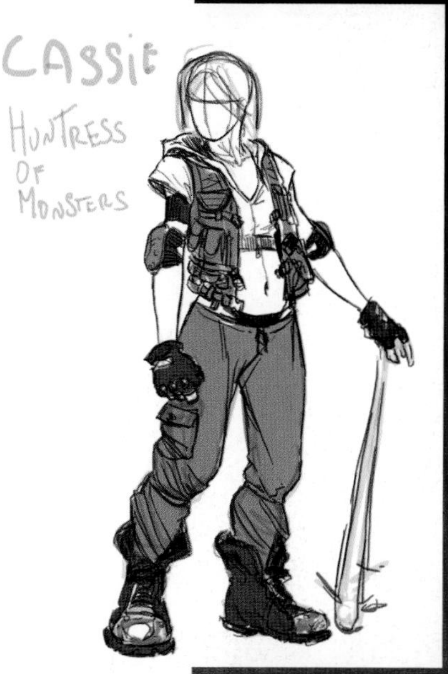
CASSIE
HUNTRESS
OF
MONSTERS

CASSIE HACK REDESIGN BY TIM SEELEY

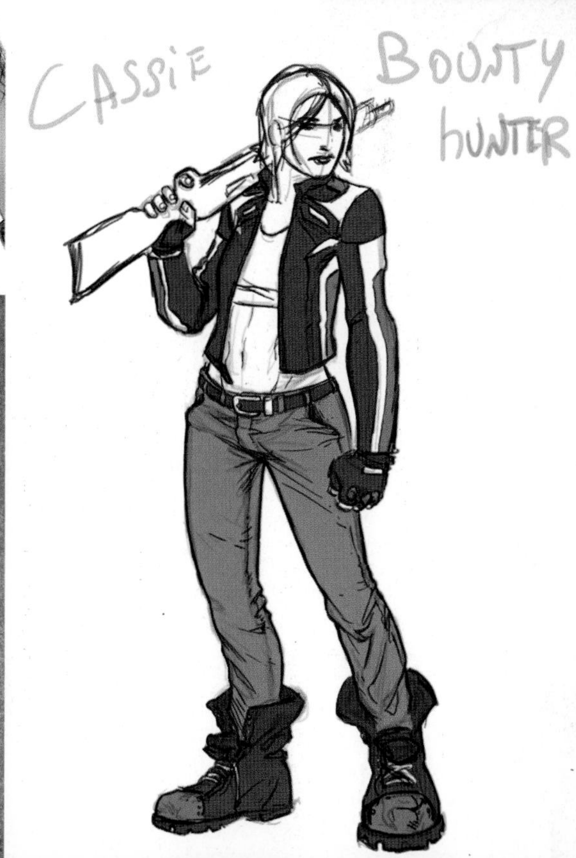
CASSIE
BOUNTY
HUNTER

CASSIE HACK REDESIGNS BY EMILIO LAISO

CASSIE ART AND GOD BEAST DESIGNS BY EMILIO LAISO

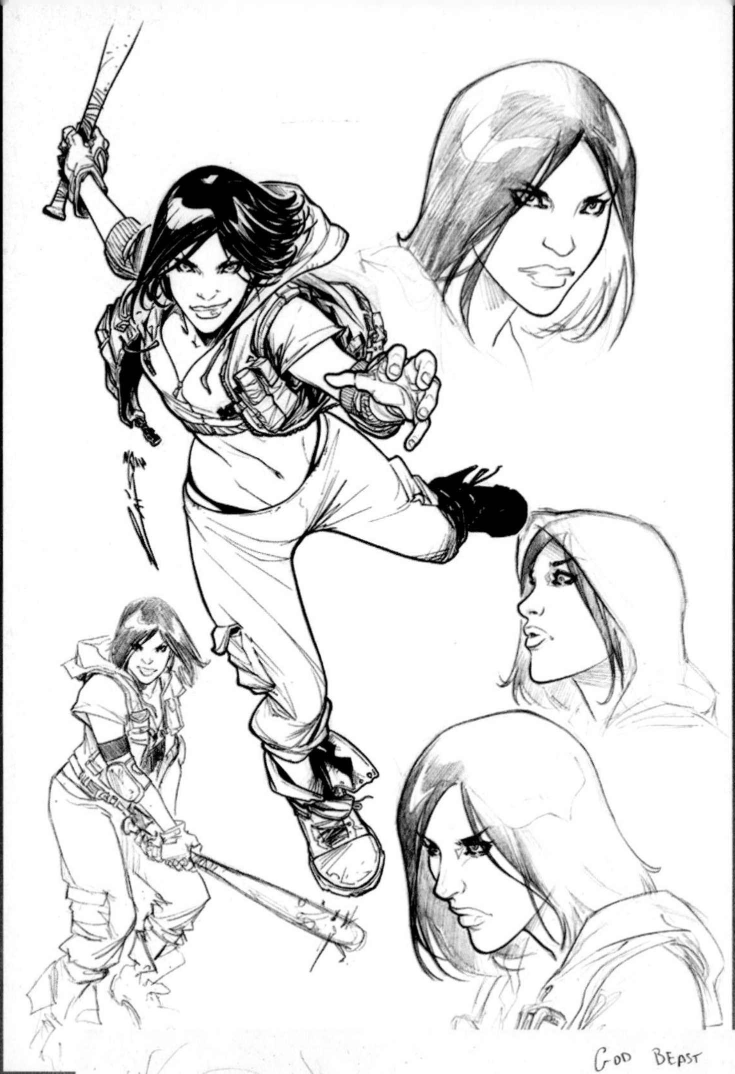

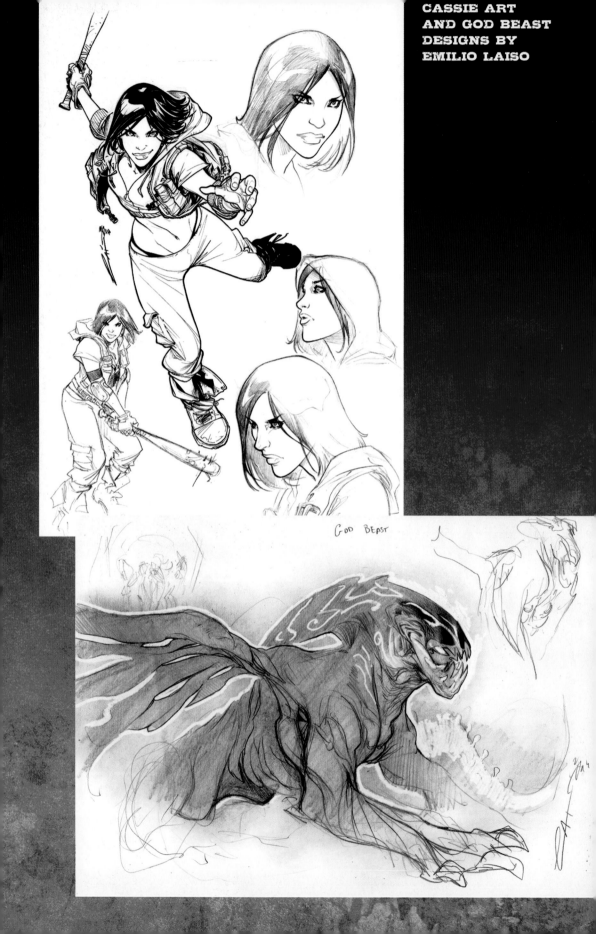

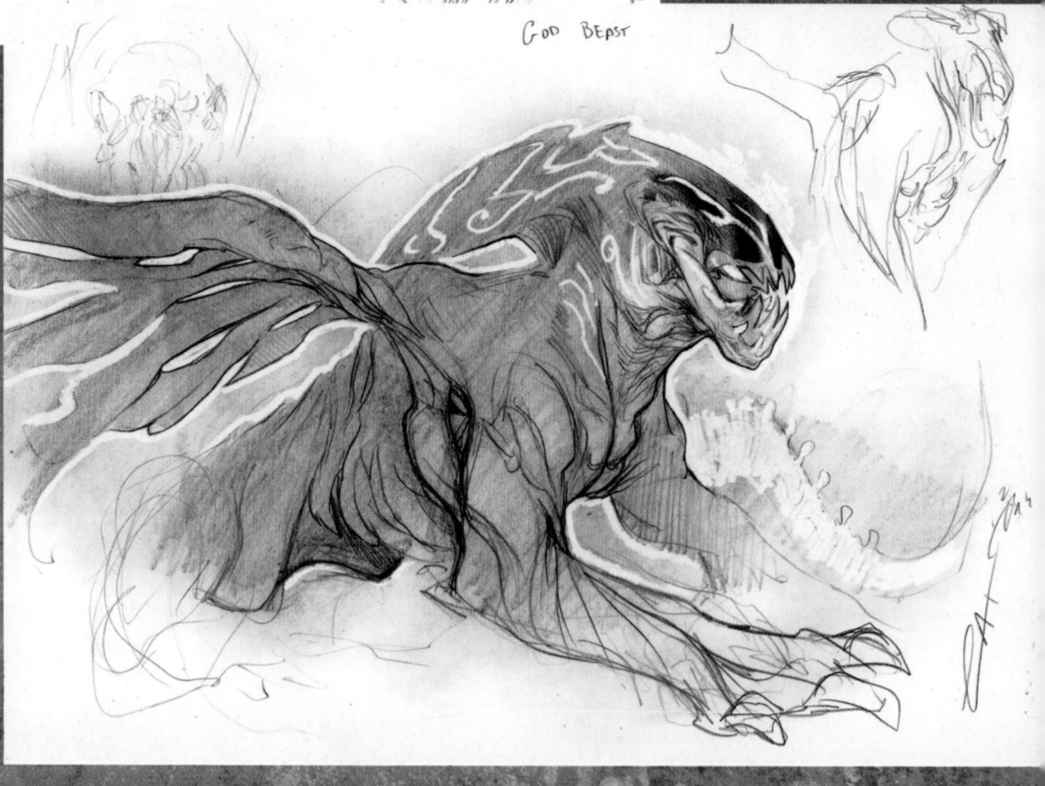
GOD BEAST

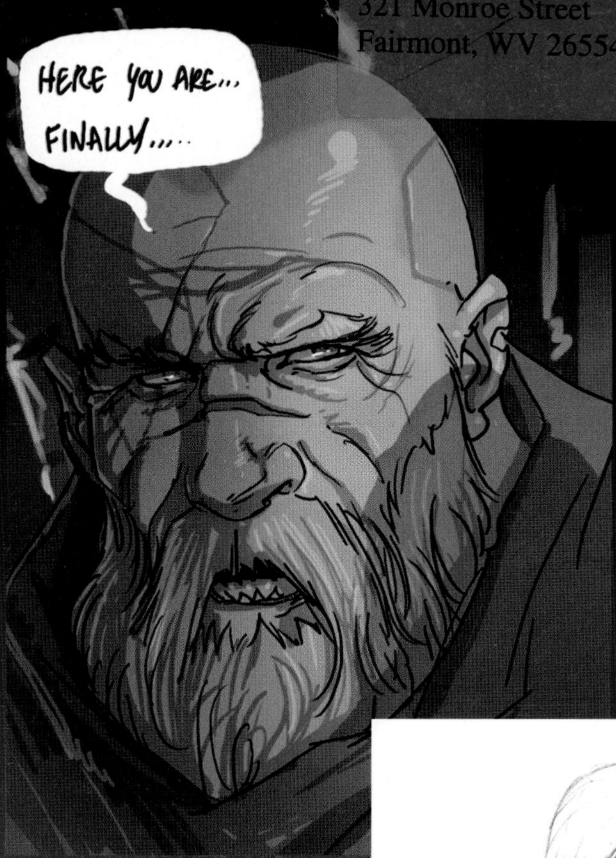
HERE YOU ARE... FINALLY....

DELROY DESIGN
BY STEFANO CASELLI

CASSIE ART BY
EMILIO LAISO

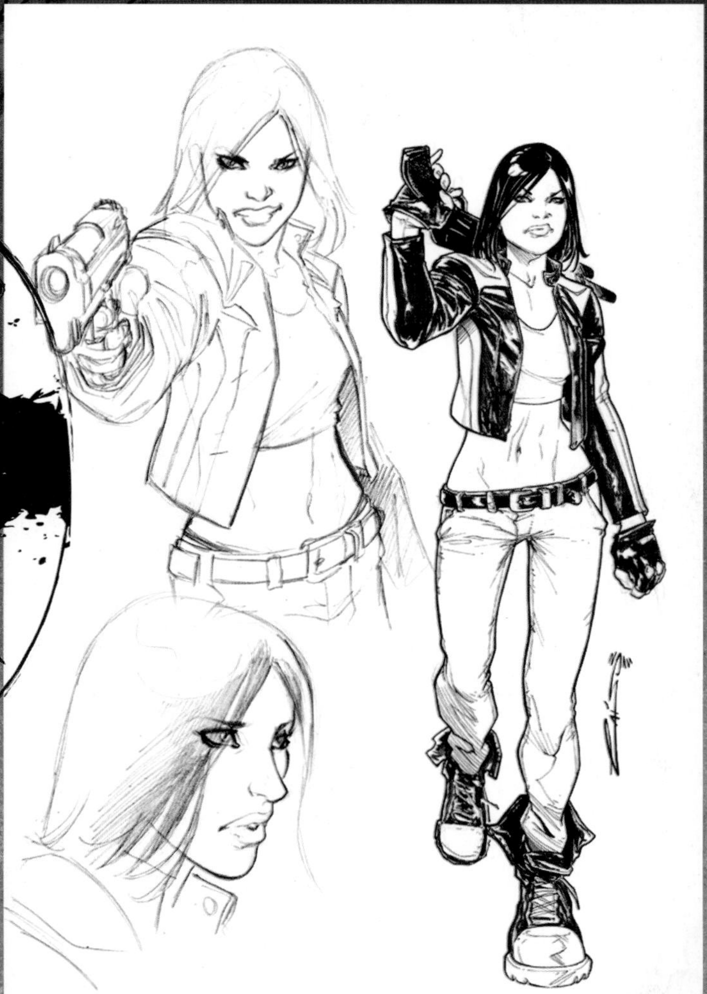

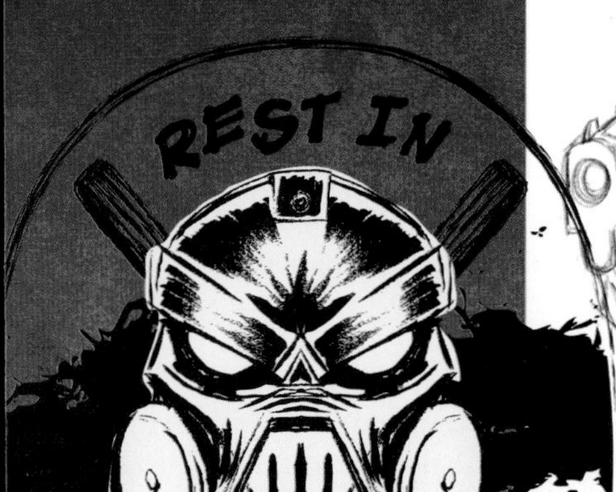
REST IN
PEACE

VLAD TATTOO
DESIGN BY
BRIAN CROWLEY

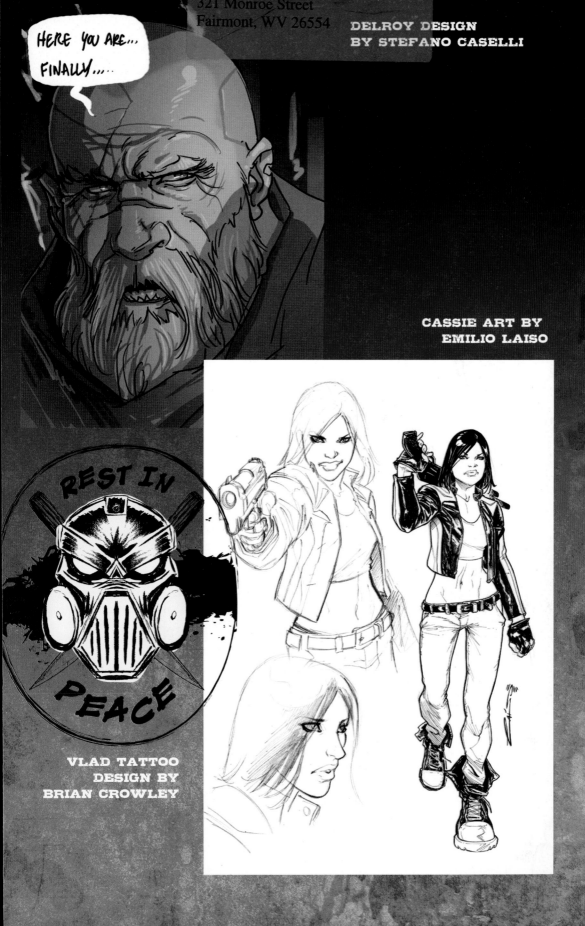

PITCH/SERIES OUTLINE
BY MICHAEL MOREC

Hack/Slash

After reading the ideas passed around so far, which are really great, I think I have a way to weave some of the threads together and build it into a story that, hopefully, we're all satisfied with—enough, at least, for us to collectively build off of.

For starters, I'd have more time pass between where we last saw Cassie and the beginning of this arc. We want there to be enough of a space between then and now to absorb the idea that Cassie is a changed person, that not only have the events of the Samhain battle made her different, but so has the path she's taken. I'd go three to four years. Plus, it makes her older. 26 to 27, no big deal. 26 to 30, there's a difference there.

When we find Cassie, she's working as a bounty hunter, tracing and capturing various lowlifes. Kind of JUSTIFIED, in a way. It's dirty work—it's not glamorous, it doesn't pay well, and it's dangerous. But it keeps Cassie moving (we retain Tim's idea to keep her alone, separated from Georgia and Sandra, and for real—there's no going back).

It's on one of her hunts that Cassie is herself hunted—by Delroy, our aging monster hunter. Think of a hybrid of FEAR AGENT's Heath Huston and any character ever played by M. Emmet Walsh (or Tommy Lee Jones in NO COUNTRY). He's a big Texan who has been at the monster-hunting game for too long, though we don't make him a caricature. He may seem like a slow-minded Texas hillbilly, but Delroy is very smart and, underneath the gruff exterior, a good man who imparts a lot of wisdom to Cassie.

Now, this is where we really have to tie the worlds of Cassie and Delroy together in a convincing way. It's a tough sell, saying that monsters have been around in the Hack/Slash universe the whole time. I don't think any of us what to start and ground zero and say monsters didn't exist, but now they do—it's too convenient.

That said, we're going to have to rely on two things: One, the strength of Delroy as a character. His job, as he explains to Cassie (who doesn't believe monsters exist—she'll be a surrogate for our readers, in a sense), is to keep monsters out of the public's minds. (He's also good comic relief, to maintain the levity the series is known for.) Same as Cassie with slashers. You deal with them quickly and quietly. When you don't, that's when people start to die. Also, while Cassie hasn't a clue about Delory, Delroy has known about Cassie for years, and that's what brings us to point 2, which is:

Delroy needs Cassie, and her skills, for a specific purpose: The monsters and slashers are starting to unite, and he can't stop them on his own.

Delroy and Cassie's journey takes them across the border, to Mexico. Here, we'll start digging into our core monster myths. We're in Juarez or thereabouts, which will give us not only an awesome gritty feel, but a great visual look as well. In Juarez, as you all likely know, the murder/disappearance rate is off the charts (Tim, this is where your BRIDGE reference, a show I love, comes into play)—many of the victims are absorbed into the Underground City of Morinto (I'm going to dig into Mexican folklore and whatnot to add some credibility to this). Here, they become nocturnal servants to Morinto, our first monster.

Note: I agree with Stefano in staying away from mainstream, classic monsters, at least at first. If we go right into a werewolf or Dracula or something, it's going to be campy as hell.

PITCH/SERIES OUTLINE
BY MICHAEL MORECI

Cassie and Delroy learn some specifics of the monster/slasher union, at least enough to know this is the tip of the iceberg. Also, more importantly for now, Cassie is personally struck to learn that the slashers cavorting with Morinto is the group The Way of the Alchemist, of the Black Lamp Society. And, even more devastating, the group has in its possession an eight year old boy—the Son of Samhain, October.

Note: I made October eight because six might be a little too young, if only for physical maturation.

The rest plays out as to be expected and as Tim laid out. Cassie rescues Ocky, and Delroy kills Morinto, with Cassie's help. We have a scene where Delroy is about to sacrifice himself so Cassie can escape and live, when she interferes. "No one is sacrificing themselves for me again," she says, calling back to Vlad. Cassie, Delroy, and Ocky go on the run, which is unusual for Cassie—she's usually the aggressor. But now she has to both protect Ocky and help him control his urges as well as unravel the monster/slasher plot.

The first arc, as I see it, will work more as an introduction to this new world/threat and less of a strict "Son of Samhain" story. That will be a big part, don't get me wrong, but we'll focus more on the transition into the new Hack/Slash universe. Assuming we'll go beyond an initial arc, the Cassie/Ocky relationship will be developed over time. We also develop a world of strange monsters, much like Mignola has done with Hellboy, and broaden Cassie's network. Like Stefano says, we really work on developing a tight, underlying threat that's bigger and badder than what we've seen before.

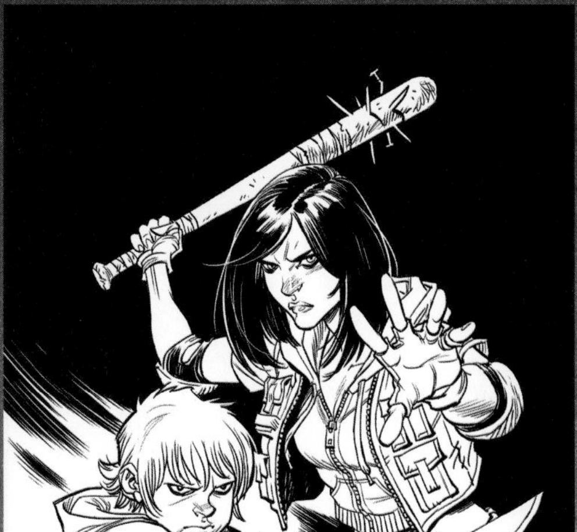

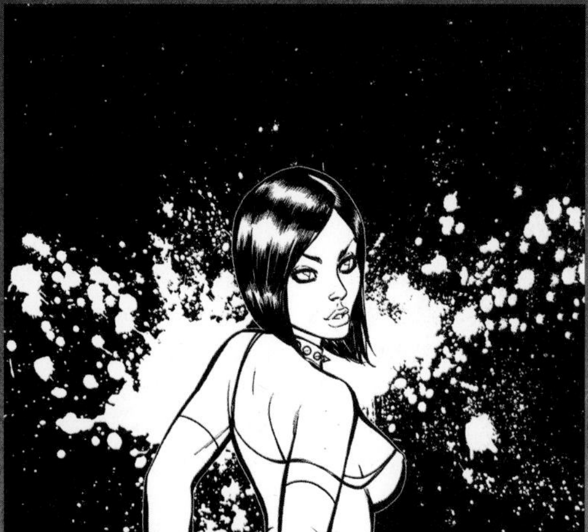

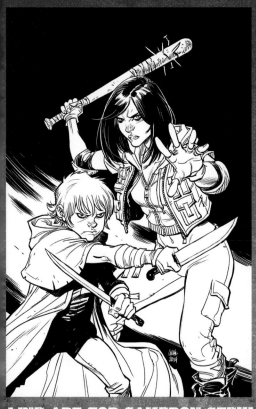

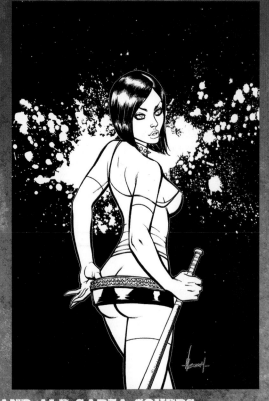

LINE ART FOR CAMERON STEWART AND ALE GARZA COVERS

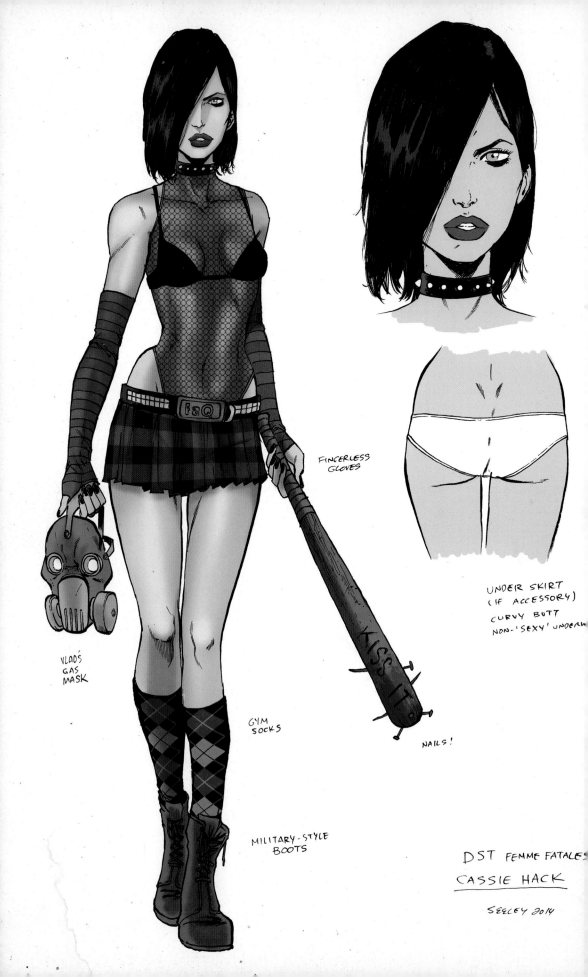

FINGERLESS
GLOVES

VLAD'S
GAS
MASK

GYM
SOCKS

MILITARY-STYLE
BOOTS

UNDER SKIRT
(IF ACCESSORY)
CURVY BUTT
NON-'SEXY' UNDERW

NAILS!

DST FEMME FATALES
CASSIE HACK

SEELEY 2014